Raven's End

Raven's End

A NOVEL BY

BEN GADD

Sierra Club Books

San Francisco

Copyright © 2001 by Ben Gadd

All rights reserved under International and Pan-American Copyright Conventions. No part of this book may be reproduced in any form or by an electronic or mechanical means, including information storage and retrieval systems, without permission in writing from the publisher.

Published by Sierra Club Books
85 Second Street, San Francisco, CA 94105
www.sierraclub.org/books

Produced and distributed by
University of California Press
Berkeley and Los Angeles, California
University of California Press, Ltd.
London, England
www.ucpress.edu

SIERRA CLUB, SIERRA CLUB BOOKS, and the Sierra Club design logos
are registered trademarks of the Sierra Club.

First published in Canada by McClelland & Stewart, Ltd., Toronto, Canada

Library of Congress Cataloging-in-Publication Data available from Sierra Club Books

Map by Ben Gadd
Illustrations by Lawrence Ormsby

07 06 05 04 03

10 9 8 7 6 5 4 3 2 1

This book is for Cia, my Molly

Written in memory of Richard Cole, John Kula,
Bugs McKeith, Ekhard Grassman, John Lauchlan,
Laura Jasch, Heidi Schaefer, Mark deLeeuw,
and all the rest

Raven's-eye View
of Selected Places in the Canadian Rockies

Columbia Icefield

To Jasper

Castle Mountain

Banff

Mount
Rundle

Carrot
Creek

Princess Margaret Mountain

Wakonda Buttress

Raven's
End

Yamnuska

Bow River

N

Morley Flats

Map by the author, 2000

Contents

PART ONE

Yamnuska

I

He had never had a dream like this before. He was falling – falling so fast that the air was roaring in his ears and tearing at his feathers.

"*Pull up!*"

He opened his eyes. He spread his wings. They almost ripped away.

"Awk!" cried the raven, fully awake now. He extended only his wingtips, which slowed him a little. He spread his tail, which slowed him more. He spread his wings wider –

But here was the ground, close by! He was going to hit –

Flump!

The raven looked up through the juniper bush that had broken his fall. He blinked, opened his bill and said, "Crawk!"

" 'Crawk' is right." Another raven, big and black, was striding toward the bush. "I can't believe what I just saw. Are you okay?"

"I, uh – my bill hurts." The raven struggled out of the juniper. Checking, he found that he had lost some neck-feathers and one wing-feather.

"Looks like you went in headfirst. How's that right wing?"

The raven stretched out a wing.

"No, no. Your other wing."

"Oh. Sorry. I – I'm feeling very confused."

"Bump on the head. Don't worry about it. Just sit tight. I'll hang around."

"Thanks," said the hurt raven.

"My pleasure," said the other. "I don't believe we've met. I'm Zack C.C., from the Raven's End Flock. And you?"

"My name? My name is . . ." The raven's bill began to chatter. "Oh, no! I can't! I –"

"Oh, you're just a bit addled. I would be, too, after a crash like that." Zack's voice was reassuring. "Are you from around here?"

The other bird looked about. He was resting on a mountainside. Beside him the juniper bush gave off a piny fragrance. Down the slope he could see spruce and aspen trees. He turned his head, noting that his neck hurt, and peered up the slope. With a start, he realized that he was at the base of a cliff. The cliff seemed very high, reaching up and up until the gray rock met the blue sky. As he watched, a cloud appeared at the edge, moving past the cliff. In a strange reversal, the cloud seemed to stop and the whole cliff seemed to topple backward. The earth itself felt like it was moving. The raven fell over on his side.

Zack rushed over and prodded him with his bill. "Hey, let's not be passing out, whoever you are!"

"I feel awful," said the nameless raven. "Everything is so strange." He looked desperately to the other bird. "Do you have any idea what happened to me?"

"Not the faintest," said Zack, glancing up, "but what's happening right now is that a coyote is headed over here. If I were you I'd try to get airborne right away."

Sure enough, a beast that looked like a long, lean dog was approaching. Padding along, head low and eyes fixed on the ravens, it began to trot, then to run. Zack spread his wings and easily hopped into the air. The coyote leapt after him, but Zack was well out of reach.

"Try again, fur-brain!" he yelled.

And try it did, turning toward the other bird. The crash-landed raven was hobbling away downhill, trying to take off. The coyote saw its next meal there, an easy catch. It gathered itself for the pounce.

Then it felt something stab the base of its tail. The coyote yelped and twisted around. There was Zack, a few wisps of tawny hair in his bill, headed skyward as fast as possible. And there was the other raven, now climbing slowly away with frantic, badly coordinated wingbeats.

Zack swooped over to him. "That was close. You're in worse shape than I thought. We've got to get back to the cliff."

"Thanks – *huff, huff*," said the bird, breathless from fear and effort. "I think you just saved my life."

"Twice, actually. First time was when you were falling. Remember?"

Zack tilted his tail and changed direction toward the cliff. The other raven made a wide, skidding turn but managed to follow Zack as he flew on.

A gust of wind blowing up the slope caught both birds and lofted them upward. They had only to hold their wings out; the trees dropped away beneath them as the wind carried them higher and higher. Soon they were coasting toward the shadows cast by the cliff. Once there, the birds seemed to disappear, dark on dark.

Zack soared beside the vertical rock. He turned his head this way and that, his eyes scanning the cracks and ledges for a special spot. When he was almost level with the clifftop, Zack tilted a wing down and slid sideways toward the wall. He drifted over a tiny spruce growing in an alcove, put out his feet, flapped his wings twice, and landed neatly on a branch. The other raven followed, grasping the same branch awkwardly. Tired and sore, too exhausted to speak, he settled onto his perch.

"Now," said Zack, "I'm going to take my afternoon nap. And so are you."

Both birds fell asleep.

II

When the raven awoke, he knew his name. There it was: "Colin."

Over the dark hills on the eastern horizon a bright spot of pink was growing where the sun would rise. Colin extended his wings, stretching the sleep out of them. The soreness was gone. He felt fresh, like the mountain breeze that ruffled his feathers. Evidently he had slept right through the afternoon, and on through the night.

Now – about yesterday. About that accident. What had caused it? He thought hard, but nothing came to mind. He couldn't remember anything about the day of the crash, or the days before, or where he had lived, or . . . or anything. An uneasy feeling grew within him, creeping toward panic. He raised his wings, feathers trembling, as if to flee.

Then the feeling changed. It softened and warmed, gently nudging the fear away. The feeling was telling him not to worry, to stop asking those questions for now. Everything would be fine. Everything would sort itself out. Colin let his wings relax.

Zack was stirring beside him on the branch. He raised his head, making the feathers under his chin fan out in a kind of ragged beard. "Gro," he said, which Colin knew meant "hello" to a raven.

"Gro," said Colin.

"How're you feeling today?"

"Much better, thanks."

"That's good to hear." Zack gave his wings a half-flap over his head. "You slept all afternoon, you know. And right on past roosting time. I wasn't sure you'd ever wake up."

"And you waited here? All this time?"

"Yes."

"Thanks for looking after me like this, Zack."

"No problem. Would have done the same for any bird."

"Oh – my name is Colin."

"Ah, remembered your name? Thought you would. Now then, where are you from?"

"I still can't remember. But I'm trying not to let it bother me."

"The right thing to do. All in good time, eh?" Zack reached down with his bill to rearrange a feather on his belly. "Care to join me in hunting up some breakfast?" He leapt off the spruce branch, spread his wings and soared away.

Colin followed. Really, it was easy. Just jump outward, fall briefly to build up some speed, then get your wings out. And what a joy as the feathers caught the wind! The wind would hold you up, carry you places, tickle your neck-feathers, flip you sideways in a sudden gust. What fun! Colin felt immediately sorry for any creature that could not fly.

The first flash of morning sun shot over the foothills. It caught the birds in flight, a squirt of pure warmth soaked up eagerly by every jet-black feather on their bodies. The heat spread inward, flowing deep and strong, loosening their muscles, transferring its energy to their flesh and bone. The two ravens accepted it gladly and flew on.

Zack was bound for the meadows below the cliff. He lost elevation quickly in a shallow, tucked-wing dive. Colin followed, taking care to keep his speed down. At treetop height the birds levelled out and began flying slowly along the cliff base. Colin recognized the site of yesterday's crash. He looked for the coyote, but it was gone.

Abruptly Zack wheeled and landed, attracted to something square and pale lying on the ground. He examined the object closely, then tore into his find, gesturing with his bill that Colin was welcome to have some, too.

Colin touched the square thing with his own bill. He found that it was soft. It smelled wonderful. He picked off a piece, felt it on his tongue and swallowed it. Yes; it was delicious.

"What is this?" he asked.

"Shanwish," said Zack, mumbling through his food. "Peenuhbudder 'n' jam. Humansh eat 'em." He swallowed. "The humans walk up this trail to the cliff. They get hungry, so they open their packs and eat these things. They're messy buggers, so they always leave some crumbs. 'Course, we're lucky to get a whole sandwich."

Zack bent down for another bite. Then he saw a bright-yellow bag lying nearby. "Hey-ho! Could be potato chips!" He hopped over and stepped on the bag, clamping it to the ground with his outstretched toes. Grabbing a patch of the slippery plastic in his bill, he pulled upward. The bag popped open, showering the birds with chips and orange-colored barbecue flavoring.

"All right! My favorite kind!" Zack gobbled down several chips, then looked at Colin. "But they do make a bird thirsty."

Crunching away at the chips and ripping off pieces of the sandwich, Colin was lost in pleasure. Such food, lying about for the taking! These humans, whatever they were, must exist just for the benefit of ravens.

A thumping sound close by interrupted Colin's thoughts. Zack jumped backward into the air, and Colin did the same, following Zack to the safety of a tree. Looking down, Colin saw several large animals walking slowly up the trail together.

"Whew," said Zack, as he watched them go by. "I'm losing my grip. They got *way* too close before we heard them."

"What were they?" Colin asked.

Zack's head swivelled toward Colin. His bill opened and closed in disbelief. "You don't know?!"

"Um . . . not really. I guess you do, though."

"You bet your bum-feathers I do. Humans!" Zack looked in the direction they had gone. He shook his head.

"Are they dangerous?" asked Colin.

"Bloody well right they are," said Zack. "Most dangerous things around. You can't trust 'em at all."

"But they leave this food for us –" Colin began, unable to believe that these slow-moving, ponderous creatures could pose a threat to a raven.

"Yeah, and I've seen 'em *poison* it, too." Zack looked suspiciously in the direction the humans had gone. "I always take just a small bite first, to make sure it's okay. Before I get right into it." He looked from his perch to the remains of the sandwich. "And since this is fine," he continued, "I'm going to take some home for Molly." He coasted back down to the ground.

About half the sandwich was left, and Zack grabbed it in his bill. Rather than doing a vertical takeoff, he was forced to run downhill with it. A few powerful flaps put Zack into the air – and straight into an aspen tree. The sandwich fell from his bill, came apart in midair, and both halves landed jelly-side down in the dirt.

"By the Trees, you moldy lump of wormwood!" Zack swore. "What the blazes are you doing in my way?!"

Colin alighted beside the sandwich, trying not to laugh. "Let's each carry half," he suggested. "We can still give it all to . . . to whoever it was you were going to give it to."

"To Molly," said Zack, preening a twisted wing-feather back into line, "who is my nestmate, if you care to know." He looked irritably at

Colin. "You're awfully smart all of a sudden, for a bird who could hardly fly only yesterday, let alone *think*."

Colin saw that Zack's pride was suffering, so he said nothing. He picked up one of the slices of bread and wondered whether he could fly with even half of what Zack had been carrying. Perhaps some additional tail-spread would compensate for the extra weight in his bill. It worked, and soon both birds were heading back the way they had come – back along the cliff toward the east end of the mountain called Yamnuska.

III

Of all the limestone mountains along the eastern front of the Canadian Rockies, Yamnuska has the longest, straightest, steepest cliff. For this reason Yamnuska has always been home to ravens, and it was homeward along Yamnuska's great South Face that Zack and Colin flew, carrying a hiker's discarded lunch.

Zack passed by last night's roost. He led Colin farther east along the face, then he landed on a ledge. There, still sleeping, was another raven. This, Colin thought, must be Molly.

Molly pulled her head from under her wing and blinked in the morning sunlight. She joined Zack in a dance. Both birds hopped about on the ledge, raising and lowering their heads. The dance ended with Zack putting a small piece of his sandwich right into Molly's open bill, as if she were a youngster being fed. Molly ate slowly, delicately, to show how much she appreciated the gift. Then she turned toward Colin. Colin was about to offer his own piece of sandwich, but Zack interrupted.

"Molly, this is Colin C.C.," he said.

"Gro," said Molly.

"Gr – *augh*," said Colin, choking on the food he still held in his bill. He dropped it quickly at her feet and turned away. "Excuse me," he said, in a small voice.

Molly and Zack laughed. They laughed as ravens laugh, a sort of "craw-ha-ha," their bills held high, their bodies prancing around in silly little steps.

"Craw-ha!" laughed Zack. "Molly, this bird fell right out of the sky over the South Face yesterday. Got a bump on the noggin from it. Kind of mixed him up, you know? But he's really quite decent. Should be okay in a day or two. Do you mind if he stays with us? Just until he's back to normal?"

Molly took a bite out of the sandwich and looked Colin over carefully. "He's certainly polite. At least he tries to be." She smiled at Zack. "Of course I don't mind. For a few days." Molly reached for another bite of breakfast.

Suddenly a dark body flew between the birds and the sun. It seemed to pass over the ledge in a black flash – and Molly's meal was gone.

"*Awk!* Dolus!" Zack was on the wing instantly. In five beats he caught up with the thieving raven and they grappled in mid-air, locking feet. Zack pecked Dolus in the breast and raked him with his claws, but Dolus would not give back what he had stolen. He swallowed most of it and spat the rest out. As Zack swooped to chase the falling food, Dolus called after him, "If I can't have it, you can't have it either, Zacky!"

From the ledge Colin watched all this in horror, but Molly just sighed. "That's Dolus for you," she said. "No one can stand him. He does stuff like this all the time. And he's big and mean. Watch out for him, Colin. He can really hurt a bird."

Zack was plummeting downward in a full wing-tuck, hoping to intercept what was left of the sandwich. But the gob of food fragmented as it fell, and Zack snatched up only a few crumbs before he had to give up the chase. By this time, Dolus had flown off. Zack returned to the ledge in a rage.

"By the Trees, I'm going to get that bird! First chance, I'm going to get that bird! I'm going to – I'm going to – I just don't know what I'm going to do to that bird!"

Molly smoothed Zack's feathers, clucking sympathetically. "Never mind, dear. We'll complain at the Flap."

Zack regained his composure. "Molly, I'm so sorry he got your breakfast. I just didn't see him coming."

Molly gave Zack a loving touch with her bill. "I know, I know. Nobody could have done a thing."

"Uh . . . what's the 'Flap'?" asked Colin.

They both looked at him dumbly.

"You don't know what the Flap is?" Molly was astonished. "Where are you from, anyway?"

Zack explained. "He has no idea. It was that crash-landing. Can't remember anything that happened before then. Must be very hard for him."

Molly's eyes looked kind. "Forgive me, Colin. Imagine – forgetting your whole life! Come along with us to the Flap, and then you'll remember, I'm sure." She turned to Zack. "It's at Raven's End this morning."

The three birds hopped off the ledge and started eastward into the warm morning updraft. The cliff became lower as they followed it, and then it ended abruptly. At its foot a long, rounded ridge continued eastward toward the prairies. This, Colin decided, must be "Raven's End."

Other ravens were gathering there, arriving in ones and twos. They were walking about on the bits and pieces of gray limestone that had fallen from the cliff and now lay heaped against its base. Tall pines and spruce trees stood here and there. Brilliant orange lichens encrusted the cliff, and wildflowers bloomed on every ledge. A small gray bird sang from its perch at the top of the tallest spruce, repeating the same musical-sounding one-note call: "Morn, morn, morn."

It was a special place, Raven's End, a place like nowhere else in the mountains, and for countless centuries the ravens of Yamnuska had gathered there. They met each morning to discuss the things ravens care about – where to find food, mainly – and to hear the news.

Molly, Zack, and Colin joined eight other ravens on the ground, forming a rough circle. They shifted their feet, bobbed their heads and greeted each other, saying "gro." They turned their big bills this way and that. They spoke in low, serious-sounding croaks and high-pitched giggles. At length a very large raven swooped down into the middle of the circle. Every bird became quiet.

The Flap had begun.

IV

Colin stood next to Zack in the circle. He watched as the big raven extended a magnificent set of wonderfully ragged neck-feathers and looked each bird briefly in the eye. Colin was impressed. Might this be the leader of the flock?

"Gro," said the raven, in a deep, rich voice.

"Gro," replied the other birds. Colin turned to Zack and asked, very quietly, "Who is that bird?"

"Our Main Raven," Zack replied in a whisper. "I forget his real name. He doesn't use it, anyway."

The Main Raven spoke again. "First," he said, "we shall have the news. Maya?"

The flock looked up, toward the gray bird atop the spruce. Maya was a Townsend's solitaire, with white rings encircling her eyes. She finished her warmup – a few more of those wistful "morn"s – and broke into a long, complicated song. She trilled on and on in a high voice, her eyes bright, her daily report spilling out.

Maya's soul was that of the journalist. She loved events and activities, gossip and intrigue. Anything that happened on Yamnuska became known to her. She could understand any bird, no matter how difficult the language, and she could follow the communications of many other creatures, too: the musical talk of the frogs; the grunts, whines, and howls of the mammals; the buzzing high-speed data transmissions of the insects. Maya spent her days collecting information, and every morning she proudly, happily passed it on to the ravens. News addicts themselves, the ravens were one of the few species that could understand her, she talked so fast.

"Overnight weather was cool – wood rats report frost on the summit rocks – but winds were light – a pair of snipes in the Willow Marsh lost a clutch of eggs to a mink last night – first mink seen there this summer – flowers reaching height-of-bloom this week include brown-eyed susan, goldenrod, and fireweed – last year's spectacular display of arnica is unlikely to be repeated this summer."

She stopped, took a breath, then went on.

"The cougar killed a porcupine in the North Valley yesterday – her other recent kills here include an elk calf and a female bighorn sheep – she apologizes for the number of kills but cites her unusually large litter of kittens – says they're hungry all the time."

Another breath.

"Moving to the world of avifauna – the Brewer's sparrows are worried about the rain we've been having – some report brood failures from it – but most pairs are still optimistic."

The pitch of Maya's voice rose higher and higher. Her eyes widened until it seemed that her eye-rings might burst. She was at full speed, now, turning this way and that, leading up to the most important item of the day.

"And this just in from a red-tailed hawk who happened to be cruising the central South Face yesterday afternoon – a human has been killed there – fell all the way from the top while climbing – another human, apparently with it at the time, was uninjured but spent the night on a ledge – other humans rescued the survivor – as usual, they took the body away before anyone could eat it –"

At this point Brendan, a young raven, interrupted impulsively. "Hey, wow! Eating a human!"

"I wonder what they taste like?" another young raven wanted to know, leaving Maya to burble away unheeded.

"Oh, really weird, I bet," said Brendan.

"Please, please," the Main Raven called out. "Let us afford Maya the attention she deserves."

By this time Maya was reaching the end of her newscast. She finished with a prediction for tomorrow's weather, courtesy of the toads, who were very sensitive to changes in barometric pressure and relative humidity. Her commentary trailed off into the same repetitive, one-note call she had started with, a rather sad sound reminding her audience of the burden Maya bore: day in, day out, the news was mostly bad. As usual, no one thanked her for her report. Soon she nodded off on her perch. Later she would make her rounds.

"Now, then," said the Main Raven. "The next item is complaints. Does anyone wish to register a complaint?"

"I do," said Molly. "I wish to complain about Dolus."

The ravens groaned. Not Dolus again. Somebody was always complaining about Dolus. There he was, part of the circle but given plenty of room by the birds on either side, neither of whom wanted to stand too close. Dolus grinned mischievously.

Molly refused to look at him. "Dolus stole some food from me this morning, and it was a present from Zack."

"That's right," said Zack. "Swiped it right off our ledge. Gobbled as much as he could, and then – can you believe this? – he threw the rest away when I caught up with him."

The other birds clucked disapprovingly.

"Well, Dolus?" queried the Main Raven. "Have you an excuse for this behavior?"

Dolus looked down at his feet. He spoke in a low croak, out of the side of his bill. "Aw, Molly's making this up. Zack brought her something she didn't like. She pushed it off the ledge. I just caught it and ate it."

"Liar!" roared Zack. In two hops he was across the circle, bill-to-bill with Dolus. Zack sleeked his feathers back – a threatening gesture – and clacked his bill.

Dolus did likewise. "Come on, Zacky. Just try it," he growled.

Infuriated, Zack attacked. His head shot forward, and his bill struck Dolus hard on the breast. Dolus immediately struck back. The two locked feet, pecking and biting each other, flopping about in the rising dust as the circle moved back to give them room.

"Stop it! Stop it!" shouted the Main Raven. But the fight went on. The other birds became more and more upset, flapping their wings and calling "Craw! Craw!"

Suddenly another bird jumped on Zack. This one had been cheering for Dolus. Now it was pulling feathers from Zack's back. That was too much for Molly.

"You! You leave my Zack alone!" she screamed, running up and pecking the other raven on the tail. It sneered at her and hopped away.

By now Dolus had ripped several feathers from Zack's wings, and a spot of blood was showing on Zack's breast. Breathing hard, Zack looked to be in danger of losing the fight. But then Dolus took a stab at Zack's eye – a low blow among ravens – and missed, giving Zack a chance to get his bill around Dolus's throat. He bore down hard, and the other birds gasped. Zack could kill Dolus this way. Zack was considering doing just that when he, Dolus, and every other bird in the flock suddenly took to the air. Humans were coming, headed right for the circle. And they had a dog.

That was the end of the fight. Dolus and his ally flew off by themselves. Zack, Colin, and Molly alighted high in a pine beside the cliff.

"It was on a leash, thank the Trees," said Molly, eyeing the dog from the safety of her perch. The humans, a male and female with a child, were now sitting right where the ravens had been fighting. The dog was sniffing among the shrubbery, chasing squirrels up the trees, barking at the birds, lifting its leg on the boulders.

Zack was a mess. His feathers stuck out all over, and he had nasty bites on his legs. The wound on his breast oozed pink. He sat stiffly, not saying a word. Molly went to work on his feathers, tenderly straightening them and pressing them back into place. "Oh, Zack. My poor, brave Zack. If those humans hadn't come along, I don't know what might have happened. You're not the type to kill anyone. But I wouldn't have minded a bit if you'd hung onto Dolus long enough to do the job!" She raised her eyebrow tufts and looked in the direction Dolus had flown. "That Dolus has got to go. And that other bird – what's his name? Garth, that's it – that other bird always takes his side. They've *both* got to go!" She stamped her foot. "They just arrived here one day, uninvited, and they won't leave."

Zack still sat speechless, his eyes shut against his pain and anger. Molly's bill continued to stroke and soothe him. Colin had kept quiet since the fight started, surprised that such a well-mannered, civil event as the Flap could have ended the way it did.

From a neighboring spruce, Maya watched and listened. She would really have some news to pass on today.

V

Zack and Molly excused themselves to go back to their roost. Maya flew off. The other ravens had already left, disgruntled by the outcome of the Flap and not caring to hang around the humans – and their dog – too closely. Only Colin remained, alone on a dead branch atop the pine.

Brilliantly sunny a few hours ago, the day was now going dark. A bank of low clouds had moved in from the east, and tiny drops of rain were making black speckles on the ground. The humans pulled their jackets from their packs – Colin was amazed to note that humans carried extra plumages with them – and they talked excitedly, looking up and pointing. At the first rumble of thunder they hastily packed up, called the dog, and headed back the way they had come. The rain started in earnest, and Colin had Raven's End to himself.

He enjoyed the sensation of the drops hitting his body. They rolled off rather than penetrating, for Colin's feathery covering was practically waterproof. Opening his bill and leaning his head back, he caught some rain directly from the sky. It tasted of clouds.

He thought about things. Here was a flock of ravens. He wasn't really a member of the flock, and he wasn't sure he wanted to be. But what else could he do? He'd have to stay with them for a while. He needed their help until he got himself sorted out. Zack and Molly certainly had been kind to him. As for the other birds, well, they seemed decent enough – except for Dolus. He'd have to stay out of the way of that bird.

Lightning hit a neighboring peak. It sent a wave of thunder bumping through the valley, rolling back and forth between the cliffs. Colin looked up. The undersides of the clouds had joined themselves into a solid ceiling as gray as the rock, and now the ceiling was coming down. It touched the top of Yamnuska and crept farther down the cliffs. Tendrils of mist caressed the pinnacles and explored the corners. A gust of wind carried the mist over Raven's End, and Colin's perch was suddenly in fog. He could hear the dog barking, now far below, but the fog was so thick that he couldn't see beyond the next tree. The world became very small.

Colin felt as if the mist were alive. Its cold presence brushed by him, stroking his wings, curling between his toes, throwing tiny flecks of moisture into his eyes. He blinked.

Then the fog started to speak to him.

"There is a mountain," it said softly. "A mountain with feathers."

The voice of the fog was wispy and high, the sound of vapor moving over stone. It came from everywhere at once, and it kept saying the same thing, over and over.

"There is a mountain. A mountain with feathers. Feathers on the mountain. The mountain has feathers. Feathers. On the mountain there are feathers . . ."

This message from the mist, Colin knew, was meant for him. He knew it more surely than he knew anything else – which was comforting, considering how little he understood of the world around him.

As the voice went on, he tried to imagine what a mountain with feathers would look like. An image flickered through his mind, but he couldn't see it clearly. He grew sleepy. His eyes closed. He tucked his head under his wing and dozed off in the rain.

VI

While Colin slept, the weather ran its course. The sun had worked very hard in the morning to generate the storm, heating the air masses and pushing them this way and that until they crashed into one another and spilled out their rain and lightning. But now, late in the afternoon, the sun was bored with the whole business. It shone lazily near the horizon, letting the clouds drift away.

Colin awoke. He shook off the remaining droplets. Where was he? Ah, yes: at Raven's End on Yamnuska. Things were becoming more familiar now. His memory, at least for recent events, was improving. He recalled the fog. The fog-memory recalled the dream-memory, and then the message in the dream.

"What a crazy idea," Colin said to himself. "Mountains with feathers? I'm still not right from that crash."

"Eek," came a sound from below.

Colin looked down.

"Eek," came the sound again, exactly as before. It was raspy, as if some animal were making it through its nose.

Then Colin spotted the source: a small gray creature crouching on a boulder. The boulder was gray and the animal was exactly the same color, so it blended in perfectly – as long as it didn't move. And it wasn't moving. A few moments went by as the animal stared at Colin, and Colin, turning his head from side to side, looked at the animal. It was fat. There was no tail. Its round ears were edged with a thin line of white fur. Its black eyes didn't blink.

Colin was beginning to have designs on this creature, whatever it was. It looked like the sort of animal a raven could eat, and Colin was hungry.

"Eek."

Colin now realized that the animal wasn't shrieking "eek" from fear or surprise. It was *saying* "eek." This must be its normal voice. So it wasn't really afraid of him. Maybe it was trying to tell him something.

He decided to speak to it. "Gro," he said.

"Eek," said the animal.

This conversation was going nowhere, thought Colin. Maybe he should just hop down there and have the thing for supper. But he delayed. He wanted to know what kind of animal this was even more than he wanted to eat it. He spoke to it again.

"Uh, hello there. I was just wondering what kind of animal you are."

"I'm a pika," the creature said plainly. The way it said *pika* sounded a lot like "eek."

"Oh, a pika. Of course," Colin replied, as if he had known all along.

"We live among boulders," the pika went on, "and we are not rodents. Please do not confuse us with rodents. Rather, we are lagomorphs, which are relatives of the rabbits and hares." The pika recited these facts without emotion.

"Oh, I wouldn't confuse you with a rodent," Colin assured the pika, wondering what a "rodent" was.

"Yes, you would. Everyone does."

Colin decided to change the subject. "I'm feeling a little hungry," he said, socially. "How about you?"

The animal ran down from the rock and disappeared underneath it. The next "eek" had a tinge of alarm.

Now that was stupid, Colin thought. He'd scared it off. Oh, well; that was that. He jumped off his perch and glided down to the ground, where, he recalled, the humans had been having a snack earlier in the day. Sure enough, there were goodies lying around. In the hikers' haste to escape the storm, they had left behind a plastic bag with several cookies in it. Colin grabbed the bag in his bill and picked it up, spilling a cookie onto the ground. He regarded his find, lying there with its chocolate chips staring up at him. Now what had Zack said about human food? Oh, yes: taste first before eating. It could be poisoned.

He nibbled a corner. Sweet; dry. He picked at a bit of chocolate. Wow! No wonder humans ate this. Colin planted his bill in the centre of the cookie, breaking it up, then he wolfed down the pieces. He ate another cookie, and a third and fourth.

"Eek." The pika had crept up on its rock again. Here it was, only a wingspan away, watching him.

"What's your name?" Colin asked, feeling more friendly toward the woolly little rock-rabbit sitting across from him on the boulder. He was no longer interested in making a meal of the pika. The cookies had taken care of that. And the pika knew it.

"My name is Okotona," said the pika. It spoke without expression. "All pikas are named Okotona," it added.

"What?" Colin couldn't believe what he had just heard. "You all have the same name?"

"Yes," replied Okotona. "But we all have different names, too."

"Now, wait," said Colin. "If you all have the same name, how can you have different names?"

"Oh, it's easy. We change them every day. Today we're calling our-selves 'Edward.'"

Colin started to giggle. "And tomorrow?"

"Well, for tomorrow we were thinking of using 'Maxine.'"

This was too much. Colin threw his head back, opening his bill. "Craw-ha-ha!" he called, dancing about on the rock, wings shaking with laughter. "Craw-ha-ha-ha! Edward, is it? Maxine? And what were you all yesterday? Craw-ha-ha-ha-ha!"

"'Emily.'" The pika didn't laugh.

"Craw-ha . . . ahem." Colin's wings rustled down onto his back. He looked away from the pika, trying to understand. He couldn't, so he looked back. "Why is it that you pikas don't keep the same names? I mean aside from the one you all have?"

"It's because we're all so much alike. Besides, we don't last long enough to make it worthwhile having separate names," said the pika.

Colin was shaken. "You mean – you mean you don't live very long?"

"That's right," said Okotona. "Myself, I'm doing pretty well. Almost a year now. But not too many more days, probably."

"How do you know that?"

"Well, the weasels got an Emily last night, and a hawk picked off a Harold the day before. There's only a few of us left here at Raven's End."

"How terrible for you, to lose your friends that way."

"Oh, it's okay," said the pika. "That's the way of the world. We've got lots of little ones coming along. My mate had a pretty good litter this spring, and she denned with another female. When one of them gets it, the other will look after all the youngsters. Of course, there will be fewer to look after as the days go by. So everything works out, you know."

Colin mulled this over. What a fatalistic existence! Did these pikas just let themselves be eaten? Didn't they even make an effort at self-preservation?

Of course they did, he reminded himself, recalling how Okotona, or Edward, or whoever it was, had run away when he had blurted out his intentions. Still, this animal seemed awfully easy-going about matters of life and death.

"Have you ever wondered what happens after you die?" he asked.

The pika didn't reply right away. It thought for a minute, then it said, "I have. Just now."

"Well?"

"After I die. Let's see. After I die, then I'm dead. But lots of other pikas are still living. Pikaness goes on."

"Pikaness?"

"Yes, the essential thing about being a pika. Pikaness."

"But you, personally, are dead."

"Personally dead, yes, I suppose, but then there are all the others. And we're all really the same, so –"

Colin couldn't help interrupting. "What do you mean, you're all the same? You can't all be the same."

"Of course we are," said the pika. "Just look at us. Same size, same shape, same color. Same habits, too. Pikaness."

"So it's this 'pikaness' that matters most to you? More than your own personal life?"

"Certainly. When one of us dies, pikaness goes on. Isn't it the same with ravens?"

"Well . . . no," Colin replied, feeling strangely selfish. He would need to consider this further. He tried to grasp the implications clearly. Now, if *all* pikas thought of themselves as the *same* pika, then any *particular* pika would –

Before he could complete the thought, his eye caught the shape of a shadow sweeping over the ground toward them. Small and black, the shadow stopped exactly overhead. Okotona cried "eek!" quite loudly and scuttled away toward the edge of the boulder. But the shadow grew suddenly bigger, there was a whistling sound, and the pika was gone, wriggling in the talons of a large brown-and-white bird. The bird skimmed away at high speed as it turned the motion of its vertical dive into a long horizontal glide out over the trees. Colin heard its voice.

"Falcon Mate, this is CZE. Stoop complete. Have taken on fuel. Am now over Raven's End on heading oh-one-niner, returning to base."

VII

As the brown-and-white bird departed, a black one arrived. Colin flapped off the boulder, out of harm's way, but the bird turned out to be Zack.

*

"That was amazing, Colin! Pretty close encounter for you, eh? Imagine having a prairie falcon grab its dinner right from under your bill!"

"Is that what it was? A prairie falcon?"

"Yes. Lives across the valley. *Very* fast bird. Fortunately doesn't kill ravens – although you never know with hawks and falcons. I try not to make too inviting a target. Not that you can see a falcon coming, it dives so fast. Flies high. Sees something. Drops like a rock falling off the South Face."

"Zack," said Colin, "what do you know about pikas?"

"Not much," Zack replied. "Never talked to one. Cute little buggers, though. No trouble to anyone. Hey, Molly, did you see the falcon?"

Molly lowered herself out of the air with a couple of reverse flaps. "No. They're gone before you know it. But I did see one earlier, cruising over the summit, and it could have been the same bird. The one from over on Bilbo?"

"That's the one. The Main Raven told me they confabbed once. Something about hitting a raven by mistake."

"Let's hope he never makes a mistake with *us*," said Molly, shivering. "What a way to die! Knocked out of the sky, then those talons crunching into your belly. Oh, oog." She shivered again.

"He got a pika," said Colin.

"Poor thing. That pika will be nothing but a scrap of fur by morning. And a bony pellet dumped under the roost."

"Not that I'd venture anywhere near a falcon's roost," said Zack. "Especially while it's eating. I hear they don't take kindly to that."

"Well, you stole half a deer mouse from a red-tailed hawk once," Molly reminded him, proud of her mate. "And you got away with it."

"Aw, those red-tails. Especially that pair nesting at the west end. They're nothing but a bunch of puddleducks. I've seen 'em on the ground eating *worms*."

Colin laughed. He pictured a large, fierce-looking hawk hopping around pulling up worms like a robin. Then he became serious again. "What kinds of things *do* attack ravens?" he asked. "Besides coyotes."

"This bird still isn't in his right mind," Molly whispered to Zack. "How could he even *ask* that?"

Zack whispered back. "Considering everything, I think he's functioning pretty well."

"Considering what?" Colin said loudly.

Zack looked down at his feet and replied, "Oh, considering that you're still alive."

"You've got to smarten up, Colin," Molly said. "That falcon incident was scary. It might just as easily have been an eagle."

"So eagles hunt ravens." Colin at least had his question answered. "What else?" He knew that this was another dumb question, but how was he going to survive if he didn't know what to watch out for?

Molly decided to humor him. She ran through the list. "Foxes, coyotes, wolves, martens, fishers, lynx, bobcats, cougars, goshawks – now *there's* a frightening bird – and golden eagles, of course."

As Molly spoke, Colin was surprised to discover that he could picture each one of these raven-killers. The tawny coyote, with its bushy tail; the fox, like a small coyote but redder, with a white tip on its tail; the wolf, bigger yet; the marten, a pointy-eared weasel, but not as big as the fisher, which was another kind of weasel; the lynx, a big cat with a short tail and tufted ears; the bobcat, similar but lighter-colored and faintly spotted; the cougar, biggest of the cats; the goshawk, a powerful gray bird with red eyes; the golden eagle, enormous and brown. So many enemies! But ravens were lucky, he realized. What if he were a pika? The list for pikas must be even longer.

"What did I leave out, Zack?" Molly asked.

"Humans," he said.

"Oh, yes. Humans, the worst of all."

"Why the worst?" Colin queried. Might as well learn as much as he could, while Zack and Molly were willing to explain.

"They kill everything," Zack explained. "Doesn't matter what it is, they kill it. They even kill *trees!*"

"No!" Colin was genuinely shocked. Deep in every raven was an abiding love for trees.

"Yup. Cut through 'em at the base of the trunk and take 'em away."

"Where?"

Molly answered. "Who knows? And I don't *want* to know, either. Imagine – cutting down trees." She closed her eyes and shook her bill back and forth.

"You know what's really awful?" Zack continued. "Humans kill without eating. Just for fun. I've seen them do it. Remember that raven last year, Molly?"

"Indeed I do." Her tufts rose in anger as she remembered. "It was Dolores, visiting from Kananaskis. Very enjoyable bird. I spent a morning with her. A human killed her with a stone not two hops from where we're sitting right now. Just left her lying there. You can imagine how her nestmate took it."

Colin was nonplussed. "But why do they do it – all this killing?"

"Naturally mean. Just naturally mean." Molly clacked her bill. "I wish they'd all go back to wherever it is they come from. There are more of them every year."

"Although, uh . . ." Zack was looking sly. "You have to admit that we benefit by them, Molly."

She rolled her eyes up and looked away. Zack turned toward Colin. "Molly won't admit this, but humans provide us with a lot of food. What they leave, we get. They'll kill a sheep, say. Cut off the head and leave the rest to rot. Well, guess who's there the minute they walk away? Pretty good eating, bighorns. Especially after a couple of days in the sun." He opened his bill and ran his tongue along the edges. "Been a long time since I've had sheep guts," he said, savoring the memory. "Maybe this fall, when the humans are hunting . . ."

"But we always wait until the hunters are long gone before we move in," Molly cautioned. "They can kill you from a long way off. They just point at you with a stick. Bang! You're dead."

"How can they do that?" asked Colin.

"Don't know," said Zack. "But I can tell you this: expect the unexpected around humans." Then he looked up. "Hey! It's the Evening Flight!" he shouted. "Gro! Gro! Up, up, and away!"

Overhead, Colin could see the whole flock of ravens soaring on the updraft high above the summit of Yamnuska. Ten spots of black against the sky, they were circling, doing shallow climbs and dives, playing in the wind. Colin could faintly hear them calling to one another up there. He understood immediately – for a change – that this was the evening equivalent of the morning get-together. In the evening the ravens did their socializing in the air, not on the ground.

Molly and Zack departed noisily for the Flight, croaking loudly and flapping hard to catch up. Colin hesitated a moment, wondering if he were welcome to join in. Then Zack looked back and called to him. "Come on, Colin! Get a wing on it, C.C., or you'll be left behind!"

He'd have to ask Zack about this "C.C." business, Colin thought as he leapt into the updraft. What did "C.C." mean, anyway? But he soon let the thought go; the sheer rapture of flight drove everything else from his mind. He could feel the breeze tugging him skyward.

VIII

The late-summer sun was setting behind the Canadian Rockies. It slid down at a shallow angle, coasting northward as it sank, skimming the tops of the peaks, winking out behind a summit and reappearing on the other side, dropping lower and lower. The last golden rays streamed eastward through the valleys, out across the foothills to the prairies.

High over Yamnuska, the Raven's End ravens played in the pink warmth of the atmosphere at day's end. They chased each other happily, dodging left and right, climbing and diving, dancing through the sky.

"Gro! Gro!" the birds called to one another. "Where have you been all the day?"

"Over by Mount Fable, eating ants!"

"Up Fort Creek, grabbing minnows in the Willow Marsh!"

The fight, the storm, everything sorry and cold and negative was forgotten. How could a bird not feel glad in a sunset such as this? Colin's heart filled with joy. His bill opened, as if by itself.

"Gro!" he called. "I found some human food at Raven's End!"

Without even thinking, he had caught up to Zack and Molly.

"You're a strong flyer," Molly said.

"Yes," Zack agreed. "You must be getting over that crash. Hey – let's do some aerobatics! Molly, I touched your tail-feathers!" Zack nipped Molly's tail playfully with his bill, then he tucked both wings and dived.

"*Rawk!*" he called. "Nyaaa, nyaaa! Catch me if you can!"

Molly went after him. She folded one wing under, and the other wing snapped straight up as she half-rolled into pursuit. Catching Zack with ease, she pecked him lovingly at the base of his tail. Then they both went after Colin.

"You're it! Craw-ha-ha!"

Colin copied Molly's half-roll, but he was awkward. Molly and Zack swooped by him, simultaneously cupping their wings to send a ripple through the air. The ripple hit Colin and he flipped upside down, like a puppy bowled over by a bigger dog. He stumbled about, amazed at what Zack and Molly could do with the air itself. He watched as they locked feet.

"Here we go!" croaked Zack. Pulling in their wings, both birds plummeted downward, spinning around, shrieking with delight as the air roared past. Colin watched them falling and falling, becoming a single dot of black far below. Then the dot separated into two. Molly and Zack veered apart, feathers whistling loudly from the speed. As they levelled out, the pair glided this way and that, hunting for an updraft. They found one and rode it back up to Colin.

"Want to go for a tumble?" Molly asked him. "Do you remember about tumbling?"

"Uh, no, I don't really remember." Something about this scared him. But he wasn't going to show it. "I'd like to try, though."

"Just keep your wings tucked until I let go," she instructed. "I'll let go just a little way down, in case you can't remember how the tumble works."

"Okay – I guess."

He and Molly locked feet and tucked. Off they went.

"*Awk!*" yelled Colin as they picked up speed and the horizon spun around.

"Craw-ha!" laughed Molly. She released him quickly – but Colin continued to fall.

"Oh, my!" she cried. "Colin, stick your wings out!"

His eyes had closed tightly. His mind had jumped back to . . . to what?

"Pull up! Pull up!" he heard a voice saying. But he couldn't help himself. He was falling – falling so far, so fast – into the darkness below, where death lay –

Something seized him. He felt himself dragged to a stop, then carried gently sideways. He opened his eyes. There was the Main Raven.

"My word," came the deep voice of the big bird. "You were certainly headed for a mishap, my friend." He was carrying Colin in his claws, keeping them both airborne with great sweeps of his wings.

"Thank you, sir."

"I've seen this before," the Main Raven said to Molly, as she and Zack came flying near. "These young ravens, you can't tumble with them. Sometimes they just freeze up from fear."

"It's my fault," Molly apologized. "I didn't realize."

"He seems to be feeling better now," said the Main Raven. He looked at his cargo. "Shall I release you, then?"

"Yes, please," said Colin. The Main Raven let go carefully, one foot at a time. Colin righted himself, coordinated his wingbeats and kept flying with the three other birds. He was still a little dizzy.

"Who is this bird, pray tell?" the Main Raven asked Zack. "Is he the one you brought to the Flap?"

"That's right, M.R.," said Zack. "He's new to Yamnuska."

"Indeed," said the Main Raven. "Perhaps he would like to introduce himself." He looked squarely at Colin with the same eye-holding expression he had used at the Flap.

"My name is Colin."

"Colin? Just *Colin?*" demanded the Main Raven.

"Uh, yes, sir. Just Colin."

The Main Raven gave him a withering look. His eyebrow feathers were rising, and he clacked his bill once. Turning away from Colin, he boomed out his growing anger. "Isn't this a bad-mannered bird! Here

I've just saved his life, but you'd think he didn't care a wing-mite! Well, of all the –"

Suddenly Zack was at Colin's side, whispering in his ear. "Say 'Corvus Corax,' you idiot! 'Colin Corvus Corax'! Quick!"

"Colin Corvus Corax!" Colin shouted, just as the Main Raven was starting to lecture Molly about the company she kept.

The Main Raven turned back toward Colin. "Ah, 'Colin C.C.' is it? How *nice* of you to favor me with your full name." His eyebrow feathers still stood out.

"Please don't be too hard on him, M.R.," Zack said quickly. "He's recovering from a pretty bad accident. Can't remember things."

The Main Raven turned to look at Colin more closely.

Zack kept explaining. "Two days ago he got into some kind of scrape and crashed at the foot of the South Face. He must have got a bump on the head. He couldn't remember about the Flap, or – or anything, really. Didn't even know his own *name*, for the Trees' sake. I'm sure he meant no harm."

"Zack and I are looking after him until he gets better," Molly joined in.

The Main Raven looked from Zack to Molly and back. He looked over at Colin. "Well, let's hope he remembers the social graces soon," he said coldly, "or he won't last long in *this* flock."

With that, the Main Raven dipped a wingtip, changed course and flew off to join some other birds soaring nearby. They had been watching the incident.

"Whew," said Zack to Colin. "You really got his tufts up."

"I'm so sorry! I didn't realize –"

"And now we're in trouble, too," Molly added. "Wait 'til word gets round that we've befriended a boor."

"He's no boor! He's just mixed up! Give him a few more days and he'll be fine!"

"And what makes you think that, Mister Smart-Tail?!" Molly was getting angry. "I knew this wouldn't work out the minute you brought him home! You're always doing that! And it just makes trouble for me!"

Zack blinked several times, trying to think of what to say. Colin started to fly off in the other direction. Zack collected his thoughts, then he spoke in a small voice meant only for Molly's ears.

"Molly, Molly. Please be patient with him. I have a feeling that everything will be okay." She turned her head away. "No, really," he insisted, "something tells me that, well, maybe the flock actually *needs* this bird, you know? Remember when *Greta* came along? Remember how messed up she was?"

Molly's expression changed completely. Quickly, she began to chase after Colin in the darkening sky. "Colin! Colin, come back! I'm sorry!"

Colin was miserable, headed who-knows-where. He'd made a scene at the Flight, and he'd embarrassed the two birds to whom he owed so much, right in front of the Main Raven. Now he'd just keep flying until he encountered another flock somewhere.

IX

"Colin, wait!" It was Molly, and Zack was right behind her. "Come back," he said. "Never mind the Main Raven! Everything will work out! We need you!"

Colin had plainly heard only the words "we need you," but that was enough. He turned around.

"I know how hard this must be for you," Zack said as Colin drew near. "It's hard for all of us. But listen, bird! I know something you don't know, and it would be better for everyone in the flock if you tried to stick with us until you get yourself sorted out."

Colin couldn't imagine why Zack would say that, but at this point he wasn't going to ask. "Okay, if it's what you really want," he said morosely. "I'll try not to foul up like that again. I hope."

He felt very tired. What a day this had been, all ups and downs. With darkness at hand, he wanted only to sleep. "I have to go somewhere and roost," he said.

"Sure," said Molly, soothingly. "You can roost with us tonight, if you like."

The three birds flew purposefully toward home – toward Yamnuska, which filled the northern sky, huge and black against the lavender of oncoming night. As they drew closer, Colin wondered how they were going to locate Zack and Molly's ledge in the maze of shadows. Yet without hesitation, the pair flew straight to their familiar roosting spot. They settled down next to each other. Backed up against the rock, invisible in the darkness and high above their predators on the valley floor, they were as safe as any birds could be.

Colin found a comfortable spot at the opposite end of the ledge. He fluffed his feathers out against the chilly evening breeze and noted that the rock was still warm from the day's sun. He felt himself relaxing. Well, at least he knew what this "C.C." business was all about. Tomorrow would be better.

Just before Zack and Molly fell asleep, they heard Colin say something. It was a question, asked aloud – although not really directed toward anyone.

"Who's Greta?" he muttered.

Molly whispered to Zack. "How does he know about Greta? He couldn't have heard you mention Greta's name, could he?"

"Well, what did I tell you?" Zack whispered back. "This bird is something special."

A nighthawk cleared the cliff edge above them. It called "veentz, veentz" as it slipped softly through a night sky full of moths. Far below, somewhere out in the Bow Valley, a coyote howled. The stars grew brighter. The birds slept.

X

Greta arrived a little late for the Flap, but no one seemed to mind. A small raven, she was also an old raven. Her feathers had lost their sheen. Her bill was rough along the opening, worn from years of use, and it had a prominent scratch along one side. She flew feebly and landed awkwardly.

But her eyes! Her lovely brown eyes, thought Colin, were so clear, so deep – her eyes shone with intelligence and wisdom far beyond that of any other bird in the flock.

The Main Raven called the Flap to order and Maya gave the news. This time there were no complaints, but the Main Raven lectured the flock about fighting.

"Fighting," he said, "is a highly detrimental activity. It wastes our energy. A caring, well-adjusted raven cooperates in matters of sustenance. When a Raven's Ender finds food, he or she is expected to inform the rest of the flock of its location. And never, *never*, is there to be any stealing. Granted, sometimes we make a game of chasing one another when we have food. This is done in fun, and it is acceptable. But stealing a flockmate's breakfast is a different matter entirely. I appeal to all C.C.s here to practice these important principles."

He raised and lowered his head grandly as he talked, extending his impressive neck-feathers when making important points, and occasionally unfurling one wing or the other. Now he glanced around the circle. "Of course, the birds for whom these directives are especially intended are not here to receive them this morning."

Indeed, Colin thought, Dolus and his friend were absent. Where were they?

Knowing that everyone was wondering the same thing, the Main Raven spoke before the question was actually asked. "After yesterday's unfortunate incident, I discussed with Dolus and Garth the idea that perhaps they should be away for a while. I suggested that they return when they are feeling a little more agreeable."

The other birds nodded their heads. Colin looked over to Zack, who whispered to him. "Main Raven's kicked 'em both out for a couple days. Standard thing after a fight. He'll lay into me next."

Sure enough, the Main Raven looked sharply at Zack. "And now, Zack C.C., have you anything to say to us about your role in this altercation?"

"Yes, I do," said Zack. "I'm terribly sorry to have started it. Dolus did provoke me, but I shouldn't have taken the bait. Got what I deserved, too," he said, lifting up his breast-feathers to display his scabbed-over wound.

Before any of the other birds could interject something about how much Dolus deserved the attack, the Main Raven closed the matter. "Well," he said quickly, and more brightly now, "Zack, while you have the floor, how would you like to introduce your visitor?"

Zack raised his bill high and flapped his wings once. "Gro!" he called. "Molly and I have made the acquaintance of a very interesting C.C. He arrived somewhat unexpectedly, by crashing into a juniper bush."

"Craw-ha!" a couple of birds laughed. Zack was known for his wit at the Flaps.

"And he seems to have lost his memory in the process. But he wasn't hurt otherwise. He's a cheery bird, very good-natured, and we have offered to put him up until he remembers where he was going and moves on."

Zack poked Colin with his wing. Earlier he had explained to Colin what was going to happen, so Colin took the cue.

"Gro to all the C.C.s of the Raven's End Flock!" Colin called out loudly, raising his head high and showing his neck-feathers. "My name is Colin Corvus Corax, and I bring you greetings from – from –" Here his voice dropped, and he looked around, apparently bewildered. "Well, from wherever it was I came from!"

Zack had told him to say this, in exactly this way, and it had the desired effect. Several birds laughed.

"Craw-ha! What a funny bird!"

"Craw-ha-ha!"

"Oh, craw-ha! Did you catch that? 'From wherever it was I came from'? He can't remember! Craw-ha-ha!"

Then Colin threw in the kicker. "Of course, wherever I came from, I'm sure they don't miss me there!"

That did it. Every bird in the circle cracked up. Even the Main Raven, given only to quiet chuckling and always in socially correct circumstances, came out with a loud guffaw. He had to give credit to Zack, the Main Raven thought; that bird really knew how to make the best of an awkward situation. And this Colin had no pretensions. Well done.

The Main Raven held his wings out, calling for order. When everyone had got over the joke, he spoke. "Welcome to Raven's End, Colin C.C. We hope you enjoy your stay."

A young bird couldn't help himself. Trying to suppress his laughter, a sort of high squeak came out, and then he said, giggling, "I wonder if he can remember – craw, craw – if he can remember anything about us when he *leaves!* Craw-ha!"

Again the flock lost its decorum, craw-ha-ing away until the Main Raven raised his ear tufts a little, quieting the birds. "That will be enough, Brendan," he admonished gently. Then he spoke to everyone. "I would be pleased if all Raven's Enders would personally extend their greetings to our visitor after the Flap. *After* the Flap. We shall now move on to the last item on the agenda."

This was the daily report on food locations. It was given by Marg, a bustling, businesslike raven. She had been scratching with her feet, making little notes to herself in the dirt.

"Hi, everybody!" she said. Her voice, loud and brassy, was full of enthusiasm. "Today we've got a really great menu. The cougar's finished with her sheep over in the North Cirque, and there's lots left. And Greta tells me that the dead elk in the lower valley is a day old now, so the cougar won't be on it much longer. She's a strong cat, though, and she's dragged it into the trees. You'll have to get there fast, in case she decides to bury it." Marg opened her bill and smiled widely around the circle. She loved giving these reports. "Now, here's the topper, gang: Cathy's found *raspberries* under Frodo Buttress! Yes, and even with all the rain. Cathy, please tell us, dear. Exactly where are they?"

"Uh, well . . ." she started, in a tiny voice. The only surviving member of a family that had perished together when lightning hit their nest, Cathy seemed permanently frightened.

"Speak up a little, would you please?" asked the Main Raven.

"Uh, okay. Sure. Well, uh . . . they're not actually under Frodo Buttress. They're more like under the Runes." She stopped.

Marg prodded her on. "And where under the Runes, dear?" she asked brightly.

Cathy looked around the circle, her head low, her wings starting to flutter involuntarily. "I, uh . . . well, right there, I mean, right under the

Runes, sort of. Wait – what I mean is they're in that gully – the one that comes out from the Runes – just right at the bottom of it, you know, that one – oh, poop, I just can't explain it." She shut her eyes.

"That's fine, Cathy." The Main Raven spoke in sympathetic tones. "I'm sure we'll be able to find them quite well from your excellent directions." He turned to Marg. "Was there anything else?"

"No, that's all for this morning," she said, finishing up with another big smile. "Have a nice day, everyone."

The Main Raven smiled back. "On that note I think we'll adjourn." He walked grandly away from the centre of the circle, turning his head from side to side and ruffling his neck-feathers. The others made room for him along the edge. "May we have a Motion?" he asked.

All the birds in the circle unfurled their wings. Colin was unprepared for this, and he quickly stepped back out of the way. The Raven's Enders held their wings outstretched, as if they were about to fly. But no one took off.

Viewed from above, as this display was meant to be viewed, the effect was striking: what had been a loose circle of ravens looked like a solid black ring as the wings of the birds overlapped one another. To the ravens, this was symbolic of unity in the flock, and it was always the last thing they did before ending the Flap. The Main Raven waited for a moment, to let the feeling build, then he raised his wings straight up.

"Rawk-a-taw!" he called loudly. All the other birds did the same.

This was the flock's special call. Every raven flock has such a call; it's a cry that carries far on the wind, letting the world know that the flock is there, that it's strong and about to begin the day's foraging. Ravens in flight give their flock calls to strangers they pass on the wing. As a greeting, it's more purposeful than just "gro." Sometimes it's used as a warning. Ravens are not very aggressive birds, but each flock has its territory and it doesn't like other flocks butting in. A vigorous "Rawk-a-taw!" every morning at the east end of Yamnuska told all and sundry that the place was occupied, just in case . . . well, just in case.

Colin wasn't expecting any of this, and he didn't participate. By chance this was the correct thing to do. After all, Colin was not really one of the Raven's End ravens. But he quickly saw the significance of the Motion, and he would have liked to have joined in.

The Motion ended the meeting. As the Main Raven had asked, each bird hopped over to introduce herself or himself to Colin.

"Hi, Colin, I'm Marg C.C. We're so glad you dropped in – so to speak, craw-ha!" Marg touched his bill lightly with hers and bounced away.

The next bird was Brendan, the young raven who had laughed out of place during the meeting. He seemed very earnest now. "My name is Brendan C.C.," he said. "I'm kind of new in the flock, okay, because I just got, like, inducted, uh, this summer. I hope – I mean we all hope – you have a pleasant visit with us, and I personally hope especially, uh, that you get your memory back soon." Brendan was just reaching maturity, and this was the first time he had made a formal introduction. The Main Raven smiled at Brendan as he finished, showing that he had done well.

Another young bird came up to meet Colin. "Hi, Colin," she giggled. "I'm Sarah C.C. Marg's my mum."

Colin bowed politely at each introduction, pulling his head back and fluttering his wings a little in a submissive gesture. He was catching on quickly to the civilities here at Raven's End. One by one, he met all the birds in the circle. Even Zack and Molly reintroduced themselves, giving the formal welcome. Then each bird left for the day. Molly and Zack, the only mated pair in the flock, left together.

One raven hung back from the rest, waiting until the others were gone. It was Greta, the old one. She walked over slowly, rather than hopping up like the other birds had, and she stood facing him silently. Colin was about to speak, to end the awkwardness, but Greta spoke first.

"So this is Colin," she said. Her voice was low and scratchy. It gave away nothing of her mood. "Fell out of the sky, eh?"

"Yes, ma'am."

There was another silence while she looked Colin over, first with one eye, then, turning her head, with the other. She walked right around him, at one point prodding his side gently with her beak. She did the same under his tail, which made Colin jump. Then she spoke again, evidently satisfied. "Well, Colin, you seem healthy enough. My name is Greta. Come to me when you've got a difficult question. And pay attention to your dreams."

Without waiting for a response, she stretched her aged wings and flew slowly away. Colin watched her go, his bill hanging open in amazement. How did she know about his dreams? Who was this Greta, anyway?

XI

"C'mon, Colin, let's eat!"

Zack and Molly were headed for the cougar's kill. Colin joined them as they jumped off the rocks at Raven's End and coasted over the meadows to the north. Wild gaillardia was blooming there, looking like hundreds of big yellow daisies on the grassy slopes.

Soon they reached the centre of the valley, where the forest sloped gently down to the edge of a stream. Here the trees were taller and the woods less dense.

"There's the elk!" Zack called. He flared his wings, putting on the brakes, and descended to the edge of the creek in tight circles. Several other Raven's Enders were already there, clustered around a reddish lump lying beside the water.

"Looks like she dragged the thing right through the creek," Zack said to another raven.

"Strong cat, eh?" the bird replied. "I sure hope she's not hangin' around, like." He looked about warily. Colin landed beside him, trying to remember his name from the many introductions at the Flap. Ah yes, this bird was called "Scratch." Why was that?

Then Scratch did what he was named for. Tucking his bill under his belly, he scratched himself with it. "My bugs is terrible today," he complained.

"So go jump in the creek," Molly suggested.

"No way. You guys knows how I hates water, Molly."

"So do your bugs," Molly said, as she hopped over to the carcass.

What had once been an animal the size of a small horse now lay as a low mound of red meat, white sinew, and glistening bones. Loose hair surrounded the dead elk, so much hair that the meat seemed to be heaped on a brown carpet. The cougar had eaten much of the elk already, leaving the ribcage empty of the parts she liked best – the heart, liver, and lungs – and she had also torn off a rear leg and carried it home to her kittens. This had left most of the animal free for scavenging until the cougar returned.

A family of coyotes had arrived first. They had quickly opened up the elk's head, chewing through the hide, cracking the skull with their sharp teeth and eating the brains, which they enjoyed most. The eyes were soon gone, and the tongue after that. The coyotes were gone, too, for the moment. Having stripped the major muscles from the neck, breast, and the remaining legs, the coyotes had wandered away to a boulder up the slope and flopped down in the shade behind it, so full of meat they could hardly move. All four were sound asleep. Still, as the ravens approached the carcass they glanced around constantly, watching to see whether the coyotes were waking up.

And the Raven's Enders were wary of the meat itself. Despite their hunger, they didn't simply start eating. They treated the dead elk quite differently from, say, a discarded peanut-butter sandwich. They walked up to the carcass nervously, taking small, jittery steps. A bird would come close – dancing forward and backward – then abruptly leap up, stumbling and flapping backward as if the elk had suddenly twitched to life. Having shown such fear toward something obviously dead, the raven would come a little closer, perhaps this time actually touching its meal before doing another jumping-jack and then backing off.

Eventually, though, one of the birds took the first bite. That was the signal; everyone moved in for breakfast. And as they did, they discussed their ritual.

"Oh, nicely done, Marg, nicely done!" complimented the Main Raven. "An excellent Lead, if I do say so myself."

"Thanks. I hope I wasn't too quick."

"No, no, just right. I particularly liked your wing-work on that last jumping-jack."

"Oh, it's nothing. Molly was better last week. I could have waited a little longer, I think."

"So could we all!" chuckled the Main Raven.

"But first things first."

"Precisely, Marg. First things first. As Greta always says, 'Do things right, live 'til night.'"

A couple of birds walked boldly into the ribcage. There they could expect to find delicacies: a bit of the lungs, a little chunk of the spleen that the cougar and the coyotes had missed. But they wouldn't have much warning of approaching danger.

Molly was too cautious to go into the ribcage. Perching atop it, she took hold of a strand of meat in her bill and ripped it free. She swallowed the morsel. "Not really ripe, but not bad," she pronounced.

Colin saw a tasty-looking blob of red clinging to the lower jawbone – maybe a shred of the elk's cheek – and he grabbed it with his bill. He pulled, but the piece stayed attached to the carcass. Clamping onto it, he pulled again, harder. Still he couldn't tear the meat off. This was stupid, he thought. Here he was with all this food in his bill, and he couldn't get it loose to eat it! He tried once more, tugging with all his might – and his bill slipped, sending him flopping over on his back.

As he clawed the air, the other ravens danced with laughter. "Craw-ha! Colin's trying to eat the whole elk at once! Craw-ha! What a crazy bird!"

Colin fluttered back to his feet. This was making him angry. He stepped up to the carcass again and looked at it closely. The piece he wanted had torn partway through. He saw the point at which it was still attached, and he nibbled at it with the tip of his bill. A little blood ran out of the meat as he cut away at it, and he tilted his head back to let the red liquid run down his throat. Glorious! He worked furiously now, suddenly very hungry, and then the meat came away – a good-sized chunk, too much to swallow.

Colin realized that the other birds were still watching him. He turned around to face them, carrying his reward sideways in his bill.

"Hey! Wow!" Scratch said. "Breakfast in one bite, eh?" He looked admiringly at Colin's prize. Like the other birds, Scratch had been picking at tiny strips and flakes of meat, eating as he went, not having the patience or the presence of mind to think of sawing off a virtual steak as Colin had. "You's one smart bird," he said.

"Oh, much smarter than I am," said a small, scrawny raven, hopping up. Colin noted that one of its legs was missing. The bird, who hadn't been present at the Flap, spoke to him again. "With only one leg, I could never hope to accomplish what you just did, even if I had the brains to do it, which I don't. And I'm terribly hungry. Terribly."

Colin looked at the bird. Touched by this combination of compliment and appeal, Colin snipped off a strip of his meat and gave it to the bird, saying, "Here you go. I don't mind sharing."

At this, Scratch sniggered. "Good ol' Wheedle strikes again."

"You've been had," Molly whispered to Colin. "Don't let him do that to you. Wheedle will say anything just to get a bit of whatever *you've* got."

Colin flinched. "Aw, that piece was too big for me, anyway," he said, trying to hide his embarrassment. He held the remaining meat under his foot, tore it in two and swallowed half. "Anybody else want some?" he said, casually.

"I do," said a voice from the trees.

XII

The birds jerked their heads toward the sound, hearts beating furiously as they leapt into the air. They hadn't been paying proper attention, and now they might suffer the consequences.

One raven – Brendan – was inside the ribcage. In his panic Brendan jumped up and almost knocked himself out against the breastbone. "*Awk*," he cried, flapping about.

But Zack saw where the voice was coming from. He settled back on the ground. "It's okay," he said. "It's only Perry."

A smallish gray-and-black bird glided softly down on stubby wings. His eyes were large, dark, and friendly. "Scared you, did I?" Perry asked, landing atop the carcass. His short black beak probed eagerly between the ribs, extricating a choice tidbit that had been missed by the ravens.

Marg turned to the other birds. "You know, that could have been the coyotes," she scolded.

Perry swallowed his find. "No problem," he said gaily. "I was watching out for you."

"Well, thanks, then," Marg continued, "but that was still a lesson for all of us."

Deftly poking about in quick little motions, Perry snagged another bite. He looked up, cocked his head and listened for a moment. He had better hearing than the ravens did. "Actually," he said, swallowing the meat, "the coyotes *are* waking up. I'll just have one more helping – not bad, this elk – and then I'll say toodle-oo."

A moment later he was gone, vanishing into the woods as soundlessly as he had come.

"What kind of bird was that?" Colin asked Zack, quietly, so the other ravens couldn't hear.

"Gray jay," Zack replied. "He's a relative of us ravens. Jays are, uh, the *second*-smartest birds in the mountains."

"He seemed smarter than any of us that time."

"Well, maybe Perry *is* as smart as a raven. Sometimes I think so. But jays are awfully dumb about humans."

"What do you mean?"

"They come right up to 'em. I've seen Perry, there, actually land on a human's *hand!*"

"Oh, all the time," Molly added. "They're terribly cocky, those gray jays."

"Well, if you was as quick as they was, you'd be cocky, too," said Scratch, picking at something under his wing. "Put it this way, like. Have ya ever heard a' one a' them jays gettin' *caught* by a human?"

"No," said Molly. "I guess humans just can't kill them."

Greta joined the conversation. "It's not that humans *can't* kill them," she added. "It's that they don't *want* to kill them. Gray jays are just too cute to kill."

She stopped to eat as the ravens laughed at her remark. How could you not like gray jays? Friendly, honest, helpful and, yes, cute in their soft gray-and-black plumage – and they had those big eyes and that cheery voice.

Greta struggled with a strip of rib meat, then held it dangling from her bill. "I'd love to stay and eat this, friends, but we had better go," she said. "The coyotes are just across the creek."

No one had seen Greta look over that way, but sure enough, the coyotes were slinking through the undergrowth, only their ears showing. The animals would soon be dangerously close.

All the birds leapt at once, flapping into the trees surrounding the kill. Now safe, they watched the coyotes jump across the creek for another go at the meat. Two of them seized a front leg in their jaws and pulled at it, growling, until the skin tore away. Then both of them went for the exposed flesh. The other two also latched on, and soon all four animals were fighting over the leg, snapping and baring their fangs. The biggest one snarled nastily and nipped at the others, driving them back. Then he settled down to gorge himself.

"Disgusting," Molly said, turning her bill away. "I don't know why they have to eat like that. And they don't care a bit for each other."

In the days that followed, Colin and the flock began to adjust to each other's ways. The flock thought him odd for asking stupid questions all the time, but at least he was friendly, and he went out of his way to be helpful. He spent much of his time exploring the valley, and one morning he came to the Flap reporting a new carcass. It was a small find – a marmot – but it had died of natural causes and nothing else had scavenged it. So the flock had first pick, enjoying delicacies that usually would have gone to a predator.

Maybe, some of the birds thought, Colin would never remember where he came from. And that would be fine with them.

PART TWO

Autumn

I

All in a day, summer ended at Yamnuska.

Molly knew it first. She awoke on a cold, gray morning and said, as the first statement of the day, "That's it."

"What's it?" Zack asked, scattering a few drops of dew off his feathers. Like couples who have lived together a long time, the two birds seemed to fall asleep and wake up simultaneously.

"That's it," Molly repeated. "Summer's over."

"You know, I think you're right," Zack agreed. "It's time."

Colin slept on, crouched at his corner of the roost, his head turned far back under his wing. He dreamed uneasily of black things moving in whiteness, of cold and silence.

"First it's going to rain," Molly said.

"Then the rain will turn to snow," Zack continued.

"And that will be it," Molly concluded.

Indeed, that *was* it. The rain started. Colin's dream began to include wet things as well as cold things. He woke up. "Gro," he said, stretching out his wings. "Gee, it's cold."

"Ought to be," said Zack. "It's summer's end today."

Molly turned to Colin and noted his puzzlement. "You don't remember, do you?" she said, gently. "Well, it happens the same way every year. We get a day like this – soggy and chilly – and then the rain turns to snow, way up here on Yamnuska. And that's *really* miserable, wouldn't you say, Zack?" He nodded. "But the snow melts away," she continued. "Then it warms up again, and it's, you know, autumn."

The rain continued all morning, right through the Flap. The birds spoke of nothing but the weather, and Maya's meteorological report confirmed what everyone was thinking. The temperature fell as the rain continued. By late afternoon scattered flakes of wet snow were tumbling out of the clouds along with the rain. Then one of the sharper peaks poked a hole in the belly of the cloud deck. Down came the contents. By dark the rocks were white. By the next morning everything was coated thickly. All the warmth in the world, it seemed, had been lost, and just as Molly had predicted, the birds were miserable.

"By the Trees," Zack complained loudly, shaking off the accumulation from his wings, "I can't get used to this. Happens every year, and every year it's bloody unbearable!" He stalked around the roosting ledge, picking up first one black foot, then the other, flicking off slush.

Colin's thoughts were on his crop. How could he and the others find food under the snow? "What do we do?" he asked, growing worried.

"About what?" Zack replied in an irritated voice.

"About breakfast," Colin continued. "How are we going to find anything to eat?"

Zack saw the fear in Colin's eyes and reassured him. "Not to worry. There's still plenty to eat. That elk carcass isn't gone yet, and that sheep up the valley – well, there's lots left on the sheep."

"But what about the snow?" Colin persisted. "How can we find anything under the snow? Everything looks different today."

"Oh, I see." Molly said sympathetically. "You can't remember about snow. Well, my first snowfall, I was scared, too – terribly scared. All the landmarks I knew were gone. No, not gone. They had *changed*. The trees didn't look familiar. And even Raven's End looked so strange, as if I'd never seen it before. But it's okay, Colin. The snow will melt. But even when it comes back – and it will, you know, because winter's coming – even then you'll get to know all the places here just as well as you know them now. Every bird does."

To prove her point, Molly coasted off directly toward the elk carcass for breakfast. She found it easily enough, but Colin lost his bearings and had to follow her. Most of the flock was already there, leaving their big three-toed tracks in the snow as they walked about the cougar's kill, now well picked-over. Still, the birds found a bit of this and a bit of that. Something red clinging in a crevice between two ribs, or something unidentified adhering to the skull. The meat was powerfully ripe by now, and even a small piece was enough.

Back at Raven's End with their crops full, the birds felt somewhat better. Still, the Flap started out sorrowfully, with lots of complaining and petty squabbling.

"We didn't have snow this early *last* year."

"Oh, yes we did. Don't you remember?"

"That was the year before, dummy."

"Who's a dummy?!"

The Main Raven said reassuring things about the long-term outlook for carrion availability this season, the quality and quantity of the various fall berries and so on, but nothing improved the humor of the meeting – until the sun broke through the clouds. Suddenly the mood of the flock changed. The cold mass of insecurity in every bird's heart melted instantly as heat and warmth beamed down between the clouds. Colin blinked. What had been a coating of frigid desolation was now a carpet of blinding white light.

Without another thought the flock made the Motion. The blackness of their outspread wings gathered the sun's power into their daily wheel of unity, and with a mighty "Rawk-a-taw!" they all leapt into the air at once, surging upward as fast as they could toward that hot spot in the sky – the spot that every bird knew to be the most important thing in their lives, as it was to all living creatures on Yamnuska, to all living creatures in the Rocky Mountains, in all the mountains and on all the plains and over all the oceans of the world.

A few hours later the sun had turned the snow to dripping water. A day later the rocks were dry again. But the work of the weather had been done. The storm was a signal, and the plants got the message. The poplarlike aspens, especially, took notice. They had been waiting for this. In the spring they had responded to a different signal, one that had said "grow." And dutifully they had grown, sprouting beautiful spring-green leaves, strong and bright, full of brand-new chlorophyll. All through the summer those leaves had worked hard, using sunlight to turn water and carbon dioxide into starch, cellulose, proteins, and wood fibre; growing thicker trunks, heavier branches, new twigs, new roots. But by late summer the leaves were wearing out. They had gone from the shiny, vigorous green of spring to the dull, weary green of late summer. Their enzymes and hormones and catalysts were drying up. Instead of feeding the tree, the leaves were now feeding mainly the insect larvae that nibbled at their edges and chewed serpentine tracks through their centres.

The leaves were glad to feel the snow. They were ready to retire. This they always did in style, by having the Show.

That's what the ravens called it: "the Show." They had a saying about it: "First the snow, then the Show."

"Oh, Zack," Molly called on the second morning after the end-of-summer storm. "There's a streak of yellow over there!"

Across the Bow Valley, a large grove of aspen had come into its fall color. Since every tree in the grove was joined at the roots to every other tree, they all got the word at once – "Do it! Now!" – and they did. They let the chlorophyll in their leaves go from green to colorless, and the yellow carotene, present all the while in the leaves but masked by the green, emerged from hiding. Every aspen in the grove went gloriously gold.

Yes, the Show was on. And it grew better by the day. The evergreens contributed by darkening their needles to afford maximum contrast against the aspen patches, which spattered the foothills with yellow. On the forest floor, too, the Show erupted. This was wild-rose country, and countless thousands of rose bushes went from summer green to autumn red. Every rose leaf, half the length of a raven's bill, blushed brighter by the hour.

In flight, the birds could look down to the dots of red, each advertising the rose hips – the fruits of the roses – weighing down the plants. Those rose hips were glossy red and swollen with seeds, good for a bird.

Good for Colin and Zack and Molly as the bright-blue days of fall drifted on. They feasted on rose hips and raspberries and gooseberries and all the other gifts of that prickly tribe. They plucked the last of the chokecherries off the bushes that grew by the edges of the woods. They climbed with the updrafts to higher elevations, where the leaves of the low-bush cranberry presented the reddest red of all. In dry places along the sunny banks of the Bow River the birds found snowberries, pure white and tasting of winter. Black twinberries ripened in cool, shady spots, where the morning frost stayed longer. The frost soaked into every kind of berry – bearberry, blueberry, dewberry, huckleberry, buffaloberry, crowberry, elderberry, bunchberry, cranberry, gooseberry, grouseberry – and the frost broke down the cells and released the sugars. Night by night, all this food grew sweeter.

Black bears ran from one bountiful shrub to the next, eating urgently. They ripped at the fruit-laden boughs with their claws and stuffed the berries into their mouths, leaves and all, chewing only a few times and swallowing hard, driven by a powerful hunger. Each bear had to grow very fat if it was to survive the winter-long sleep that was soon to come.

Overhead, the great fall migration began. Millions of birds – ducks, geese, robins, sparrows, warblers – followed the eastern edge of the Rockies on their way south. The eagles cruised over the rough gray ridges of the front ranges, while the hawks preferred the rolling green-and-yellow swells of the foothills. Some migrants journeyed west instead of south, across the mountains to the Pacific coast, where they could winter by the sea.

A few of these travelling birds would stop each night at the east end of Yamnuska, where they were welcomed by the ravens as interesting visitors with tales to tell of summers spent in the taiga of mountain ranges far to the north, or on the tundra of the High Arctic.

"Shall we join them?" Colin asked.

"Join who?" Molly countered.

"The other birds. The birds flying south. It sounds like fun."

"Oh, Colin, you're hopeless." She giggled. "Ravens don't fly south!"

"Why not?" Colin persisted.

Molly was laughing too hard to reply, so Zack answered the question, trying not to show his amusement.

"We don't need to, Colin. Ravens already live in the best places in the world. Like here at Yamnuska. And really, you know, we can live anywhere at all. Those other birds *have* to leave, or they'd starve in the winter when the bugs are gone. But we won't starve. We can eat practically anything. So we stay put."

"But think of what we're missing! Those tropical forests – they sound really great!"

"Yes, indeed," Zack replied patiently, "but first you have to get there. And then you have to get back in the spring. Now, think about it. Of all those migrating birds, do you know how many make it back here? Fewer than half." Colin blinked. "We stay, and with good reason," Zack stated firmly, letting Colin know that the subject was closed.

Frost glazed the yellow aspen leaves every night, but it vanished every morning. There was no new snow, no rain. Afternoons were warm and lazy. The sun covered its daily circuit without passing behind any clouds. Soon to lose its heat to the pale cold of winter, the sun provided all the living things below with a farewell treat.

The ravens thought of the sun as a hole in the sky that poured out heat and light. The sun thought of the ravens as tiny moving specks in the atmosphere, specks of black – the sun's favorite color, for nothing loves the sun's warmth as much as the color black – and so the ravens were the sun's favorite birds. This was no surprise to the ravens, who knew it all along.

Autumn swept quickly along the length of the Canadian Rocky Mountains. In only a few days the signal, written in gold, had travelled from one end to the other; from the red-and-green argillite peaks surrounding Waterton Lakes to the shaly brown ridges sloping down to the Liard River, far, far to the north. The message was simple: to everything there is a season. Turn, turn, turn.

II

Colin spent much of his time that fall on the wing. He loved to fly, and he flew for hour after hour. He would climb for thousands of wing-beats, until his big flight muscles ached; he would soar, gliding from the top of one invisible column of rising air to the next, hunting out the thermals over and over until he could find them instinctively. From on high he would look down, memorizing the lay of the land.

Then he would dive, fast and far. He would dive so fast that he could barely open his eyes against the scream of the wind – his private gale, made by his own plummeting body. He could feel his hollow bones strain against the air-pressure change. As the ground rushed up he learned to flare his wings carefully, a feather at a time, and thus to pull out of these plunges under control. "No more juniper-bush crashes for me!" he shouted into the roaring slipstream.

He practiced to perfection the half-roll, the barrel roll, the somer-sault, the mid-air stall, and all the other stunts and tricks he had seen the Raven's Enders do. He invented new ones. At the Evening Flights he was eager to show off his growing skill, chasing about the sky with Molly and Zack and the others, who were astonished by Colin's rapid advancement in flying. Zack had to admit that Colin now flew better than he did, which was saying a lot, for Zack was one of the stronger birds in the flock. The only bird Colin couldn't catch was the Main Raven, and day by day, chase by chase, Colin was gaining. How did he keep improving? It was the sort of progress that one saw in a fledgling, not in an adult bird.

Molly asked Greta about this. Greta's reply was to ask another ques-tion: "If you had no idea where you came from, wouldn't you at least want to know where you were going?"

"Yes, but what does that have to do with –"

"And wouldn't you want to become strong enough to get there?"

"Well, I suppose. But Greta, I don't really understand –"

"There's no need to understand. Just have fun thinking about it." And Greta flew off.

A raven has extraordinary vision, which is a good thing, because a raven's sense of smell is rather weak and the bird has to locate food mainly by sight. Colin was soaring above Raven's End one morning when something in the image on his retina tripped a switch in his brain. The switch turned on a message: "Hey! What was that?"

Colin dived like a black thunderbolt. The image grew larger. An object down there was pure white against the gray limestone, and it was moving.

As Colin whistled by, the white thing took fright. It bounded under a boulder.

"Sorry to frighten you," Colin called as he landed on the boulder. "I was just checking. Not hungry at all. Really."

"Well, you could have been a little more *polite*," came a small voice from under the rock. Colin apologized again, promised that he wouldn't attack, and the white thing came out into the sun. This animal looked to be made of snow, thought Colin, gazing incredulously at it. Much smaller than a raven, its body was long and thin, and it was all white – except for the tail, which had a black tip. Its eyes and nose were black, too. What was it?

Colin continued the conversation by offering his own name. "I'm Colin C.C.," he said in a friendly way. "What's yours?"

"Optimistic Molt," said the creature. It wiggled its white whiskers.

"Beg pardon?" Colin asked.

"That's my name, like it or leave it. An ermine can't be too careful about her name. Those who know me well sometimes call me 'Oppie,' for short. But you can't."

"I wouldn't think of it," said Colin, noting how irritated the ermine sounded. And irri*tating*, too. The voice was high and the tone was sarcastic, almost sneering.

"Tell me," Colin continued, trying to ignore the unpleasantness, "where did you get such a str – I mean, such a *fascinating* name?"

"Oh, it's just a little something I thought up. You probably already know that weasels get really boring names at birth. Mine was 'Mustela Erminea.' Isn't that awful? So I got rid of it. Everybody told me that my coat changed color earlier in the season than anyone else's here at Weasel's End, which stands to reason, because I'm way ahead on everything, so I chose 'Optimistic Molt.' Quite a pretty name, don't you think?"

"Uh, sure," Colin replied, thinking just the opposite. "A charming name, really. But did you say, 'Weasel's End'?"

"Of course. Weasel's End. Where we are right now."

"But isn't it called 'Raven's End'?"

"Oh, no, no, no. Absolutely not. Nobody ever named anything for *ravens.*" She peered down her nose and curled her lip. "How vulgar. No offense intended, but you can see what I mean, I'm sure."

Colin stifled a laugh. "Oh, of course," he agreed, sounding earnest. "We ravens understand that quite well."

"You do?"

"Well, this particular raven does."

"It's about time one of them did." Optimistic Molt began licking her front feet.

"Would you mind explaining to me how your coat changes color?"

"Humph." Optimistic Molt looked up sourly. "I've met *smarter* ravens. Surely you must have heard that I am the reddest of all the weasels around here in summer and the whitest in winter. Everybody says so."

"But it's not really winter yet," Colin said.

"So what? We've had snow on the ground already this fall, haven't we? I'm just getting the jump on everyone. Especially on that nasty long-tailed weasel down along the ridge, who thinks that *she's* some kind of gift to the world."

Colin thought for a moment. "You're white in the winter so no one can see you against the snow, right?"

"Hey, the bird has some brains after all! Of course. Just remember that in the winter you are to refer to me as an 'ermine,' not a weasel. I'm a weasel in the summer only." She turned her head coyly. "Or, if you like," she added, "you can call me a 'stoat' in the summer. Those of good breeding call me a stoat. And an ermine when I'm all white."

"Certainly," Colin agreed. "But why is the tip of your tail *black?*"

"That is a very elementary question, and I will answer it for you only because you seem nicer than most ravens. There is a dreadful creature – I won't mention its name – that actually kills weasels."

"No!" Colin said, sounding shocked.

"Yes! Despite the good we do, getting rid of all those mice every year. Why, if we weasels didn't, uh, 'manage' them, they'd reproduce themselves right out of business. The whole valley would be full of stupid little rodents, and then where would we be? I mean, really."

Optimistic Molt hesitated, giving Colin time to interject another question. "This creature that dares to attack weasels," he said. "What does it look like?"

"Well, it's a bird. A big one, and it flies at night. But that's all I'm going to say about it. Except that it's fairly stupid. And it falls for the old black-tail trick every time."

"What's the black-tail trick?"

"Oh, it's a wonderful trick. No one else has it except us weasels. You see, the owl – oh, dear, I *did* use its name!" The weasel suddenly looked frightened. She flattened herself on the rock, at the same time bunching her body up in the middle, as if she were about to jump away. Then she regained her composure and continued talking.

"Yes, well. The – shall we say, 'savage attacker' – comes down to grab the poor, defenseless ermine in its talons. But at the last moment the ermine flicks that black tip, and the killer is *distracted by it!* It strikes at the tip. But the tip, you see," and here the weasel started to giggle, "the tip is just *hair!* No bones! So the stupid owl gets nothing! Hee hee! Oh, dear, I've said it again." Optimistic Molt cowered once more. "I'm going," she said. "This place is just too exposed for my taste. That horrible prairie falcon could be around. Oh, dear, I've said *its* name, too. I really must be off. How nice to have met you. Let's not meet again. Goodbye."

And Optimistic Molt was off. Rather than running quickly away, the little weasel seemed to melt into the landscape. Her long white body bent this way and that, worming through the spaces between boulders. She would disappear under a rock, then reappear on the other side. Her head would pop up, whiskers wiggling; her tiny black eyes would peer quickly here and there. Then she would vanish again.

Colin watched, fascinated by the way the animal moved. So this was an ermine – the terror of the small-mammal population, he supposed. That skinny, slinky body could easily slip down the burrows of the deer mice. Or enter the grass-lined runs of the pikas. Hadn't that pika – what was its name? Ah yes, Okotona – hadn't Okotona talked about danger from weasels?

Optimistic Molt stopped for a moment atop a smallish boulder. She squatted, then she moved on. Colin flew over to see. There, on the rock, was a fresh dropping. Fairly long and very dark, it lay between orange and yellow lichens, draped, Colin felt, in a way that indicated some forethought as to its placement.

As Colin contemplated the dropping, Optimistic Molt called out from some distance away. "Nice arrangement, if I do say so myself."

III

Later that morning, playing in the rapids of air gusting around the South Face of Yamnuska, Colin heard something falling down the cliff.

Bonk, clonk, PING!

"Heads up!" came a human voice. "I dropped a 'biner!"

"One of those new ones?" came another voice.

"'Fraid so."

There were two humans halfway up the South Face. He hadn't seen many climbers since the end of summer, but today seemed especially warm, so it was no wonder that humans were out and about in the mountains. Both of these were dressed in red sweaters. With their yellow helmets, they stood out brightly against the sombre limestone. One climber was directly over the other, higher up. A blue rope ran between them.

The climbers were in one of Yamnuska's big inside corners, where two slabs of rock came together at an angle, like two walls on a tall building. Colin swung in close to the cliff, alighted on a projecting pinnacle of rock, and settled down to watch and listen.

"John!" one of the climbers called up. "No more rope!"

"Okay," came the reply. John was going to have to find a stopping place, because all the rope between him and the other climber was used up. John looked around, located a small ledge in the corner and stepped over to it. He did something with one of the shiny items hanging at his waist – climbers carried lots of shiny things, Colin noted – and called down to the other climber. "On belay, Linda!"

Colin looked toward this "Linda" creature. Brown braids swung from under her helmet. "Climbing!" she called to John, then upward she went.

Colin was surprised at how agile these humans were. From where he was sitting the rock looked blank – nothing to hang onto – but Linda was moving up nonetheless, and she was not using the rope for help.

John took up the slack as she climbed toward him. She straddled the corner, one foot on each wall, a little way out from where the two sides met. Her fingers ran over the rock surface, coming to rest on small holds. She took little steps, carefully shifting her weight with each move.

Linda quickly and gracefully closed the gap between herself and John. Soon they were together at John's stopping place. It was so small that only one of them could stand there at a time, so Linda didn't wait long. She took all the shiny things John was carrying and started upward again. John let the rope out as she moved above him.

When Linda was a couple of body-lengths above John she stopped. She was practically level with Colin's perch and only a few steps away, but she was so preoccupied with her climbing that she didn't see him. She looked into the crack at the back of the corner, as if searching for something. Then she took a little silvery item from the climbing gear at her waist, stuck it into the crack, fiddled with the rope and climbed higher.

An instant later Linda fell.

"John!" she yelled.

"Awk!" Colin cried. This would be the end of her! Humans couldn't fly!

But hardly had she started falling than she stopped. Instead of smashing into the boulders at the base of the South Face, she was dangling on the rope only a little way below the point at which she fell.

This was incredible, Colin thought. If the humans hadn't figured out how to avoid falling at all, they had at least figured out how to avoid falling very *far*.

Linda seemed surprisingly unflustered. She rested for a moment in the corner, all her weight on the rope, then she got back onto the rock.

"You okay?" John called up.

"Yeah," Linda replied, almost casually. "Hold broke."

"That must have been what hit me in the helmet," John said. The little chip of rock had put a new scratch there, among many old ones in the yellow plastic. "Didn't hurt, though."

"Okay, I'm trying again."

"Gotcha."

Linda climbed back up to the place where she had fallen. She hesitated there, put another item in the crack and continued climbing. Every couple of body-lengths she put something else in the crack, until John called up, just as Linda had, that the rope was fully extended. Linda found a ledge and sat down on it. Using yet another bit of gear, she hooked a loop of the rope to something sticking out of the cliff. Now John climbed up to Linda. She took up the rope as he climbed, and he collected all the little shiny things that Linda had put in the crack. Nothing was left behind.

So this was how it all worked, Colin thought. Humans may be crazy to climb on these cliffs, but they were awfully *smart* in their craziness. Yet why did they climb on Yamnuska in the first place?

Linda's ledge was big enough for both climbers to sit on. Tied securely to the rock, they dangled their legs over the edge. A warm breeze was flowing up the face. It was now midday, and all morning the rock had basked in the sun. Yamnuska was warm to the touch, in turn warming the air that touched it. The heated air rose in a thin sheet caressing the rough limestone; this was the friendly breeze felt by the climbers. They took off their sweaters. John carried a small pack, and now he opened it. Out came lunch.

Colin was immediately very interested, and he flew closer to the two. Perched nearby, he saw and smelled his favorite human food: a peanut-butter-and-jelly sandwich. He croaked hungrily, and the climbers heard him.

"Gee, that bird's sitting awfully close," John said.

"What kind is it? A crow?"

"Naw. It's a raven. Look how big it is."

"Here, Mister Raven." Linda threw Colin a bit of her sandwich. Colin gobbled it down.

"Wow!" said John. "He sure ate that fast. Let's try some gorp on him."

Linda pulled a plastic bag out of her pack and reached into it, withdrawing a handful of tasty-looking peanuts, raisins, and chocolate chips. Some of it spilled down the rock, and Colin immediately flew down to intercept what he could of it. He caught a raisin in mid-air.

"He got it!" Linda cried delightedly. "Neat!"

Colin came even closer. He hopped onto the same ledge the climbers were sitting on.

"Hey, I've never seen that before," John said. "Ravens don't usually get this close to people."

"Maybe it's really a crow," Linda said, defending her earlier opinion.

"Well, a crow wouldn't get this close, either." John reached out his hand. In the centre was another hunk of sandwich.

Colin started to hop over to take it – when he suddenly remembered what Zack and Molly had said about humans. Quickly, he backed off.

"See, he's not dumb," John said. "He won't eat out of my hand."

"I'll just leave him some over here." Linda set down a corner of her sandwich on the ledge. Colin crept over warily, seized it, and flapped over to his perch to eat.

Linda pulled a plastic bottle full of water out of John's pack. She took a long drink from it and passed it to him. He was thirsty, too, and drank the rest. John closed up the little pack and they prepared to climb on. Linda took the lead again. "Bye-bye, Mister Raven," she said, looking over at him with a smile. "See you on top, maybe."

Colin watched the climbers all afternoon. They reached the summit of Yamnuska just as the sun went down. They didn't stay on top for long; in a hurry to descend the mountain before dark, they coiled their rope and jogged off down the hiker's trail on the north side of the peak.

The summit of Yamnuska was marked by a cairn – a stack of rocks – and Colin sat on it after the climbers had left, wondering again why they did what they did. If they just wanted to reach the top, they could have walked up the trail. If they had been looking for something to eat, they wouldn't have carried their lunch with them. Maybe that was it! Maybe humans had to carry their food to places like the South Face, well away from everything, in order to eat it. Their food was so good; perhaps other animals, or maybe other humans, would steal it if they could. So humans had to come up here to eat. That must be it. Colin croaked a self-satisfied croak.

He decided that he liked these climber-humans. He croaked again, thinking of the wonderful food they had given him, and to his surprise he was answered. Looking southward he saw the whole flock of Raven's Enders dancing out into the great empty space off the South Face. The mystery of why humans climbed cliffs had to be put aside; now it was time for the Flight.

Molly had called to Colin as she passed over the summit. That bird, she had thought. There he was, sitting all by himself. He'd been gone the whole afternoon. Doing what? Perching on the summit cairn? She'd never understand what went through his mind. But he was always thinking; she was sure of that.

The flock soared and wheeled in the sunset. Ravens were arriving from every direction, greeting one another – "Gro!" – and announcing where they had been that day. Brendan had made quite a trip, flying south right across the Bow Valley in search of rose hips.

"Oh, hey – you should see the hips over there!" he called. Most of the birds moved closer to Brendan. "They were, like, *mega!*" he continued, doing a barrel roll for emphasis. "Awesome. Really excellent. I'm going back tomorrow for more. Who's going with me? Sarah?"

Sarah, like Brendan, had fledged that spring. The two had taken some flying lessons together from the Main Raven, and they liked each other. Sarah replied to Brendan's invitation. "Sure! I'll go. Hey, Mum! Can I go?"

"If you don't mind me coming, too." Marg had a sweet spot in her crop for rose hips, especially if they were as good as Brendan said they were. Besides, she thought she'd better come along anyway, to look after the youngsters in case they ran into trouble.

IV

It began as an ordinary autumn day in the Canadian Rockies. At the morning Flap, Dolus and Garth were back in the circle. They had been away longer than expected – a few days in exile was normally enough punishment for fighting – and both seemed changed. They spoke in friendly voices, and Dolus said he was very sorry for stealing from Molly. Zack apologized to Dolus for taking the first peck during the fight. Dolus apologized to Zack. With genuine affection the banished birds were welcomed back.

Colin felt that there could be no better bunch of C.C.s in the whole world. He had given up hope of remembering where he had come from originally, and even though this bothered him from time to time, it was bearable now that the Raven's Enders had taken him in. Zack and Molly were good friends, and he was coming to know the other birds better as the days passed. When the flock made the Motion, spreading their wings toward each other and creating that wonderful wheel-shape of solidarity, Colin knew he could now join in. What a privilege to be considered a Raven's Ender, even if it was only temporary. Rawk-a-taw!

As usual, Colin flew off on his own after the Flap. He made his way lazily up the valley behind Yamnuska. Many things about this place were starting to make sense. Yet the more he learned, the more he wanted to know. Humans, for example. What were humans all about? Colin had talked at length about humans one day with Zack and Molly, and he hadn't learned much – except that Molly considered them terribly dangerous and Zack considered them terribly stupid.

"They do the dumbest things," Zack had said. "Throwing away food, beating down the ground where they walk so nothing grows on it, letting these idiot dogs go everywhere with them. I tell you, Colin, I've even seen them sticking *fire* into their *mouths*. Would you believe it? They must burn themselves inside. Smoke comes out!"

Colin was trying to imagine this when something caught his attention down below, on the back side of Yamnuska. There, on the trail to the summit, were a couple of hikers. Fancy that, he thought; start thinking about humans and there they were. He changed course.

Having been warned repeatedly about approaching humans too closely, Colin glided by at a safe distance. He hadn't told any of the other birds about the afternoon he had spent with the climbers. Molly, particularly, would have been shocked to learn that he had been right on the same ledge with them.

These humans might be climbers, too, Colin thought as he looked them over. They had on bright red jackets, like some of the climbers wore, and red hats, too. They carried packs, and they also had sticks with them. Hikers on Yamnuska often carried walking sticks, but climbers didn't, he recalled; they carried ropes instead. Colin couldn't see any ropes, so he decided that these were hikers, not climbers. Both kinds of humans always carried goodies in their packs. And often they had gorp.

The thought of gorp – that exquisite mixture of raisins and nuts and chocolate chips – lured Colin on. He sailed close by the hikers. As he did, he saw that one of the humans was carrying something that made smoke, just as Zack had said. Colin flapped ahead of the hikers and landed on a boulder beside the trail. He wanted a close look at this fire-eating.

As the humans approached, he saw that the fire was in a twig that one of the hikers held between its fingers. Smoke came out the end of the twig, which was white, as if the bark had come off and the twig had lain in the sun a long time. Or maybe it was a little piece of bone, Colin thought. It was certainly white enough to be bone.

The hikers were now very close, but Colin was so fascinated that he didn't fly away. The hikers stopped. One of them spoke.

"Well, I'll be gol-darned, Phil. This here crow is just settin' there. I could reach out 'n' grab it. You ever seen the like?"

The one with the fire-bone, which is what Colin decided it must be, stuck the thing into its mouth and sucked on it.

"I never seen a crow like this, neither. Pretty bold crow." Smoke came out of the hiker as it spoke.

Colin jumped back in horror. The human really was on fire!

"Whoa," it said, smoke puffing through its lips. "Don't fly off, now, birdy."

The human stuck the fire-bone back in its mouth. More smoke came out as it continued talking. "By golly, that wind is cold." The smoke blew away quickly, for the day was indeed getting windy. The wind came from the north, across the valley behind Yamnuska and up the slope the humans were hiking across. "Them clouds are lookin' pretty ornery. Wanta stop here awhile, Frank? Kinda watch the weather?"

Colin and the humans eyed each other. Then, Colin noted happily, the hikers took their packs off. This was a good sign that eating would come next. Sure enough, out of the pack came a brown paper bag, and out of the bag came sandwiches. Colin could see the peanut butter and jam oozing out. Oh, joy! He hopped right over.

Sitting there, the humans didn't know how to react. Colin was a large bird, with a wingspan almost as broad as a human's outstretched arms. His body was as long as a human's forearm and hand; his bill was almost as long as a finger. And here he was, at arm's length from the humans, looking intently at the sandwich one of them was eating.

Colin didn't wait to be offered a bite. He reached forward with his bill and grabbed.

The human holding the sandwich fell backward in fright. The firebone in its mouth fell out. "Cripes! It's attacking!"

"Hang on, Phil!" the other one shouted. "I'll get it!"

The humans were yelling and jumping around. Colin decided he'd better leave. He leapt up, flapping hard, trying to carry the whole sandwich in his bill. But it was too heavy and he couldn't get airborne.

"Oh, man! Look at those wings!"

"Get clear, Phil! Get clear!" One of the humans had picked up the stick it had been carrying. Uh-oh, thought Colin. He dropped the sandwich and leapt again.

BANG!

Colin heard the loudest sound he had ever heard, and at the same moment he felt something tear through his right wing.

"*Awk!*"

"You got him!"

Colin fell to the ground. He fluttered about, his wing completely numb. He ordered it to flap. "By the Trees, *flap!*" he cried aloud. The wing quivered, but it would not obey him.

"Rip off my sandwich, will you? Shoot it again, Frank! You only winged 'im!"

BANG!

The rock next to Colin's bill shattered. Everything was ringing. Pain roared into his wing as the numbness left. There were bits of stone in his eyes. His brain was shrieking a single thought: "Fly! Fly!"

"But I *can't* fly," Colin told his brain. "Can't fly!"

"Then *run!*" screamed his brain. "If you can't fly, run! Run away up the rocks! Go, go!"

One of the humans was waving its stick around. "Missed. Stupid bird won't hold still."

Colin's legs were doing what his injured wing could not. Desperately they carried him up the rocky slope of Yamnuska. He scrambled over boulders, hopping, falling, scratching his shins, breaking his feathers, running, running. The wind was helping, blowing him uphill. It carried something with it. Snow.

Bang!

The sound was farther away, now. But again the rock exploded, underneath him this time, tiny chips stinging into his body from below. A smell came with the pain; the sulphurous odor of shattered limestone, the same smell a falling rock makes as it tumbles down a cliff, battering itself to bits as it falls. To bits – bits of snow – the wind so strong now –

Bang! Something stung Colin in the tail. "*Awk!*" Run! Run!

And there, ahead of him, was the ridgeline. Rock against sky. A million flakes of snow blowing him toward it. Only a little farther, now –

"Dang. He's gonna get away. But he'll die anyhow. You got 'im twice for sure, Frank."

"Wisht I had me a shotgun. That'd do it."

"Since when did you go carryin' a shotgun way up on Yamnuska? Ever shoot a sheep with a shotgun?"

"No, but now I'm gonna pack one anyway. 'Cause of the birds. Haw! Birds're bad up here, eh, Phil? Haw haw! Take a guy's sandwich right outta his hand!"

"Hee hee! Better go *armed*, eh? Hee hee hee!"

A heavy gust of wind spun the humans around.

"It's blowin' a blizzard. Let's get the heck off this boulder pile."

"For sure, for sure. I can't hardly even see the trail."

The same gust caught Colin on the ridge. It picked him up, all agony and confusion, and flung him over the South Face.

V

Brendan was out in front as he, Sarah, and Marg flew southward across the Bow Valley. This was his idea, his trip, and he wanted to make sure that he, not Marg, led the way. He was ready for this, he thought, since he was all grown up.

And he was, nearly. Coming into the world in April of that year, Brendan had been strong and smart from the start. He was the first in his brood to hatch, the first to fledge. He had arrived at Yamnuska from farther north along the mountain front, where his parents were members of the Black Rock Mountain Flock. His mother was one of Marg's sisters, and when Brendan was still in the nest his mother had told him wonderful stories about Yamnuska: about riding the thermals along the South Face, about sunrise at Raven's End, about the flowery meadows and the Willow Marsh and the beaver ponds. As soon as Brendan was able to fly the distance – some would have said a little *before* he was able to fly the distance – he had set off alone to visit his relatives in the Raven's End Flock. He had barely made it. But he had also found that what his mother had told him was true, and he had stayed on at Yamnuska, which seemed an even more agreeable place after he met Sarah, Marg's only fledgling that year.

Marg had lost her nestmate in the spring, just after the brood hatched. That made it very unlikely that any of the young birds would survive, for it took both parents to feed them. Marg tried to carry on, but she soon realized that it was hopeless. All of the nestlings were starving. Still, she noticed that one of them – Sarah – was stronger than the others. She made a difficult decision. She chose Sarah over the rest. She kept Sarah fed as the others died, and thus Sarah had lived.

When Sarah left the nest, Marg had the bittersweet satisfaction of producing at least one fledgling in a year that should have given her none. She considered this, watching Sarah and Brendan flying happily with her that morning. Yes, it had been the right thing to do.

Marg thought about Brendan. Of the many young birds she had known, Brendan had outstanding qualities. But he was also impulsive, ready to try any sparrow-brained idea. Yet he was so well-intentioned and quick to take direction from the older birds . . . well, Brendan had promise. Marg remembered being like that herself: young, keen to show off, wanting everyone to listen to *her*, not to the Main Raven or Greta or the other old fuddy-duddies in the flock. Well, she'd be there to help if his exuberance got him and Sarah into trouble. Sarah, now, was different. Quiet. More careful. Studious. It was Sarah who had caught the first grasshopper of the year and brought it to the Flap, wondering what it was. Everyone had laughed, and poor Sarah was embarrassed to a croak. Even that idiotic Main Raven had laughed. But Marg had comforted Sarah and demanded that the flock apologize. Here Sarah had come to them seeking help, and what had she received? Ridicule! It just wasn't fair.

By this time the birds were about halfway across the valley, right over the Bow River where it passed through a particularly wide, flat stretch called Morley Flats. Morley Flats was a place where the glaciers had dumped enormous quantities of stones. Trees shunned the place; the stony ground would grow nothing but grass.

Marg noticed that the grass was waving in the wind, and that her ground speed was picking up. All birds are sensitive to this; if the ground goes by more quickly than it ought to, then there must be a tail wind. And quite a tail wind it was. Since the ravens were flying south, and getting kicked along smartly as they did so, the wind must have been coming from the north. Something about that north wind worried Marg. She couldn't quite get a wing around that worry, but there it was. Something.

Sarah and Brendan, too, had noticed the tail wind. Now they played in it, climbing and diving as they tried to find the faster currents. "This is *great!*" Brendan croaked, catching a particularly powerful gust. He coasted right by Sarah and Marg.

"Hey! Wait for me!" Sarah called, flapping furiously. She, too, caught Brendan's gust, and the two left Marg behind for a moment. Then both the young birds were amazed to see Marg breeze by. She seemed to have found an even faster stream in the rushing atmosphere.

But Marg wasn't enjoying the wind. She was troubled by it. They were now a long way from Raven's End, and they would have to come back home against that wind. Well, maybe it would die down in the afternoon. Think positively, she told herself. There was no turning those kids around; Brendan wouldn't hear of it. And they were too old to order about. She just hoped that everything would be all right.

"That's the spot!" Brendan pointed his bill down to the left. By this time they were over the foothills flanking the south side of the Bow Valley. The slopes below were a patchwork of meadows, divided by groves of aspen and stands of spruce. The birds pulled in their wings and dived toward one of the meadows. They had to lose elevation quickly or be blown past their objective. As it was, they missed it and had to haul themselves back northward against the wind.

Just before landing, Marg cautioned her charges. "Now, remember. You should always perch a while before landing on the ground in unfamiliar territory," she instructed. "You never know. There might be a coyote in the willows over there, or maybe a marten behind that rock."

"Aw, we know, Mum," Sarah complained. "You don't have to tell us everything."

"Sorry, kids. I just can't help it, I guess. But we must be extra careful, this far from home."

They were sitting in a small aspen. Its golden leaves were gone – most of them had blown away that very day – and the wind was strong enough to rock the tree. The meadow grass below was brown, and everything had the look of late fall. After waiting and watching for what seemed like much too long to Brendan, Marg fluttered down to the ground. She performed the ritual of the Lead, doing jumping-jacks over to the patch of wild roses.

Just as Brendan had said, the rose hips here were magnificent. Red and plump, they were huge – too big to swallow whole – and taut with goodness. Brendan pulled one off its stem. He burst the hip in his bill, then tilted his head back and let the mealy, seedy insides tumble down his throat. "*Galargle! Galork! Skoonsh!*" he said through the enormous mouthful.

"Say what?" Sarah queried.

"*Gulp* – I said," Brendan repeated, "there's some *saskatoons* over there!" Not waiting for the reaction, he hopped across the meadow, nearly getting blown over in the wind. A patch of purple saskatoon berries waved like heavy wheat; somehow this prize had not been found by any other creature since it had set fruit many weeks ago. And now, sweetened wonderfully by the frost, it was all theirs. They fell to it greedily, downing berry after berry.

"You kids look like waxwings in a feeding frenzy," Marg scolded. "Let's watch our manners." But it was hard for Marg to control herself, let alone the young ravens. They might as well enjoy this late-autumn treat, she reasoned, and try to remember the place when winter came.

At this thought, an icy chill ran up her spine. She realized now what had been bothering her so much about this wind. She jerked about and faced into it, focussing her eyes as far in the distance as she could.

What she saw terrified her. A wall of cloud, full of snow, cold and white as death, was already halfway across Morley Flats, coming in low and fast.

"Oh, no!" she cried. "It's a Cold Blow! Kids! Stop what you're doing! We've got to get out of here!"

VI

The Evening Flight was cancelled that day, for the weather had turned suddenly and utterly bad. Zack and Molly huddled on their roosting ledge, buffeted by wind and snow, wondering where Colin was.

"He could be anywhere," Zack offered. "That bird flies so far. I just hope he found someplace to hide when the Cold Blow hit."

"It really is a Cold Blow, isn't it?" Molly replied, wincing as a gust threw snow into her eyes. "And Maya never manages to predict it."

"You'd think she would. We get a couple of these every year."

"Oh, Zack!" Molly cried. "I forgot! Marg and Sarah and Brendan flew right over the Bow River today! They might be way across Morley Flats!"

Zack blinked. "I hadn't thought of them, either. They could be in serious trouble. There's no place to hide over there." He gripped the rock tightly with his feet and tucked his head under his wing as another snowy blast tried to tear him from the ledge.

Molly shook off an instantly applied coating of white. "The poor things! It's just lucky they had Marg along. She won't panic. She's steady. She would have turned them around the minute she saw the Cold Blow coming." Molly kept worrying. "I just wish they were back – including Colin. It's getting dark."

"Oh, he can take care of himself," Zack said. "You know, Molly, I don't think Colin needs us like he used to."

"I just hope he wasn't involved in that shooting up near the summit this afternoon."

"Did you hear that, too? I was off in the North Valley. Didn't see anything. By the time I got over there, the Blow was coming in and the humans were leaving."

"Well, I didn't see anything, either. But you know how humans are. They were certainly trying to kill something."

"Hey – with any luck they shot a sheep! Maybe they didn't take it away! We'll get it!"

"Oh, Zack, I hope you're right. That would be a great way to start the winter." Molly was hungry. She hadn't eaten much that day because she didn't like flying in heavy wind, and it might be another day before the birds could go out scavenging. "All the same, I'm worried about Colin. Maybe he can't remember what a Cold Blow is like. Maybe he'll try to fly home instead of weathering it where it catches him."

"Well, we'll just have to see. But I wouldn't be surprised if he arrives in the middle of the storm – and in the middle of the night. He's strong enough to do it."

VII

Colin wasn't arriving anywhere. Wounded and desperate, he was in the grip of the north wind, which had tumbled him over the crest of Yamnuska.

The wind was very angry, as the leading edge of a cold front always is. This particular weather system had raged out of the Arctic and down the Rockies, battering the peaks, snapping off trees, killing the small songbirds caught in it. It tried to kill Colin. It saw that some of his feathers had been broken by the gunshots and it broke a few more. It felt around Colin's tail, found a sore spot and stung it with sharp crystals of ice.

Colin realized that he must be falling. He could see nothing through the roaring grayness of the storm, but he could feel the air chambers in his bones creaking. Soon he would feel something else: the pain of the crash. Twice he had plunged out of control from Yamnuska's heights. Zack had saved him the first time, and then the Main Raven had saved him. But this time no one could save him but himself.

As Zack had assured Molly, Colin was indeed a very strong raven. So strong that even a bullet through the wing hadn't stopped him. And now he showed another kind of strength, the strength of his will. What he did next hurt a great deal. He croaked out loud, it hurt so much. But he did it anyway. He straightened out his damaged wing and held it firm in the snow-filled fury of the storm. The bone, it seemed, had not been broken.

With both wings extended and at work, Colin regained control. Now he could ride *with* the wind instead of plummeting through it. Now he could survive.

VIII

Sarah had been eating saskatoon berries, relishing the sweet goo inside each one, when she heard her mother's cry. She turned in Marg's direction and saw a white wall of wind and snow coming at them. "Mum!" she cried. "What're we going to do?"

Brendan, too, had now seen the Cold Blow approaching. He tried not to show it, but his voice quavered in fear. "So can we just fly home now?"

Marg had collected her thoughts. "We'll never make it home against that. We've got to get to a safe place, and quick. Brendan, Sarah – listen to me. When this storm hits we'll hardly be able to see each other in the blowing snow. So stay close to me. Really close, okay? We'll go with the wind, trying to keep ahead of the worst, until we find some shelter. Got that?"

"Yes, Mum," Sarah said, her bill opening wide and closing with a frightened click.

"Brendan! Are you listening?!"

"Yes, ma'am."

"So here we go! Stay close!"

The three took off into the wind. It blew them backward as soon as they jumped up. Marg and Brendan recovered enough to stay in the air and turn south, but Sarah tumbled over a buffaloberry bush and struck the ground. She jumped again. This time she cleared the shrubbery, but just as she began to gain elevation her left wingtip brushed against an aspen branch. The wind spun her around. Her head struck the trunk of the tree. She went limp and fell to the ground.

A blast of wind swept through the clearing. It rolled Sarah over and over across the meadow until she caught against an outcropping of rock. There she lay in the dead brown grass. Like the grass, she too was soon covered with snow.

IX

Colin and the wind came to an understanding.

"I'm very angry," said the wind, "and I won't tolerate anyone flying with me! Get out!"

"No way!" Colin retorted. "I'm alive, in spite of everything, and you can't hurt me any more than I've been hurt already!"

"In that case, you have my admiration," said the wind. "You are a strong-willed bird, indeed. But that doesn't mean I have to *like* you."

"Then don't!"

"It's a deal!" shrieked the wind.

"All right!" Colin shouted back. And on he went, carried southward into the night on the back of the storm. "This is amazing," he said to himself. "I've been talking with a tempest!"

X

Marg and Brendan didn't look back; once above treetop level the wind was so fierce that it demanded all their attention. They didn't notice that Sarah was no longer with them, as they shot southward with the wild gusts, sometimes kicked up or down, or sideways, or even backward. The forest passed below in a green blur, now going gray as the sky around them filled with snow. Adding to the grayness was darkness. The wind seemed to be blowing away the remaining daylight. Marg knew that they had to find shelter, and soon. Night was falling fast. She had been right; the thing to do was go with the wind, hoping that it would carry them to a leeward slope where they, like the snow in the wind, could find a place to settle. She wondered where that place might be.

Despite the storm, Brendan stayed close to Marg. He knew that his life depended on it. And when he saw her fighting to descend, he fought his way down, too, down through the crazy currents of the cold front. Just as the last light of day was lost, Marg saw what she had been looking for: a cliff facing southward. A cliff on the far side of the foothills rimming the Bow Valley. A downwind haven for three ravens in trouble.

She turned to look for Brendan and Sarah. Barely visible in the whirling snow, there were two other ravens following her. But one of them – one of them didn't look right. Something was wrong with either Brendan or Sarah; the bird was holding its wings in a strange way, as if it were injured. Well, she would soon find out. It was only a little way now. Already the wind was more manageable, here in the lee of the cliff. She would just guide the other two toward what looked like a sheltering break in the rock. If it was what she thought it was, they were going to survive.

At that moment the bird with the injured wing caught up with her. It was bigger than Sarah, or Brendan, or even herself. It was Colin!

But where, oh where, was Sarah?

XI

Sarah lay beside the rock outcrop, snow sticking in her feathers and piling up around her. Groggy from hitting the tree, too weak to try another takeoff, she felt the snowflakes covering her legs, her wings, her head. She closed her eyes. Perhaps Marg and Brendan, at least, had found some shelter. Perhaps they would live to tell the rest of the flock what had happened to her. Dying wasn't hurting as much as she had imagined it would. Her thoughts grew hazy, and she passed out.

Snow piled up at the foot of the rock, and soon Sarah was covered entirely. It was a cold blanket, to be sure, but it kept the icy wind from reaching through. Would she freeze to death under that white coverlet? No doubt. But it would take a long time. She slept, dreaming of her sun-warmed roosting ledge on Yamnuska, with Marg and Brendan pressed close beside her.

XII

The break that Marg had seen in the cliff turned out to be a deep crack, just what she had hoped for. She, Brendan, and Colin landed on a great block of rock jammed into it. The three ravens stepped cautiously back into the gloom, ready to turn and fly if something rushed toward them. But they found the shelter unused – at least not in use that evening – and then, out of the wind, safe and dry, they let their exhausted bodies sink down over their feet. Speechless, they fluffed out their feathers to keep themselves warm against the deepening cold. They tucked their heads far back under their wings and fell asleep.

Marg dozed fitfully. Fear kept seizing her dreams, turning them to nightmares. Once, she awoke fully. She looked out from the crack, where a strip of midnight-blue sky hung between the blackness of the rock walls. The strip was covered with stars. The wind had dropped from a howl to a whisper. All was well, she thought; the storm had passed. But then, like claws closing over her body, came the knowledge that somewhere out there, lost and probably dead, was Sarah. Marg let out a soft cry of anguish.

At this moment, Colin also awoke. Marg's cry had ended a vivid dream. He recalled every detail. In the dream, a sleeping raven lay on the ground. Snow fell, covering the bird. He, Colin, could see this as if he were soaring above. Then the scene began to move. It moved away from him – no, he was rising above it – and he could see a rock outcropping at the edge of a meadow. Then the meadow grew smaller, and he could see that it was on a hillside. Higher still Colin's dream took him, until he could see that the hillside was part of a low ridge forming the southern boundary of Morley Flats. Yet higher he went, and he could see the other side of the ridge, where the very cliff in which they were sheltering came into view. "Marg," he said quietly, "don't worry. I know where she is."

Marg was shivering, not with cold but with grief. "Sarah – oh, my dear, lost Sarah –"

"Marg," Colin repeated. "Marg, I know where Sarah is. And she's alive. Tomorrow, if I can fly at all, we'll go there."

XIII

"I'm hungry."

It was Brendan speaking. Brendan had said "I'm hungry" as his first message to the new day ever since he had hatched. He still said it out of habit, without thinking. But this time he shook his head and peered around. Where was he? Panic sent him jumping to his feet as he looked at the unfamiliar surroundings.

Then he remembered. Yesterday had started off so beautifully. He and Sarah flying together across the valley. Finding the rose hips in *exactly* the right place. He and Sarah eating them together. But then it had ended so horribly. Here he was, perched on a cold block of rock in a crack in some cliff, far away from Yamnuska. Well, at least they were all here, safe and sound. Marg had found this place. How had she done that? It was amazing to be able to do that. Hey, that had been a close call. But they'd made it. Yesterday was a lesson learned. Now they would fly home to Raven's End and tell the flock about it. He and Sarah and Marg. All right! Maybe they'd let *him* tell it!

He stretched forward, noting how much longer his neck-feathers were growing. Soon they would be just as long as those of the other adult birds. He stretched his wings. And in so doing he jostled Colin, who was roosting close by.

"*Awk!*" Colin cried, waking to the pain of something brushing against his injured wing.

Brendan jumped back. "You're – you're not Sarah!"

"No, I'm not Sarah. Ooo, I'm sore." He shook himself, gathering his wits. "Sarah's not here. We have to find her, and quickly, before the coyotes do. Marg!"

Brendan was stunned. Sarah not here? But where? And Colin? Where had Colin come from?

Marg woke up slowly. First one eye opened, then the other. They seemed less bright than usual, Colin thought. Marg was still tired from the events of the last evening, and she had slept uneasily, worried all night about Sarah. But as she became fully awake she didn't have to be told what the first job of the day would be. She rose to her feet without a thought for her empty stomach. "Colin! Last night – last night you –"

"Yes, last night I told you I knew where Sarah was. And I still do. She's on the other side of the ridge, at the edge of a clearing beside a ledge. Is that where you left her yesterday?"

"Well, I – we didn't *leave* her there, Colin – but yes! That's where I saw her last! We'd been eating berries when the storm came in. I thought we all got away, but I guess Sarah didn't. It's all my fault. I didn't notice anything wrong until it was too late. Oh, I feel so awful about this whole thing." Marg's wings were fluttering. "It's my fault, it really is. I –"

"No, Marg, it's not your fault," Colin comforted. "You did your best. And you found this place, too."

Marg's expression changed to one of confusion. "But, Colin – how did you know about Sarah? How did you come to be here with us? What's going on, Colin?"

"I got caught in the storm too," he said. "After a human hurt me with some sort of stick thing. In my wing."

Carefully, he stretched out the damaged wing. "Awk! That hurts!" He pulled the wing back.

"You poor thing," Marg said, moving closer to him. "Let me see."

Colin extended his wing again. It hurt less to do it this time, but he couldn't stretch it far. Marg looked at the wing carefully. She could see blood on it – a big, dark clot of blood that stuck the feathers together.

"Oh, Colin. How could you fly at all? I'll bet those humans shot you with a gun! You're lucky you weren't killed. They shoot lots of ravens." She looked at his tail. Two feathers were missing there. "Does that hurt?" she asked, touching him lightly with her bill.

"Awk! Uh, no, not much," Colin replied. "Oh, rat poop, Marg, I'm sore all over."

"They shot you in the tail, too! We'll have to get Greta to look at you when we get home."

Brendan was becoming more and more agitated, hopping about. "But Sarah?! What about Sarah?!"

Colin flapped his wings and twisted his tail, trying to work out the stiffness. He had to fly, that's all there was to it. He hopped over to the front of the crack, took a deep breath and jumped off the cliff.

Oh, it hurt! It hurt to the core! But yes, he could fly, missing feathers and all. The injured right wing wasn't very strong, but at least it went up and down a little. The other wing would simply have to work that much harder.

"Colin," said Marg, "Dear Colin. You are a brave, strong bird." She had followed him out of the crack and was now flying beside him. And here came Brendan.

"Let's go find Sarah," Brendan said. "Then let's eat."

XIV

Back at Raven's End, the flock assembled for the Flap. It was a subdued group of ravens. The storm had been most unpleasant – there wasn't a single roost on Yamnuska that was really protected from it – and although the wind had died, the temperature had dropped considerably. The sun was only a spot of brighter gray in the overcast sky. Slate-colored clouds of ice crystals drifted among the snow-covered peaks. The scene had no warmth and no color. Winter had arrived, and brutally.

But the birds had more than that on their minds. What had happened to Marg, Sarah, and Brendan? And where was Colin? Rumors passed from bill to bill, but nobody really knew anything definite.

The Main Raven convened the Flap. He tried to sound cheerful. "Gro, C.C.s. And a very good morning it is, wouldn't you say?"

As he peered around the circle, looking at each bird briefly, the Main Raven saw nothing but worry in their eyes. Few said "gro" back to him.

"Maya seems not to be with us this morning, so we shall have to dispense with the news."

Indeed, Maya had not turned up. Most of the Townsend's solitaires in the valley migrated south for the winter, but a few, including Maya, stayed behind to live on juniper berries. Maya loved Raven's End too much to leave it, even during the cold months. This was her first absence ever at the Flap, and the other birds knew what that implied. Their spirits fell even further.

"Well," the Main Raven continued, "how did we all weather the storm? I'd like to hear each bird's own story of this exciting event."

Zack wasn't going to wait for his turn. He spoke up immediately. "I'm very worried about Marg, Brendan, and Sarah," he stated. "They went over to Morley Flats and haven't come back. Would anyone like to go with Molly and me to look for them?"

"I'll go," said Scratch.

"Me, too," said Wheedle.

"Okay," said Zack. But he was thinking that this wasn't a particularly strong search party.

"Anyone else?" he asked.

"You can count me in," said Dolus.

"If Dolus is going, then I'm going, too," said Garth.

Uh-oh, Zack thought. He was wary of these two birds. They hadn't been seen much since returning to the flock a few days before, and they hadn't said anything at the Flaps about what they'd been doing. Why the sudden interest in a rescue trip? But if they wanted to help, he could use them.

"If Dolus and Garth are going, I'm *not* going, and neither are you, Zack." It was Molly. She was more than suspicious of Dolus's motives; she was certain that he was up to no good. She voiced her opinion in the form of a question. "Dolus, exactly why are you so interested in joining this search party?"

"Oh, I'm just concerned for the welfare of my fellow flock members," he replied, his eyes flicking around the circle. "Just trying to help out, that's all."

At this point the Main Raven interrupted. "Well, that's a most heartening attitude, Dolus. I'm pleased to hear it. Now, if you six want to be off, the rest of us wish you well –"

"Just a moment!" Molly interjected. "I'm not finished yet!" Her eyes were small and hard as she looked at Dolus intently. "What were you doing over on Wakonda Buttress two days ago, Dolus?"

"Uh, you mean with Zygadena?"

At the mention of "Zygadena," several ravens twitched, involuntarily hunching their shoulders and opening their bills.

"Yes, with Zygadena. What were you doing with Zygadena?"

"Oh, just talking. We were only talking."

"What were you eating, Dolus? What was it?"

"Oh, that. Well, Zygadena had found a dead – a dead bird over on

Wakonda Buttress, and we were just looking at it. Not really eating it. Not really."

"Was it a black bird, Dolus?" By now Molly's eyes were tiny slits, and she hissed out the words.

"Yeah, a blackbird. A red-wing blackbird, sort of."

The flock began muttering and whispering. What was Molly driving at?

"Couldn't have been a *raven*, could it?!" she shrieked.

The other birds opened their eyes wide. A raven? Dolus and Zygadena, eating a raven? How horrible! Surely Molly couldn't be implying that Dolus would actually eat another raven?

Dolus looked around the circle. His pleading expression told everyone what he was about to say. "I – I guess it, uh, it might have been a raven, once. Part of one, anyway."

This was serious. The Main Raven took over the questioning. "And did Zygadena eat any of it?" he asked Dolus.

"Yes," Dolus said, looking down and scratching in the snow with one foot. The wind swirled through the flock, ruffling their feathers. Every bird felt a chill, both from the steady north breeze and from the scene they were witnessing.

"And now, Dolus," the Main Raven said, striding over to him, "I want to know something else. Look at me."

Dolus turned toward the Main Raven. The Main Raven looked at Dolus, and the two birds locked eyes. "Did *you* eat any of it, Dolus C.C.?"

For a long moment the only sound was the whisper of snowflakes skipping around the feet of the Raven's Enders. Dolus stared at the Main Raven and the Main Raven stared at him. Finally Dolus broke loose from the Main Raven's gaze. He looked down again, and he spoke in a voice that could barely be heard. "No. I didn't eat any." With that, Dolus spread his wings, leapt into the air and flew away. So did Garth.

The other birds started breathing again.

"See?" Molly said. "It's just what I expected. Dolus has been hanging around with Zygadena. And you know what she does with any dead raven she . . . finds." Anger hardened her voice. "Zygadena's a menace.

She knows what she's doing. I think she's tried to get Dolus and Garth hooked on the stuff."

Zack looked at Molly, considering. Then he spoke, saying what every other bird was thinking but afraid to say out loud. "Molly, did you think that Dolus wanted to come along" – here he stopped, searching for the words – "that he was hoping to find Sarah and Brendan and Marg – *dead?*"

The flock shifted its attention to Molly. Her eyes flashed. "Yes. That's exactly what I was thinking. And the way Dolus looked just now confirmed it."

The other birds all began talking at once, either stating that they, too, had figured out what Dolus was up to, or that no, Dolus would never do anything like that. Or would he?

"C.C.s! Please, C.C.s!" the Main Raven croaked. "Order, order!"

The other birds quieted.

"Before we all jump to conclusions, let us be reminded that it is unnatural for a raven to, uh, ingest another raven, and we cannot assume that Dolus has engaged in this highly inappropriate – in fact, prohibited – activity. The freedom to eat what we please is one of the Three Freedoms enjoyed by all ravens, but" – and here the Main Raven looked very grave – "cannibalism is not included in that freedom."

Scratch spoke up. "Zygadena's always eatin' dead ravens. I seen her myself. Real scary ta watch, too. She just rips right in, guts 'n' everythin'. Real disgustin', an' –"

"That will do, Scratch," the Main Raven interrupted. Cathy had listened to the discussion with her bill hanging open, horror-struck, and now she was wobbling on her feet. Molly threw a wing over her.

"Now then, Cathy," he went on, "rest assured that Zygadena never comes over to this side of the valley. You have nothing to fear from her."

"Bloody right she never comes over here. The Main Raven and I see to that." Zack was croaking loudly, his wings set back, his head thrust forward and his neck-feathers ruffled out. The Main Raven did the same.

Just then a small, gray bird fluttered out of the wind and landed atop the biggest spruce at Raven's End. With its longish tail and its lovely white eye rings, it could only be –

"Maya!" croaked all the ravens together.

"Hello, everyone," Maya said. "Sorry to be late. But several stories just came in, and the wind kind of slowed me down getting here."

"Oh, Maya, I'm so glad to see you!" Molly called. "We thought you'd been lost in the storm."

"Well, you may not be so glad when you've heard the news. Here goes." And she began her routine, starting with several single, wistful notes. Then, as if rolling off a printing press, page after page, came her report.

"At the top of the news this morning – the weather – an Arctic frontal storm hit the area late yesterday afternoon – winds reached gale force, bringing blowing snow and reduced visibility – the overnight low froze the beaver ponds completely across, and the voles report enough new snow to begin preparing their winter runs underneath – the winter solstice is still many days away, but everyone expects this snowfall to last, even on south-facing slopes."

Maya stopped for a breath. Molly heard the sound of raven wings behind her, and noticed that Greta had arrived. Why couldn't she ever get here on time? Molly thought of coming right out and scolding her a little, but then Maya started up again.

"Optimistic Molt, the weasel, saw a member of the Raven's End Flock killed yesterday –"

At this the other birds gasped.

"She reports having a conversation with Colin C.C. a few days before in nearly the same place – yesterday she watched him approach a pair of hunters on the human footpath up Yamnuska –"

Oh, Colin, thought Molly. She had told him over and over. Never get near humans. And now he's dead. Zack was right about hearing the sounds of humans shooting. Shooting Colin. Her wings began to flutter in grief.

"According to Molt, Colin C.C. actually grabbed an item of food away from one of the humans, at which point the other one shot him in the wing – he tried to run up the slope, when he was hit again – he was last seen falling over the South Face –"

Cathy began to wail. Molly couldn't help herself, either. She croaked a long, slow cry of sorrow. "Crraaawww . . ."

Maya had to stop until the Main Raven asked for calm. The bad news wasn't over.

"This tragedy is compounded by the disappearance in the storm of three other Yamnuska ravens – Marg, Brendan, and Sarah C.C., all of the Raven's End Flock – early reports indicate that the trio were overtaken by the cold front while on the south side of the Bow Valley, well downwind of Yamnuska, and they haven't been seen since –"

Molly was beside herself. She called out in grief again. "Crrrraaaaaaaaaawwwwwww . . ."

And this time Scratch and Wheedle joined in, croaking and cawing so miserably that even the Main Raven couldn't contain himself. He hadn't ever been known to cry, but now he gave forth a long, deep, velvety groan that perfectly expressed the misery sweeping over what remained of the flock.

Maya stopped and looked down at the birds. She was surprised at how badly they were taking all this. Having passed along so much bad news over the years, she was personally immune to it. Perched impassively, she simply waited for the crawing and groaning to stop. Eventually it did. The ravens were growing numb with the shock of losing four flock members overnight.

"Moving to other news –" she started again. But Greta interrupted her. Her voice was not loud, but whenever she spoke everyone stopped to listen. She had not been crying. "How typical of the press," she said. "Just take the copy and pass it on, no questions asked. Well, most of the time Maya's pretty good. Pretty factual. But this time I'll have to correct her."

Maya was stunned. No one had ever questioned the accuracy of her reporting. Her bill dropped open, and a single note fell out – "morn?" – a wistful question mark.

Greta continued. "I suggest, friends, that you take a look to the south and tell me what you see."

The other birds swung their heads toward the Bow Valley. Through the icy haze hanging over the Rockies they could just barely make out four ravens flying toward them. One was flying very awkwardly, favoring its right wing, and another seemed to be limping through the air, too. All flew weakly against the oncoming northerly breeze, but they were gradually getting closer.

"Oh, Zack, could it be?" Molly cried, trying hard not to believe her eyes.

"By the Trees, Molly, I can see Marg!" Zack called excitedly. "And there's Brendan! And Sarah, and – by golly, Colin is with them!"

The flock was instantly in an uproar. All the birds were hopping about, flapping their wings, dancing with delight. Some of them leapt into the air and flew off to escort the four lost ravens, now so close that everyone could hear them croaking their own happiness at making it home. The entourage landed at Raven's End in a great flurry of wings. Amid the ensuing hubbub each flock member personally welcomed back the Raven's Enders who had been given up for dead.

"Oh, Sarah," said Molly, touching the young raven's bill tenderly with her own.

"Oh, Marg," said Cathy, doing the same to her adult friend.

"Colin, you big lunk," said Zack, "I'm so glad to see you. Tell me what happened."

After a time, when the essentials of the story had been related, the Main Raven brought the meeting back to order. "My friends! My friends! Let us end this morning's Flap with the most joyous Motion we have ever shared!"

"Hear, hear!" called several birds. The flock formed a circle once again, wingtip to overlapping wingtip, and each bird filled its lungs with crisp mountain air. Then, all together, they raised their wings and let forth a mighty roar of raven strength and common power.

"*RAWK-A-TAW!!*"

Never had the Raven's End Flock meant it more. The sound shook snow loose from the trees surrounding the circle. The sound rode south on the breeze, across the wooded slopes below and out over the Bow Valley. Every wild thing within earshot – and a long earshot it was – stopped for a moment, hearing and considering what it heard: the sound of the ravens of Yamnuska, telling the world at large that all was well.

All wasn't completely well for Colin. He couldn't raise his right wing much, and the pain of trying had resulted in him saying "awk" instead of "rawk-a-taw." But the thunderous outburst from the rest of flock made him feel wonderful anyway.

Maya looked down from her perch, taking notes on the whole event. This was definitely going to require a special edition.

XV

When the rest of the flock had gone, Greta looked at Colin's hurts with a clinical eye. She prodded him here and there with her bill, saying "breathe in," and "breathe out," and "raise that wing higher. I know it hurts. Higher." At length her examination was complete.

"Well, you've been 'winged,' as the humans are so fond of saying," she stated. "Nasty wound in the right flight muscle – can't see how you got home on that. Bullet went right through. Missed the bone somehow. Got a bruise on your tail, but no bleeding there. Three primaries gone, two tail-feathers and half a dozen secondaries, and you're stuck with a fair number of bent shafts and dinged-up tips until the spring molt."

Colin looked down. "It was all my own fault," he said miserably. "I'll never trust humans again."

"Indeed," Greta replied. "So take it easy for a few days and let that wound heal." Then she muttered something under her breath. Colin heard it anyway: "They always learn hard."

"What?" he said. "Who learns hard?"

"Oh, all you ravens who think you know everything. But don't."

"Greta," Colin said, ignoring her insult, "I had a strange experience during that storm."

"Ah. Let me guess. Did the wind talk to you?"

"Yes! How did you know?"

"Oh, it's happened to me, too. What did it say to you?"

"It was terribly angry with me."

"Typical cold front," Greta declared. "They're always like that. Can't reason with them at all."

Colin continued. "But we made a deal, Greta. We actually made a deal. We decided not to fight each other. I made a deal with the wind!"

"Yes, and that's nice. But don't get carried away with yourself. In point of fact, you barely survived that whole episode."

Colin looked away, embarrassed. But he quickly turned back. "Oh – that's the other thing I wanted to ask you about, Greta. I had a dream last night, in the crack in the cliff. I dreamed where Sarah was. I knew exactly where to find her, and it was because of that dream."

Greta looked hard at Colin. She came close and peered right into each of his eyes. Then she croaked softly and hopped back. "Colin," she said quietly, "there's a word for all this dream stuff. It's called 'second-sight,' and I can see it in your eyes. It's both a blessing and a curse. But there's nothing you can do about it. You'll have to get used to it, that's all. Act on it when the need arises, like with Sarah. You'll know when. And remember this – don't talk to the other birds about it. They'll think you're crazy. If you must talk about it with someone, talk about it with me. Just me. No one else. Okay?" Her voice was as serious as he had ever heard it. But it was friendly, too. Confiding.

"Okay," said Colin. He looked over to Greta, now clumsily preening her back-feathers. First she had understood about his dreams. And now she had offered him a kind of companionship that no other flock member could. Henceforth he would treat her differently. He knew, as surely as he had known where to find Sarah, that he could trust Greta completely.

"Thanks, Greta," he said. And he meant it.

"You're welcome." She flew gently away, her old wings beating slowly.

XVI

It took several days for things to return to normal at Raven's End. Colin couldn't fly much, and neither could Marg, who seemed exhausted mentally as well as physically. Sarah was still nursing the worst headache of her life. (After examining her, Greta had remarked that the only reason Sarah had any brains left was that she had so many to begin with.) Brendan was the only one who had come through the experience undamaged. In fact, he was already looking back on it with pride. The whole thing, he decided, was a kind of test – and he had passed.

"It was awesome." Brendan was talking with Garth, who was about his own age. "I mean, there I was. The wind, the snow, everything. And, like, I'm still here. I can handle anything, now."

Garth looked at him out of the corner of his eye. "Oh, yeah? There may be a few things you can't handle, Brendan."

"Huh? Like what?"

"Oh, like – well, like a whole other side of life you don't know anything about."

Brendan glanced back at Garth and lowered his voice. "So you're going to tell me you've been nesting somebody, right?"

Garth looked down. He scratched in the snow with one foot. "No way, Brendan. Nesting time is a long way off. You know that."

"So, what's this 'other side of life'?"

"I can't tell you anything more. Dolus and me, we –"

"Dolus! Dolus! You hang around with that bird like he owns you!"

"No way. I can quit any time I like."

Brendan's head jerked up. "Quit what?" he asked.

"Oh, nothing. Forget I said that." And Garth flew off.

Brendan was wondering what kind of trouble this implied, when Sarah settled down beside him.

"Hi," she said. She looked at Brendan, then she looked away. She started preening herself, running her bill along the edges of her folded wings.

Brendan hadn't seen much of Sarah the last few days. She had been staying with Marg since the incident in the Bow Valley, and they roosted farther west along Yamnuska than Brendan did.

"Oh, hi," Brendan replied. "How's your head?"

"Lots better. Way better. Well, the sun still hurts my eyes, though."

"That was really close, Sarah," Brendan said soberly. "What did you think about, lying there on the ground?"

"Couldn't think about much," she replied. "My thinker was all messed up, sort of. I passed out."

"Did you, like, have a dream?"

"Oh, yes – I dreamed I was back at Yamnuska, all safe and everything. But really, I guess, I kind of knew I was going to die."

"Wow. You really thought you were – really going to *die?*"

"Uh huh. For sure."

"And what did you think when we – when I – came for you?"

"Oh, Brendan, that was wonderful! Like, I was buried in the snow, okay? And I woke up under all this white stuff. It was really weird. So then I try to move, and I can't, 'cause the snow is too deep. And I'm trying to keep it together, 'cause I'm getting really scared, and I don't know where I am, and then there's this, this big *bill* shoving me in the back, and then there's another one, and I see it's ravens, and I'm thinking, this is so *cool!* I'm buried in the snow, but somebody's digging me out! And then –"

Here she stopped. She looked at Brendan, whose glossy brown eyes were staring intently into her own. "And it was you, Brendan. You and Colin and Marg and – mostly you, I guess. It was you."

Brendan raised his head and unfurled his wings. He fluffed the feathers out under his chin. Tilting back and forth, he croaked happily several times.

"And Brendan –" Sarah said, still gazing at him.

"What, Sarah?" Brendan looked into her eyes. He saw his own reflection there, and she must have been seeing her reflection in *his* eyes, the two of them together, just the two of them, here at Raven's End, looking so deeply into each other's eyes, beginning to glimpse all their secrets and their passions, getting ready to tell them to each other. "Go on, Sarah. You can tell me anything. Anything you want."

"Brendan, the part I don't get was the snow kept me warm all night. I mean, how could it do that? Snow is cold, okay, and so how could *snow* keep a bird warm?"

Brendan's neck-feathers snapped back down under his chin. His bill clicked shut. His wings returned to their usual parking place atop his back, and he looked down at the snow. It was full of raven tracks, his and hers, two tangled patches where their feet had been going up and down excitedly as they talked.

"Well?" she asked. "Do you know anything about that? I guess I could ask Greta. I mean, it's interesting, isn't it?"

Brendan managed to smile.

PART THREE

Winter

I

Zack was speaking at the Flap. "We ought to consider a trip west," he said. "Food's getting scarce around here. Worse than last year. Or even the year before. I think we should go to the Park."

The other ravens had noticed the scarcity, too. There weren't many berries left around the east end of Yamnuska, except for the bitter juniper berries, which the ravens would eat only in desperation. And none of the valley's big predators had made a kill in weeks; at least, they hadn't made a kill the birds could find. The coyotes or the cougar might have got something, but light snow fell almost every night, hiding any new carcass, and the days were now so cold that a kill was frozen and practically odorless. Several birds had searched hard, trying to spot something, but even Colin had come back empty-billed.

The flock had come to depend on Colin for finding meat. He seemed to have a sixth sense about it. The fact that he hadn't been able to locate a fresh kill convinced Zack and Molly that there just weren't any around.

The Main Raven took the sense of the meeting. "My friends, we haven't been to the Park for some years. Zack C.C. proposes that we do so at this time. How does the flock wish to proceed?"

Marg spoke first. "Hi, everyone," she smiled. Then her expression grew serious. "Well, I don't see why we shouldn't go," she stated, looking straight at the Main Raven. "In my opinion, for the good of the flock we had better get into the Park before we get weak for lack of food. Myself, I've been on seeds for three days now, and that's not good."

"Yeah," Scratch agreed. "I'm fer boogyin'. Me and Wheedle, we're real hungry, like."

One by one, all the birds in the circle presented their views. As usual, Greta spoke last.

"Well, then," she said. "Seems everyone is hot to trot. Me too. These old wings need something better than snowballs to keep them flying. I'll lead the way, if you like."

The Main Raven cleared his throat. "It would appear that we have a consensus," he said. "All that remains to be settled is when we leave."

Several birds spoke at once.

"Right now! Right now!"

"Hey! There's Optimistic Molt!"

The little white weasel was trying to sneak through a corner of the clearing on its way over the ridge. Against the snow she was practically invisible, but the dark-colored load she carried in her mouth gave her away.

"Hey, Oppie!" one bird called.

The weasel stopped. She started to speak, but her mouth was too full and the words came out as a muffled squeak. She dropped the furry lump in the snow. "Who's that?" she demanded.

"What've you got?" was the reply, as a half-dozen hungry ravens came hopping and flapping over to investigate.

"All right, all right! Back off!" Optimistic Molt was up on her hind legs, standing over a dead meadow vole. She had taken a chance that morning, passing so close to the flock. But she hadn't really been hunting; she'd been spying on the long-tailed weasel, her disliked neighbor down the ridge. And the vole? The vole had blundered right into her as it scratched away noisily under the snow, digging a new run. She had only to make one dive, and then she had it by the neck, biting through the tiny bones, ending its life in one quick movement. But then she had to get the body back across the ridge to her own home – a burrow she had taken from a deer mouse earlier that fall – and in her haste to get across the territory of the long-tailed weasel without losing her prize to it, she was about to lose it to the ravens instead.

All this went through her mind as she confronted the circle of birds. She hissed and bared her teeth.

One of the ravens reassured her. "Hey, Oppie! We don't want the vole! We just want to talk to you!"

It was one-legged Wheedle. He was lying, of course. He had no intention of talking. Only grabbing.

"Any closer and I'll bite your skinny black leg!" the weasel screeched. To make her point clear, she lunged at him.

Wheedle jumped back, exaggerating his surprise. This was all part of a plan. "Oh, aren't we fussy this morning? Is that any way to treat a gentlebird come calling?"

Infuriated, Optimistic Molt lunged again. By now she was a body-length from the vole. Scratch had been working his way around behind the weasel, and now he edged closer.

Several of the other birds caught on to the scheme. They stepped over beside Wheedle. "You know, dear," he said in a syrupy voice, "I saw the long-tailed weasel yesterday, and it had the most *darling* winter coat. Much whiter than yours."

"Yeah, and I'll bet she was all over Weasel's End showing it off, too. Oh, of all the nerve! And you, you –"

She sprang straight for Wheedle, who leapt nimbly into the air, pulling up his one leg as the weasel's teeth clicked together under him. At the same time, Scratch grabbed the dead vole and flopped off in the other direction. He needed a run to get airborne with the vole, which was quite fat and rather heavy. The whole flock was right behind him.

Optimistic Molt was left behind in the snow, enraged. She thrashed about, stamping her feet and growling, snapping her teeth at the departing flock. "You big bullies! You're all thieves! Oh, I hate ravens! I'll get even with you for this! Some night you'll be sleeping, and CHOP! – there goes a leg! Your *other* leg, you, you –!!"

Colin was flying beside Zack as Optimistic Molt flung out her final insult. He heard Zack let out a nervous laugh. "What's so funny?" Colin asked.

"She doesn't know how right she is," Zack replied.

"Right about what?"

"Right about Wheedle. That's how he lost his leg. A marten got it. Same thing – teasing."

"And he still does it?"

"Yes. That's what he's good at, living by his wits. He's smart, that bird. But maybe a little *too* smart once, and it cost him dearly."

Colin and Zack caught up with Scratch, who was getting tired of carrying the vole, and all the birds descended on a big boulder sitting in the meadow north of Raven's End. The wind had blown the snow off the boulder, and in the centre lay the vole, looking delectable. How beautiful, thought Colin. The brown fur against the gray rock, and the white snow all around.

Among ravens, food stolen from some other animal always sets off a game of chase. There isn't enough meat on a meadow vole to give more than a couple of billfuls to anyone, so getting fed is not the object. The idea is to chase and snatch, keeping a nibble for yourself before someone else grabs the booty.

Scratch was the first snatcher and nibbler, and thus the first to be chased. Tiring, he dropped the vole on the rock. Wheedle grabbed it. No sooner had Wheedle stolen a taste than Brendan took it from him; then Marg from Brendan, Molly from Marg, Sarah from Molly, and on and on. By this time there wasn't much left. But the whole flock had enjoyed the unexpected treat, and it really *was* fun. Fun at the expense of another species.

What strange birds we are, Colin thought. We care so much for each other, yet any other creature can be robbed at will. He wondered if other animals had the same view of things. Was the whole world this way? If so, how could it function? The apparent contradiction crept up his back and made him shiver.

And then the most contradictory bird in the flock reminded the rest of them exactly what they had been doing when Optimistic Molt showed herself to this bunch of opportunists. "Shall we go?" Greta asked.

"Huh? Go where?" Brendan asked.

"West," Greta replied. "To the Park. Remember?"

II

West to the "Park," indeed. West to Banff National Park. Greta explained what it meant to Colin as they flew along.

"Humans invented the Park," she said.

"What do you mean, they invented it? Wasn't it there all along?"

"Well, yes, I suppose it was. It's just a place in the mountains. But the humans think of it as a special kind of place, and they call it the 'Park' for that reason."

"What do they do there?"

"Oh, they do the kinds of things they can't do in their cities. They walk for days without crossing a highway or stepping on a sidewalk. They eat lunch on top of mountains. That kind of thing."

Colin had no idea what a city was, or a sidewalk. But he had seen hikers and climbers eating their lunches on Yamnuska. "What's a 'city,' anyway?" he asked her.

Greta thought for a while, soaring. The birds cleared the ridge at the head of the valley behind Yamnuska. They cruised over the long, slabby slope on the other side and flew straight on, across the next divide to the valley of Exshaw Creek. Each time they went over a ridgeline, they caught the updraft there, feeling an air-cushioned kick under their wings.

At length Greta replied to Colin's question. "A city is a place only for humans. I went to one once. More humans there than you can possibly imagine, and they live all together like bees. I had to get out of there. Human cities are poisonous to most everything but humans – except for the kinds of animals that humans prefer."

"Like dogs?" Colin had often seen dogs accompanying hikers on the trail up Yamnuska.

"Yes, dogs. And cats." She noted Colin's quizzical look. "Cats are like little cougars, Colin."

"But if these cities are poisonous to everything except dogs and little cougars, what do humans eat there? Do they eat dogs and little cougars?"

"No, they don't. They have all kinds of food – you know, you've eaten some yourself – and they bring all this food into the city, and then they eat it there."

"But, Greta," Colin began, "you just said they like to eat their lunches somewhere else —"

Greta interrupted with a laugh. "Colin," she chuckled, "humans have to have everything in opposites. They are all opposites themselves. Cruel and kind, smart and stupid, loving and hating. For all their poisonous cities, and there are lots of them, they have to have a place that's exactly the opposite. And that's what the Park is. They just leave it alone, more or less, so it's not at all like a city, and they go there whenever they're tired of the city."

"So they go to this 'Park' place, and they eat their lunches there?"

"Yes, they do. And they walk around a lot. And mainly — I guess this is the most important thing — mainly they don't kill anything."

"Molly says that humans always kill everything. I didn't believe her, and I should have, because they almost killed *me*."

"True enough, but they wouldn't do that in the Park."

"No?"

"Well, it's not likely. Some of them might still try. But not with guns."

"Why not?"

"Because the humans have decided not to allow guns in the Park. Otherwise, they really *would* kill everything. Molly is right, in that sense. But humans kill everything only when they have guns. When they don't have guns, lots of animals can escape."

"But Greta," Colin said, now more confused than ever, "why would humans give up their guns and let things escape?"

Again, Greta took her time before replying. In the meantime the birds sailed over the chisel-point summit of Mount Fable. This was a higher peak than Yamnuska, and the west wind poured across its ridge with greater power. The constant flow of air had blown the snow away, exposing bright-orange patches of lichens growing on the shattered gray rock. The birds could almost touch the lichens with their feet as they struggled over the mountain.

Greta flapped doggedly upwind toward the summit. She alighted there for a moment to rest, and Colin sat down beside her. He was still waiting for an answer to his question about humans and guns.

"Greta — about those guns . . ."

"Whew." She caught her breath. "Oh, yes. Guns. Humans live nearly everywhere on earth," she stated, "and that means that nearly every place has guns."

Colin wondered what Greta was driving at. She took another long breath and continued. "So if guns were everywhere in the world, then the humans would kill everything in the world, right?"

"I suppose so." This was going to be one of Greta's weird answers, he thought.

"Now consider this, Colin. If they killed everything, then what would happen?"

"Uh . . . I don't know."

"Yes, you do. You know very well what would happen. Think about it."

Colin thought, and he thought fast, so Greta wouldn't fly off and leave him puzzling. The answer hit along with a gust of wind that nearly blew both birds off the summit and back the way they had come. "Oh, I know! If they killed everything, then they would starve, because there wouldn't be anything left to eat!"

"That's right," said Greta. "*Now* do you know why they have these places where guns aren't allowed?"

"Well, is it so they can make sure not everything gets killed? Or – or poisoned?"

"Exactly," said Greta. "It's so they can save part of the world from themselves."

"I see what you mean about them being stupid and smart at the same time."

"Very."

"But I still need to know something else, Greta. We can get away from them on Yamnuska, even if they have guns. But we don't really have to go to the Park to be safe, do we?"

"That's true," Greta said. "Ravens are smart enough to avoid getting killed by humans. Most of the time." Her eyes met Colin's. He looked down. "No, we go to the Park for a different reason."

"Yes?" In her circuitous way, Greta had finally brought the discussion around to what Colin really wanted to know.

"We go there," she said, "because there are wolves there. Outside the Park the humans kill them, but in the Park the wolves are safe."

Colin had heard of wolves, but he had never seen one. Zack had told him that they resembled coyotes, but they were bigger. They hunted in packs, and they killed large animals such as elk and moose. Which would mean – so quick was the realization that he twitched in the air – carcasses! "Greta! In the park there must be lots of carcasses!"

"Indeed."

"Thanks, Greta," Colin said. "I understand now."

"Any time," she replied, lifting off into the wind rushing up the western side of the mountain.

III

By now the flock was farther from Yamnuska than Colin could ever remember being. Flying very high, scattered about the sky like bits of black cloth, the birds needed Greta's guidance from this point on. Everyone moved closer together to follow her. Even though Greta was the slowest, clumsiest flyer in the flock – someone had once said that the only difference between Greta's flying ability and that of a fledgling was that the fledgling had hope of doing better – still, it was Greta who led the way on any long trip. Despite her ungainly style, she had been just about everywhere in the Canadian Rockies.

More importantly, she always remembered where she had been. The other birds might explore new territory, but they seldom penetrated far, and when they returned they found it difficult to recall where they had gone. Ravens, after all, are not migratory birds. They don't fly great distances north and south each year as many other birds do. They're essentially homebodies, criss-crossing their particular patch of mountains or prairie or desert or tundra, but not venturing far beyond it.

Except for Greta. Greta had the traveller's restless soul. She would disappear for several days at a time – once she had been away for the better part of a summer – and then she would return as if she had left that morning. The flock always welcomed her back noisily, with lots of croaking and flapping, for the Raven's Enders loved her dearly and always it seemed that *this* trip might be the one from which she would not come back. The Main Raven would give a long speech, reciting events that had occurred in her absence, and then Greta would be asked to tell of her experiences.

She wouldn't have much to say – at first. "Oh, I was over at Mount Assiniboine," she had reported the previous year. "Not much happening, really. Although that forest fire along the Simpson River is acting up again, and there's been a landslide at Marvel Lake."

Then, without fail, Greta would tell of some event that astounded and delighted her audience. "Of course, there was that thing with the mountain goat."

"Tell us, Greta! What about the goat?"

"Well, I thought it was dead, so I kind of popped by for a look, you know."

"And?"

"Strangest thing. It wasn't dead at all. I mean, it *should* have been dead. Appeared to have fallen down the cliff. Pretty torn up. No head left on it. But then it spoke to me."

"It *spoke* to you?!"

"Indeed. Knew my name, too. Said 'Greta, come here.'"

At this the younger birds looked around uneasily. Those on the fringe of the circle moved in closer.

"Ooo . . ."

"Like, *I* wouldn't have got any closer, that's for sure."

Greta continued. "Oh, heck – a decapitated goat is a decapitated goat. There's no way the thing could *hurt* me. So I walked right up."

Here, Greta entered one of her renowned pauses. Her eyes closed for a moment, as if she had just dropped off to sleep.

"And what happened then, Greta?" one of the birds said after a while.

"Hmm? Oh. That was the funny part," Greta replied, looking innocently at no bird in particular. "Inside the goat was a wolverine I knew."

At this the whole flock cracked up.

"Craw-ha! There's a wolverine in the goat!"

"Imagine! A wolverine in the goat, and it talks to Greta! Craw-ha-ha!"

"Oh, Greta, you tell the greatest stories!"

"That's what I'm here for," she said, as the other ravens pranced around her.

IV

What Greta was here for today, though, was to put some of her traveller's knowledge to use. She was leading the flock to Carrot Creek, a place where she had seen wolves on her last outing of the fall. The flock spent time in Banff National Park every few winters, but they had not been to Carrot Creek in living memory.

And now, a couple of hours after they had started their flight, the ravens were nearly there. Greta had led them straight west at first, across the snow-speckled gray ridges of the front ranges. Beyond Mount Fable she had turned northwest, passing over the wonderfully twisted strata of Syncline Mountain (Sarah noticed this), then on to the headwaters of Cougar Creek, where the ridges were rugged and gray on the east side and gentle and brown on the west; then over Cougar Pass to the headwaters of the Ghost River, wherein lies Wraith Lake, so high in the mountains that it's frozen most of the year; then over the Ghost Plateau, where flocks of bighorn sheep spend the summer grazing in that enormous alpine meadow, safe from predators in the valley below. Safe from wolves – the wolves that live along Carrot Creek.

"There's one!" Marg called out. She had spotted a doglike shape crossing the gravel flats far below them.

"Naw – that's jest a coyote," Scratch called back. "Too small fer a wolf."

"Oh yeah? What's *that*, then, Mister Know-It-All?"

The whole flock could now see what Marg was talking about: another wolf had crossed the gravel. This one was jet black, and there was no such thing, the ravens knew, as a black coyote.

Colin was nonplussed. The first animal had been a different color. Zack was flying nearby, and Colin was about to ask him how some wolves could be gray and some wolves could be black, when Zack brought up the subject on his own.

"Look, Molly! A black one and a gray one! All we need now is a white one!"

"They look well fed, too," Molly noted. "Lots of muscle."

At this point a white wolf *did* walk out of the woods. "Hey, there we go!" Scratch cried. He did an excited half-roll. "With a white one in that there pack, we got it made this winter! Sneak up on them elk, no problem. Once I seen a white one creep up ta within a wingbeat a' fangin' distance before the elk knowed it was even there. Big sucker, that wolf. Had that elk down right smart, it did. Got it right on the windpipe, like so."

Scratch threw his head back and made a choking sound, then fluttered in mock agony.

The birds all circled downward to see where the wolves were going. It was still early in the day, and perhaps the wolves had not yet eaten. Maybe they were going to lead the flock to a kill right then and there. Meat – elk meat, too, thick and bloody, full of protein – was exactly what the birds needed. They had flown the whole way without stopping to find food.

With Colin in the lead, and the Main Raven not far behind, the flock sprinted through the air in the direction the wolves were heading, hoping to arrive at the kill, if there were one, before the pack got there. Greta fell far behind, of course, and she would have plugged along all by herself, had not Marg broken away from the race to coast back and fly with her.

"Ooo, those birds make me so mad," Marg said, clacking her bill. "Here you take them all the way to this place, and we find the wolves, and then what do they do? Do they thank you for it? No! They just flap off, every bird for himself, like you didn't exist. Ah!"

"Never mind, Marg. I'm a terrible flyer and I know it."

"I *do* mind, Greta. It's just not fair. Not fair at all."

"Pretty hard to be fair when your crop is empty," Greta said.

Meanwhile, Colin had spotted something up ahead. "Hey! There it is!"

The Main Raven saw it, too. "I daresay it's a kill, all right. But I find it awfully *dark*-looking to be an elk, don't you think? We'll all just have to go and see."

The Main Raven's words were wasted on the wind, for the other ravens had furled their wings and dived.

"By the Trees," Zack croaked, as he landed in a poplar overlooking the kill. "It's a moose!"

Colin perched beside him. He had never seen such a large kill. Even half-gone, it was enormous. There was meat here for a hundred ravens. "So this is a moose," Colin marvelled.

"Well, it *was* a moose," Zack corrected. "Didn't you ever see a moose?"

"Uh . . . no. Not that I can remember."

"True enough. Hasn't been one at Yamnuska for a long time. But we're sure seeing one now. Let's dig in. Haven't got much time before the wolves get here." He dropped to the ground and edged over toward the kill. Brendan was ahead of him, though, doing raven jumping-jacks in the approved manner. He danced forward and back, closer and closer, until he actually touched the meat.

"Well done, Brendan!" complimented the Main Raven. "Your first Lead. I think we should all recognize Brendan's achievement." He croaked heartily, as did the other birds. Brendan fluffed out his head-feathers as a sign of appreciation, and glanced over to Sarah, who produced a single "tock!" – the call of female admiration – which Brendan noted proudly. Then all the birds hopped over to the carcass and began to eat.

Zack plunged his head into the body cavity, reaching for an enticing bit of red dangling under the backbone. All the other birds were picking and pulling, stripping food away furiously. Most hadn't eaten meat for many days, so their bodies craved the protein, the fat, and the salt it contained.

Then the wolves showed up.

"Wolves're back!" Scratch shouted, leaping into the air. Everyone followed. Colin jumped far and fast, not knowing how quick the wolves might be. But he needn't have worried. The three wolves didn't lunge for the birds. They arrived at a slow trot, ambled over to the carcass and began feeding.

"They're not like coyotes, are they?" said Colin. He, Molly, and Zack were sitting on the same bare branch of the poplar.

"No, not at all like coyotes," Molly agreed. "Coyotes are quicker and sneakier."

"And wolves don't kill ravens," Zack added.

"Never?" asked Colin.

"Oh, sure, if a bird is foolish enough to get too close. But you have to be *really* close. I've been right on the ground with them, a couple of hops away, and they've paid me no attention."

"Wolves are naturally more generous than coyotes," Molly said. She looked down at the carcass. "They can afford to be. They can kill one of these every few days if they like."

To Colin it looked as if the generous wolves were about to kill one another. The three of them were snarling, wrinkling their lips back and showing their teeth as they tugged at the moose. One wolf – the white one – seemed a little larger than the other two. It didn't growl very loudly or show its teeth much. Yet it got whatever it wanted from the kill because the gray one and the black one deferred to it. Those two, on the other hand, spent much of their time trying to intimidate each other.

"So the white one's in charge," Zack said, noticing the same thing.

"I'm not surprised, Zack," Molly said. "It looks really tough."

"They all look really tough," Colin offered. Not much would stand a chance against these animals, he thought, noting their big heads, their strong jaws, the heavy muscles in their necks. "I wouldn't want to be on the receiving end of that."

"Nor would I," said Greta. She had finally caught up. "Any left?" she asked. "Oh, phooey. The wolves are on it."

"Still bound to be plenty when they finish," Zack said. "There's only three of them, and they'll be full pretty soon."

Just as Zack had predicted, the wolves were slowing down, both in their eating and in their quarrelling. Presently they walked away together and flopped down in the snow not far from the moose. Colin could see bloodstains on the white wolf's muzzle. He could see its black nose, raised and twitching, savoring the scent of the kill. He could see the wolf's yellow eyes, steady and cool, showing the intelligence behind them, the cunning.

Then Colin saw Wheedle glide down to the carcass, Scratch hot on his tail-feathers. The Main Raven also flew down, and soon all the birds but Colin were pecking away again. The wolves lay nearby and watched. How could the birds feed so close to such killers? Colin stayed in the tree. But the wolves never moved a paw to chase the ravens. Instead, they curled up and went to sleep.

"You're right, Zack," Colin said, as he sheepishly joined his friends on the ground. "They really are different."

Zack had his bill full of moose brains and couldn't answer. So Molly did. "Oh, they'll be asleep for quite a while," she said. "It's time for their morning nap."

Colin looked up from his meal to check his surroundings. He could see the north wind rocking the trees farther up the mountainside, but on the narrow, protected valley floor it was calm. He noted the cloudless sky, yet the sun provided little warmth. He turned back to the carcass, stoking his own furnace with fuel from the body of another creature.

Winter was here, all right, and it was chasing the heat of summer farther and farther south. Soon, anything still alive in the Canadian Rockies would shiver through the long, deathly cold nights of the winter solstice – and the truly arctic conditions that were sure to follow.

V

Colin awoke. Like the wolves, he and the other ravens had eaten their fill. Zack and Molly were perched beside him in the poplar tree, still dozing, their heads beneath their wings.

"Zack," Colin croaked softly. Zack opened one eye, but he didn't move his head.

"Zack, I'm going to explore the valley. See you later."

"S'ya later," Zack mumbled, going back to sleep.

Colin soon discovered that the valley of Carrot Creek held a spectacular canyon. The creek had cut through massive layers of limestone here. Begrudging every bit of erosion, however, the rock had forced the water to flow through a narrow gorge, like a saw-groove in hard wood.

The dead moose was just upstream of the canyon, and as Colin flew along the creek, into the gorge, the gray rock walls rose quickly on either side of him. Every ledge was covered with green moss. This morning a dusting of snow lay on the moss, vividly white on green. Trees grew on the ledges, too, little ragged spruces that somehow had found enough soil for their roots. Living here wasn't easy for these trees. Every winter the accumulating snow tried to squeeze them off their perches and into the gorge. Every spring the melting snow threatened to wash the shallow roots away. Every summer the moisture on the ledges was barely enough to sustain them. Growth came hard, and the little spruces decorating the cliffs were much older than they looked. Carrot Creek Canyon was a tough, rocky, difficult place, but like the rest of the world's difficult places it was also very beautiful.

Colin could appreciate the canyon on the wing, from midway up. Above he saw a strip of blue sky between the canyon walls. Below he saw a strip of white ice and snow on the narrow canyon floor, interspersed with pools of open water. Thirsty from eating so much meat, he dropped down to one of these pools for a drink. The water rippled at the base of a sluiceway in the rock, a trough worn perfectly smooth by summer after summer of sand and pebbles riding down it. Only a trickle flowed here now, in early winter, but that was enough to keep the pool from freezing. Looking into the water, Colin could see some of the pebbles on the bottom – black, gray, pink – and a tiny fish picking at them. Colin wasn't hungry, which was lucky for the fish.

"This is an amazing place," Colin said aloud to himself, thinking that "amazing" was a word he used far too often. But then, the world was so interesting, so . . . amazing. What else could he call it?

"Sounds like the right word to me," said a voice Colin had never heard before.

Colin's wings whipped out in fright. He leapt up. From treetop height, which he reached in an instant, he tried to locate the voice. His eyes searched the canyon as he cocked his head warily up, down, sideways. Still he could see nothing but rock, snow, moss, trees, and sky.

Then the voice came again. "Gro, Colin C.C.," it said.

This was unmistakably the voice of a raven. But where was it? The voice seemed to come from someone flying beside him, but no bird was there. It was a strong voice, and deep like that of the Main Raven. But it wasn't the Main Raven. And how did it know his name?

"Uh, gro, whoever you are," Colin replied.

"Don't bother looking for me," it said. "You can't see me. I'm not really here."

Colin's heart started to race again. What was going on? "But, but –" he stammered.

"Now, don't be frightened," the voice reassured him. "I'm a friend."

This was not terribly reassuring. A disembodied voice claiming to be a *friend?*

"A friend of Greta's," it said.

A friend of Greta's? Colin landed in a tree to mull this over. He said nothing, and for a time all was silent in Carrot Creek Canyon. However, at length Colin came up with a question for the voice, if it was still there.

"Um – how do you know my name?" he asked.

The voice replied immediately. "I thought you'd ask me that. They all do. In point of fact, I've known of you for some time, Colin. And as for Greta, well, I've known Greta for – let's see – maybe fifteen years?" Then the voice abruptly changed the subject. "Great canyon, eh?"

Colin couldn't think of what to say in reply, so he just agreed with the voice. "It sure is." He wondered what turn this strange conversation was taking. But he wanted to keep it going. "I've never been in a place like this," he offered.

"Oh, there are lots of others in the mountains," the voice went on, sounding interested. "Canyons, I mean. Even better ones than this. There's one with a huge waterfall at the top, and another one that has clear springs you can look way down into . . ." The voice trailed off for a moment, then came again. "But I know how it is. Your first canyon – that's really the best one. Nice weather we're having, too, don't you think?"

What Colin thought was that here he was, making small talk with a voice that had no bird to go with it.

The voice didn't wait for a reply. "Not a bad time of year, you know," it said. "Snow covering that depressing brownness of late fall. Still, winter seems to come later every year. And it ends sooner. And I thought another ice age was coming. Must have been wrong about that."

Not knowing what an "ice age" was, Colin stumbled for a reply. Before he could think of one, though, the voice indicated that the conversation was over. "Well, I guess that's all, Colin. You're doing fine. I'll look you up again, okay?"

Colin wasn't sure whether he wanted to be "looked up" again or not. Before he could catch himself, he blurted out, "It's kind of strange to be talking to a bird that isn't there."

"I know, I know," the voice said, not offended at all. "You'll get used to it. Maybe even enjoy it. Most of them do. 'Bye now."

VI

Carrot Creek Canyon regained its silence, except for the sound of water running down the stone sluiceway and into the pool. Colin looked. The fish was still there, making its rounds, going from pebble to pebble. He lowered his head to watch it closely, and it saw him. With a flip of its tiny tail it hid under a rock.

Colin waited for it to come out, and it did. The fish seemed to have forgotten what had just happened. Colin knew, from his own experience in catching fish, that as long as he didn't move, the fish wouldn't realize he was there. He tried to fool the fish by moving very slowly, so slowly that the fish wouldn't notice. Colin was succeeding, coming almost bill-to-fin with the fish. It would be so easy to reach in and lift it out, feeling the squish of its body against his tongue, a little burst of fishy taste, maybe some tiny eggs inside –

Splash!

A large black bill plunged down right beside Colin's and caught the fish. Standing next to him, water dripping off his head, was Dolus.

"Scared you, right?" Dolus said, eating the fish. "What were you doing there, anyway? Just *watching* the bloody thing? Fish are to eat, not to watch." He took a drink from the pool. "You watched. I ate."

Colin's surprise turned to anger. "For your information, I *was* watching, because it was interesting, and I learned something, too. And maybe I *was* about to eat that fish, but I see that you've eaten it *for* me."

"Always happy to oblige a buddy. Let me know if I can be of further service." Dolus knelt and extended his wings slightly, rustling them in mock submission.

Before Colin could react to this teasing, Garth alighted beside them. "Hey, Colin! The fishing's great, eh? Dolus and me, we've done the whole canyon. Every pool. I'm so full I can hardly fly."

"Colin is *watching*, not fishing," Dolus sneered.

"Huh?" Garth looked puzzled. "Watching what, Colin?"

"Oh, this little fish that Dolus just ate from under my bill."

"C'mon, Dolus, that was Colin's fish."

"Aw, he wasn't gonna eat it. Fish was gonna go to waste. Had to grab it myself, before it got away from this dummy."

Colin felt his anger rising again. Dolus could get a bird's tufts up so quickly. He was always looking for a fight. Well, maybe Dolus was going to get what he was asking for. "Dolus, take that back. That bit about 'dummy.' Just because someone is *studying* something doesn't mean that he's stupid." Colin raised the feather tufts above his eyes. He sleeked the rest of his plumage and clacked his bill.

Dolus responded in kind, but Garth defused the situation. "Hey," he said, "let's not get into an uproar. We're all way too stuffed. Anyway, I'm sure Dolus appreciates what you were doing, Colin. Every raven can take the time to learn something new, right, Dolus?" Before Dolus could reply, Garth continued. "Look – I've got an idea. There's a bunch of bighorns rutting a little way down the canyon. Wanta go watch?"

"Yeah, okay," Dolus growled.

Colin was immediately interested in the sheep. What was this "rutting" business? "Sure. I'll go," he said, glad to be doing something with Dolus and Garth other than fighting.

The canyon walls grew even taller and closer together as they flew through the gorge. It was colder here, where the sun didn't penetrate.

Raven tracks around the pools showed where Garth and Dolus had been fishing. At some of the pools they had been forced to punch their bills through a thin layer of ice to reach the water.

Then, as the birds banked around a sharp bend, they saw the sheep. The birds settled down on a ledge overlooking the flock. A half-dozen bighorn rams and perhaps twice as many ewes were milling around at a wide spot in the canyon. The bighorns wore their thick gray winter wool. In the cold, little plumes of vapor came out of their nostrils. Colin picked out the males, the ones with the large, heavy horns curling around the sides of their heads. The ewes had shorter, thinner horns that stuck up from their heads in gentle arcs. The ewes were smaller and lighter-looking generally, and they had no trouble eluding the rams, who were chasing them, Colin realized, all over the place.

A ram would come up to a ewe from behind. The ram would stretch its neck out, turn its head sideways and sniff the rear end of the ewe. Then it would throw its head up and wrinkle its upper lip back in what looked like a sneer, holding the expression for a moment.

Colin started to laugh. Birds don't generally go poking about each other's behinds, considering this place private and naughty, and the fact that the rams would do this so openly, making such a show of it, seemed wonderfully absurd. Colin let out a mild "craw-ha."

Neither Dolus nor Garth laughed. "Look at the size of that ram," Dolus said.

Garth nodded his agreement. "I'll bet he's number one in this flock," he said seriously.

"Yeah, maybe. Hey, look! Here we go!"

Another ram had walked over to the first one. The two stood side-by-side, eyeing each other. They weren't moving much, but judging from the amount of vapor coming from their noses, they were certainly worked up about something. Perhaps they were comparing the size of each other's horns. Both had impressive sets.

Then the challenger made his move. He turned sideways to the first ram, reached out with a front leg and tapped it under the ram's belly.

Aha, thought Colin. That must be some kind of insult.

The first ram butted the challenger smartly across the horns. Clack!

"All right, all right! Teach that upstart!" Garth was taking sides. Dolus joined in. "Yeah, show him who's boss."

The sheep drew apart, and Colin figured that the contest might be over. After all, there were plenty of ewes. There was no need to fight over them.

But what happened next was a surprise. Having backed away from each other a couple of sheep-lengths, the two rams reared up and charged each other. This time the impact of their horns was a lot harder, and the sound – CLACK! – echoed down the canyon.

"Good one!" Dolus said.

"I'll bet they're both seeing stars," Garth put in.

"That must really hurt," Colin remarked. "I wonder if they get a headache?" He chuckled to himself, thinking how ridiculous the scene was. Here were two large animals banging heads. The females didn't even seem to notice. Why didn't one ram just *bite* the other one? It would be a lot less work, and certainly less hard on the brains inside those skulls. If – and he couldn't help it; he laughed aloud – if there were any brains at all! "Craw-ha! This is great!" Colin croaked merrily.

Garth also started to laugh, but Dolus silenced him with a peck to the back. "It's not funny," he said emphatically. "It's about being the boss. Number One. I wish *I* could be as tough as that."

Colin cocked his head to the side. What was he hearing? A raven who wanted to butt heads like a sheep? That in itself was funny. He started to chuckle again.

Dolus was on him in an instant. He grabbed Colin by the throat and pushed him over on his side. Utterly helpless, Colin realized that Dolus could strangle him then and there.

"Did I hear you laughing, Mister Raven-Come-Lately?" Dolus said through his half-closed bill. "Did I hear you making fun of me?"

Colin could speak only in a whisper. "Not of you, Dolus. It just seemed like a funny idea. A raven butting heads like a sheep."

Dolus tightened his grip. "Well, it's *not* a funny idea, and you better not laugh. I want to hear you say you're sorry!"

Colin had no choice, but he delayed replying until Dolus closed his bill a little farther. By now, the pressure was really painful. "Okay, okay. I'm sorry."

"Tell me again!" Dolus said, clamping down on Colin's neck even harder, and digging into Colin's side with his claws.

"I'm sorry! I'm sorry!" Colin squeaked. Dolus still held him down.

Garth intervened. "C'mon, Dolus. He's apologized. I think he means it, too."

"He'd better mean it," Dolus grunted, letting go of Colin and stepping back. "He'd bloody well better."

Below them, the sheep charged each other again, head to head.

CLACK!

VII

At dusk the birds gathered at the dead moose. Most had stayed nearby, spending the day picking at the carcass. The wolves had also remained near their kill, eating, sleeping, playing tug-of-war with one of the moose's legs they had gnawed off, or just cavorting about for no apparent reason.

Then the sun went down. On this cloudless day it departed in fine style, spreading a wash of pink over the peaks above Carrot Creek. The color tinged the cliffs of Mount Peechee and the long, rounded slopes of Princess Margaret Mountain. Evening shadows crept up from the valleys, following the fading sunlight.

Tired from their long trip that day, and too full of moose meat to hold the Flight, the ravens wanted only to roost. The whole flock flew over to a huge spruce growing beside the creek. The birds sat in twos and threes, here and there, trying to get comfortable on a roost they had never used before. There was a lot of fussing. Scratch and Wheedle abandoned their branch for another because "it just didn't feel right," according to Wheedle, and the Main Raven kept moving up the tree in order to have the highest perch.

The younger ravens were restless on their first night along Carrot Creek. They tucked their heads back as if dozing off, then one would start giggling uncontrollably and the others would join in. Marg spoke to them sharply a couple of times, and they finally tittered off to sleep.

Colin wanted to roost with Greta. Usually she roosted alone, but when Colin asked to sit with her she agreed. He had something to discuss.

"Greta, a strange thing happened to me today."

"I heard about it. Dolus did a number on you."

"That's true. He did. But that's not the thing I'm talking about."

"Dolus took too long to hatch," Greta stated offhandedly. "I think he got poisoned in the shell, and he's been nasty ever since. His *parents* are certainly nice enough birds."

"Greta –"

"So expect the unexpected around Dolus. He's not to be trusted. Hasn't killed anybody yet, but you never know. Did I tell you that he came from the Wedge Flock, down in the Kananaskis? Dolus and Garth both, chucked out for bad behavior. Same thing'll happen here, probably."

"Greta –"

"Yes?"

"A really strange thing happened to me today."

Greta turned toward him. Her eyes seemed to shine in the dimness. "Tell me about it, Colin," she said softly.

"Well, it was a raven. I mean . . . a raven's voice. Just the voice. No raven, if you see what I mean."

"I think I may. No raven at all?"

"No. At least I couldn't find it. Maybe it was hiding, trying to fool me. But I looked high and low, Greta, and the sound just came from everywhere at once. In fact, the voice told me that it wasn't even *there*. Isn't that strange?"

"Depends on who was speaking. Did it give you its name?"

"No. But here's the really weird part. It said that it was a friend of *yours*, Greta. It told me not to be afraid, because it was a friend of yours."

"Ah. Then I know who it was."

She paused. Colin waited expectantly. When Greta spoke again, she offered one of her cryptic statements, albeit a reassuring one. "Colin, you're doing fine." And with that she tucked her head under her wing and dropped off to sleep.

Colin thought this over. He repeated Greta's last statement over and over to himself – "Colin, you're doing fine. Colin, you're doing fine" – and as he drowsed off, it came to him that those four words were exactly what the voice itself had said to him.

VIII

Dawn at Carrot Creek came with clouds. Spidery filaments of cirrus appeared from the west, and long before the sun cracked the horizon the high clouds lit up, filling the sky with pink streamers. One spot on the silhouette of Princess Margaret Mountain grew impossibly brilliant. From it a sheet of sunlight shot across the front ranges, then reached gradually down into the valley of Carrot Creek.

In the enfolding boughs of the big spruce, the ravens awoke slowly, especially the young ones, who had stayed up too late being silly the night before. Marg was the first to open her eyes. She looked out from her perch near the trunk, noting that everything not covered with snow yesterday was covered with frost this morning. Carrot Creek was quiet. It had babbled by in the afternoon, emitting noisy splashes from many open spots in the ice, but the overnight cold had closed the remaining holes and now the sound was gone.

Marg heard something else. She turned to her sleeping daughter. "Sarah, wake up. There's a bear."

"Huh? Gro? Mum?" Sarah pulled her head from under her wing, blinking in the sunlight. In the shadows below, a shape was moving.

"There, right under the tree. See? It's a grizzly, I think."

Sarah looked down. The shape passed into a circle of sunlight. Tawny-colored, the bear seemed frosty itself, for each hair in its long winter coat was tipped with silver. It brushed through a patch of willows, sending a few dried leaves fluttering to the ground.

Sarah was awake now. She had never seen a bear like this.

"How come it's not black, Mum? Bears are black, right?"

"Not this kind, dear. This is a grizzly bear. Most are brown, but others are pale, like this one. They can be black, too. And combinations."

The bear had followed its nose to the moose carcass, and now it settled down beside it. Tenderly, it nudged the red mass with its muzzle. Its tongue came out. It licked the meat a couple of times. It raised its massive head and opened its jaws to make a sound that instantly woke every bird still sleeping in the tree.

"*Uhhhhhhhhhhhh.*"

"What was that?!"

"Did you hear something?!"

"Over there. By the kill. Look at the size of that bear!"

"My word, it's a big one."

"Is it going to, like, eat all our breakfast?"

"Where are the wolves?"

Marg looked around. The wolves had bedded down for the night a little distance from their kill, and she could see them trotting softly over to it now. They saw the scavenging bear and stopped, their yellow eyes calculating. Taking on a full-grown grizzly was risky. Pack members could be injured. The wolves sat back on their haunches and watched, along with the ravens.

The bear flipped the carcass over in a single easy motion. It grabbed a flap of flesh and pulled. Effortlessly, a long, thick strip of meat came away. The bear gobbled it down.

"Whoa," Brendan said. "Save some for me. I mean, for us," he added, looking over to Sarah.

Licking its lips, the bear went back for more. In a few minutes it had cleaned most of the remaining meat from the ribcage.

"Zack – this bear, this grizzly bear," Colin began, for he had overheard Marg explaining what it was, "will it eat all the meat on that kill?"

"No," Zack replied. "Bears are sloppier eaters than wolves. There'll be plenty left for us."

One of the wolves whined. The bear looked toward it and growled.

"Smart of those wolves to lie low," Zack continued, "Nothing messes with a brute like that. Strongest thing in the mountains. Except maybe for the odor of a wolverine."

Colin started to laugh. But a little noise from his crop stopped him. He was hungry. How long would the bear keep the birds from breakfast? He had his answer a moment later, when the bear got back to its feet and ambled away.

"Hey! Yay!" Brendan gave a cheer, unfurling his wings. "It's leaving!" He leapt off his perch and started gliding down.

But the moment the bear left, the wolves were on the kill. Brendan's glide turned quickly into a climb. "Aw, heck," he said, and settled back on his perch.

"It won't be long, kids," Marg reassured them. "Remember that ravens have to be patient."

And they were. A little plaintive croaking, maybe, and a few low passes over the wolves to vent their frustration. But eventually, the birds knew, they would get their morning meal. Still, tedium mixed with hunger was a foul combination, and tempers in the spruce were growing short. Luckily, another visitor arrived – a friendly one.

"Perry!"

"Hi, guys."

It was the same gray jay that had fed with the ravens last fall, on the elk kill in the valley north of Yamnuska. Flying softly across the clearing on his short gray wings, Perry perched next to Molly in the spruce. He looked quite petite next to the much-larger raven.

"Gro, Perry. You're a long way from home," Molly said.

"Gro, Molly. So are you," Perry replied. His gray-and-white head tilted to and fro as he exchanged greetings with the other birds in the flock. His large eyes kept flicking down to the moose carcass, to see whether the wolves were finished.

"What brings you to Carrot Creek?" Molly asked.

"Oh, I've been here a lot lately. My sister is nesting with a jay from Banff, and I've been hanging around at the hot springs most of the summer. Talk about good eating!"

"Like what, Perry?" a couple of birds asked at the same time. Everyone was hungry.

"Human food. Scads of it. Hamburgers, buns, french fries, you name it."

Ravens can't drool, but if they could, they would have. The spruce rustled as the Raven's Enders edged back and forth on the branches, thinking about it all. Few of them had any idea what a "hamburger" was, or "fries," but the way Perry said the words told them all they needed to know.

"Hmm. Banff isn't very far away," Greta said. "We could nip over there for the day, if we liked."

"Yeah!"

"All *riiight!*"

"Let's do it!"

"Let's go!"

Perry looked around at the ravens. "Sure. I'll show you where the goodies are. Mind you, most of the tourists have gone home."

Colin was wondering what a "tourist" was. Another kind of bird, maybe? But he lost his train of thought as Perry suddenly swooped down onto the kill, practically under the nose of the big white wolf.

"Oh, no – he's had it!" Colin croaked.

"Not that little guy," Zack said. "Just watch him."

The wolf lunged for Perry, but he dodged easily by jumping sideways off the carcass and then fluttering upward out of reach. He settled just as quickly at the opposite end of the kill and grabbed a bite there before one of the other wolves snapped at him. He kept hopping about on the moose, picking off tiny bits between wolf-lunges. Soon the animals gave up chasing him, and Perry ate his fill. He flapped heavily up to his perch beside Molly again.

"You know," he said, wiping his bill on a branch, "it never fails. Just about the time I've eaten so much that I'm getting clumsy, the wolves figure they can't catch me and they leave me alone."

"Same with coyotes?" Molly asked.

"Oh, yeah. A dog is a dog. They're all the same. Though I wouldn't trust a coyote quite as far as a wolf." He wiped his bill again. "And dogs that live with humans," he added, "are completely unpredictable. Fortunately they're also completely uncoordinated."

Molly, Colin, and Zack all laughed. Having watched many dogs stumbling over the boulders on Yamnuska, they could vouch for that.

IX

"Hey! Let's go to this 'Bann-iff' place!"

It was Brendan. The wolves had moved away from the kill, and the ravens were finishing their delayed breakfast. Brendan was always keen to travel, and the long trip to Carrot Creek had been easy for him. Now, full of moose meat, he felt that he could fly for days.

Sarah heard him. She wiped her bill on a willow stem, hopped over and asked excitedly, "Who's going? Who's going?"

More of the ravens joined in.

"I'm going!"

"Hey, yeah – I'm ready to fly right now."

"How far is it?"

"Does Perry really know the way?"

"Friends, friends. Shall we have the Flap first?"

The Main Raven was worried that everybody would take off before the flock had gathered for its first Flap at Carrot Creek. He was right to worry; Perry was already being begged to take the flock to "Bann-iff." The Main Raven sighed. So much for the Flap. And he had no interest in going to Banff.

The other birds were growing more and more excited.

"Perry, you'll take us, right?"

"Gee, guys. I'm really a slow flyer. You sure you want to follow little old me?"

Indeed, the ravens realized that it would be a slow trip with Perry leading the way. Too slow, maybe. But Scratch had an idea. "Hey, Greta – *you* knows the way, right?" Even Greta flew faster than Perry.

Greta declined. "I've been to Banff already this year," she said, tired from the previous day's trip and needing a rest. "I won't be going again for a while. But the rest of you will love it. Just keep an eye on the younger ones around the hot springs. Don't let them eat too much. Tourists feed the birds the most *awful* stuff there."

The reminder about the availability of human food was all it took. Several ravens hopped over to Perry again, urging him to lead them, never mind the speed.

Perry backpedalled still. "You can find it on your own," he said, realizing that the other birds would push him too hard on the flight. "It's not very far, and you can see the town as soon as you come around the corner of Mount Rundle. Just follow Carrot Creek down to the highway and turn right. You can't miss it. You don't really need me."

"We do! We do! There's nobody who could show us better than you!"

Perry was not immune to flattery. "Well, maybe if you promise not to fly fast, so I don't get a wing ache . . ."

"Oh, we promise!"

He eyed the group. "Really, you promise?"

"We really promise, Perry. Like, really, really."

"Well, okay. Follow me, you C.C.s!"

"Aw, Perry. What a bird, eh? Eh?"

"Rawk-a-taw!"

And away they all went, leaving Greta and the Main Raven to spend the rest of the day together.

The Main Raven wasn't going to let the opportunity pass. "I say, Greta. It seems that we shall have the opportunity to discuss a few things that the ordinary birds – I mean the other birds – would have little interest in. Such as the finer points of governing, and whether or not my speeches are proving effective, and so on."

Greta gritted her bill. "Oh, wolf-widgets," she said to herself.

X

Down Carrot Creek Perry went, a small gray bird pattering along, several flaps and a glide, more flaps and a glide, surrounded by hulking black ravens. Soon this odd-looking crew had reached the canyon, which was new to most of them. Ravens love to fly in such places, so Perry's slow pace allowed the flock to spend time swooping down by the creek and soaring up along the walls. The sheep, Colin noted, had gone. Their tracks showed where they had climbed out of the canyon in a side gully.

The ravens followed the creek onto the valley floor and through a stand of aspen, where a few brown leaves fluttered in the wintry air. Then they were over the Trans-Canada Highway. Carrot Creek was forced into a culvert beneath the road, and the creek grumbled its way through before emerging with a happy splash.

At the highway Perry indicated a right turn, westward along the valley of the Bow River past Mount Rundle, a long-ridged peak. Little Perry was getting breathless from trying to keep up with the ravens. "You just – *pant, pant* – follow the river," he gasped. "It'll take you – *whew!* – right into town."

"Slow down, you lunks," Marg called out to the younger ravens, now charging ahead. "It was nice of Perry to lead us this far, and I think we should show our gratitude by not tiring him out so much."

"Gratitude is for wimps," Dolus croaked back, picking up the pace. Garth and Brendan joined him in racing ahead, while Zack, Molly, and the others heeded Marg's request and eased back to an airborne jog. Sarah started to fly off with the other youngsters, but then she thought better of it and turned back to be with the adults. "Why hurry, anyway?" she said. "We'll just get there all tired and everything."

"Wait for us at the edge of town, kids," Marg called to the break-aways as they were getting out of earshot.

"They'll have to," Colin said. "They don't know the way to these 'hot springs,' whatever they are."

"Oh, the hot springs," Sarah said. "Greta told me about them. It's going to be very funny, I think."

"Why?"

"I forget, exactly. Greta said it was something about humans."

A few minutes later, having come around the corner of Mount Rundle, Colin asked, "What's that thing in the valley?"

"What thing?" Perry replied.

"That big bump. Like a big rock."

"Oh, the hotel. That's a place for humans. Whole thing is full of humans."

"Sort of like a beehive?" Colin was thinking of the human beehives that Greta had talked about when she had described cities to him.

Perry laughed a little wheezy jay laugh. "Whee-ooo! You don't know how right you are!"

Soon they were flying over the hotel. It was very large, with hundreds of windows. Sure enough, there were humans going in and out of it.

Colin had another batch of questions, but for the answers he picked Zack instead of Perry. "Are they all different?" he asked.

"What?"

"The humans. The ones coming out and going in. Is it the same humans going in and then coming out? They don't stay inside for very long, do they?"

Zack decided that this was a *Colin* sort of question, and he told Colin rather gruffly to figure out the answer for himself. Colin obliged, dropping away from the flock and angling down to the hotel. It overlooked the Bow River, and many humans were standing around on the sunny terrace.

Colin was taking no chances. He was going to keep his airspeed up, in case any of the humans had guns. This couldn't be the Park, he thought. There were far too many humans here. Maybe it was a city.

He zoomed low over the terrace, wings whistling in a half-tuck. One of the humans saw him coming and cried out in alarm. "Malcolm – look out!" The human covered its head with its hands.

"Jeez, Agnes! That bird came really close!"

"Big black one. A crow, maybe?"

"Musta been. Mighty big crow, though."

Colin flew around the corner to the other side of the hotel. There he saw some humans going in the entrance. Keeping his momentum up, he did a circle of the building, finishing again at the terrace. He looked toward the door. "Aha. Humans going out, all right," he said to himself.

Rejoining Zack and Molly, who had avoided the hotel altogether, Colin reported his findings. "They go in and they come out," he stated.

"Eh?" Zack thought that Colin might be losing his grip entirely. "What's this all about?"

"The humans," Colin explained. "They go into that hotel thing and then they come out."

"Oh for the love of – I could have told you that," Zack said testily.

"No, no – I saw a bunch go in, and they came right out. They must change their plumage inside. And quickly, too, because they look different when they come out."

Zack laughed so hard he stumbled in the air. "Craw-HA! Colin – by the Trees, Colin! You say the funniest things!"

"What's so funny?" Colin asked.

Perry interrupted. He was clearly in need of a perch. "Hey, everyone – *pant, pant, pant* – the hot springs – *pant, pant* – are just up there. See? On Sulphur Mountain."

He pointed with his bill. Mist was rising from the mountainside. Colin could see another building there, and the mist seemed to be coming from it.

"Look – *pant, pant* – I'm really all in." He lit atop a Douglas-fir. "I'll meet you guys at the hot springs later, okay?"

"Sure, Perry," Sarah said, in her most grown-up manner. "We of the Yamnuska Flock, like, really appreciate all you've done for us today."

"My pleasure," Perry called after the ravens, as they flew on toward the misty spot. "'Bye!"

The younger birds had managed to find the hot springs on their own. They were all perched in a big lodgepole pine overlooking the pool.

"Get a load of this," Brendan said to the others as they arrived. "It's far out."

Colin settled on a branch and furled his wings. He looked warily around, uneasy about sitting in a tree so close to all these humans. What if some of them had guns? "Zack, I'm worried about guns," he said.

"No need," Zack replied. "We're in the Park, here."

So this city *was* in the Park, after all. But if the humans came to the Park to get away from their cities, why had they built a city in the Park? Colin was mulling this over when he heard Zack chuckle. He looked over toward the hot-springs pool, where Zack was gesturing with his bill, and he croaked in amazement. Here was a pond of some kind, and it was full of humans. The humans didn't look the way they did when they hiked or climbed on Yamnuska. Humans on Yamnuska were all different colors. Sometimes their top halves would be red, say, and their bottom halves would be brown. Or green and blue. Or orange all over. They came in endless combinations. And Colin knew that they could change their colors whenever they liked, because they carried extra plumages in their packs. The humans in this hot-springs pool, though, all looked pretty much the same: shades of pink or brown.

Colin turned to Marg. "I've never seen humans looking like this," he said with a questioning look.

"Neither have I," she replied, "but I remember now what Greta said about them. She said that when humans go in the water they take their plumages off."

"You mean, this is what humans look like without any feathers at all?"

"Yes! Isn't it a scream?" Marg started laughing. Molly and Zack joined in.

"Hey, wait," Colin noted, "They *do* have plumages on them. Little ones. See? Some have just one, where their back legs come out."

"Oh – and there's males and females in there," Molly said.

"How can you tell?"

"The females have mammaries."

"What?"

Sarah explained. "I know! I know! They have these, like, bumps, for giving milk to their young. They're mammals, okay? Greta said so."

Colin hadn't considered that humans belonged to any biological family. "Mammals? Like wolves and elk and such?"

"Yeah."

Colin's eyes opened wider. "Sarah, I didn't think they were even *animals!*"

"Well, they're not, sort of. Greta said –"

Sarah was interrupted by a shriek from one of the humans. It had got out of the water and was rolling around in the snow by the edge of the pool. It made loud sounds, then jumped back into the pool.

Other humans were watching. One of them yelled, "Yay! That was great! Who's next?"

"Al, you try it."

"Not on your life! My heart would stop!"

"Under all that blubber? You're insulated like a whale!"

"Haw, haw, haw!"

Another human climbed out of the pool. It had two bits of plumage on – very small ones – and Colin thought it might be a female. It rolled around, getting snow all over it. A couple of other humans joined it, shrieking.

"What is this all about?" Colin said to any bird who might be listening.

"I – I think they like getting hot and cold," Sarah ventured. "The water is hot, okay, and the snow is cold. They sit in the hot water, and then they get out and get cold in the snow. Hey, look – the first one to do it? It's doing it again."

Sure enough, the first human was back in the snow. It picked some up and threw it at another human in the pool.

"Tweet!" went a whistle.

All the yelling stopped. Everyone, including the birds, looked over toward the building beside the pool. A door in the building was opening. "You! No throwing snow!" shouted an angry-looking human, leaning through the door.

The snow-thrower put down its second handful and crept back into the water.

"That must be their Main Human," Molly offered.

"Some kind of pompous type, that's for sure," Marg added.

"See, Garth? They obey each other." It was Dolus speaking. "Every human in the pool has to obey the one behind that door."

"What's the harm in throwing a little snow?" Colin asked.

"Maybe the Main Human, like, doesn't want the pool filled up with snow," Brendan offered.

Sarah sniggered. "But the pool *can't* fill up with snow, dummy. It just melts."

Brendan looked embarrassed. "Oh. Right," he said. "Cool. Can't fill up. Yeah."

"So, to summarize what we've learned so far," Colin pronounced, surprised at how pompous he himself sounded, "humans go into hotels, change plumages and go out. They come here to this pool of hot water, and they wear very small plumages. They like to get hot and cold. They're not allowed to put snow into the pool . . . oh, I know why!

The snow is cold and the pool is hot, so putting snow into the hot pool would make it cold, right? And they don't want it to get cold."

The other ravens had been listening to Colin's recitation, and they nodded their heads.

"That's gotta be it," Garth said. "Gotta be it."

"Shut up," said Dolus.

At that point something moving below their tree caught Molly's eye. She looked and saw a human standing right below the birds, pointing something at them. It made a sudden flash. "*Awk!* Guns!" she cried.

The ravens leapt into the air and scattered. They came to rest high up in other trees nearby, badly frightened – especially Colin. So much for what Zack had said about there being no guns around here, he thought. Never mind that the gun hadn't made any sound; it couldn't be anything else.

The human that had shot at them walked over to another human and said something. From where Colin was sitting, he could just make it out.

"Well, at least they held still long enough to get their picture taken."

"What were they, anyway? Crows?"

"I guess. Really big ones."

Then the ravens heard a familiar wheezy little laugh ringing through the woods, coming their way. "Whee-oo! What a pack of scaredy-birds! What's this, running from a camera? Whee-ooo! Whee-hee-hee!"

Perry, the jay, had arrived. He perched atop a leafless poplar a little distance away, and several of the ravens joined him, landing high among the bare branches. Perry looked up at them. "It's okay, you guys. Those cameras can't hurt you. Humans just use them to look at things. It's okay."

The ravens glanced at one another, croaking uneasily. Perry left the poplar, calling back as he flew, "Come on! Goodies in the parking lot!" He was headed toward a clearing in the woods a little distance away.

Goodies? Food? Human food? Well, that put a new light on things. One by one, the ravens left the security of their high perches and followed Perry.

XI

The clearing turned out to be a place where humans, in Colin's words, "got into nests and came out of them, but the nests moved around. Not like hotels."

Molly laughed. "Oh, Colin. You mean cars!"

"Is that what you call them?" He'd seen cars parked at the foot of the trail up Yamnuska, but he hadn't known the proper name for them.

"Yes, you silly bird. *Cars.*" She laughed again.

"Cars," Colin said to himself. "Cars. Cars."

Perry didn't have to explain further; the other ravens knew what to do. They located the trash barrels in the parking lot and happily began exploring them.

"Oh, jolly," Wheedle called out. "French fries!"

"There's 'bout a whole hamburger in this here barrel," Scratch replied.

"Awesome. This is really awesome," Brendan said. "The humans around here are totally cool."

Zack and Molly were working together on a particularly large barrel. Zack was inside, issuing reports as he picked over the contents with his bill and his big feet. Molly perched on the rim, acting as lookout.

"Okay, Molly, we've got a doughnut here." Zack hopped up onto the rim and presented a piece to Molly.

"Oh, thank you, dear," she said, dipping her bill in appreciation. "Such a thoughtful bird."

Colin was watching Perry. He had gone over to where some humans were eating something in their car. The window was rolled down, and one of the humans kept throwing scraps out. Not at all shy, Perry landed on the pavement under the window and started scavenging. Each time he picked up something he flew off with it. Colin knew what he was doing: hiding the food. Colin considered following him, but then realized that to do so would be impolite.

On each of his trips back to the humans in the car, Perry became bolder. Now he was perched right on the windowsill, and the humans were delighted.

"Hey, it's sitting right here," one of them said excitedly. "Myra, look at this."

"I can see it, Art. Kids, can you see the bird?"

"Yes, Mother. We see the bird."

"I'm going to feed it something. Here, birdy, have a bite of sandwich."

Colin watched the human hold out a bit of bread in its fingers. Perry flew up, hovered in mid-air and grabbed it.

"Hey, neat-o, Dad!"

"Let me try that!"

The other windows in the car were rolling down. All the humans were now reaching out toward Perry with offerings of their lunch. Perry became very busy, grabbing this and that, flying off to hide it, returning for more.

"I wonder if he'll sit on my hand, Mom!"

"Well, I don't know . . ."

"Oh, it's okay, Lissy. He won't peck you."

One of the smaller humans placed a marshmallow in the centre of its hand and held it as far out from the window as it could reach. Perry lighted on the outstretched fingers and took the marshmallow.

"Hee hee! He's got ticklish feet, Dad!"

So it was true, Colin thought. Gray jays really would perch right in a human's hand. Well, maybe Perry could do that, but he, Colin, would never try it. Thinking about this, he pictured a raven trying to perch on a human's hand. He laughed at the thought: a bird three times the size of little Perry, trying to find room for its feet! Craw-ha!

Meanwhile, Marg was over in a far corner of the lot where there were no cars parked. She was pecking at something on the ground. "Cheesy worms, kids. We've got cheesy worms," she called out.

Instantly Brendan, Sarah, Dolus, and Garth were there. Marg had a bag of crunchy yellow things held under a foot, ripping it open with her bill. "Golly," she said excitedly, "they left us a full one."

The bag spilled open and all the ravens hopped around, picking up the scattering contents.

Brendan: "Thish – *crunch* – shtuff ish – *crunch, crunch* – jush great – *gulp*. Like, these choppy worms are really, really excellent."

Marg: "*Crunch, crunch* – 'cheesy worms,' dear."

Brendan: "Whatever."

"I don't care what they are," Sarah said, when her bill was empty. "They must have been, like, invented just for ravens."

Dolus made a grab for the bag, still half full.

"Dolus! Don't you dare!" Marg gave him such an evil look that Dolus hesitated. Then he clamped a corner of the bag in his bill and flew off with it.

"Dolus! Dolus!" the other birds called after him. Garth started to fly away, too.

"Oooo – I'm going to have to speak to the Main Raven about this," Marg said. Then her voice softened. "But never mind, dears, there's still plenty lying around here."

In fact, there was now plenty of food everywhere, because Dolus had flown off with the ripped bag hanging open downward. Cheesy worms fell through the air, bouncing on the pavement when they hit. A trail of yellow led across the lot to Dolus, now sitting in a tree, infuriated. By the time he'd noticed what had happened, the bag was empty.

Sarah laughed in his direction. "Craw-ha! Serves you right!"

"I didn't want 'em anyway," Dolus yelled back.

"That's fine. We can take care of them."

"I'll take care of *you*."

"Try anything and Zack and I will personally pick your tail-feathers out," Marg croaked angrily, her eyebrow feathers fully erect. "Zack!" she called. "Get over here."

"Aw, Zack doesn't scare me," Dolus sneered. "I beat him up already."

Zack landed. "What's happening?"

"Oh, Dolus is just being Dolus. I thought I might need some help in dealing with him." She explained about the botched theft.

"He's been stupid. And you saw it. No bully can bear that. But I don't think he'll take us both on." Zack looked over to the trees. Dolus and Garth were sitting there, speaking to each other in low tones.

At the other end of the parking lot, Colin, Perry, and most of the other birds had gathered around a car. Sitting inside was a cat.

"What's that?" someone asked.

"Don't know," another replied. "I've never seen one."

"That," said Perry, "is the most dangerous little predator that ever stalked a bird."

"How so? It's not very big."

"But it's very, very *fast*," Perry continued. "Watch this." He hopped up to a mirror on the car.

In one smooth motion, so quick that the birds had to jerk their heads to follow it, the cat was on the dashboard, shooting its paw out at the glass. It opened and shut its mouth, showing a set of sharp teeth. The birds could hear a muffled yowl.

"Hoo-whee!" Scratch said as he arrived. "Them cats! One a' them dang near kilt me up in Yellowknife."

"What happened?" Colin asked.

"Jumped me when I was down in a trash can. Just like today. Waited 'til I was comin' out, like. Zip! Got a claw into me right here." He pointed at his belly. "Dragged me right offa that can and onta the road." He shuddered. "I got away, though."

"How did you do that?" Colin couldn't imagine escaping such a creature at close range. He looked at Perry, calmly sitting right on the other side of the window from the cat, which was still pawing the glass, its tail swishing side to side, its mouth twitching.

"Car come down the alley and run over it." Scratch laughed. "Cat was too busy tryin' ta bite me. Didn't notice the car, like. Squoosh."

"Did you eat some?" Brendan asked.

"Are you kiddin'? I blew outta there like poop out of a gull!"

Everyone laughed.

"Not too bad a town, Yellowknife," Scratch mused. "Not bad at all. 'Cept fer it had cats."

XII

"Shall we be heading home, everyone? I mean, back to Carrot Creek?" Marg was thinking about the time of day. If they were going to be back before dark, they would have to leave soon.

"Naw, let's stay here for a few days," said Brendan. "The food is really good here."

Perry spoke up. "Uh, guys, there's something I should tell you about. It's okay to *visit* here, but, well, it might not be too smart to stay."

"Why not?" asked Brendan.

"Well, there's other ravens," Perry replied.

"So?"

"So they don't mind another flock in town for a day, but they take exception if you stay longer."

Dolus began to perk up. He stopped moping in his tree and joined the others. "Just how tough are these other ravens?" he said, fluffing out his neck-feathers.

"Oh, pretty tough. And there's a lot of them, and they have a way of keeping Banff more or less theirs."

"Well, I'd like to meet some of these supposedly 'pretty tough' ravens." Dolus tilted his head up and let out a loud "Rawk-a-taw!"

Marg didn't like that. "Dolus, the flock call is only for making the Motion. You shouldn't be doing it here, so casually like that."

Marg had no sooner spoken than a couple of strange ravens landed among the Raven's Enders. Perry said, "See you later, guys," and flew away.

"Gro, C.C.s," one of the Banff ravens said. It was large and glossy, obviously strong and well fed. The Yamnuska birds were quick to notice that its eyebrow feathers were ever so slightly raised.

"Gro," Zack replied, trying to sound friendly. He kept his tufts down.

"So. You're just visiting, right?" the big raven said.

Dolus opened his bill to say something, but Marg quickly interrupted. "Yes, that's right," Marg said. "Just visiting. We're from Yamnuska."

"Ah, the Raven's End Flock." The big raven relaxed a little. "We've had a visit from one of you. 'Rita,' or 'Grittle,' or something like that. Nice old bird."

"'Greta' is her name, if it's all the same to you." Dolus had barged into the conversation.

"And what's your name, my young friend?" said the big raven, his eyebrow tufts rising again.

"Dolus C.C. Have you got a name?"

This was a very insulting thing to say to a stranger. But the big raven let it pass, realizing that Dolus was young and hot-headed. The other Banff ravens, however, started to sleek their feathers. One of them clacked its bill. Things were not going well.

Zack tried to calm the situation. "Oh, pay no attention to Dolus. He's always unpleasant. We've had a lovely day here at the hot springs. We admire your mountains very much, and we'll be off shortly."

That did the trick. Everybody felt more at ease. The ravens took to greeting each other individually, with many "gro"s, and pretty soon the birds were all chatting amiably together.

"Hi, I'm Marg C.C."

"How pleased to meet you. I'm Salvelina C.C. You remind me of a raven I once met by Barrier Mountain."

"Why, yes! Salvelina! Of course! We shared some fish guts by the lake there, didn't we?"

Brendan, too, was trying to make friends. "Gro, gro," he croaked, turning in a circle. A young Banff raven walked over to meet him.

Colin was attracted to a friendly-looking raven standing on the fringe of the circle. He hopped over to introduce himself. "Gro. My name is Colin C.C., from Raven's End."

The reply was spoken in a dialect that took Colin by surprise. "Gro, then, Colin, laddie. They ca' me Boogs C.C."

This raven rolled his *r*s and pronounced his words in way that Colin had never heard. He was immediately charmed. "You have a wonderful way of speaking, uh, Boogs."

"Och, aye, that's whit they a' say. Mysel', I never could tell whit the difference was."

"Are you from around here?"

"In a manner o' speakin', laddie. In a manner o' speakin'. And yersel'?"

The conversation was interrupted by ominous sounds. When Colin swung around to look, he was horrified to see Dolus squaring off with the big Banff raven. Both birds were in full threat display – bills open, feathers sleeked hard to their bodies – except for the eyebrow tufts, which were standing way out. Marg was pleading with Dolus to stop. "Please, Dolus, he didn't mean anything. You stepped on his foot first."

Dolus croaked in a low, nasty voice. "The jerk did it on purpose. Walked right in front of me. Thinks he's so tough." And at that Dolus pecked the other bird squarely on the nape of the neck – a sensitive spot.

"*Awk!*" The fight was on.

Dolus struck again, this time at the Banff raven's leg. He missed, and the other bird bit Dolus on the wing joint.

"Now we're even, you bad-tempered lout," said the Banff bird. "Peck me again and you'll really regret it."

Dolus was in a fury now. He opened his bill and shot his head forward to bite the other bird back. But just as Perry had warned, the Banff ravens were accomplished fighters. The big bird nimbly stepped aside and seized Dolus's bill with his own. He shut it hard, the sharp tips coming together like a pair of scissors. Suddenly Dolus was screeching, and blood was coming from the corners of his bill.

"*AWK! AWK!* I'm hurt! I'm hurt!" The other bird freed him, and he hopped around, flapping in pain.

Garth looked about in amazement. He had been urging Dolus on, assuming that Dolus would win. Now he clacked his bill and shouted. "Everybody get that bird! Look what he did to Dolus! Get him!" He started to hop over toward the big Banff raven.

"No way! No way! Get back, Garth!" Zack ran in front of Dolus's friend. "You keep out of this, or we're going to have a free-for-all here!"

He had noticed the other Banff birds edging closer, sleeking down, clacking their bills. Several were just as big as the one that had beaten Dolus, and the last thing Zack wanted was an all-out, flock-on-flock fight. He looked over to the Banff contingent and spoke quickly. "I'm terribly sorry about this. We're really quite friendly, and our meeting was going fine, until – until Dolus here had to spoil things. You've given him what he deserves, you really have."

"Aye, laddie, we understand," said the one called Boogs. "It's jist a wee bit unfortunate. Now ye and yer mates be off, an' no hard feelin's."

"Right. Away we go then, Raven's Enders. It's a long way back to Carrot Creek."

Dolus had moved off to be by himself. He didn't fly with the rest of the flock. Garth went over to him, but Dolus was in such a terrible state that he took a peck at Garth, saying "awk!" again when his injured bill closed. Garth flew off to join Zack and the others, not knowing what to do about his friend. Dolus soon took wing as well, for he noticed that the Banff ravens were starting to walk toward him.

"I'll get even," Dolus said to Garth after he caught up with the flock. "Those ravens had better watch out. I'm going to kill every one of them, starting with the big one."

Garth said not a word.

XIII

Colin was over the Trans-Canada Highway, trying to get the Banff incident out of his mind, when a welcome distraction caught his eye. He alerted the others. "Hey! The sheep are here!"

They were milling about on the road shoulder, the rams chasing the ewes, the ewes trotting away from this suitor or that, the head-butting contests ongoing. This was interesting in itself, and Colin decided to perch in a tall aspen where he could get a good view. Sarah settled beside him.

"Are you planning to stay long, Colin?" It was Marg, circling near.

"Oh, just for a while. I'll catch up."

"Sarah, are you staying with Colin?"

"Can I, Mum? So I can see what's going on here?"

"Okay. But only for a little while."

"I'll catch up."

Marg flew off after the rest of the flock, leaving Sarah and Colin with the sheep.

"I didn't know you were interested in things like sheep-watching, Sarah," Colin said.

"Oh, I'm interested in everything," she replied. "Hey, look! The sheep are licking the road!"

A couple of the big rams had taken a break from ewe-chasing. They might have been trying to knock each other's horns off a moment ago, but now they were standing side-by-side, apparently the best of friends, licking the surface of the highway.

Colin was mystified. "Now why in the world would they do that?"

Sarah cocked her head to the side. "Okay," she said, "let's describe what we know – that's what Greta says, 'Describe what you know' – and what we know is that the sheep are licking the road. Thus," she continued, borrowing a word that Greta used sometimes, "thus they must be hungry for something on the road."

Colin turned to Sarah and blinked. This was one logical bird! "Yes, go on," he encouraged.

"So, like, what could be on the road that the sheep want? They must want it a lot, 'cause they stopped fighting to go after it."

"What, indeed," Colin said, trying to sound studious without admitting that he hadn't the faintest idea.

Sarah kept on talking, thinking aloud. "Sheep eat grass, okay, but there isn't any, like, grass on the road" – here she giggled – "so it isn't grass. Hey! Maybe it's the road *itself!*"

"The sheep are eating the road?" Colin considered this idea. No, that couldn't be right. They were licking it, not attacking it with their teeth. He was quick to report this observation to Sarah. "They're not *biting* the road, Sarah – they're licking it, as if there was some water on it, or something."

"That's it!" Sarah croaked excitedly. "See? Each place they're licking, they've melted through the icy part! They're just licking little spots, and they melt away the ice! To get the water!"

"Yes, but . . ." Colin knew there was something wrong with this argument, but he couldn't quite figure out what it was.

Sarah did it for him. "Oh, wait. No, no. There's plenty of water in the creek. Right beside the road they've got all the water they want. I must be wrong."

By this time Sarah's idea had taken a turn in Colin's mind, and he knew she was on the right track. "Hang on, Sarah, you may be right. It's not ordinary water they want. It's *road* water. There must be something about the water that they melt from the ice on the road. Something like –"

At this point they were interrupted by a truck coming down the highway. It was a yellow truck, going slowly, and it had a light flashing on the top. Something was coming out of the back of the truck.

"It's going to hit the sheep!" Sarah cried. "Oh no, Colin! The sheep!"

But the truck simply moved over to the other side of the highway and went around the sheep. The sheep didn't flinch; they just kept licking the pavement.

"Gee, sheep are dumb," Colin said. "There's no way *I'd* stand there like that."

Sarah was watching the sheep intently, now. They had stopped licking and were walking over to the place where the truck had passed them. They started licking again. "Colin," Sarah began, "do you see the sheep going over to the other side, where that yellow thing went?"

"Hey! They did move over there!"

"That means they're after the stuff that came out of the yellow thing." Sarah ruffled out her neck-feathers and stretched her wings. She knew she had the right answer, and she was proud of it.

"Let's go see," Colin said.

The two birds jumped off the aspen branch, leaving it bouncing on the tree, and they coasted down to the road beside the sheep. The surface there was gritty, covered with sand and pea-sized pebbles.

Sarah was disappointed. "Aw, it's just little rocks. Sheep wouldn't eat this stuff, would they, Colin?"

"Umm – probably not, Sarah." Colin had never seen sheep eating anything but grass. But then he had another thought. "Hey! Maybe they need it for their gizzards!"

"Oh, Colin – sheep don't have gizzards. You ought to know – you've eaten them." She pulled her head in. "Oops! Sorry. I didn't mean to sound that way."

Colin was too lost in thought to be offended. He picked up a bit of gravel in his bill. "Well, a bird could use this," he said. "Just the right size for gizzard stones." He swallowed one and picked up another. Then a car came by, honking. The birds leapt into the air and lighted again on the shoulder. The sheep didn't move, even though the car came so close to them that their winter wool fluffed in the breeze.

"Those poor dumb sheep are going to get hit," Colin said. "Humans kill everything."

Sarah had begun to notice a strange taste in her mouth. These were no ordinary rocks, she thought; they tasted like, like –

"Colin, the rocks that came out of that thing are *salty*."

And in a flash, both birds knew they had what they'd been looking for, the true explanation. They both started babbling at once.

"Sheep love salt," Colin began.

"And the humans have these salty rocks," Sarah continued.

"And they dump them on the road."

"And the sheep know that."

"And the sheep lick the salty rocks!"

"We got it! Colin, we got it!"

Sarah croaked. She let out her throat-feathers again and raised her head high. Colin did the same. Then he had another thought. "Of course, they were licking the road *before* the salty-rocks thing came along."

"Oh. Maybe licking the road makes the salty-rocks thing come by," Sarah offered.

"Sure. Why not? That makes sense."

Both the birds croaked happily and stretched some more.

"It's really, really nice of the humans to give the sheep those salty rocks," Sarah said.

"Well, Greta was saying about how this was a Park, and the humans didn't kill things here, so maybe that's why they're kind to the other animals."

"The humans we saw around the hot springs were nice. Leaving all that food and everything. They didn't seem to want to hurt us," Sarah recalled.

"Well, except for that cat."

"Okay, but there weren't any humans in that car. It was, like, a *cat* car. Cats aren't humans, so maybe they don't have, you know, the same rule about not killing things in the Park."

Colin was by now very impressed with Sarah's reasoning power. He was about to tell her so, when a very large truck came into view around a bend in the road. It was going fast, and the birds barely had time to flop off the pavement as it approached. They could hear the big airhorn howling.

Then, BLONK! The truck hit the flock of sheep. As before, the sheep had stood right in the way. Now they were rolling along the road. As they came to rest, blood began to pour onto the pavement. The truck slowed down and stopped. A human got out. It walked around to the front of the truck and looked at the bumper. It peered back down the highway at the mutilated animals lying there. Then it climbed back into the truck and drove away.

"By the Trees," Colin said. His bill has hanging open.

"That was the scariest thing I've ever seen in my whole life," Sarah said. Her wings were fluttering like those of a fledgling. "Colin, let's get out of here."

"Okay," Colin agreed. He couldn't decide which was more shocking: the way the truck had killed the sheep, or the fact that it hadn't come back to eat some of its prey. Eating? He turned to Sarah. "Of course, we could eat some sheep meat before we leave . . ." He looked back nervously at the remains of the rams.

"No," Sarah replied firmly. "I'm not hungry. I just want to go home."

"Back to Yamnuska?"

"Yes. It's not safe here."

"We can't go back to Yamnuska, Sarah. It's too far."

"Then back to the big spruce, Colin. Come on, let's go. It's getting dark." She looked around, her wings still fluttering.

Colin hadn't noticed that the sun was down, and that it had been down long enough for the purple curtain of evening to appear in the east. "Okay, let's go. There's still time to reach the roost. We can come back tomorrow for some sheep meat. It'll be better by then anyway."

"Hurry, Colin. My mother is going to be worried about me." The birds flew quickly up Carrot Creek, leaving the carnage on the highway behind them.

Not long after Sarah and Colin had gone, a brown pickup truck stopped at the scene. It had two flashing red lights on top that went round and round brightly in the early evening. A human in a green uniform got out. It put on its wide-brimmed hat and walked over to one of the dead rams lying on the pavement. The ram's tongue hung out of its head into the slippery red stain surrounding it, as if it were licking its own blood.

The human picked up a pebble lying on the road, said something loud and threw the pebble down hard. Then the human sighed and dragged the first sheep off the highway. Methodically, as cars stopped and other humans got out to watch, it dealt with the others.

XIV

"All good things end in horror." Greta was speaking at the Flap the next morning. Colin and Sarah had recounted the story of the sheep and the truck, after Zack had described the fight in the hot-springs parking lot. Dolus wasn't at the Flap. Garth said he wanted to be by himself.

"All good things end in horror," Greta said again. "I'm glad I didn't go."

The other ravens looked morose. Truly, Colin thought, life was like that; terrific one moment, awful the next. For every good time there would be a bad one.

"But it was fun, don't you think?" Marg was trying to cheer the flock up. "The trip, I mean. All told, I really enjoyed that trip."

Brendan joined in Marg's enthusiasm. "Oh, for sure. I'd go back, like, any day. Banff is really a cool place."

"Yeah! Me too," said Cathy, the shy young raven. It was unusual for Cathy to speak up at the Flap. All the ravens turned to look at her. "Yeah. Uh – really. Um . . . really cool," she said.

Marg hopped over to Cathy. "Cathy, my dear, do you have something you want to tell us?"

Cathy stooped and pulled her head in, trying to look small. "No. Not really. Well, not really much, I guess."

"C'mon," said Marg. "Sure you do. I'll bet you've got something really neat to say. I'd like to hear it – wouldn't you, Molly?"

"Yes, Cathy. Of course," Molly replied in a motherly voice. "There's no need to be shy. It's just your flockmates here."

Other ravens urged Cathy to speak, saying "Yes, yes!" and "Tell us, tell us!" They picked their feet up and put them down expectantly. If

Cathy was going to speak, which she hardly ever did, then she must have something very important to say.

Cathy looked around nervously, opening and closing her bill. She edged closer to Marg. Then she spoke in a small voice. "I'd like to say – tell all of you – just – oh, I'm having such a great time here. Here at Carrot Creek, I mean."

The other ravens stood silently. From the way she said it, Cathy wasn't finished.

"And, well, I brought something back from Banff, sort of." She looked at the other ravens in an embarrassed way, then hopped over to a juniper bush nearby, reached into the centre and retrieved a shiny object. Bobbing from the end of her bill, it sparkled in the sun. "This is what I got in Banff."

Cathy had carried this all the way from Banff? Tucked into her bill, where no one could see it? The other ravens were impressed. They stepped over to look.

The thing was round, and about the size of a sparrow's egg. It hung from a chain of little silvery pieces. The other birds had never seen anything like this. They inspected it closely, their brown eyes going momentarily white as they blinked at it. Wheedle pecked it gently with his bill. "It's not edible, anyway," he pronounced.

"I like it 'cause it makes a noise," Cathy said. "You have to be really quiet to hear it."

All the birds stopped talking. And indeed, they could hear a noise: *tick, tick, tick, tick.*

"Hey! Excellent!" Brendan said.

"I seen one a' them somewheres," Scratch recalled, looking away and narrowing his eyes as he tried to remember. "Hmm . . . coulda been up around Dawson Crick, mebbe. Real purty doodad, eh?"

Greta hadn't paid much attention to these goings-on, but now she hopped up to Cathy. "Where did you find this?" she asked, looking worried.

Cathy began to back away from Greta, stuttering. "It, it – it was, just, just lying there, okay? I – I – I mean in that big flat place where the cars were? You know, by the hot springs?"

"It's all right, kiddo," Greta said, having had a good look. "I've seen these before. Some humans carry one on their bodies. Every once in a while they hold it up and look at it. I think it's harmless. But still, I must remind you that this ticking thing is something human. And I've warned you all about messing with things human."

The other ravens became suddenly quiet. They looked at one another. Then they looked at Cathy. From the time they were nestlings, they had been told of the danger implicit in anything human. The fear had become automatic. Cathy crouched, feeling shame. Brendan felt embarrassed for her. Was Greta going to make a lesson of her? Poor Cathy. Brendan was glad he wasn't Cathy right now. Everyone was staring at Cathy.

Greta put Cathy at ease. "Now, don't think I'm mad at you, Cathy. I'm not. Not at all." Instead of scolding Cathy, she looked over to Brendan. "Brendan?"

Uh-oh, Brendan thought. She's got that look –

"Brendan, does this remind you of something that once happened to you?"

"Me? No way, Greta. I never saw a ticking thing before."

"But what about the *can*, Brendan. Don't you remember the can?"

"Oh. That. The can. Yeah, I remember about the can." The other birds were all looking at *him*, now. Brendan dropped his gaze to the snow under his feet. "I, uh, got my head, uh, stuck in a can." His eyes widened with the memory. "I was really young, okay, so I didn't know any better. My dad got me out. It was really, *really* scary."

"Tell us exactly what happened, Brendan," Greta insisted.

"Well, I stuck my head in, 'cause it smelled really good in there, but I couldn't get it out, okay? 'Cause of the lid." He shook himself. "It was *super* scary."

"Exactly." Greta had made her point. "Humans leave all kinds of traps around. Sometimes on purpose, sometimes not. The best thing is to leave everything human alone. Even food. But there's not a hope in hellebore that any of you will listen to me about that."

The ravens shifted guiltily. Greta was right. Every member of the flock adored human food.

To get over the awkward moment, the Main Raven summed things up. "This morning's Flap has turned into a lesson on safety, thanks to Greta. And thanks, of course, to Cathy, who brought up the matter indirectly by showing us her new, uh, ticking thing." He hesitated a moment. "Is it all right if she keeps it, Greta?"

"Why not? As long as she doesn't choke on it. I wouldn't carry it around in my bill, if I were her."

"Well, Cathy?"

"Sure, okay. I'll just kind of stash it somewhere." She lowered the ticking thing to the ground and put her foot on it protectively.

"Well, then," the Main Raven said in a businesslike way, "if there is no other business, we can end the Flap. May we have a Motion?"

Quickly the ravens formed a circle. They spread their wings, overlapping them to generate their beloved wheel. "Rawk-a-taw!" they called. The sound carried down Carrot Creek Canyon, where a bighorn ram, at that moment following closely behind a female, heard it and looked up.

As the circle broke up, Greta walked a few steps away and glanced back at Cathy. Brendan, Sarah, and Garth were standing with her, admiring the ticking thing on its chain, talking excitedly about how wonderful Banff was. Greta opened her bill a tiny bit – the raven equivalent of a sly smile. She spoke quietly to herself. "Ah, kids," she said. "They just can't leave Banff without a souvenir."

XV

And so the days at Carrot Creek went by. Each morning the Raven's Enders scattered through the snowy woods and meadows hunting for food. Each evening the ravens returned through the pinkish-gray December sundown to gather above the canyon and to report, as they soared and played in the day's last light, on their adventures in new surroundings.

A week passed, then another. There were fewer and fewer hours of daylight. Night became an adventure in itself, although not a pleasant one. The darkness lasted longer and the cold ran deeper, reaching through the birds' feathers to leave trails of shivers. One or another flock member would wake long before dawn, glance into the freezing blackness beyond the boughs of the big spruce and fluff its feathers out. Then it would push its head even farther back under its wing, hoping to stay asleep until the morning sun drove the cold away.

One day the birds awoke to find that something was different. It was the way the air smelled. Molly noticed it first. "Zack – it's going to snow," she said.

Zack opened his eyes. He had been dreaming of rain in green forests. He looked out from his perch, snug near the trunk of the spruce, and considered the landscape. A sameness lay over it, a monotone of dark-gray trees, medium-gray clouds, and light-gray snow. There were no shadows, because the sun had no hole in the clouds from which to pour out the daylight. "You're right, Molly," he said with a sigh, "and it's going to snow a lot."

Indeed, the sky was simply one enormous cloud made of uncountable billions of snowflakes. The base was indistinct, a fuzz of snow trying to reach the ground.

As Molly looked across the valley to Mount Rundle, she noted that the mountain was disappearing. The dark, tree-covered lower flanks were hazy, the upper slope was fading away, and the ridgeline was exactly the same color as the sky. Where did the mountain end and the sky begin? Molly looked hard. She had seen that ridge crest sharply defined in sunset after sunset over the last few days, but now she had to admit that she couldn't say for sure where it was. How odd, she thought. Something as solid as a mountain can vanish into something as soft as a cloud.

"These clouds are absolutely packed with snow, Molly," Zack was saying. "What do you think? Biggest dump of the winter?"

"Yes, it certainly could be." Molly was shivering.

"Aw, well. Heavy snow is a lot of fun. You can't see very far, and everything looks weird. I love flying around in that."

"And you can get *lost* that way, you dumb cluck," Molly said sharply. "Remember last winter, when you didn't show up for a day and a half?

You had me worried sick, Zack C.C., out there in that" – she spread her wings and fluttered the tips to make her point – "*wonderful* snow!"

"There, there, Molly. You're right. A bird has to be careful in a snowstorm."

And a snowstorm it was. Mount Rundle eased out of sight entirely as the storm front drifted across the Bow Valley. The first flurry arrived, whitening the big spruce in moments. Then the flakes poured down as heavily as a hard rain.

"This is great! Whoopee!" Brendan hopped out to the end of the branch and turned his head up. Snowflakes bounced down his breast feathers. He opened his bill, eating from the sky. "Hey, Sarah! Try this!"

Sarah didn't reply to Brendan. "Mum, how are we going to get to the kill?" The wolves' latest acquisition lay some distance away in the forest, hidden by the falling snow. "Shall we all fly together?"

Marg smiled at her daughter. "Exactly right, Sarah, dear. You get more with-it by the day. You really do."

They were first on the carcass that morning. The wolves had already come and gone, leaving their tracks in the snow. Each paw-print was as big as an elk's hoof-print, and it was rapidly filling with new flakes. Sarah and Brendan picked and pulled at any redness remaining on the bones. There wasn't much.

"We're – *oof* – going to have to – *umph* – find another kill soon," Brendan said, tugging hard at a tendon. "This moose thing is about used up."

"And anyway," Sarah added, "what'll happen when it's buried under all this snow? How are we going to find it?"

Scratch arrived and answered her question. "Oh, the wolves'll do the findin', sweetie. You guys don't have ta worry none. We stick with the wolves, we're okay. Gotta follow 'em, like. Make sure they don't take off somewheres we can't find 'em."

Most of the flock had now arrived, including Wheedle.

"Oh, Sarah, you look so cute working on that charming little piece under the shoulder blade. My – it *is* a difficult one. Want some help? I've an idea how to get it loose for you." He hopped over. "Here. Just stand aside and I'll –"

"Oh no you don't, Wheedle! You just want it for yourself!"

"Hee hee," chuckled Scratch. "Wheedle, yer dealin' with one smart hunk a' female birdflesh, there. Whaddya take 'er for? Somebody as dumb as me?"

And so it went, the banter of birds eating their first meal of the day. Afterward they returned to the roosting tree, unwilling to fly far in the storm. Some dozed the day away. Others carried on long conversations with friends. A few, including Scratch and Wheedle, kept busy at the kill through the afternoon, eating more and more. A deep, unremitting hunger kept them at it.

Scratch stopped for a moment to pick a mite from his wing. He ate it. "Always seems kinda *extra* hungry, eh? In a storm, eh?"

Wheedle, too, took a break. "Scratch, my entomological friend, you're never lacking an excuse to overdo a meal, are you?"

"Can't deny it." He scratched his breast with a greasy foot. "But I ain't been as ferocious hungry as this in a heckuva while."

Other Raven's Enders fluttered back onto the carcass. By this time the kill was a small island of red in a sea of fresh snow. Black shapes walked around on the island, tugging at this, pecking at that, landing and taking off.

"This is more snow than I've ever seen," said Garth.

"Yeah, well, so what," said Dolus, shouldering him out of the way to get at the joint Garth was working on. "A little snow never hurt nobody."

Colin, too, was impressed by the amount that had fallen. He picked up his feet very high, but the snow was so light, as well as so deep, that he floundered. The only way to get anywhere was to fly. "And thank the Trees birds can fly," he said out loud to no one in particular, "because we're built too close to the ground to *walk* through this stuff."

From out of nowhere, or perhaps from out of everywhere, a voice replied. "Not a bad solution, considering the obvious design flaw," it said.

"*Awk!*" Colin cried. The other birds wheeled around to see what was the matter. Several had already leapt into the air in fright. "What's happening?!" Marg called.

"Did you hear that?!" Colin shouted back.

"Hear what?" Marg replied. "I didn't hear anything. What's the matter, Colin? Is something coming?"

"No, no. That voice again. Like in the canyon." Colin closed his bill, remembering what Greta had said about keeping such things to himself.

Dolus was quick to interject. "So, Mister Colin-of-the-Canyon," he said, "are you remembering the lesson I taught you that day? Need another one? Need one about getting everybody worked up for nothing?"

"Uh, sorry, C.C.s." Colin crouched, fluttering his wings submissively. "I thought I heard – I might have heard the wolves coming back. Or something." He edged away from the flock, out of earshot.

The voice spoke again. "They can't hear me, you know. Only you can. Sorry to embarrass you there. But you handled it pretty well."

This time Colin made of point of not reacting.

"Oh, and Greta," the voice continued. "Greta can hear me, too. Forgot to mention that."

"Greta's not here," Colin said in a low voice, noticing her absence.

"Napping somewhere, probably. When you get to be her age you need your naps. I'll just check. Back in a moment."

And the voice was gone. More than the voice, Colin realized, the *presence* of the voice was gone. It had a feeling that went with it. He could tell when it was there and when it wasn't, even though he couldn't see whoever it was who was speaking.

The presence of the voice returned, then the voice itself. "She's asleep down the canyon," it said. "Took a daytime roost by herself for some reason. Funny old bird. Just waking up. Should be along shortly. Never gets lost in a snowstorm, that one."

"Greta told me a little about this," Colin said.

"About what?"

"About you, whoever you are."

"Oh? What did she say?"

"Just that she knew who you were."

"That's all?"

"That, and she told me – just like you did – that I was 'doing fine.'"

"Good for her. That's exactly the proper thing to say."

Colin was still perplexed. "Look – I really need to know what's going on here. Who *are* you? And how come you talk to me like this?"

"Okay, okay. I'll tell you."

The voice paused, much in the way Greta did. While he was waiting, Colin realized that, deep and resonant as the voice was, there was something *female* about it.

"I'm somebody you can't meet just yet. But you will. If you do things right. I like you, Colin. You're doing fine. Oh, sorry – I've told you that before. But really, I mean it. Just be careful, because you're cocky. Think ahead, okay? Especially over the next couple of days. These storms, you just can't trust them. They're not as openly angry as cold fronts, like that one that got you on Yamnuska –"

"Hey! You know about that, too!" Colin shouted so loudly that the other birds turned to look at him.

Molly hopped over. "Colin, what's the matter? You're still confused?"

"I guess so," Colin said. "And so would you be, if you'd heard what I just heard!"

Molly flinched. She look around, crouched, ready to jump.

"Calm down, Colin," came the voice. "I'm going, okay? Toodle-oo."

Colin realized that he was upsetting everyone all over again. "It's okay, Molly. It's going."

"Who's going?"

"Oh, there's this bird that keeps bugging me."

"What bird?"

"What's the matter with Colin?" Other ravens were coming over.

"Hah! The jerk's gone crazy," said Dolus.

"He's worried by the storm, that's all," said Molly. "I'll bet he can't remember what it's like to be in a snowstorm."

"Leave me alone, okay?" Colin was getting angry, as well as severely embarrassed. At that point Greta arrived.

"What's going on?"

"It's Colin," Sarah said. "He keeps saying weird things." Sarah liked Colin, especially after the evening watching the sheep, but she was beginning to wonder about him. As was everyone else.

"Oh." Greta looked at Colin closely. "Wouldn't be similar to what happened in the canyon the other day, would it?"

"Exactly. Exactly!" Colin was thoroughly exasperated now. "And I don't like it one bit!"

Greta turned to the other birds. "You're right. He's upset, and probably on account of the weather. Nothing to worry about. He'll be fine tomorrow. Just leave him to me." Then she turned to Colin. "Come with me, you mixed-up C.C. We'll talk this over."

Greta flew back to the sheltering spruce and moved far in, right to the trunk. Colin followed. When they were both comfortably perched, Greta re-opened the conversation. "Same voice, right?"

"Yes. It's really annoying, Greta. It just breaks in, from out of nowhere, any old time, busting into my life, messing things up."

Greta nodded her old head and looked at Colin. Her eyes shone in the dimness. "Oh, Colin, Colin. It's hard having this gift of yours, I know. When I was younger . . ." She stopped for a moment, thinking back. "When I was younger, it was the same thing. And way back then, an old bird in the flock told me what I'm going to tell you now." She stopped again – one of her famous pauses.

"Tell me what? Greta, please! I can't stand this!"

Greta answered. "Good things happen to the raven who waits. Be patient. You want to avoid embarrassing situations? Then don't talk back to the voice whenever it's embarrassing to do so. It will know that you're busy and leave you alone."

"That's good to know, Greta, but –"

Snow fell from the branches above as the rest of the flock arrived at the spruce. The bland grayness of the snowstorm had given no indication of the time of day, but the birds could tell by the failing light that evening had arrived. They were ready to roost. The spruce, now deeply covered in snow, offered protected pockets under the boughs. Soon everyone was settled.

"Greta –" Colin began.

"Hush, now," she said softly. "No more on this tonight. Just remember, when you're feeling strange, that everything will eventually make sense. And consider yourself lucky, Colin. Very few ravens have the gift that you do." She touched his bill with hers. "Yes, lucky indeed. Sleep well, kiddo."

Remarkably, he did.

XVI

All night the snow fell heavily at Carrot Creek. It snowed hard at Banff, at Yamnuska, and throughout the Canadian Rockies. Just as Molly had predicted, this was the biggest storm of the winter.

It had got its start over the Pacific Ocean, on the other side of the mountains. A big, greedy low-pressure cell, it had sucked up as much moisture from the sea as it could. Then it had staggered inland. Unable to lift its heavy clouds over the peaks of British Columbia, the storm had to barter its way through, trading snow and wind for the right to move eastward across the ranges. Along the way the storm had lost much of its power, but there was still enough moisture left for a goodly snowfall over the Rockies.

The small furry creatures needed that snow. The temperature could drop to forty degrees below zero, but at the base of the snowpack the temperature remained steady just a few degrees below the freezing point. A myriad of mice, voles, and lemmings tunnelled their way from one tasty patch of dried grass to the next, using what they didn't eat for making cozy nests. They could survive the winter that way, and the thicker the snow-layer overhead, the better.

When the snow stopped falling at Carrot Creek three days after it started, survival was much on the minds of the ravens wintering there. Even though they were protected in their big spruce throughout the storm, the Raven's Enders knew that death by starvation – death by cold, really, because a hungry bird couldn't keep warm enough to survive – was always a strong possibility in winter. A raven had to eat every day, and eat well, or the cold would overwhelm it.

It was the deaths of other living things that kept the Raven's Enders supplied with rich, sustaining meat. But now little remained of the current carcass, and this was worrisome.

"We haven't been keeping track of the wolves," Molly said to Zack on the morning the snowstorm ended. "They'll be gone. And we'll go hungry."

"Don't worry, we'll find 'em. I'll bet Colin spots the whole pack right away. Look – he's gone already." Zack peered into the pale pre-dawn light, noting Colin's empty roosting spot on a nearby branch.

It was Colin's habit to leave the roost early and go scouting. The rest of the flock had come to expect this. By the time it was broad daylight and the other birds were assembling for the Flap, he was always back, and often he brought news of where to find breakfast. Today he had left even earlier than usual, wondering, just as Molly had, about the wolves. He had found them farther down the valley, at the wide spot in the canyon where the sheep had been rutting. And overnight they had brought down a ram.

"Good jobs, you guys!" Colin had called down to the wolves as they fed on their new kill. Fighting over the dead ram, the wolves were too busy baring their teeth and snarling at each other to reply. Not that they ever spoke to him anyway. Colin had yet to strike up a conversation with one of these haughty creatures that treated the ravens like so many flies on their meat.

"I've got to pursue this," Colin said to himself. "A wolf ought to know a lot of really interesting things about –"

Suddenly he felt a surge of fear. He looked around, spreading his wings to leap.

"*Awk!*" he cried, as the fear came again. It came like a white wave – yes, he was actually *seeing* a white wave, seeing it in the same way that he heard voices and spoke with the wind – and then the feeling swept from his second-sight to his heart, which began to beat faster, and it swept to his brain, which told him to fly. Oh, fly like you have never flown before, it shouted. Fly back to the flock! Now! *Now!*

The other birds were just stirring when Colin arrived. "Fly! Quick!" Colin screamed as he swooped past the spruce. "It's white! It's coming! It's death! Fly! *Fly!*"

And fly they did, all at the same time, as if the tree had shaken them out.

Then the tree actually *did* begin to shake. It whipped forward and back once, then splintered into pieces as the biggest avalanche in a hundred years roared down the side of Princess Margaret Mountain and smashed everything in its path.

Far up on the mountain, on a cliff overlooking a particularly steep gully, a stone had fallen. It was a chunk about the size of a raven. When it plopped into the gully it sent a small force out into the surrounding snow. There was enormous power in that snow. Each flake was a crystal of latent energy, one among billions, piling up day after day, covering the slopes, filling the gullies, getting heavy, getting ready . . . As the stone hit, the interlocking flakes – just barely touching each other, all prickly and uncomfortable – started to slide.

The avalanche was small at first, quietly carrying the stone slowly down a single gully. But the slide began to move faster, as more and more snowflakes fell into step, until the gully was wall-to-wall with churning whiteness, snaking through the narrow places and flinging itself into the air as it bounced around the corners.

The slide overflowed the gully. Cracks ripped across the slopes on either side as the snowpack collapsed there, too. A gigantic slab boomed as it broke loose, a mountainside of snow moving faster, faster. The front reared up, pushing the air forward, generating a wind so strong that when the blast hit the trees they snapped off. The snow carried the shattered wood and limbs and branches and needles farther, down and down with a noise like thunder.

Colin saw the avalanche a moment before it hit. His wings gulped huge bites of air as he climbed for his life out of the way. Looking down, he saw the other ravens doing the same, thrashing skyward at top speed, their groggy minds telling them that *up*, as always, was the way to safety.

Then the wind blast struck the birds, throwing them out of control in choking white powder. Behind came the main mass of the avalanche. It was piling up in the valley, now, burying whatever it caught, suffocating it, tearing and crushing.

The last of the slide reached the flats and stopped. A sprinkling of conifer needles settled over the huge heap. There, sitting on the surface, was the stone that had started it all.

The stone had come to rest directly over Carrot Creek. In the spring it would melt out of the avalanche debris and drop into the stream, where it would be tugged, tumbled and rolled for centuries toward the Bow River, then on to the Saskatchewan River, the Nelson River and eventually the salt waters of Hudson Bay. "Gee," the rock said to another stone, lying beside it in the snow, "the system works!"

XVII

Rosy in the dawn light, Princess Margaret Mountain looked incapable of producing the mess that lay at its base. Broken tree trunks and torn evergreen boughs stuck up through the deadly mass of white. Over the slide the Yamnuska ravens flew back and forth, croaking piteously.

The Main Raven gathered his wits. "Attention, everyone," he said loudly. "Attention, please. Let us land over there on that outcrop and discuss the situation."

Most of the birds didn't hear him. Their eyes still wide with fright, they kept circling aimlessly.

"C.C.s! May I have your attention!" the big raven called again, this time louder and more confidently. "Let us gather out of harm's way for the Flap."

The word "Flap" got through. The flock seized upon the idea – something familiar – and followed the Main Raven, who was now flying with purposeful strokes to a rocky pinnacle nearby. Sarah, though, still numb from her second trial by snow, seemed not to hear. Marg flew back for her. "Sarah, dear, it's all right. The snowslide is over. Come with me." And she did.

As the birds alighted on the rock they looked at one another, counting heads. Who was there? More to the point, who *wasn't* there?

The Main Raven opened the meeting. Speaking from the centre of the gathering, he said, "C.C.s, a most grievous episode has come and gone. The, 'snowslide,' as Marg calls it, seems to have started from up there" – he pointed with his bill toward the summit – "and finished, as you can see, down there." He pointed to the slide heap below the birds. "Are there any questions?"

Everyone started talking at once.

"Oh, by the Trees, that was the scariest thing I ever saw in my life!"

"Did you feel that *wind?*"

"I'll never forget that as long as I live."

"Well, we almost didn't live long enough to forget anything!"

"Who yelled the warning?"

At this, the birds stopped talking. Indeed, who *had* cried out as the slide approached?

"Oh, it was me," said Colin.

"You?" Dolus called. "Crazy Colin, who talks to birds that aren't there?"

"I don't care who he talks to, he just saved our lives," Zack replied.

"Yessir," Scratch said. "Whoever they was, you was sure talkin' ta the right guys that time," he stated. "And I thank ya kindly fer givin' old Scratch another chance at stayin' alive, so's he can get killed more normal-like later on." He picked at himself, tenderly removing a tiny red mite from under his wing. "Even my bugs is pleased with you, Colin C.C."

Molly was looking at Colin in a curious way. She cocked her head to the side and asked him to explain how he knew the slide was coming. "You must have had some sort of warning," she said. "Did it make a noise?"

"Well, actually I was a fair distance down the canyon. I just had a feeling that something was wrong, a really strong feeling. Almost as if I could see the slide before it happened, you know? So I flew back as quickly as I could. I wouldn't have bothered all of you if it hadn't been a really strong feeling." Colin was looking around anxiously.

Molly blinked and looked at Zack. Zack looked at Molly and nodded, then he addressed the other birds. "I tell you, friends, this C.C. has a very special talent. I think we should be grateful for it."

Several birds voiced agreement. The Main Raven had been convinced, too. "I think it incumbent upon us to recognize the contribution of this, uh, unusual, member of the flock," he said.

"Oh. I almost forgot," Colin said quickly. "There's a new wolf kill down the canyon. Bighorn ram. Really nice one."

"Hurrah for Colin!" Marg shouted.

"Yeah! Let's hear it for Colin!" Brendan croaked in his deepest, most authoritative voice. It cracked halfway through. Sarah smiled at him.

Zack stepped forward and thrust out his neck-feathers. Raising his bill high, he addressed every bird in the group. "I move we accept Colin C.C. as a full member of the Raven's End Flock," he said. "He's not your typical raven, and I, for one, am glad of it. We needed this bird today, and we'll need him again. By the Trees, C.C.s, I'm *sure* of it."

"Hear hear!" Wheedle called. "I'll second that!"

"All in favor?" said the Main Raven, pivoting in the centre of the circle to see how each bird felt about Zack's idea.

"Me!"

"Me too!"

"Yeah, right on!"

"Oh, for sure, for sure."

"By all means. And it's about time, too."

On it went, each bird voicing his or her approval of Colin's membership in the flock, until only two birds had not spoken.

Dolus and Garth stood by themselves and wouldn't look at the Main Raven. He walked over to them. "I take it you disagree," he said.

Dolus picked in the snow with his foot. He looked over to Garth, who was looking back at him. "I say we throw him out," Dolus said with a guttural croak. "He's not like us. I don't trust him."

Dolus poked Garth with his bill, and Garth started speaking. "Yeah, and he does weird stuff all the time. I think he's crazy. We don't need any crazy birds in this flock."

The Main Raven knew how to deal with dissent, and he dealt with it now. "Well, Dolus, you have the right to your point of view. A raven can say anything he wishes, as you know. That's one of the Three Freedoms. And we won't think ill of you for it. A strong flock is a tolerant flock, and much as I wish our acceptance of Colin were unanimous, we can certainly live with your point of view. And yours, too, Garth."

"So," he continued, turning now to the other birds, "let us welcome Colin C.C. to the Raven's End Flock. All together, then. A Motion. A Motion in honor of our newest member, Colin Corvus Corax."

Wingtip-to-wingtip, the birds formed their circle. But this time there was a difference. Colin was pushed into the centre, and the birds gathered so closely that he had to duck under their overlapping wings. The feathery canopy covered him like a shield, symbolic of the protection afforded by the flock.

All the birds filled their lungs and let forth a heartfelt "Rawk-a-taw!"

Touched, Colin wasn't sure how to respond. "Thank you," he said humbly. It was the right thing to say.

XVIII

"Where's Cathy?!" Marg suddenly asked. "Cathy! What's happened to Cathy?"

Molly looked wildly about. "And Greta – where's Greta? Oh, no! Greta!" Involuntarily she let out a short "awk!" of panic.

"Now, now," the Main Raven said. "Let's not be too hasty, here. Let's be rational. Now. Let's start with Greta. She often roosts alone. Has anyone seen her?"

"She wasn't in the spruce last night," Zack recalled. "At least I didn't see her."

"Me neither," said Brendan.

"She wasn't perched by me," said Wheedle, "and I was way up by the top."

As if to answer the question, Greta herself came flapping into the circle.

"Greta!" Molly was overjoyed. "Oh, Greta, we're so happy to see you!"

Greta perched on the rock and caught her breath. When she spoke, it was clear that she was just as shocked as everyone else. "What a scene. Hornets and yellowjackets, what a scene."

"We're all enormously grateful that you're safe," said the Main Raven. "But where were you when the avalanche hit?"

"Down the canyon, where I've had to go most nights because these young 'uns keep gabbling away after dark like a bunch of brainless vireos." Greta seldom spoke ill of anyone, and a statement like this showed just how upset she was. "Sorry I wasn't here when you needed me," she said. "Dumb. Dumb."

"Greta – was Cathy roosting with you?" Marg asked, a tremor in her voice.

"Cathy? No. Cathy wasn't with me." Greta looked down. "You needn't look for her, I'm afraid."

The circle was silent for a moment, then Marg opened her bill. The saddest sound in the mountains, the sound of a raven crying, began to come out. "Craaaawww . . ."

The rest of the Raven's Enders looked over to the slide heap, deep and cold, a tomb for anything in it, and they, too, began to mourn.

Even Greta, old Greta, witness to more suffering and death than any other member of the flock, was moved to join them.

"Craaaaaaaaaaaaaawwwwwww . . . craaaaaaaaaaaaaaaaawwwwwww . . . craaaaaaaaaaaaaaaaaaawwwwwww . . ."

She knows, Colin thought. She knows about Cathy. She knows Cathy is lying under the snow, just as I knew about Sarah under the snow. But Sarah was alive. And Cathy, poor Cathy, is dead. His sigh became a sob of despair.

Marg looked up to the path of the avalanche on Princess Margaret Mountain. The track was dirty brown against the rest of the slope, for the snow had been peeled away right down to the scree and rock beneath it. To Marg it looked as if something huge and vicious had clawed the mountainside, dragging everything to the pile at the bottom. Marg flew off to be by herself. She flew with her eyes barely open, seeing little but the image of her young friend, feeling nothing but her pain.

She was drawn to a gnarled whitebark pine. As she approached it, something shiny caught her attention. It hung on a dead twig. Marg looked at it, and as she realized what it was she threw her head back in a new outburst of grief. It was Cathy's ticking thing.

XIX

Later that morning the birds flew down the canyon to the new wolf kill. Normally this would have been a joyous flight, full of excited chatter, but today the birds flew sadly to their breakfast. Still, with some bighorn sheep in their crops, the weight of the day's events began to lift.

After all, these were ravens. Like other birds, they lived a bird's life, and the reality was that a bird's life was usually short. Despite Greta's best efforts at educating the flock and tending to its injured members, a couple of Raven's Enders perished every year. Especially the young ones. Only two or three out of five or six survived for long after they left the nest. Cathy, for instance, was the only one in her brood to reach adulthood. Cathy's parents had died during the lightning strike that had killed all her nestmates. Now the family was gone entirely.

Ravens think deeply about things, and they feel deeply about things, but they have learned not to think or feel *too* deeply – or too long. Creatures of the wilderness live in a world stained often by the blood of their relatives and friends. Dwelling on it doesn't help. In fact, dwelling on it is dangerous, for a bird preoccupied is a bird likely to become another creature's meal.

After a while, Marg left Cathy's ticking thing hanging in its tree. She sighed a long sigh and flew back to the rest of the flock.

Marg noticed two things along the way. One was the sky. This morning there were no clouds. The weather was perfectly clear, with no wind. The other thing Marg noticed was the air temperature, which was low. She knew, as all the older ravens knew, that after a winter storm comes the cold.

XX

The day wore on, but rather than warming, as it normally would, it grew colder. By afternoon one bird after another was remarking about the drop in temperature. Most had flown up the south-facing valley wall, out of the shadowed depths and onto the sunny slopes higher up, where the sun could reach them over the top of the opposite ridge. But the sun had little heat to offer.

"Going to be cold tonight, M.R." Zack was speaking to the Main Raven. They were perched in a dead pine. The sun was going down.

"Indeed," the Main Raven replied. He looked thoughtful. There was something he was supposed to be doing. Something he was supposed to remember. The Main Raven looked down to where the big spruce had stood a few hours ago. Now the spot was altered beyond recognition. What a day it had been! And now night was falling.

Zack was looking in the same direction. Suddenly he exclaimed, "Oh! By the Trees – we've got no roost tonight! The spruce is gone, and we've got no roost!"

Ah, that was it, thought the Main Raven. *That's* what he was supposed to be doing: looking for a new roost. Zack had reminded him of his duty before it was too late. "Indeed. I, ah, was just thinking that it was about time to locate something suitable. I must be off."

"Want some company?"

"By all means."

The two birds cruised down the valley, heads swivelling this way and that, sizing up the lodgepole pines and the Engelmann spruces and the subalpine firs.

Colin arrived from the other direction. He turned around to join them. "Any good roosting trees down that way?" inquired the Main Raven.

Colin thought for a moment. "Umm . . . well . . . oh, yes! About halfway down the canyon, right on the edge. Really big Douglas-fir. Want to see it?"

"Douglas-firs are usually too thinly foliated to make good winter roosts," the Main Raven said doubtfully.

"This one's different," Colin replied. "Broken off at the top, but really bushy below."

They flew on, Colin in the lead. "There, just ahead on the right. What do you think?"

"Worth a look," Zack said, swooping by. Satisfied that nothing dangerous lurked in the tree, all three birds landed on the dead branches jutting from the top. Sure enough, the foliage below was very thick, with lots of limbs. The whole tree was dense with evergreen needles and well covered in snow.

"Good tree, Colin. Capital tree." The Main Raven was pleased. "Couldn't have found a better one myself. Not that I, uh, wouldn't have found this one in a few minutes anyway." He stretched his neck-feathers and produced an eloquent croak, claiming the tree for the Yamnuska Flock. It looked like an easy claim to hold; there were no fresh droppings there from other birds. And no hawk nest, either. The place was perfect for ravens, winter or summer.

"Shall we start the Flight?" Colin asked.

"*I* shall start the Flight," the Main Raven replied testily. Zack chuckled to himself. Colin the upstart, was it?

"And I choose to call it now," the Main Raven concluded with a laugh, leaping up and striking off powerfully for higher elevations. Zack couldn't keep up, but Colin could. It turned into a contest. The Main Raven climbed faster and faster. Colin, although smaller, had no trouble with the pace. In fact, he could have passed the Main Raven with ease, and he knew it. But he stayed a few lengths behind, out of respect.

A thousand wingstrokes above Carrot Creek the birds came level with the ridgelines on either side. They could look far in any direction. Down the valley lay the Lougheed Peaks, north-facing and grim, their cliffs winter-darkened. In the opposite direction lay the friendlier south slope of Cascade Mountain, its rock layers bent into a smile, for it caught the sun for more hours of the day than any of the surrounding mountains.

Zack and Colin and the Main Raven noted the beauty about them and decided to climb higher, to sample the day's last direct sunlight. Like swimmers breaking the surface, the birds popped up above the shadows and into the brightness. Instinctively and all together, they inhaled deeply. Sure enough, Colin thought, sunset air was noticeably better than the regular stuff. They soared, turning their wings to the sun, letting the rays hit them all over as they wheeled and rolled. The black pigment in their feathers picked up the photons, each one a packet of solar energy flung to them from very far across the reach of space. Warm now, the ravens croaked their satisfaction. Today's tragedy? Never mind. They had almost reached tomorrow.

Colin looked down, wondering if the other birds had seen them. Indeed, Marg had looked up and spotted her flockmates far above, black on pink. She called to the others – "Evening Flight!" – and now they were all flapping and croaking eagerly upward. Invisible at first in the darkened part of the landscape, the Raven's Enders burst into the light in ones and twos, calling happily as they twirled and eddied.

"We've got a roost," Zack said to Molly as she drew near. "Big Douglas-fir down the canyon. Even better than the spruce, I think. Colin found it. And – and M.R. approved it," he added hastily, as the Main Raven drifted over to give him a hard look.

"A Douglas-fir. That's nice," Molly said, savoring another lungful of sunset air. "It's been ages since we roosted in one of those. I like the feel of Douglas-fir bark under my feet. It always feels warm, somehow."

"Well, we're going to need any warmth we can find tonight," Zack commented. "Just look at it, down there – everything iced up like the end of the world."

"It *was* the end of the world for Cathy."

Zack looked pensive. "That poor bird . . . I kind of figured she wouldn't last too long."

"Zack! How can you say that?!"

"I don't mean to be unkind. Just an observation, you know? Cathy was just plain unlucky, right from the start. There but for fortune . . ."

Molly dipped her bill, acknowledging the truth in what he said. She added a thought of her own. "If that's the way the world works, then why do we fight it? Why do we ever leave the nest? Is there any point to anything at all?"

"Aw, Molly . . ." Zack's attempt at a soothing reply died away as he gazed down to the bleak landscape below. He soared, stiff-winged and contemplative, and Molly did the same beside him. Colin, looking increasingly morose, made it a threesome. Then Molly spoke again.

"Really, Zack – I don't think there *is* any point to it. The world is nasty and violent, that's all, and it doesn't care a bit about us. Not even the Trees really care about us. It's just every creature for itself."

Someone had overheard Molly's dark pronouncement. "Oh, goat-trinkets, my dear." It was Greta. She came nearer, flailing her way through the air, as clumsy as ever. "Whew," she puffed. "This gets harder by the day." She coughed. Then she smiled. "But what the heck. Even for me, as old as I am, there's at least *one* good reason to keep on living," she said. "One very good reason."

"What's that?" Colin asked, brightening. He sensed one of Greta's famous utterances in the making.

"To be part of all this," she said simply, stretching her wings out in a sweeping gesture to the world around her. With that she did a shaky, geriatric half-roll in the fading light and dropped off into the gloom muttering, "Ooo, it's cold down here."

XXI

The birds arrived at their new roost en masse, each hoping to pick the best spot. There was a lot of petty squabbling.

"Wheedle, you got th' inside perch last time!"

"Well, the inside perch was *worse* last time, remember?"

"I don't care. With you it's just take, take, take!"

"I wouldn't if you were inclined to *give* a little."

And on and on, well past the hour of darkness.

"Mum, I just can't sleep at all. It's so cold." Sarah fluffed her feathers out farther and settled lower over her feet. She and Marg sat close together on the same limb.

"I know, dear. It's the same with me," Marg replied. "When it gets to be this cold, any bird has trouble sleeping." She likewise fluffed and settled. Then she had an idea.

"Greta?" she called. "Would you tell us a story?"

Greta had actually dropped off to sleep, despite the cold, but she awoke at the sound of her name. "Gro? Story?"

The other birds had been listening, and now they joined in.

"Oh yes, Greta. A story. We haven't had a story in ages."

"You sure do tell real fine stories, Greta. Don't have to be a long one. If you're bushed, like."

"Hey, yeah! Tell us one, okay?" Brendan had decided immediately that a story would be just the thing. "Like the one about the Great Raven or something."

"I think we should all allow Greta to make up her own mind on this issue," chided the Main Raven. "It is rather late to be asking her for this sort of thing." He, too, had gone to sleep – grateful to escape the cold – and he was annoyed at being awakened into it. But then, a story by Greta was worth a little discomfort. He knew that she would oblige, for Greta loved telling tales. And he, like the other Raven's Enders, loved to listen to them.

"Okay," Greta said, shaking herself fully awake. "The flock ought to get more stories."

"Yay!" Sarah hopped down from her perch to get closer to Greta. Brendan followed. "All *riiiight!*" he croaked.

Soon all the birds had crowded around Greta, preening and gabbling, eager for the first story-telling session in a long time. The Main
Raven hushed them. "If we all wish to hear from Greta, then it
behooves us to give her our full attention."

Greta turned her head sideways and looked thoughtful. "How
about . . . how about the Great Raven story?" she asked. This was
strictly pro forma; the other birds knew that she would start with the
Great Raven story.

"That's the one! Give us that one!"

"Yes! 'Great Raven'!"

"Great Raven?" The last voice was Colin's. Who or what was the
"Great Raven"?

"Well," Greta said, answering his unspoken question and beginning
her story in the same breath, "the Great Raven was the first of the birds.
Recall that the birds were invented by the Trees, because –"

Brendan blurted it out: "Because the Trees got itchy, okay, and –"

The Main Raven cut him off. "Shhh. Greta is telling this story, not
you." Sarah giggled. Brendan pulled his head in. "Sorry."

Greta started again. "Yes, Brendan, the Trees did invent the birds.
And all the other animals. But let's go back further." All the birds snuggled closer together. "Before the Trees there were the rocks, and before
that there was nothing."

Sarah twitched. "You mean, like, just *nothing?* Nothing at all?"

"Well, Sarah, I know what you're thinking. There had to be *something*,
of course. But it wasn't anything that made sense. A lot of weirdness
and darkness, then a lot of noise and fire. That sort of thing. No birds
were there to see it, not even the Great Raven. So we don't know much
about it. One day maybe I'll find out more, and I'll let you know.
Remind me to, Sarah." Sarah smiled.

Greta continued. "Eventually there was rock, and that was solid,
giving us the world. But the world didn't look the way it does now,
with Yamnuska and Carrot Creek and all the places we know. No, first
we had to have *ice*. Ice came along after rock. And there was lots and
lots of ice. Ice covered everything, and it was very heavy, and it moved
– sometime I'll take you all down to see the glaciers by Kananaskis
Lakes – and it carved the mountains out of the rock. And then, after a

long time, came the first Trees. And those first Trees, as you all know, were the smartest things in the world."

Greta looked up to see if the other birds were listening. Sure enough, their brown eyes gleamed intently back at her, reflecting the starlight that filtered through the branches of the Douglas-fir. Greta wheezed a little in the cold air, then continued.

"But the trees had a problem. As smart as they were, they were still rooted in the ground. Couldn't walk around. Couldn't even move their limbs. And if you can't move your limbs, then you can't scratch an itch. You know how it is, right? If you hold still for even a few moments, you seem to get an itch somewhere."

At this point Scratch started picking at himself furiously. The other birds noticed and laughed along with Greta. She had to stop and catch her breath. Then she started again. "Anyway, the first Trees, poor things, *did* get itchy. So what were the Trees to do? Well, they –"

"I know!" said Brendan, interrupting again. "They –"

"Brendan!" The Main Raven was getting angry. "This is the last time that I'm going to warn you!"

Brendan clamped his mouth shut. Greta went on.

"Now. As I said before, the Trees were smart. And, being smart, they soon figured out how to solve their itchiness problem. They solved it by inventing something to scratch the itch. And that something was the first bird."

Practically all the ravens knew this part of the story well, so they nodded their heads. Colin, though, couldn't remember hearing it, and he was delighted. Of course, he thought. Wow! He almost said it out loud, but caught himself just as his bill was starting to open.

"The bird would fly around and land on a Tree. It hardly ever landed on exactly the same branch, and that was part of the plan. Without knowing it, the bird was designed to land on precisely the itchiest spot on the itchiest branch. And we've been doing it ever since. You've got to admire the Trees for it – this was a very clever plan."

All the Raven's Enders took a moment to admire the Trees.

"Now, that first bird was a raven. A female raven. And wouldn't you know it, the Trees decided to make more of them. So they provided her with a nestmate. Only he didn't look like the original raven. The original raven was dark green, to match the color of conifer needles – the Trees wanted the bird to match – but the male raven was bright red."

Here Sarah giggled. Imagine! A bright-red raven! She stopped herself and looked over anxiously to the Main Raven, who was smiling at her. Giggling, as long as it wasn't too loud, seemed to be acceptable.

"This puzzled the first raven. She asked the Trees about it. 'How come he's red and I'm green?' she asked. 'Oh,' they said, 'it's for the other ravens coming along. If you two do your job, there are going to be lots more ravens, and they'll need to know which is male and which is female, so they can nest properly and produce plenty of branch-scratchers for us. You can nest with a different male every year if you like.'

" 'But color isn't necessary,' said the first raven. 'What I want is a friend as much as a nestmate. I'm not going to pick a new one every year. He'll always stay with me.'

"The Trees were impressed with this loyalty. 'Then we shall make ravens of both sexes the same color,' they said to her, 'which is less work for us. And the color will be black.'

" 'Black? Why black?' she asked.

" 'Because black is the color the sun loves best. If you're black, the sun will keep you warm. We plan to make a lot of other kinds of birds, to go with all the different kinds of Trees, and we'll save the colors for birds like warblers, who are going to pick new mates every year. By the way, since you're the first raven, we've decided to make you immortal.'

" 'Immortal? You mean I'll never have to die?'

" 'That's right. You've turned out pretty well, so we're going to keep you around. We hope you don't mind.'

" 'Of course not,' said the first raven, 'but I do have a request.' "

At this point Greta paused. All the ravens leaned forward expectantly, most of them having heard this story many times and knowing that this was the most important part. They also knew that it would be handled in Greta's tantalizing, maddening way. But they hoped that maybe this time she would add to it.

"And, as you know, the exact nature of her request has never been discovered."

The other birds groaned. Not again!

"Oh, Greta," Molly said, "somewhere in your wanderings you've got to find this out for us."

"Well, perhaps I will, my dear. But don't hold your breath." She smiled to herself. "So, to finish up," she continued, "the ravens nested, producing lots more ravens, and the Trees proceeded to make many other kinds of birds, some of them just to look at, like the ducks, but mostly birds that fitted nicely on various sizes of branches, for the best scratching. And that's the end of the story." Greta wheezed noisily in the cold air. "*Hooh!*"

"May I ask something?" It was Colin.

Greta wheezed again. She caught her breath. "What did you say, Colin?"

"I have a question," he repeated.

"Sure. Always okay to ask a question *after* the story," she said, looking at Brendan.

"My question is: why do you call her the 'Great Raven'?"

"Oh, what a dumb question," said Dolus.

"And look who's asking," said Garth.

"Now, now," Greta scolded them gently. "Please keep in mind that perhaps Colin hasn't heard this story – or more likely he forgot it on account of his accident. But I'm so wheezy that maybe somebody else had better explain." She coughed.

"Okay," Scratch offered. "It's like this here. The Great Raven is real great 'cause she was the first one, see, and that's why she's so great. Simple."

"Wrong." Wheedle was shaking his head. The other birds turned to hear him. "The first raven became known as 'Great' because she was older than any of the others. She had her nestlings, then her grand-nestlings, then her *great*-grand-nestlings, and her *great-great*-grand-nestlings, and so on, until there were so many 'greats' that everybody just called her 'Great Raven.' It was easier than adding all those 'greats.'" He stopped, enjoying the surprised looks on the faces of the other birds. "And also because," he added, "in case any of you didn't notice, the first raven had no name at all."

Wheedle had just one-upped the whole flock. Colin was impressed. He wanted to make sure, though, that he had the story straight. "Now, tell me if I've got this right, Wheedle," he said. "She was immortal, so she would outlive all the others, getting older and older, and having all these grand-nestlings and great-grand-nestlings and so on."

"Exactly," said Wheedle, looking smug.

"Then, then . . ." Something about this was still bothering Colin. He turned to Greta, who was looking at him with those wonderful eyes.

"Well, if the Great Raven could live forever, but she wanted only one nestmate, how could she have that? Her first mate wasn't immortal, was he?"

Now it was Zack's turn to be impressed. "By the Trees, Colin C.C.! You may ask dumb questions sometimes, but that wasn't one of them!" He turned to Molly and said, quietly, "I wonder how Greta is going to answer that."

Greta smiled a little half-bill smile. No one else had ever asked this question. But she knew that Colin – had *expected* that Colin – would ask it, if not this evening, then some other time. "Hmm . . . how could the Great Raven solve her problem with mortal mates, eh?" She looked away into the darkness. "Haven't really thought about that," she said. "But I will, if you like."

That answer wasn't good enough for Colin, and he started to object, but she spoke again before he could pester her further. "And you should think about it too, Colin. You've got the brainpower."

This was more than dodging the question. It was intellectual praise that Greta rarely gave, and the other birds recognized it as such. Wheedle made a whistling sound. "Oho – the promising young student is given a difficult assignment by the teacher!"

"Okay," Colin said, disappointed that no easy answer was forthcoming, but pleased to be complimented in this way. "Okay, I *will* think about it."

"Me too," said Sarah, brightly.

"Uh, me three," said Brendan.

"But not me," said Zack, lifting his wing to tuck his head under it. "Just starting to think about that kind of thing sends me off to roost-land."

Molly was already asleep. One by one, the other ravens turned their heads back and down, breathing the warm air under their wings. Soon the flock was still. Silvery shreds of starlight fell across their feathers. Some time later, far up in the night, high above the highest mountains, something began to happen in the sky. Not a bird noticed the shimmery curtains of color, fading here and brightening there, pale green and faintly pink, so thin that the stars shone through.

Down the valley the white wolf awoke. Curled up tightly against the cold, it raised its big head from under its tail and looked up. It saw the northern lights. It howled.

XXII

Having stayed up later than usual listening to Greta's story, the Raven's End Flock slept late the following day. By the time Colin took his morning flight down Carrot Creek to check on the wolves, it was broad daylight. But it was a day without warmth, a day without heat. The pale winter sun seemed only to dribble light down from the hole in the sky, not enough reaching the earth to warm it.

Dense and achingly cold, the air lying over the Rockies had been born in Arctic darkness far to the north, where the sun stayed below the horizon for months on end. That air had chilled the great glaciers of Greenland. It had frozen the ice of the Beaufort Sea and hardened the permafrost of the Arctic islands. The air mass had grown and spread southward, and now it lay over all of western Canada.

Colin's wings swished loudly through Carrot Creek Canyon, and his eyes blinked constantly in the frigid wind generated by his own speed.

Crack!

Instinctively Colin altered his course upward, away from the sudden noise. It had sounded like a gunshot. He looked back to see an aspen tree shaking loose what little snow lay on its bare limbs. The cold had split the trunk in half, straight down the middle.

Colin landed on a ledge overlooking the dead bighorn. The wolves were already on the kill, trying to get their teeth into the hard-frozen meat. Their breath left little clouds of frosty vapor around their heads.

Colin, too, produced twin puffs of steam from the nostril holes at the base of his bill. A larger plume came from his mouth when he called out to the big white wolf.

"Leave some for us, craw-ha!"

"Take off, you black maggot," the wolf called back, chewing.

Before Colin could reply, Wheedle landed beside him on the ledge. "My word. The dog-king speaks," he said. "Usually they don't talk to us. Unless it's an insult."

"Well, at least it replied."

"Very stuck on themselves," Wheedle continued. "Arrogant lot. The whole tribe have decided that they are the Trees' gift to the world."

The white wolf walked a little way off from the carcass and lifted a back leg over the snow. Immediately the other two wolves ran over to sniff the yellow stain. Adding their own urine, they enlarged the spot to a sizeable patch. All three animals then pawed vigorously, sending snow flying everywhere.

"And such delightful habits, too," Wheedle added.

Scratch had arrived. "Well, I hates ta admit there's anything good about wolves," he said, shaking his head, "but we'd be lost without 'em. Mind you, some of us get lost on *account* a' them guys." He looked into the distance. "Friend of mine up in Hay River, he figgered he was faster 'n them. Only he found out he weren't. Big raven. Made a pretty fair meal fer that pack."

Colin shifted uneasily on his perch. "I'm not going down there until they're good and full," he said.

"Nor I," said Wheedle. Looking around, he noticed that none of the other ravens was on the ground, either. "Take that white fellow, there. He's big *and* quick. He's caught the odd raven in his time, I'll wager."

"Prob'ly has," said Scratch. "But I'm gettin' real hungry. This is just stupid, waitin' around like this. Let's play a trick on them suckers." He looked over to Wheedle. "You with me, ol' buddy?"

"Depends on the trick," Wheedle replied. "What do you have in mind, Maestro?"

"Let's do that there Wolf-in-Trouble number."

"Splendid! We haven't done that one for quite a while! I'm in! I'm in!"

Before Colin could ask what the "Wolf-in-Trouble" was, the two friends had left. They flew down the canyon, around a corner and out of sight. The wolves saw them go, and the white one turned up its nose disdainfully as they flew by. Then it went back to crunching up a rib bone. The other wolves – two gray ones and a black one – were scattered around the clearing, lying in the snow as they gnawed noisily on various parts of the sheep.

A few minutes passed. The Raven's Enders spoke quietly among themselves, looking at the wolves and tittering. Except for Colin, they seemed to know what was going on. None of them followed Scratch and Wheedle down the canyon.

Then a strange sound came from the direction in which the birds had flown. Low and moaning, it was the howl of a wolf – but a weak howl, as if it were suffering.

The big white wolf stopped eating. It looked at the rest of the pack. They were looking back at it. Without a word, all the wolves got to their feet. With the white wolf in the lead, they padded away down the canyon toward the sound.

The sound came again, this time from farther down the canyon. The wolves broke into a run. As they disappeared around the corner, Wheedle came into view, flying back high up along the canyon rim. Scratch followed soon after.

"Never overestimate the intelligence of your average wolf," Wheedle said, yawning. "That lot will certainly be away for quite some time." He flew down to the sheep carcass. The other birds followed, and soon all were busily picking away at the meat. Just as Wheedle had said, the wolves were well occupied, giving the flock plenty of time for a hearty breakfast.

Except for Wheedle himself. With his single leg, and because he was so small, he had to work hard to pull even the smallest bit of meat from the sheep. He was forced to eat more slowly than the other birds, and now he was trying desperately to fill his stomach before the wolves returned. Colin noticed him struggling, walked over, and tore a large piece free.

Wheedle seized the bite hungrily. He spoke with his bill full. "*Galarg. Gulp.* Much appreciated. Really."

"No problem. I didn't know you could imitate a hurt wolf."

"Well, truth to tell, Scratch is better. He taught me, actually."

"How come both of you went?"

"Ah, that's essential to the game." Wheedle swallowed the last of his billful. "Scratch, you see, flies farther away from the pack than I fly. I go just far enough to get out of sight, and I give the first howl. Along come the wolves, and I let them see me. I sit there looking as if nothing has happened. Now, at this point they're thinking that maybe I was pulling their leg – love that expression, means a lot to me – then *Scratch* lays on another howl. This convinces our friends that I'm innocent, and off they go."

Now, however, they were back in an angry flurry of snow. Led by the white wolf, they jumped high, snapping after the birds flying up from the kill. But their efforts seemed to tire them out, for they soon left the carcass and went to curl up in the snow among the trees nearby. Wheedle couldn't resist a final tease. Landing in a pine immediately above one of the sleeping wolves, he plucked an old, hard cone from a dead branch. He stepped this way and that on the branch, cone in bill, lining it up exactly. Then he dropped it right on the wolf's head.

The head popped up and the wolf looked groggily around. "Huh? What?" it said. Then its eyes closed, its head dropped back on its paw, its tail flopped over its nose, and it began snoring.

XXIII

The cold weather had continued. For the last three days the Raven's Enders had stayed by the wolf kill, eating what was left of the sheep.

"Keep it up, kids," said Marg, addressing Sarah and Brendan. "You need all the meat you can eat. Let's just hope this cold snap doesn't last too much longer."

"How much longer?" asked Sarah.

Brendan was quick to reply. "Aw, Greta says we're gonna get a shnook, or something. Going to warm up."

"What's a 'shnook'?" Sarah asked, downing a bit of greasy sheep fat.

The three birds were picking away together at a leg joint. The snow here, and everywhere surrounding the carcass, was now covered with the hatchmark pattern of raven footprints.

Marg answered Sarah's question. "The word is 'chinook,' dear," she said. "The wind starts to blow. And it warms up very quickly. But I don't think we're due for one any time soon. So don't get your hopes up. In the meantime you'll want to eat as much as you can and fly as little as possible. It saves energy. And in this weather we need all we've got just to survive. Remember what Greta always says: 'A wingbeat saved keeps a bird just that much farther from its last flight.'"

"Hey – d'ya think Greta will tell us another story tonight?" Brendan asked. "About the Great Raven or something? I really like those stories."

Marg looked over to where Greta was pulling at a slim red thread dangling from the side of the carcass. "She might. Especially if you ask her yourself, Brendan. She thinks the world of you, you know."

Brendan fluffed out his throat-feathers and walked over to Greta, leaving yet more tracks in the snow. "Hi, Greta. Would you tell us a story again? Like that one the other night, okay?" Then he added, "Only longer?"

"*Longer* he wants it! And when is old Greta supposed to sleep, eh?" She pulled the meat free, gulped it down, and wiped her bill in the snow. "All right, then, Brendan C.C., you handsome young raven, you. A story tonight. A long one."

"Hey, cool! Thanks, Greta. Can I tell everyone?"

"Sure. That way they won't have to pester me individually."

Brendan walked back over to Sarah and Marg. He fluffed up his neck-feathers again. He spoke in his deepest voice. "I, uh, suggested to Greta that a rather long story might be in order," he said. Sarah began to smile.

"And she agreed," he continued, pointing his bill first to one side, then to the other. "Further, she said I was handsome. Handsome, indeed."

Sarah giggled. "Oh, Brendan, you sound just like that silly old Main Raven. Craw-ha!"

"I do?" Brendan replied, using his normal voice. "Really?" He sounded pleased.

The next thing they knew, the Main Raven himself was calling in a loud voice. "Attention, C.C.s."

The other birds looked up. Some began walking across the snow toward the big, elegant bird. He turned round and round, picking up his feet deliberately, ruffling his neck-feathers, raising his bill and flopping it from side to side, just as Brendan had done. Sarah let out another giggle, but Marg shushed her. When most of the flock had arrived, the Main Raven made his announcement.

"Colin tells me that he spoke with a lynx today, and –"

The other birds started to mutter.

"A lynx! Haven't seen a lynx in ages."

"Like, what's a 'lynx'?"

"Big cat. Got a short little tail. Eats bunnies."

Colin's thoughts turned to the encounter itself. He had decided to fly *up* Carrot Creek rather than down the creek into the canyon, as he usually did. He had passed by the roosting tree, and then before he knew it he was over the site of the avalanche. The avalanche. He hadn't thought about it for many days. But now, as he circled above the slide heap, he thought of Cathy's body down there, dead and frozen somewhere in all that snow. The thought made him shiver.

It was then that something on the periphery of his vision moved. His head snapped around.

An animal was prowling about at the edge of the slide heap. He looked at the thing with one eye, then with the other. The image brought up a word: *cat*.

"Big cat," he had said aloud, comparing it in his mind's eye with the smaller cat he had seen in Banff earlier that winter. "Really big cat."

This sound had caught the attention of the beast, which looked up at him. They locked eyes, the cat and the bird. For a long moment, Colin held fast to those two yellow eyes. There was something about them, he thought. Something he could feel. Something, he realized, that he could actually *hear*.

I am a lynx, said the eyes.

Colin found himself replying in the same way, without speaking. **You are beautiful,** he said. The words seemed to come by themselves.

Of course, said the cat. **Would you not like to land near me, to see me better?**

Colin could not break away from the gaze of the lynx. Involuntarily, he started to descend. **Yes,** he said through his eyes. **Yes, I would like to come closer.**

Oh, by all means, the lynx replied. **By all means. Come closer. Much, much closer. I am waiting.**

Colin had almost touched the snow before every alarm in his brain went off.

Up!

He leapt a split second before the cat would have caught him. Even so, one of its paws slashed by so close that it sucked the cold air after it and almost threw him out of control. That paw had been very big, with long, curved claws stretching out far beyond the fur.

"*Awk!*" he had cried, this time with his real voice.

The lynx laughed. It used its real voice, too. "Ha! Close one, eh, Corvus?"

"You are one – *whew* – incredible predator!" Colin was breathless, perched in a pine well out of reach.

"Best there is," said the lynx, licking one of its lethal feet. "Almost had you, didn't I?"

For all his fear, and despite the close call, Colin could not help but admire this creature. "I saw a smaller cat a while back –" he began.

"Housecat. Not as fast as I am." The lynx inspected its paw. "Doesn't do too badly, though. It's very good, in fact, at catching **birds.**"

This last word had been said by the animal's eyes, and Colin felt the peculiar power falling over him again. He replied in his proper voice – "I'm going!" – and headed down the creek.

"Oh, forget it," the lynx called after him. "Look – I'm not really hungry. Just finished a hare over in the trees there. Still got bunny blood on my whiskers. See?" Indeed, Colin could see red streaks on the cat's face. He noticed the long tufts of black fur on the ends of its ears, the dark ruff under its chin. The lynx sat down. "I just couldn't resist a crack at you. Sorry, in a way. Would have been pleasant to chat."

Colin tilted his tail and swung round, his curiosity aroused. Well, he thought, now that he knew what to watch out for . . . "I would like to chat, too," he had said. "But none of this *eye* stuff, okay? Or I'm off." He perched in a tree – a tall one – overlooking the lynx.

"Okay. No eyes." The cat looked up at him. This time the yellow circles projected nothing dangerous. How curious, Colin thought; they looked downright merry. How could such an accomplished killer be so likable? He decided not to lower his guard. Not even a little.

"Can't stay long," the lynx continued. "Cat I know came by this way – see her tracks, there?" The lynx looked over toward a set of faint impressions in the snow. "Believe I'll follow her for a while. She likes me. Might want to mate next spring."

So this lynx was male, Colin thought. He decided to ask it the one question he really wanted an answer for. "That thing you did with your eyes –" he began.

"Hey, I just promised not to do it to you."

"No, no. I don't want you to do it. I just want to know *how* you do it."

"Um – I don't really know. It just comes naturally. Every lynx does it. Basic way of catching hares, really. They can't resist it. Walk right over to you sometimes, or just sit there long enough for you to pounce. Same with, uh, birds." The lynx looked up to Colin. Its eyes maintained their neutrality. "But it was interesting how you did it right back at *me*."

Yes, Colin realized. He had. It had been in imitation of the lynx. No thought required; quite spontaneous. This, too, was curious.

"And," continued the lynx, "you're the only creature, aside from another lynx, that has replied, so to speak."

"Really?"

"Yup."

"And that's why you wanted to talk?"

"Sure. Never talked with a bird before. Only ate 'em."

Colin didn't know what to say next. Neither did the lynx. "Well, let's talk again some time," it suggested, getting up.

"Sure," Colin replied, knowing that doing so would be very risky. Better not to chance it. The big cat was too tricky, too fast. It started to pad away into the trees.

"Oh. One last thing," said the lynx, turning back toward him.

"Yes?"

"Tell your friends in the flock they'd better fluff up well tonight."

"What makes you say that?"

"Just some friendly advice. You were kind enough to share a little tête-à-tête with me, and I appreciate it, so I'm doing you and your crew a favor. Tonight is going to be the coldest night of the year."

"What? How do you know that?"

"A cat knows," the lynx said, walking into the trees. "A cat always knows. 'Bye." It seemed to vanish among the shadows.

Colin opened his eyes. He was back with the Raven's Enders, and the Main Raven was still speaking.

"And the lynx told him," the Main Raven was saying, "that tonight was going to be the coldest night of the year."

This set off a round of feather-fluffing. No one spoke.

"Now, in accordance with that prediction, I think it behooves us to conserve energy. So, with your permission, I'm cancelling the Flight. Are there any objections?"

There were none. Few of the birds cared to fly, even to catch the last sun of the day.

As forecast, dusk arrived with steadily deepening cold. The birds flew to the roosting tree early. They sat closer together than usual and practiced fluffing out their feathers as far as they could.

Molly knew what was in store for everyone that night, and she could hardly bear it. "Oh, Zack, this is going to be frightful. I'm afraid – I'm really afraid somebody might freeze to death tonight."

"Hasn't happened in a couple of years," he said reassuringly.

"Yes, and that's what worries me," Molly replied. "This is going to be the year that it does."

"We'll be all right, Molly. We can snuggle up close." He brushed against her with his feathery body and touched her bill with his.

"It's not *us* I'm worried about, Zack. It's the others. What about Sarah? What about – well, what about Sarah?"

"Marg will look after her. And she's got Brendan. Brendan wouldn't let Sarah freeze. By the Trees, there's plenty of energy in Brendan."

"Still –"

From elsewhere in the tree Brendan's voice interrupted. "Hey, Greta! How about that story you promised?"

Greta didn't reply.

"Greta!" several birds called at one.

"Gro?" She opened her eyes. She had already dropped off to sleep.

"Your story, Greta. You promised a story, remember?"

"Oh – so sorry. Yes, I did forget. But not the story. Just forgot to remember to" – here she yawned a raven yawn – "to think of a story to tell. What would you like to hear?"

"More on the Great Raven," Sarah said.

"Yeah! Like the Great Raven, totally more on the Great Raven," Brendan added.

"Uh, sure," Greta replied. "Totally sure." She sniggered a little. "Totally sure, craw-ha. Ah, to be young again. Well."

The moon rose over Princess Margaret Mountain on the coldest night of the year, and Greta began her tale.

XXIV

As the ravens cocked their heads to listen, Greta's slow, wheezy voice floated through the big Douglas-fir. "This is the story of the Great Raven and her song –"

"What?" Brendan interrupted. "Ravens don't sing – urk." Sarah had poked him with her bill, and the Main Raven's eyebrow tufts were rising.

"Well, Brendan," Greta went on good-naturedly, "you're right. Ravens don't sing. But they did, once. Or at any rate they tried to." She took a deep breath and restarted her tale.

"Here's what happened. After the Trees invented the Great Raven, the Trees gave her a nestmate, which helped to pass the time, you know."

Sarah sniggered. So did a few other birds. They liked these slightly risqué comments that Greta threw into her stories.

Greta continued. "The Trees had already told the Great Raven that they planned to make other kinds of birds, and they did. The next batch were the warblers. These were quite colorful – lots of yellow on the males – and the Trees were pleased with their handiwork. But they got carried away and decided to give them songs as well as colors. Actually, they *had* to give them songs. Everybody knows that warblers are dumber than deer droppings, and –"

"Craw-ha! 'Dumber than deer droppings'! Craw-ha-ha!" Brendan couldn't contain himself. But it was all right; the other birds were laughing as well.

"Being so stupid, they still had trouble finding their mates, even with colors to tell the males and females apart. So the Trees figured they needed songs as well. They gave each warbler a different song. Not just each species, but each individual *bird*. And you can imagine the result."

"What? What?" Now Colin was interrupting.

"The result," said Greta, turning toward him, "was chaos. They called constantly, all day long. And they kept forgetting their songs, changing their songs, losing their mates, going to the wrong nests, losing their tempers and fighting with each other – it was awful. After a few days of that the Trees simply shut everybody up. Then, of course, the warblers became even more confused. So things were not working out very well.

"At this point the Great Raven had an idea. She suggested to the Trees that each type of warbler be given a song and told to stick with it. So the yellowthroats would get their own song, the blackpolls would get theirs and so on. And, to make sure that each warbler stuck with its own mate and its own nest, at least through the summer, she suggested that no two pairs of warblers would be allowed to nest on the same tree. That would be a rule. To make sure, each pair would keep all the other pairs away. And the song would tell those other pairs that this particular tree was occupied.

"The Trees thought this was a good idea and tried it out. Sure enough, the warblers settled down, with one pair here, another there, and instead of everybody singing constantly all the time, it was only necessary to sing every now and again, when there were other warblers around. Of course, there was still a fair bit of singing, what with all the warblers. But it wasn't as bad as before. It was quite bearable. Kind of entertaining, really.

"Now, you'd think the Great Raven would be pleased as pea-pods that her idea had worked out. And she was. But she felt a little sadness as she heard all the other birds singing. Because she, herself, had not been given a song. She went again to the Trees and stated that she too wished to sing.

"'Well,' said the Trees, 'we'll have to think about that. You know how much trouble the warblers caused us.'

"'Oh, I won't be any trouble,' she said. 'I won't have to sing much at all, really, since I always know who my mate is. And ravens don't like nesting in the same tree anyway. I'd just like to be able to sing every now and again, so as not to feel left out.'

"'But are you sure you want to?' the Trees responded. 'You know what they're really saying to each other, all those warblers? "My territory! Get out! Get out!" and things like that. Even worse. We heard one the other day singing "Eat castings, nest-fouler!" over and over to the birds in the next tree. Do you want to be part of *that*?'

"The Great Raven said that there was no way she would ever sing anything unkind to anybody, and that, yes, she really wanted a song.

"'In that case, leave it with us,' said the Trees. They had one of their committee meetings about it, and afterward they summoned the Great Raven.

"'We have decided to give you a song,' they said. 'It goes like this.' And one of them sang it for her. Then the Great Raven tried it. Here's how it sounded."

At this point Greta produced something that came out as, "Tweetle-dee-rawk-CROAK-*blargh*." The other birds laughed uproariously.

"Well," she said, when everyone had quieted down, "that was more or less what the Trees were expecting to hear. After all, ravens were not designed for singing, because singing came along after we had been invented. So the Great Raven was terrible at it. Even worse than I am."

The other birds laughed again. *No one* could sing as horribly as Greta!

"So the Trees tried to take back the song. But the Great Raven wouldn't let them. 'I'm keeping it,' she said, 'unless you give me a song I can actually *sing.*' The Trees confabbed a while and, as always, they came up with something really clever."

Colin leaned forward, listening intently. This was going to be good.

"We have an alternative for you," the Trees said. "Instead of a song, we have decided to give you the power to imitate the sounds made by other creatures."

"'So what?' said the Great Raven. She had her heart set on a song.

"'And it's not just birds, you know,' the Trees said. 'We're about to bring out a line of mammals, and, as a courtesy to you, we're going to give them voices that you will find rather easy to imitate.'

"The Great Raven was getting interested in this idea. She had a streak of fun in her, just like you or me, so she said, 'Go on. Tell me more.'

"'Well, you could imitate coyotes,' said the Trees. 'We're going to invent coyotes. They'll give you some trouble, but you'll be able to tease them, too.'

"'Sounds amusing,' said the Great Raven. 'But can I try it for a while? Return it if I don't like it?'

"'Nope,' said the Trees. 'It's all or none. Take it or leave it.'

"Now, this placed the Great Raven in a quandary. Should she agree to this plan? What might happen? She wasn't sure. But what could really be wrong with the idea? After all, *she* would have control of her new power. And if she didn't want to use it, she didn't have to.

"Then she had an idea, and that idea alone convinced her to say yes to the Trees.

"'Yes,' she said. 'The answer is yes. I'll take the power of imitation.'

"'Good choice,' said the Trees. 'Here you go.' And they gave it to her.

"'Now,' she said, 'Before I try using this, are you sure that I have it?'

"'Of course,' said the Trees. 'We just gave it to you.'

"'And you're not going to take it back? I'd hate to get dependent on it and then lose it.'

"'Oh, we won't take it back. We can't, actually. You're stuck with it now.'

"'And so are you,' she said, in the exact same voice used by the Trees themselves.

"'Good grief!' said the Trees. 'She's imitating *us!*'

"'You said I could imitate anything I liked,' the Great Raven said, using her own voice now.

"'Yes, but we didn't realize, you know, that —'

"'It's okay,' said the Great Raven. 'I won't tease you. Much.'"

Greta stopped here and winked. There was mischief in her eye. "Shall we tease the Trees a little right now?" she asked.

"Hey, yeah!" said Brendan. "Let's do it! I've never teased the Trees before!"

"Okay, then," Greta said. "Here's how you tease the Trees. Make a sound like a tree swaying in the wind. Kind of like this. *Creak. Creeaaak. Creeeaaak.*"

It did sound exactly like a tree complaining of the wind, worried that it might be blown over. The other birds started imitating, too, and the effect was of a whole forest muttering away. The birds carried on for a while, perfecting their imitations, and they would have probably kept at it longer, except that a strange thing happened.

The big Douglas-fir quivered.

"Hey! We did it! It heard!" Brendan was ecstatic. "Wow! It works!"

But he shut up a moment later when a patch of snow fell from the branch above and hit him squarely on the head.

"Whoa," Scratch called out. "Let's not overdo this here teasin'! Could be the roost don't like it."

Greta replied quickly. "No, in point of fact they don't much like it." She looked up at the great load of snow hanging over them in the big Douglas-fir. "Maybe we *are* overdoing it."

"Indeed," the Main Raven said, "it would be inappropriate to irritate our wonderful roost tonight. Why don't we all make amends by giving our perches a good scratch?"

And they did, each bird flexing its feet around the limb it was grasping, running its nails over the rough surface of the old Douglas-fir. Small flakes of itchy bark fell down through the branches. The tree seemed to appreciate it, because immediately the branches felt warmer underfoot. Molly remarked on it, and Marg agreed.

"Is that the end of the story, Greta?" Sarah said, shivering. "I'm still too cold to sleep."

The Main Raven replied on Greta's behalf. "Let us consider the story finished for tonight," he said. "Greta needs her rest. And we shouldn't stay awake any longer ourselves. The thing to do is fluff up well and sit as close together as possible."

Brendan and Marg cuddled Sarah between them. "Oh, hey, thanks," she said. "That's really nice." She put her head as far back under her wing as it would go. "Yes," she said, her voice muffled as she breathed the warmth of her own feathers. "Maybe I can roost. I can try, anyway."

Throughout the tree, birds pressed tightly together in twos and threes. No one lacked a warming partner that night. Near the top, Colin and the Main Raven kept Greta snug. She wheezed in her sleep.

The moon sat high in the sky, small and white, throwing a colorless light onto the snow. No clouds stood between the earth's surface and the astronomical cold of space. Whatever heat the Rockies held that night – and it wasn't much – was drifting away into the void.

XXV

Hours later, when the moon had gone down, Sarah awoke. She felt very cold, colder even than the time she lay in the snowdrift south of Morley Flats, colder than she had ever been in her life. Down the canyon, she could hear the wolves howling. "Mum?" she called weakly. "Mum?"

"Yes, dear?"

"Mum, I'm so cold. I'm really, really cold."

"Let's cuddle a little closer, then. Here – scoot over."

Sarah huddled closer to Marg. Brendan, who was still asleep, automatically moved closer too.

"It's not enough, Mum." Sarah shivered again, more deeply. "I'm afraid."

Molly, roosting on the limb above, heard this. She spoke quietly to Zack, who was also waking up. "Zack, it's happening. Poor Sarah is freezing. And there's nothing we can do about it."

"Maybe if we all snuggled up around her?"

"How? All we can do is sit beside her on the limb. That won't help."

"You're right, Molly. She's going to have to make it on her own."

A voice from higher in the tree sifted down to them. It was Wheedle, sitting next to Scratch. "I know how she feels, I certainly do. There have been several nights in this poor raven's life when he's figured he'll be wolf food by dawn."

"Come down here with us if you like," Zack said.

"Oh, no thanks," Wheedle replied. "I've got to keep Scratch warm. And you don't want to cuddle with him and his bugs. We'll be all right. We've weathered worse than this, old Scratch and me. Besides," he added, "I've got only one leg to keep warm instead of two."

Sarah shivered and made tiny peeping sounds like a fledgling. Molly had heard this sound before, and it filled her with fear.

"Zack, I don't think I could stand it if Sarah froze tonight. Just after losing Cathy in the avalanche – it would be awful to lose Sarah, too. And she's the only young female raven in the flock. Oh, Zack, we can't let this happen!"

"Well, then we've got to do something. Maybe we could find a big flat branch where we could kind of cluster around her."

But before he could finish speaking, the wind interrupted. A gust swept through the tree, knocking snow down on everyone.

"*Awk!* This we don't need!" shouted Zack, shaking the snow off. "That wind hurts to the bone!"

"Oh dear, oh dear," Molly wailed, "this is the end for Sarah!"

Then, as the wolves started to howl more loudly, the wind swept through the tree again, stronger now, dislodging more snow. Another gust caused the whole tree to sway. It woke the birds near the top, who had been spared an eyeful of snow but now felt the frigid air pushing their feathers aside and stinging their skin.

Colin awoke in a panic. He had been dreaming of the South Face of Yamnuska on a summer afternoon, his feet resting on sun-warmed rock, his wings spread to let the breeze cool his feathers. Suddenly the wind had become altogether too cool for comfort.

"This is frightful!" he called. "I'm going farther down the tree." He left his perch and hopped down to where Zack, Molly, Marg, and

Brendan were trying to surround Sarah. She could hardly keep her grip on the branch, and everyone knew that if she fell from her perch she would die. Sarah swayed forward, her eyes closing.

"Sarah! Wake up!" Marg yelled, prodding her under the chin with her bill. "Don't fall off!"

Brendan was frantic. He squeezed hard against Sarah, willing all the heat in his body to rush through the feathers on that side and warm her. She felt cold against him. He pushed so hard that he shoved both Sarah and Marg sideways on the branch.

"It's too late," Molly said. "Her eyes –"

"No! No!" Zack cried. "Sarah! Just a little longer! The wind – the wind –"

"The wind feels *warm!*" Colin cried. "It's a warm wind! The wind is warm!"

"Chinook! Chinook!" Marg called out. "Oh, thank the Trees, it's a chinook!"

XXVI

One moment the wind was killing the birds, and the next it was saving their lives. In an instant the chinook, warm as spring, blew the Arctic cold from the valley of Carrot Creek and replaced it with milder air from the other side of the mountains – from the Pacific Ocean side, where winter was easy. The Raven's Enders spread their wings into that miraculous flow. Sarah opened her eyes and regained her balance on the branch. Brendan croaked with joy. "Shnook! Shnook!"

"The word is 'chin-*ook*,' Brendan," Marg corrected.

"Right. Shnook-ook! Shnook-ook!"

"Mum, how come it's warm all of a sudden? Am I dying again?" Sarah was finally talking.

"No dear, you're not dying again. And neither is anyone else. The chinook wind has saved us."

When the sun rose over the Rockies that morning it shone through long bands of thin cloud that held their places over the ridges. The clouds marked the wavecrests in a sea of warm, dry air that was flooding across the continental divide. Overnight the chinook had raised the temperature above freezing for the first time in many days, and the Raven's Enders now delighted in it. After the Flap they set off into the sky with pleasure. Released from the debilitating cold, they rolled in the gusts like puppies in spring grass.

"The air is so pleasant. So *sweet*," Colin said to Zack that afternoon as they soared together above Princess Margaret Mountain. "Even way up here it's warm." They were level with the summit ridge, far above the treeline. "Really good updraft, too."

"Wait 'til you check out the downdraft on the other side, C.C. Watch this." Zack let the wind carry him eastward over the crest of the ridge. Abruptly he dropped like a stone.

"Wow! Let me try that – *whoops!*" Colin was snatched away. He had never felt such a downrush of air. It pulled him earthward so fast it was frightening. "*Awk!*"

Zack wasn't frightened in the least. He tumbled happily in the currents. "Ya-*hooooo!*" But as he looked back to Colin, struggling desperately against the downward flow, he remembered Colin's near-disasters in similar situations, noted the fear in his eyes and called out to reassure him. "Just ride it out. It flattens out near the ground and rolls back up toward the peak. It's okay. Ride it out."

Colin took Zack's advice. He relaxed and let the wind fling him where it wished. He felt it carrying him down, then horizontally back toward the east face of the mountain, then up along the cliffs in a lurching, ragged way – a great rollercoaster of an air mass, plunging down an invisible track and then climbing back up for another run. This was heady adventure, a dose of fun so strong that it bordered on terror.

Above him Colin could see Zack reaching the ridge crest. Without lighting there, Zack dived back into the maelstrom and hurtled by. "Wah-*hooo!*" But Colin decided to land on the ridge before going around again on the downdraft.

"Be right with you!" he called out. "I'm just going to rest a minute!" Or so he thought. As he tried to land, the wind threw him back and down, just as it had thrown Zack. Still, this time the ride seemed less scary, more exhilarating. Soon he was levelling out and being dragged back toward the mountain, then boosted upward again. Zack came wobbling along beside him.

"Wild stuff, eh? By the Trees, it's great to be a raven! A dinky-doo chickadee could never do this! Probably get all its feathers blown off and fall out of the sky like a little pink mouse! Craw-ha!"

Colin was still a little concerned. "Zack, this wind is so strong – it's like we're stuck in it. I tried to land up there and I couldn't."

"Waste of time even to try. No, when we get tired of riding the current around and around we'll pop out of it east of here. Climb up high. It's not as strong up there. Then we can head back west against it. But right now we're coming up on the ridge again, and there's something up there I want to show you. Stay close."

As the wind pulled him up the cliff face toward the ridgeline, Zack retracted his wings halfway, losing lift. Hanging in the updraft, he slid neatly over to the rocky face of the mountain and alighted a few steps below the snowy crest.

Colin did the same. Strangely, there was very little wind here, yet he could hear it roaring loudly just above his head. Colin looked up and saw clouds of snow blowing over the ridge. He blinked the flakes out of his eyes. Looking to either side he could see a wispy fringe of snow streaming eastward all along the crest. He looked straight up again. The sun shone through the flying ice crystals, making colors in the streamers: subtle pinks, blues, yellows, and greens. The colors changed moment by a moment.

Colin watched raptly, astounded. "Zack, that is the most beautiful thing I've ever seen."

"You bet."

"This is the best place in the world."

"Sure is."

Colin looked across the Bow Valley to Mount Rundle, which was higher than the mountain they had been playing on. Enormous plumes of snow extended from Mount Rundle's long summit ridge. "I wonder what the chinooking would be like over there?"

"Terrific, most likely." Zack looked over to Colin and started to smile. "'Chinooking,' is it? This crazy sport has a name, thanks to you. 'Chinooking'! Craw-ha! I love it!"

"Shall we try it over there? On Mount Rundle?"

"Why not? This air is great for bashing around in!"

And away they went.

XXVII

On their way back that afternoon, Colin and Zack let the wind do most of the work. They were coasting over Carrot Creek when Colin looked down and saw something that made him put on the brakes. "Zack! What's that?"

"What's what?" Zack skidded around on one wing.

"Look! Down by the creek – right down there."

"I still don't see what you're looking at." Zack was tired. What was this nonsense?

"Those lines, Zack. What are those lines?" Colin was diving now, losing elevation fast. Zack groaned. Now they'd have to regain lost height. Where did Colin get the energy to be so interested in everything?

"There! Look at that!" Colin was quite excited. "Lines! Lines in the snow! And, and – humans! Zack! Humans making lines!"

"Oh, for the Trees' sake, Colin. They're just skiers."

"What?"

"*Skiers.* Humans skiing. They leave tracks like that."

By this time the birds had perched in an aspen overlooking the ski tracks. The humans were moving slowly up the snowy, frozen-up creek. They were coming toward the tree.

Zack began to explain. "They do it with their feet, see? They have special feet for walking in the snow." He modified his explanation. "Well, they don't walk, really. They sort of slide their feet. Really long feet. And the feet leave those tracks."

Colin stared intently at the skiers, turning his head from side to side, looking at them first with one eye, then with the other, the pupils widening and narrowing as he focussed as closely as possible on the scene below him. He saw something that worried him. "Uh-oh. They've got sticks, Zack. See that? They're poking them in the snow. Those wouldn't be *guns*, would they?" Colin unfurled his wings to fly.

"Not to worry, C.C. This is the Park, remember? Humans don't have guns around here. Anyway, they don't look like guns to me. I think they use those sticks to help them move along."

Colin settled back on the branch. One of the skiers, he noticed, had long brown hair in braids that stuck out from under a green cap. The other one had short hair and a beard. It wore a red cap.

"It's a female and a male, I think," Colin said.

"How observant," Zack replied, yawning.

The skiers were going to pass directly under their tree. Zack moved away warily, but Colin stayed. Something about the skiers seemed familiar. They stopped and looked directly up at him.

"That's a really big crow, John." The human with braids, the female one, looked over to the other.

"Can't be a crow. Crows fly south in the winter. Gotta be a raven." The human called John was short of breath, leaning on his poles. He had been breaking the trail through the snow.

The female human spoke again. "Remember that raven we saw on Yamnuska last summer?"

"Which raven was that?"

"You know. The one that ate part of my sandwich."

"Oh, right. The day we did the South Face Direct. Really bold raven."

"This one reminds me of that one." She looked up at Colin again. He cocked his head to the side and looked down at her.

"Aw, we're too far from Yam for it to be the same one."

"Okay, but – hey! I know what. Let's stop and eat something. Maybe it'll take some of my sandwich. Like that other one did." She stuck her ski poles firmly in the snow and pulled her hands out of her gloves, leaving the gloves hanging in the pole straps.

Colin flinched when he saw the gloves hanging by themselves. These humans had two sets of hands!

"Good idea. Let's eat." John looked at his watch. "Holy smokes –

it's two o'clock. No wonder I'm running out of gas." He parked his poles and took his pack off. "We'll have to turn around pretty soon."

"Yeah. Break some more of this trail tomorrow."

The two took their skis off and sat on them.

Colin's eyes widened. First they took off their hands, and now they were taking off their feet! He was wondering what to expect next. Spare heads?

John pulled a plastic bag from his pack, and from inside the bag came a peanut-butter sandwich. Colin couldn't restrain himself. He hopped down to the ground and strode over to the skiers.

"Wow!" John exclaimed. "This raven is really bold. Like that other one."

"I tell you, John, it *is* the other one. Look at his face."

"Ravens don't have faces."

"Sure they do. I recognize this one."

Colin, too, had remembered. These two humans were the same ones who had fed him up on the South Face of Yamnuska last autumn. John and Linda, the climbers. Today they were John and Linda, the skiers.

John broke off a corner of his sandwich and tossed it over to Colin. The sandwich bite landed practically at his feet. He jumped back reflexively, then stepped forward and seized it in his bill. Tilting his head back, he swallowed it in one gulp. As the sweet sensation passed down his throat, he uttered a happy cry.

"See? He likes it. He knows about peanut-butter sandwiches, John."

"Must be a rare raven that doesn't," John replied. "They're always looking for handouts."

Zack had been watching this from the safety of a nearby spruce. He called out to Colin. "You're taking your chances with those two!"

"I know these humans. They're safe. Want some sandwich? Peanut butter?"

Zack licked the edges of his bill. He, too, had gone for a long time without the pleasure of eating human food. He put aside his fear and glided down to the snow, but stayed well away from Colin and the humans. "Molly wouldn't approve," he said, looking around warily, wings extended.

John glanced at Linda, who was tearing her own sandwich into small bites for the ravens. "Save some of that sandwich for yourself," he advised. "It's a long way back to the car."

"Oh, it's all downhill. Besides, I've got another sandwich."

"You packed *two* sandwiches?"

"Sure. It was supposed to be cold today, remember? Extra energy. Only the chinook hit, so . . ." She reached out toward Colin, who was standing an arm's length away. He took the bite from her hand.

"Hey, all right!" John was impressed. "He ate from your hand!"

"Sure. He knows me. We're friends."

"What about that other raven?"

"Don't know that one. Its eyes are different."

"Its *eyes* are different?"

"Yeah. Look at it. Its eyes are different."

John shook his head. As he did, a small gray bird that was preparing to land on his cap fluttered aside.

"Perry!" Both Colin and Zack called the name together.

"Hi, guys." Perry, the gray jay, alighted on the snow next to Colin. "Pretty good eats?" he asked.

"Really good. These humans – I know them. They're climbers from Yamnuska."

"Best kind of humans," Perry said, eyeing John.

John was looking around and laughing. "It's bird city around here!"

Linda was laughing, too. "Oh, John! You looked so funny when that other bird tried to sit on your head! Ha, ha, ha!"

"It's a gray jay. Now *there's* a bold bird for you. Watch this." John balanced a small piece of crust on top of his cap. Perry, living up to the reputation of his species, completed his original landing, grabbed the crust and flew off into the trees.

"So much for us getting any more food," Zack said glumly. "Perry will have it all."

"Oh, I've had plenty," Colin said.

"Well, I haven't," Zack replied testily.

"Here, you are, Mister Scaredy-Raven," Linda said, tossing a sandwich bite at Zack's feet.

"See? These are terrific humans." Colin said. "They knew you were wanting more, so they gave it to you."

"You may be right," Zack said, gobbling down the bite, "but I'm sure glad Molly isn't here to see this." Linda threw him another crust.

Perry came back, having hidden his prize. He hopped right over to the humans and flew up onto one of their ski poles. "Here I am," he said, as if to the humans but really to Zack and Colin. "Look at me. I'm so *cute.*" He blinked his big eyes at the skiers.

"Aw," Linda said, "he's so cute!" She offered him another bite.

Colin and Zack cracked up. "Craw-ha! Perry, you're the greatest! Craw-ha-ha!"

Linda and John closed up their packs. They put their skis back on.

"Nuts. They're going to leave," Perry said. He wiped his bill on a fallen twig. "Believe I'll nip home now. My mate and I are set up down by the highway, at the Park gate. Good spot. Humans throw stuff out of their cars there."

John and Linda started back the way they had come. They took long strides and coasted gracefully with each step along the trail they had broken in the snow. "Yee-ha!" John whooped. "Downhill all the way to the road!"

Colin was puzzled. "Now that's odd. They were breathing hard coming this way, taking little short steps, going really slowly. But now they're sort of *running* on those ski feet."

"Yeah," Zack said. "That *is* odd. All of a sudden they're going a lot faster."

"Maybe they feel stronger since they had something to eat." Colin spread his wings, preparing to catch the wind and ride it the rest of the way home.

"Must be it," said Zack, doing the same.

XXVIII

Back at Carrot Creek, the rest of the Raven's End Flock was relishing the weather in more traditional fashion: alternately eating sheep meat and sitting in the sun. The wolves had gone elsewhere that afternoon, so the birds had the carcass to themselves.

"I can't believe I almost died last night." Sarah swallowed another bite of bighorn.

"It was very close, dear," Marg said. "You've had your share of scrapes, what with that thing over in the Bow Valley last fall. Let's hope there won't be any more."

"I'm going to be, like, super-careful from now on. If it gets cold again, let's roost right up next to the trunk."

"Now, that's a good idea. There's always a bit of warmth in the trunk."

"What are you two birds discussing so earnestly over here?"

"Oh, hello, Greta. Sarah and I were reminding ourselves that a bird has to be very careful of the winter cold. We were thinking of ways to survive."

Greta looked up at the sky. "I hate to say this, but I think it's going to get cold again."

"What?!" Sarah shivered and fluffed up her feathers.

"Not right away, kiddo. We'll have this chinook for another night anyway. Then it will snow, most likely. Then another cold snap and another chinook. Storm, cold snap, chinook. That's the pattern. Better get used to it."

Greta was right. After a few days the chinook breeze faded and the sky clouded over from the west. The same dim grayness that had brought the first snowstorm now brought the next. Again the birds took to their roost, and they sheltered under its friendly boughs as the snow sifted out of the sky and piled up all around. It snowed for a day and a night – not as much as the previous storm – but this snowfall ended with a flourish of wind at dawn, driving snow into the deepest, most protected roosting spots on the Douglas-fir.

Still, the cold spell that followed didn't seem as bad as the one before. Perhaps the birds were better prepared for it physically – they certainly had been eating a lot over the last few days – or maybe they were better prepared for it mentally, resigned to the worst and pleased to find the next Arctic air mass easier to bear than the first.

Wheedle had his own way of putting it, as he and Scratch roosted with Colin one evening.

"He who expects nothing will not be disappointed." Wheedle smiled wanly. "It's the perfect philosophy for a runt like me."

Scratch snuggled up a little closer to his friend. "Aw, Wheedle, yer not jest a runt. Yer also a bum."

All three birds laughed.

"Have you two always been with the Raven's End Flock?" Colin asked.

Scratch replied first. "Nope. Not us. We been all over. Been at Raven's End a couple years now. I think. Right, Wheedle?"

"Must be. Let's see. Yes, indeed. A little over two years."

"Where did you come from?"

"Well, I met Scratch up in Yellowknife." Wheedle looked over to Scratch. "Remember that? You were on a dead bear at the dump. All by yourself. Remember?"

"Uh – yeah. Yeah, that was it. Dead bear."

"Then we bummed south after that, across Great Slave Lake, down through Pine Point. Charming dump there in Pine Point –"

"Real great dump," Scratch agreed, his eyes closing a little as he remembered.

"And on across the Caribou Mountains, through the human camps there and on to the Peace River –"

"Oh, *bird*, Colin," Scratch interrupted again. "You shoulda *seen* that river! Never seen so many fish in my life. Why, you jest land at the edge and the fish'd flop up right there and die fer you. Rot down right on the spot, so eager to please."

Wheedle continued. "Then we drifted over to the Swan Hills. Very messy humans in the Swan Hills. They threw out more good food –"

"Lotta good food –"

"And then we kind of blundered into the Rockies, didn't we?"

"*You* blundered into the Rockies," Scratch said vehemently, prodding Wheedle with his bill. "I was all fer goin' on east ta them big grain fields in Saskatchewan."

"Aw, we'd never have made it. You were headed the wrong direction."

"Now, wait just a maggoty minute, Mister Migrator! I figgered ta hit the coast first, like, and get in on some a' them salmon runs, see, but –"

"Scratch, you were headed the wrong direction for that, too."

"Well, I woulda got it straightened out iffen you hadn't a' messed with that nasty li'l weasel there in Grande Cache."

"True enough," Wheedle sighed. "Losing one's leg does rather slow a bird down."

"Slowed us down! Cost us a whole winter!"

"Well, anyway, we were forced to lay over in Grande Cache for the cold weather, living on next to nothing until I healed up – a very thin winter, it really was – then we started south again in the spring, and –"

"But I was gonna stay, like," Scratch interjected. He sounded wistful.

"Oh, yes. That's right. You met that What's-her-name up there."

"Marguerite. Her name was *Marguerite*, eh? Whatta chick! I mean, Colin, if you coulda *seen* this bird. My, my, my!"

Colin chuckled. "What happened?"

"Oh, things kinda fell apart in the clinch, like." Scratch looked down.

"What he's trying to say," said Wheedle, "is that he gave her the mites and she threw him out."

"Now, that ain't it at all, you scandal-monger –"

"And then her regular nestmate came home –"

"That's more like it."

"And we had to leave in a hurry."

Scratch and Wheedle recounted their adventures in flying south along the Rockies. They had stopped at Jasper and found some ravens there, then soared over the huge white expanse of the Columbia Icefield, finally arriving at Yamnuska in the fall and joining the flock.

"Best Tree-blessed buncha birds you'll ever meet, Colin," Scratch said wholeheartedly, "but you knows that anyways."

"Yes, I certainly do," Colin replied.

"May never travel again," Scratch added. "Gettin' too old."

"*You're* too old?" Wheedle mocked. "What about Greta, who goes away for days and days at a time, and she's about as old as this tree we're perched in!"

"Fer sure, my irritatin' friend," Scratch replied. "She's so old she prob'ly died ten years ago an' never realized it." Then his voice changed tone, becoming reverent. "But I guess she's a big part a' the reason we hang around here. Wouldn'tcha say, Wheed?"

"As good a reason as any," Wheedle continued. "I've never known a bird like Greta. The Raven's End Flock just couldn't live without Greta."

"You can say that again," came a voice from nowhere. Colin recognized it immediately as the voice he had heard in the canyon. "Did you hear that?" he said.

"Hear what?" Wheedle looked about nervously. "I didn't hear anything."

"Oh, I guess I didn't either," Colin said. This time he wasn't going to let on. He had an idea. "Or maybe it was one of the wolves howling."

"Sure," Scratch offered, trying to reassure Wheedle. "Prob'ly jest one a' them wolves."

"Maybe I'd better check on it," Colin continued.

"Say what? Check on it? This time a' night?" By now it had grown quite dark.

"Oh, just for a minute. Just curious. Heh – you know me, right?"

"That's fer darn tootin'. If there's somethin' goin' on, you're gonna be right there, Colin C.C."

"So don't wait up for me. I'll be back when I'm back."

Wheedle caught the odd look in Colin's eye and it worried him. "Take care, Colin," he said.

"Don't worry about me, you two." Colin jumped off the branch and glided away into the darkness.

XXIX

Colin was getting angry. It had a lot of nerve, this voice, listening in on his conversations and interrupting like that. And at night, too. He flew petulantly down the canyon and around a corner, landing in an alcove on the wall.

"*Awk!*" He leapt up again. Something soft and feathery was under his feet!

"*Awk!*" It squawked back at him, and he realized from the tone of the squawk that it was Greta.

"Greta! What are you doing here?!"

"Coyotes and foxes, Colin, you sure know how to frighten a bird!"

"I'm sorry, Greta. I really didn't know you were here."

"Apology accepted. Barely."

"But now that I've found you," Colin continued quickly, "listen to this. That voice just spoke to me again. Right there on the roost. I was talking with Scratch and Wheedle, hearing their stories, really enjoying them, and along came that voice, messing everything up."

"Looks like now *I* have to apologize," said the voice.

"There! There it is again!"

"And trying to be polite, too," Greta said.

"Hey! So you *can* hear it!"

"Of course. But only when it's really close." She shook her head, trying to wake up. This was going to demand some attention.

Colin spoke directly to the voice. "I've got to get something straight. Greta can hear you. I can hear you. But no one else can hear you. Why is that?"

"Well," said the voice, "I was about to explain that the last time we talked, but it didn't work out that way. And I've been meaning to get back to you ever since. But things have been rather hectic and I just haven't had a chance to look you up again until this evening. So here goes." The voice paused. "Uh, wait. Greta?"

"Yes?"

"Does this bird know about the second-sight thing, and so on?"

"He knows he has second-sight, yes. I told him last fall."

"Okay. Now, Colin –"

"I'm listening."

"Colin, some ravens have second-sight and some don't. Those who do can hear me, and those who don't, can't. It's as simple as that."

"Do you mean to say that when I get these weird dreams about . . . about avalanches and mountains with feathers and all this kind of stuff, that you've been giving them to me?"

"Well, yes and no. Okay, the 'mountain with feathers' thing could very well be from one of my own dreams. I dream about that a lot. And sometimes I talk in my sleep. The other thing, the avalanche thing, that was strictly your own second-sight working."

"He had another one," Greta offered. "A terrific one. He found an injured raven under the snow. Sarah – do you know of her?"

"Oh, the Raven's Ender who got caught in the storm last fall? Spent the night in a snowdrift and survived?"

"Right. It was Colin who found her, and he did it by second-sight."

"Very good, Colin. That's really extraordinary. You certainly saved her life, and you can be proud of that."

Colin hadn't thought about the incident for a long time. He hadn't been terribly proud at the time, just sore and tired. Now, though, he smiled to himself and fluffed out his neck-feathers.

"Let's not get *too* proud," Greta admonished. Colin's feathers dropped back.

"Absolutely right," the voice said. "Be humble, Colin, as befits a bird with your gift."

Yes, of course, Colin thought, as the image of the over-proud Dolus came to mind.

"Speaking of Dolus –"

"What? You can hear what I'm *thinking?!*" This was too much.

"Well, no. I can't *hear* what you're thinking. I just sort of *know* what you're thinking."

"But that's not fair! My thoughts are for me only!"

"As well they should be, so I never pry. I'm talking with you now, so I'm just catching a little of what you're going to say before you say it."

"Greta," Colin pleaded, looking at her desperately, "*what is this voice?!* I've simply got to know. Right now. While you're here, and while it's here." He turned away from Greta, facing out from the alcove and croaking loudly into the night. "I can't stand this! Whoever you are, you're driving me crazy! Please, please, tell me what in the name of the Trees is going on!"

Colin's shouts echoed down the canyon. He sat sullenly as the sound died away.

Finally the voice replied. It was a question, spoken as a statement. "You want to know who I am."

Colin's reply was calm and firm. "Yes. I want to know who you are. I really do."

"Should I tell him, Greta?"

"Well . . . I think, maybe . . . yes. He's coming along very quickly. Best I've seen. It might just keep the whole act airborne and out of trouble if you answered that question directly."

"Okay, Colin. You wanted to know."

Colin leaned forward. He could feel his heart speeding up in anticipation. But nothing could have prepared him for what he was about to hear.

"Colin, I'm the Great Raven."

PART FOUR

Spring

I

It was the Flap, and from all indications it was not going to be very interesting. The Flaps had been boring lately, as had life generally. A number of weeks had passed, during which the cycle of storm, cold snap, and chinook had repeated several times. A kind of gray monotony had set in. Day in, day out, the ravens followed the wolves up and down Carrot Creek, sharing their kills. There were no further surprises in the season, which was comforting in one way – survival seemed assured – but in another way, it was, well, dull.

"Gro, my friends," the Main Raven began, "I'd like to take this occasion to achieve an important consensus." He looked around at the indifferent expressions of the flock. "Greta informs me that she has been thinking of moving back to Raven's End."

"Raven's End? Yay!" Sarah blurted out. She had been away from Yamnuska for so long that she had stopped thinking about it. Now she felt a pleasant burst of excitement – as did the other birds. Several of them croaked their approval.

The Main Raven wasn't finished with his opening statement. "I'd like you to consider this idea individually. Then, after everyone has made up his or her mind, I will ask for the feeling of the flock."

"What's to feel? Let's go!" Brendan could hardly contain himself.

The Main Raven spoke to him sharply. "Brendan C.C., this requires a consensus. We will all 'feel' about this issue *together*, if you don't mind."

"Sorry, sir."

"Now, then. Greta, perhaps you could explain."

"Oh, there's not much to explain," the old raven replied. "We've been here for a good long while, and the wolves have moved on."

"The wolves are gone?!" Sarah's eyes were widening.

"Yes. Colin saw them at dawn. They went right by our roosting tree. Didn't anyone else notice?"

The birds looked at one another. No one said anything.

Greta continued. "Anyway, Colin followed them up Carrot Creek. They were moving right along, obviously going somewhere. And if I know wolves at all, they're headed over the pass to the Ghost River. Now, there's no game over there right now – I just happened to take a peek a couple of days ago – so that means they'll keep going. Probably south, over Exshaw Pass and around the corner toward Yamnuska. And the elk are headed back there, too. Do it every year about this time. It's been quite a while since that herd had any trouble with wolves, so they're going to be dumb about our fanged friends, so if I were a wolf –"

"You'd go right to Yamnuska!" Brendan interrupted. Greta looked at the Main Raven, who was about to give Brendan a scolding for interrupting her yet again. She winked and spoke quickly, before the Main Raven could. "Yup. I'd go right to Yamnuska."

Sarah spoke next. "I'd really, *really* like to go back to Yamnuska," she said dreamily. "We had such a cool time there. It's been so long . . . I can hardly remember."

"Oh, I can remember fine," Brendan said. "We'll all get back our old roosts on the South Face, and we'll have the Flaps and Flights at Raven's End, okay, and Maya will give us the news every morning, and it'll be really excellent, and –"

"And you'll keep babbling away like a jerk," Dolus said.

"Hey, it's his job!" Garth added.

"Better a babbling jerk than a bully, Dolus." Sarah's eyebrow tufts were up. "You're just totally obnoxious, you know that? Why don't you just stay here and the rest of us will go back to Yamnuska. Without *you*."

"Please, please," interjected the Main Raven. "Let us not waste our time on negative matters. It would seem that many flock members wish to leave Carrot Creek and return to Raven's End. But, as is customary, we shall take the sense of the meeting first." He paused, glancing about the group. "We already know what Brendan thinks, and Sarah. Several others of you have spoken, but so quickly that I had trouble registering your opinions. So let us inquire individually, starting with Dolus."

Dolus looked away as he spoke. "I'll go back. This place stinks. I'm bored out of my mind."

"Me, too," Garth said. "I say we leave." He fluffed out his neck-feathers. "There's more interesting stuff to do back at Yamnuska, especially with Zy –"

"Shut up," Dolus said, digging his claws into Garth's foot.

The Main Raven turned to Marg.

"Hi, everyone. Well, I've really enjoyed our stay here, aside from the, uh, unfortunate accident after the big storm" – her eyes fell as she thought of Cathy – "but, as Greta says, we'd better move on. In the interests of the flock. I'm definitely in favor of that."

"Scratch?"

"Oh, what the hey – no wolves equals no eats. 'Bout time ta blow this here camp." He looked at Wheedle. "How 'bout it? Shall we give 'er on back ta Yam?"

"I could not have put it any more eloquently," Wheedle responded. "Colin?"

"Sure. With the wind behind us it won't be a long flight."

"Zack?"

"Yeah, it's time to go," he said. "Nesting season is getting close, and I'd hate to nest anywhere but up on Yamnuska." He looked at Molly and smiled a gap-billed raven smile.

"Oh, Zack," she said, "you big handsome C.C. Let's go back to Raven's End." She giggled.

The Main Raven summed up. "It's unanimous," he declared. "And I suspect that everyone will want to be off directly. May we have the Motion?"

The birds formed their circle. For the first time in many days, there was eagerness in the wheel of wings, and when the flock call came – "Rawk-a-taw!" – it carried a fine feeling of newness, of beginning again.

II

True enough, Zack thought as he coasted over Carrot Creek Pass, Colin was right. The return trip was a lot easier. Pushed toward Yamnuska by a brisk northwest wind, the birds had only to enter the flow and stay airborne in it. They flew in ragged formation, crossing paths, swooping up and zooming down, stalling and then flapping hard to regain airspeed, barrel-rolling off to right and left, chasing and calling to one another raucously. Like all flocks of ravens on the wing, the Raven's Enders were a travelling circus.

Soon Colin had spotted Mount Fable. Taller than the surrounding peaks, its keel-shaped summit ridge was unmistakable. "There's Fable!" he croaked happily. "Just one more ridge to Goat Buttress – and then Yamnuska!"

"By the Trees! We're going to be there in time for lunch!" Zack called.

"If there's any lunch to be had," Molly said. "What if the wolves haven't killed anything? What if they haven't even arrived?"

Zack was reassuring. "Oh, I wouldn't worry so much, Molly. It's been an easy flight. I'm not even hungry. Anyway, everybody is so fat after all that sheep meat and moose meat in the last while – heck, I could easily do a full day without anything to eat at all."

Molly brightened. "Me too, I suppose."

"Whoopee!" Sarah called, catching the updraft on the west side of Mount Fable. She skipped over the summit ridge, a razor-edge of limestone so narrow that human climbers had to straddle it. The wind had swept all the snow from the ridge, exposing the gray rock. Orange, yellow, and white splotches decorated the rock: colonies of lichens.

"Here come the birds!" said a yellow lichen colony to a neighboring orange one.

"Hey, all right! Let's hope one of them poops!" said the orange one.

"You *Xanthoria* types are such a bunch of nitrogen addicts," said a white colony. "It's disgusting."

"Manna from heaven," came the reply from the orange group. "If it weren't for the birds, we couldn't live here at all."

"Yeah – and there'd be more room for us," said the whites.

"For you? You've practically got the whole ridge as it is!"

"So what? White is a better color than orange. We deserve more than you."

"You think white is pretty?" said a yellow colony. "Hey, listen. White is the color of that bird poop you were knocking a moment ago."

"You tell 'em, guys," said the orange colony. "That white crowd has been trying to take over for about twenty years now. They grew right through Jack and Ellie's patch last summer. No manners at all."

"Aw, come on, everyone. Just because we're more *successful* than the rest of you –"

"More ruthless, you mean," retorted the oranges. "Haven't you ever heard of ecology? Live and let live!"

"Ecology is for wimps. We believe in survival of the fittest."

"Well, see if you get any help from us next time you've got substrate trouble."

"Gee, that's true," said the yellow colony. "The oranges, there – they make the best surface you ever saw. And then they leave it for somebody else."

"We do our bit," added the oranges. Then, "Heads up, everyone!"

Whop! Something splattered over the orange lichens.

"We eat! We eat!" The oranges were ecstatic. "Hey, thanks, raven! Thanks a lot!"

"My pleasure," said Greta, looking back. She made a point of unloading on the orange lichens as often as she could. She knew they appreciated it.

III

Yamnuska! The Raven's Enders could see it now. They began to hurry, and as the South Face came into view, they rushed happily toward home. Soon they were at the west end of their beloved mountain. As they flew beside the South Face it gained in size and sheerness, rising from a low cliff to a great precipice – one of the grand sights of the Canadian Rockies. Creatures afraid of heights would look at the South Face of Yamnuska and shiver. But to the Raven's End ravens it offered food, shelter, updrafts – all the necessities of life.

The sun stood due south, marking mid-day. It had some warmth to give now, in the season of the vernal equinox, and the South Face took the rays broadside. Snow still covered the bigger ledges, but it was melting away rapidly. Water ran down from each patch, making black streaks on the ancient limestone. The rock was gray where it was merely vertical, buff where it was overhanging. There was a lot of buff limestone on the South Face of Yamnuska.

"Oh, Mum, look! There's our old roost!"

"Sarah, you have such a good memory."

"Can we, like, land there right now?"

"Why not? Uh – I'd better go first, though, dear, just to see that it's safe." Marg landed on a boulder wedged into a shadowy crack on the face. "Ah, that's a relief. I was worried that something might have claimed our roost. But nothing has."

Sarah landed beside Marg and danced about on the boulder. "Oh, hey! We're really, really home! Oh, I feel so good!"

Brendan showed up. "This roost is awesome," he said, admiring the location.

"Oh, thank you, Brendan." Marg fluffed out her neck-feathers. She had discovered this roost a few years ago.

"Could I, like, could I . . ." Brendan was trying to say something, but it wouldn't come out.

Marg prompted him. "What is it, Brendan?"

He said it quickly – "Could I roost here too, sometimes?" – and looked away as if embarrassed.

"Well, I don't see why not," said Marg. She often invited other birds to roost with her. Then she realized why Brendan was asking. "Oh, Brendan. It's because of Sarah, isn't it?"

"Um, not really." He looked at Sarah sideways. "Well, okay, it would be cool to roost with Sarah" – he scratched the boulder with his foot – "but really, I'd just kind of like to roost with you two, that's all."

"Now, come on, Brendan." She looked over to Sarah, who was smiling. "I know what's on your mind. It's spring, that's what it is, and you're thinking about nesting."

The two young birds giggled.

"Oh, Mum," said Sarah.

"Oh, Marg," said Brendan.

"Oh, my," said Marg. "Nesting. Already."

Brendan looked at Sarah and caught her eye. She looked away. Then Brendan fluffed out his neck-feathers, called "*rawk!*" in the way that means "catch me if you can!" and leapt off the boulder. Sarah jumped after him. Marg started to follow, then realized that this game wasn't meant for her. It was the oldest game in the world, and only two ravens at a time could play.

IV

Farther along the South Face, Molly and Zack came to Raven's End.

"Ah, Molly, here we are. Home, sweet home. Welcome back."

"Zack, I'm so happy to be here again – and to still have you."

The two birds flew into their roosting alcove, with its flat ledge. The sun was hitting the alcove squarely. The rock under their feet felt warm.

"Zack, it's spring."

"I know, Molly."

"Do you still love me, Zack?"

"Just as much as ever, Molly. More."

"Oh, Zack." She snuggled beside him.

Zack looked over to one wall of the alcove and spotted a beetle crawling on it. This was the first insect either had seen in months. Zack grabbed it in his bill. The beetle flailed its six legs. "For you, Molly."

"Oh, Zack. The first bug of the year? For me?"

"For you."

She crouched and fluttered her wings like a fledgling being fed. Zack dropped the beetle into her open bill. She accepted it tenderly. Then she passed it back to him. "Oh, Zack. I couldn't. Here – you have it."

Zack took the beetle back. He squashed it a little in his bill. Then he passed it back to Molly. "No, Molly, this is *your* beetle. Here. I've fixed it up for you. Enjoy it now."

Molly took the beetle back, the legs no longer flailing. She crushed it and rolled the blob around on her tongue, tasting the salty beetle juice. "It's *good*, Zack. Oh, it's *so good!*"

"Only the best for my Moll."

"Shall we nest this year, Zack?"

"Yes. I want to try again. Last year I failed –"

"Now, don't blame yourself. You couldn't have known about the crows coming. Everything else was perfect. We had that nice deep crack way up on the South Face, and such a good overhang to keep the rain off – how were we to know the crows would be so quick?"

"True enough, Molly. Now we know how sneaky they are. This year I won't let 'em get anywhere near."

"Oh, Zack, if they come around we'll peck them so hard!"

"You bet, Molly. By the Trees, I can hardly wait! Take that, egg-stealer!" Zack pecked fiercely at the air. He looked toward Molly and smiled. She smiled back, her eyes radiant. "Zack, there's no better bird in the world than you."

"Aw, Molly," said Zack.

V

"It's Maya!" shouted one of the ravens.

There she was, sitting in her usual place atop the tallest tree at Raven's End. Maya, the Townsend's solitaire, had been waiting for the upcoming Flap. How did she know the flock was back? Gatherer of the news, she had her methods.

"Good morning, Maya," said the Main Raven. "How nice to see you again." It was a fine morning for the Flap. Only a little frost had formed overnight, and the day was opening clear and warm.

Maya replied with her characteristic one-note call, wistful and somewhat sad. "Morn," she said. That was all she ever said before beginning her report – although she made a point of saying it several times.

The other ravens arrived. They alighted noisily on the old familiar spot, the site of countless Flaps. Settling down on the limestone scree with much wing-stretching and croaking, the ravens were in a jolly frame of mind.

"Oh, this is wonderful," Marg said as she arrived. She looked about at the faces of her friends in the flock and spoke loudly. "I'm so happy. What a terrific bunch of birds. And we're all back together again at Raven's End."

Colin was studying his surroundings. He still couldn't remember anything of his distant past, but he could certainly remember this place well enough. Here was the low gray cliff that marked the easternmost point of Yamnuska. Here were the boulders scattered about where they had fallen. Here were the straggly, prickly spruces and juniper bushes growing in the rubble, along with a few soft-needled subalpine firs and a couple of aspens. Here was the human trail beaten through it all, coming along the pine-covered whaleback ridge that bumped into Yamnuska from the east.

To the north, Colin let his eyes run over the valley behind Yamnuska, where he had spent so many days exploring the cliffs. There were the familiar landmarks: Frodo Buttress, Bilbo Buttress, the Runes, Wakonda Buttress. He knew every crag and corner of that scenery. To the south lay the Bow Valley, a flat-floored mosaic of meadow and forest, patterned with the dark green of conifers and the smoke-like gray of leafless aspen. The patches of white, Colin knew, marked ice-covered ponds that still held snow while everything else was bare, swept clean by the most recent chinook. He could see that the Bow River had thawed. It ran clear and blue-black between wide banks of thick white river ice.

Colin looked westward, toward the mountain front. Along that mighty ridge, still heavily laden with snow, the layers and ledges and cliffs stood out gray against white. Above, the sky was the cloudless, robin's-egg blue of a fine Canadian Rockies morning. So much to see; so much to love. Colin closed his eyes. He opened them as the Main Raven called the meeting to order. "Gro," Colin replied, along with the other birds.

"As you can see," the Main Raven continued, "we have the pleasure of Maya's company this morning. She has been waiting patiently to give us her report. If you will grant her *all* your attention, I'm sure that she is ready to begin. Maya?"

The solitaire said "morn" once more, then she began her loud, trilling, warbling song.

"In the news this morning – a late-season avalanche claims two – wolves reported in the valley for the first time all winter – and the Raven's End ravens return."

Several birds croaked and fluffed out their neck-feathers at this last item.

"At the top of the news – the weather – spring is fast approaching, with mild overnight temperatures again – ice on the Bow River broke up yesterday afternoon – at only ten days past the equinox, this may be the earliest break-up in many years" – Maya stopped for a breath – "however, snow accumulations are above average, as indicated by an avalanche in the northwest gully of Yamnuska yesterday – many trees were brought down, and two mountain goats were reported lost in the slide – a pack of wolves entered the valley behind Yamnuska yesterday, and speculation is that they were wintering in the Carrot Creek area –"

"Hey, yeah! That's right! We saw 'em a lot! Oops." Brendan was shushed by the Main Raven.

Maya continued as if nothing had happened, "– with the Raven's End ravens, who returned to Yamnuska yesterday –"

At this point Brendan couldn't restrain himself, and neither could anyone else. Even the Main Raven croaked out his pleasure at making the news. "Hear hear!"

"Yay!"

"Right on!"

"We're back! We're back!"

"Hey, hey!"

Maya stopped, blinked, looked down at the cacophony below her and waited for it to subside, sounding a couple of "morn"s to pass the time. Eventually the Main Raven restored order. Maya finished as quickly as she could, in a blur of burbly song.

"In addition to the ravens, crows have been seen on migration in the Yamnuska area – gophers at Morley Flats are ending their annual hibernation – now to the forecast – light easterly winds in the morning, changing to southerly in the afternoon – little chance of precipitation overnight – expect another warm day tomorrow – and that's the news."

As always, Maya finished with several single-note calls. And, as always, she didn't expect any thank-you for her report. But today she got one. "Thanks, Maya," Colin said.

"Yes, Maya. Thanks," Marg added, smiling first at Maya, then at Colin.

"Hey!" Scratch yelled. "Did you birds hear that bit about the gophers?" He was jumping around excitedly. "Hey, let's us go on down ta Morley Flats, there, an' see if there's any comin' out beside the highway, like."

"Count me in," said Wheedle. "Nothing quite so much fun as watching rodents commit suicide."

Suicide? Colin wondered what this was all about.

"Let's get a move on," Scratch said. "If them gophers is doin' their thing, there's gonna be lots fer us ta scoop up." He stretched his wings, preparing to jump into the air. Other ravens did the same.

But the Main Raven reminded everyone that the Flap was not over. "I gather it is agreed that we shall make our way to the highway this lovely morning," he said, his neck-feathers glinting, "and in order to expedite matters I suggest that we bring the Flap to a close with the first Motion we have made at Raven's End in some time. May we have a Motion?"

"Motion!"

"Yeah, Motion! Yeah!"

The birds hopped toward one another. They were in a hurry to be off, and the resulting circle looked rougher than usual. But the "Rawk-a-taw!" that went out to the world had its usual boisterous, life-affirming quality.

Soon after the birds had left, a small animal arrived at the site of the Flap. Long and skinny, it came slinking from boulder to boulder, poking its nose out, then sitting up and looking carefully around before going back on all fours to run under the next rock. It was mostly white, but a tinge of new brown fur showed through.

"Oh, no," said Optimistic Molt, the weasel. "Those ravens. Those awful ravens have come back to Weasel's End."

VI

Flying to Morley Flats was Scratch's idea, so he led the way. A special sense of fun rippled through the flock that morning, for most of them knew exactly what they were soon going to see and do. Colin, who didn't, caught the spirit nonetheless and chased Zack across the sky. Zack was a fine flyer, but Colin caught him easily.

"Okay! Okay!" Zack yelled, laughing and panting. "I give up, O Lord of the Sky! Come peck my eyes out, O Conqueror! I'm at your mercy!" When Colin approached for the customary victory peck, though, Zack grabbed Colin's feet. "Aha! Fell for it! Oldest trick in the airways! Now you die, infidel! *Rawk!*"

The two birds tumbled downward. Zack laughed uproariously. "Craw-ha! First one to let go is a coyote turd!"

"Craw-ha!"

Soon they reached their destination: the Trans-Canada Highway. Cars and trucks passed smoothly below the birds, one after another, their motors droning. The odor of gasoline and diesel fumes rose to the flock as they peered down.

"Pee-*yoo!*" Sarah said to no one in particular. "Do we really have to hang around here?"

"Gophers are up and at 'em!" Scratch was looking at several dark spots on the pavement.

"Right you are," Wheedle said. "Breakfast is about to create itself."
He landed on a fence post beside the road. The other birds joined him
on neighboring posts, sitting in a row. "Now all we have to do is wait,"
he said, yawning.

They didn't have to wait long. A yellowish-brown rodent appeared
in the matted, salt-encrusted grass on the road shoulder. It sat on its
haunches, straight as a survey stake, tail twitching. Seeing the ravens,
it ducked down. But soon it was upright again, looking out into the
traffic. Its tail twitched faster.

"Oh, here we go," Wheedle said. "That gopher is about to take up
the challenge."

"Ground squirrel, not gopher," Greta said. She had just arrived.
"Richardson's ground squirrel. Everybody calls them gophers by
mistake. Haven't got any real gophers here. They're all ground squirrels."
She wheezed a couple of times and settled on the fence beside Sarah
and Brendan.

"Like, what's gonna happen?" Sarah asked.

"Aw, Garth told me all about it," Brendan replied. "They run across
and get squashed, okay? Then we eat 'em. Way too fresh, but they say
it's not too bad. I'm so hungry I could eat just about anything right
now." He looked intently across the road surface. "Hey! There's something red out there!"

Just as he started to unfurl his wings, Greta spoke quickly and
emphatically. "Now listen to me, you young 'uns. Stay put on this fence
until you see how it's done. I won't have you joining the flattened folks
out there on the pavement." She looked Sarah right in the eye, then
Brendan. "You hear me?"

"Yes, ma'am."

"Yes'm."

"Good. Now pay attention."

The ground squirrel that had been sitting on the road shoulder was
now at the edge of the pavement. Down on all fours, it nervously
sniffed the hard surface, moving forward and back, its tail flipping up
and down with every step. Little by little, it was moving closer to the
stream of cars and trucks.

Dolus and Garth were perched nearby. They started calling to the ground squirrel.

"Go for it, you little jerk! We're hungry!"

"Yeah, like, what are you waiting for? Get it over with!"

The ground squirrel was now so close to the traffic that its fur whipped about in the wind from every passing vehicle. One anxious step at a time, it inched out to the white line marking the edge of the driving lane.

"Dangerous territory across that line, old chap," called Wheedle. "But very appealing, I'm sure. We'll not detain you. Go ahead, then."

Colin watched with grisly fascination. He couldn't believe what he was seeing. Surely this animal realized what would happen if – *screech!* A yellow car swerved around the ground squirrel. The squirrel jumped back a few steps. It sat bolt upright on the white line, its tail continuing to twitch up and down. Its eyes, set high on its head to give it a good view of the sky, blinked. Colin reasoned that, as far as a ground squirrel was concerned, the sky contained mainly hawks. The ground contained mainly coyotes. Cars were probably not on the program.

"I can't stand to watch this," Marg said.

Molly sighed. "Me neither. But we'll both soon be enjoying the results."

"I know, I know. Yuck anyway."

The squirrel edged out over the white line again. This time it moved more confidently. A long gap in traffic allowed it to get well into the lane – almost to the centre – before the next car came along. A big black one, it passed right over the squirrel.

"Score!" Wheedle said happily. Then he realized that the auto had failed to kill. The squirrel had been right in its path, between the right and left sets of wheels, and all had tracked past harmlessly. "Oh. Missed."

"Lucky critter, that there one," said Scratch. "But not so lucky next time. Look – big ol' truck comin'. Gonna get him, sure."

The squirrel had its nose to the pavement again, sniffing about on a stain that may have been one of its kin a few days before. It was not anticipating the truck.

"All *riiight!!*" said Dolus, as the big wheels rolled over the squirrel.

"That took guts! Craw-ha!" said Garth.

The squirrel squirmed on the pavement, mortally injured, its hindquarters flattened. But its front end hadn't been struck, until a moment later a car came along and finished the animal off. The red lump that remained looked nothing like a Richardson's ground squirrel.

"Can we, like, get it now, Greta?" asked Brendan.

"No," she replied. "Wait for one of the older birds."

Scratch was already on his way. He flopped off the fence and strode up to the edge of the highway. As the other birds watched, he looked carefully in both directions and hopped out into the road. Clearly, the ritual of the Lead was not required – or desirable – in this situation. He stood over the dead squirrel, then looked both ways again before he reached downward with his bill. Part of the squirrel came away, leaving most of its insides, and Scratch picked up as much as he could. He looked up to see another truck bearing down. With only a second or two remaining before the truck reached him, he hopped neatly off the pavement and onto the shoulder. The truck howled through, ruffling his feathers, but Scratch paid no attention. He knew he was safe there. He began to eat.

"Wow!" Sarah said admiringly. "That Scratch really knows what he's doing!"

"Indeed he does, kiddo," Greta said, "and you don't yet, so keep clear."

Brendan hopped down to the ground. "That goes for you, too, Brendan," Greta called sharply.

"I'm just gonna see if Scratch will share a bit, that's all," he replied. "Hey, Scratch . . ."

Several other birds were also moving toward Scratch. It looked like a game of grab-the-meat was about to begin, but Scratch would have none of it. He placed his foot firmly over the squirrel. "Now I don't mind a bit a' fun with you guys, most days," he said in a low voice, "but by the Trees, this here's mine." He clacked his bill menacingly. Even Wheedle backed off.

Zack looked out over the pavement. "I can appreciate that, Scratch," he said. "I'll get one of my own."

Sure enough, another squirrel was nosing about on the opposite side of the road. This one didn't last long. As the birds watched, a car killed it instantly. Zack was on the victim very quickly. The body was too big to fly away with, but he managed to drag it off the highway whole. Molly fluttered over to join him.

Brendan looked over to Greta imploringly. "Okay, so what about me? When do I – when do Sarah and me get to eat?"

"You'll have to get some from another bird," she said. "And so will I. Gave up playing in traffic a few years ago." She got Zack's attention. "Spare some of that thing for two youngsters and one oldster?"

"Sure, C.C.s. Get over here."

Garth and Dolus, meanwhile, had found the remains of a squirrel that had died on the road shoulder. "Dolus, quit grabbing all the best parts. That eye was mine. Awk!"

Dolus had replied with a peck. "Bigger and stronger eats first," he said, "and don't you forget it." He helped himself to the other eye.

At that moment Wheedle was standing close to Scratch – but not too close – and speaking unctuously. "Scratch, my friend of long-standing, I must say that your approach to this squirrel was exemplary. Real *savoir faire*. Why, I –"

"Save it, moocher. I'm right bloody hungry this mornin'." Then he gave Wheedle a kinder look. "Share with ya in a bit, eh?"

Colin sat on the fence. Rather than trying the meat, he was watching the scene.

Several more ground squirrels had arrived at the highway's edge, and now they were crawling out into traffic, noses to the pavement, tails twitching. Suddenly one of them reared up and ran across the road in a series of jumps, head held high, shrieking "*tweep!*" as loudly as it could. It looked neither left nor right. The traffic was heavy, but no car chanced to run over it.

On the other side of the highway the ground squirrel stopped. It began sniffing intently. Colin flew over and landed near the squirrel. "Ahem. Hello, my good rodent."

"What's that?!" The ground squirrel leapt up in a panic, saw the raven and cowered. Its breath came in quick gasps. "Don't kill me," it said. "I just got here. Please don't kill me." Then it changed its tactic, showing its yellow incisors. "Don't get close, raven! My teeth are really sharp!"

"Not to worry," Colin reassured it. "I only eat squirrels when they're already dead." He stopped himself. "I mean, when they aren't really squirrels any more. Sort of."

"Oh, sure. Well, I know better. My sister was *killed* by a raven when she was a pup. That's what ravens are like."

"I'm just wondering about something," Colin continued. "Just wanting to ask you something."

"Ask me something?" The ground squirrel looked at him. "No raven ever *asked* me anything before." It seemed pleased with the idea and sat up again. "What would you like to know?"

"Well, if you don't mind my asking – how come you ran across the road like that?"

"Oh, the road," replied the ground squirrel. "Well, the road is just there, you know. Sooner or later you have to try to cross it. And I made it! Oh, wonderful! I made it!" The squirrel momentarily forgot its fear of Colin and romped in the grass. "Just look at this green grass! Oh, they were right! It's true! The grass really *is* greener!"

Sure enough, green blades of spring grass were showing. The slope here faced to the south, so the grass on this side of the road had a head start on the grass on the other side, which faced north. There the ground was colder.

The squirrel put its head down into the grass and began eating. At the first taste its eyes closed and it started to murmur to itself. "Yes, green grass. The road was there but I crossed it, and now I'm eating the green grass on the other side, the grass that's so green and good. I'll always stay here and be happy, so happy eating green grass . . ."

The animal had obviously forgotten entirely about Colin. He watched it for a while, puzzling over it, then something caught his eye. Here was another ground squirrel, this one working its way nervously toward the asphalt from the opposite direction.

It, too, was muttering. "Okay, okay, gotta keep going, just force yourself, that's the way, you can't go back, the others have it all, none for you, so keep going, keep going."

This squirrel wasn't paying any attention to Colin either, and it practically bumped right into him. As Colin hopped out of the way, it jerked its head up in horror. "*Tweep!*"

Colin stepped back farther, letting the squirrel know that he wasn't going to harm it. But the squirrel seemed to have lost its fear. On it went, creeping onto the road shoulder, flattening itself to the pavement, sniffing noisily and twitching its tail. It kept talking to itself, saying, "That's it, just one step at a time, be brave, won't take long, nothing to worry about, just do as they said to do."

A car came by, close enough to spray the squirrel with wind-whipped gravel. The squirrel blinked the dust out of its eyes and continued. A moment later it reared up and ran, taking the same long, jumping steps that the other squirrel had. It, too, succeeded in crossing between cars.

Colin followed, flying high over the traffic and back to the same side of the highway he had started on, where the newly successful squirrel was now exploring the grass.

"Yes, yes," it said. "There *is* green grass here! Not much yet, but there's going to be lots, I know it. Oh, they were right! And there'll be females, and denning, and I'll be so happy! Everything is so much better over here!"

Colin was now perched on the fence. He heard the squeal of skidding tires and looked up in time to see a squirrel crushed. It twisted briefly on the pavement and stopped moving. Yet another squirrel was about to make its run, this time in the opposite direction. Greta landed beside him on the fence. She cleaned her bill on the wire.

"Greta," Colin began. "The squirrels –"

"I know. Doesn't make much sense, does it?"

"Not a bit."

"You've been talking with them?"

"Yes."

"They tell you anything?"

"Not a lot that I could figure out. They don't seem to see the – well, the *futility* of this road-crossing business. I mean, some come from one side and run to the other. And some go just the opposite direction. And they *both* figure that it's better on the other side."

Greta nodded. "Oh, they're all crazy in the spring, these ground squirrels. Especially the males. Females generally stay home, and so do the older ones. It's these young males. They're willing to take the big chance."

"But why, Greta? Lots of them seem to get killed at it."

"Yeah, more than half that try, I'd say."

"So why?"

She answered with another question. "Did that squirrel you were speaking with talk about the grass being greener, and so on?"

"Yes, it did. And so did the other one – the one that came from the other direction, Greta, and it crossed to where the first one started! And it was just as pleased! I mean, of all the ridiculous –"

Greta interrupted him. "Well, maybe not so ridiculous."

Colin looked hard at her. "You know something I don't know, right?"

"Yes."

"And you want me to guess what it is, right?"

"Of course."

Colin thought hard. An idea came to him. "It's almost as if they have to *prove* something. Like they have to prove how brave they are. Hey, I know! One of them kept talking about the females . . . do they do this to impress the females?"

"You're right, Colin. Exactly right." She rewarded him with a smile. "The ground squirrels have a rule."

"What rule is that?"

"You want to pick a mate, you have to cross the road."

"No!"

"Yup. And if you don't live near the road, you have to wait until there's a hawk overhead, and then run right under it."

"Tempt the hawk?!" Colin shook his head. "That's completely nuts, Greta."

"Oh, maybe not." Greta was looking sly. "If a male is slow and gets caught by the hawk, maybe it's better that way. After all, if a female mates with a slow male and has slow babies, then the hawks and coyotes might get most of her family. See what I mean?"

"Yes! Yes!" Colin leapt up, executed a barrel roll of happiness and settled again. "Greta," he said breathlessly, "I have so much to learn from you. Can't we just perch someplace and you can tell me everything you know?"

"All in good time, kiddo. All in good time."

VII

The birds spent all day beside the highway, fascinated with its gory function and feasting on what it produced. At sundown the Main Raven reminded everyone that they had better start back to Yamnuska. The trip home turned into the Evening Flight.

Zack and the Main Raven flew together. "Quite a day, M.R. Quite a day."

"Indeed, Zack. We shall remember this one – especially the youngsters."

The two birds flew on, wingtip to wingtip.

"Uh, M.R. –"

"Yes, Zack?"

"Molly and I will be away for a while."

"Ah, yes. Nesting?"

"Right."

"Well, good luck to you. We probably won't have many nesters this year." The Main Raven looked worried. "As I'm sure you're aware, that's not good for the flock." He looked squarely at Zack. "When you get right down to it, we're counting heavily on you and Molly to succeed. Or we might not have any new members at all."

Zack looked serious. "I know," he said, those two words carrying with them the determination that any parent, whatever the species, felt about raising its young.

The Main Raven heard Zack's tone and applauded it. "Zack, if anyone can give the flock a fine batch of nestlings this year, you and Molly can."

"Thanks for the compliment. We'll do our best. But what about yourself, M.R.?"

"Me? Oh, I – well, I don't know."

"Got your eye on anyone?"

"In truth, Zack, I haven't." The Main Raven looked around, noting the other birds as they coasted and soared on a light southerly breeze. It was carrying them back to Raven's End.

"What about Marg?"

"Marg? Well, Marg's a possibility." He picked her out, flying with Sarah. "But it just seems too soon, somehow."

"Too soon since she lost her nestmate?"

"Surely. Besides, I don't think she likes me."

Coincidentally, Marg was being approached by Sarah on this very subject.

"Mum, don't you think it might be nice to check around for somebody to nest with this year?"

"Why, Sarah! I'm surprised that you'd suggest that!"

"Oh, not to be a jerk or anything, Mum. I'm just wondering."

"Well, keep on wondering. This bird still has too many fond memories of your father."

"Okay, okay, but isn't there *anyone* in the flock that you sort of *like*, Mum?"

"Of course, dear. I like nearly all the birds."

"No, no – you know what I mean."

"Well, in the *nesting* sense, I can't say that anyone interests me."

"Not even the Main Raven?"

"Oh my, no. Certainly not *that* windbag!" Marg then looked over to her daughter. "Now, speaking of nesting, you and Brendan . . ."

"Yes, Mum?"

"You and Brendan, now – I think that has possibilities."

"You do?" Sarah was flapping her wings faster but not gaining any speed.

"Well, yes. But you're both awfully young to succeed."

"Oh, Mum – do you think we should try?"

Marg thought for a moment, soaring. "Yes," she said firmly. "I do. Just understand that it's an awful lot of work, and it may be for nothing."

"Hey, wait 'til I tell Brendan!"

"No, no. Get *him* to ask *you*. That way you'll know whether he's really committed. But, just between you and me, dear, I think he could be persuaded pretty easily."

Both birds giggled, and Sarah flew off to find Brendan.

Next morning, Molly and Zack were absent from the Flap. The Main Raven explained the reason, and everyone seemed pleased.

"Good luck to 'em, then," said Scratch. "We gotta have high hopes for them two. Only ones in this here flock that've got a chance, really." He picked at a mite among his breast feathers. "Now, if there's anyone willin' to give it a go with *me* . . ." Marg and Sarah cringed.

The Main Raven continued with the Flap. "Does anyone have any more business?" No one spoke. "There being no other business, I call for a Motion to end the meeting."

It was a smaller motion than usual, with Molly and Zack away, but a cheery one nonetheless. "Rawk-a-taw!" The birds began drifting away for the day's adventures.

Before Colin could leave, the Main Raven called to him. "Just a moment, Colin. Where are you off to?" The big bird wasn't going to have Zack's company for some time, and already he missed it.

"Oh, I'm going to cruise the South Face. Down low. Might be some dead wood rats thawing out down there."

"Indeed. Mind if I join you?"

"I'd, uh – I'd be honored, sir."

"Thank you."

Now that he had the Main Raven with him, Colin thought, he was going to have to put up with him all day. Talk, talk, talk.

"Oh – if you don't mind, Colin, I'll not be saying much today. I'm feeling, well, rather subdued, really."

"Hey, that's great! Um, I mean, it's fine with me. If you're not feeling chatty, I mean. Neither am I, really. I'd just like to do some poking around."

"Let's be off."

Colin and the Main Raven departed. Scratch and Wheedle had already flown in another direction, while Greta, as usual, had gone off alone. This left Sarah, Brendan, Garth, and Dolus remaining at Raven's End.

"All the powers-that-be have split," Dolus said.

Brendan considered that statement. "Just us young peasants left, I guess." He was wondering what Dolus would say next.

Dolus had a knowing look in his eye. "Anybody wanta go for a buzz over to Wakonda Buttress?"

"Sure," Garth replied. "I'm always up for Wakonda Buttress."

"What's at Wakonda?" Brendan asked.

"Oh, a friend of mine lives there," he said.

"Who's that?" Sarah asked innocently.

"Oh, you know who that is," Brendan answered for Dolus. "Zygadena. Dolus was hanging around with Zygadena when we left for Carrot Creek. Now we're back, he's gonna do it again. Right, Dolus?" Brendan's voice showed his contempt.

Dolus stepped over to Brendan and placed his large foot over Brendan's smaller one. "My friends are my friends, Mister Brendan Smart Bird. And I'd advise you to make them your friends, too." Dolus brought his bill close to Brendan's eye as he spoke. Brendan drew his head back, and Dolus followed with his bill – big, black, and sharp. "Do you get the message, C.C.?"

"Okay, okay, Dolus. Sure, okay?"

Sarah joined in. "Really, Dolus, he didn't mean anything. We just ... well, we don't know Zygadena at all, really. Maybe she's really nice or something."

"That's better, Sarah." Dolus stepped off Brendan's foot. "Much better." He looked at Garth. "Tell them what Zygadena said to you just before we left."

"Oh, that. Well, it was real sweet. She said, 'Boys, I'm not forgetting you. When you come back to Yamnuska, be sure to look me up. We'll have a lot of fun next spring.' She said that. Those were her very words."

Brendan gave Garth a suspicious look. "'Boys' – that's what the humans say, isn't it?"

"So what?" Garth replied. Dolus put his foot over Brendan's again.

"Uh, nothing," Brendan replied, leaning away. "I just thought it was interesting. Sort of."

Dolus kept Brendan's foot pinned. "Yes, Brendan Smart Bird. Zygadena is *very* interesting. And she isn't afraid to say whatever she wants. Like maybe you are? Afraid? Like right now, when you're trying to say bad things about her? When *I'm listening?*" Dolus was pressing down on Brendan's foot so hard, digging into it with his claws, that Brendan winced.

Sarah spoke sharply. "Dolus, if you don't quit that, I'm going to tell the Main Raven. I really am."

Dolus let off the pressure. "Oh, Sarah, I'm so *sorry*," he said in a mocking voice. "You mean the Main Raven wouldn't approve? Old Wiggly-Wattles wouldn't *approve?* We couldn't have that, now could we?"

Garth looked uncomfortable. "Dolus, maybe we should go now. After all, we promised Zygadena we'd go see her when we got back."

"And we keep our promises," Dolus said.

"You bet," said Garth.

"So we'll just fly over to Wakonda and see if she's home." Spreading his wings slowly and grandly, Dolus released Brendan's foot. "The others have no business knowing where we are today," he said to Brendan. "You got that, Smart Bird?"

"Yes."

"Sarah?"

"Oh, we won't tell, Dolus."

Garth and Dolus flew off, croaking to each other.

Brendan looked at Sarah. "One day," he said, "one day Dolus is going to try that and I'm not going to take it! By the Trees, if only I'd just *grow* a little more, then I wouldn't have to take it."

"Oh, Brendan, you can't win with Dolus. He's so mean." She looked up. Dolus and Garth were now two tiny specks. "Anyway," she said, "we don't have to think about them." She looked at Brendan. "We have us."

Brendan had been staring at the scree, unhappily stabbing at it with his toes. Now he raised his head. Sarah was smiling at him. Brendan's heart started to beat faster. His neck-feathers fanned forward, and he swallowed several times. His body suddenly felt warm and strong, tingling with excitement. His bill went up. Brendan hadn't intended any of this; it just happened, along with a powerful croak that came out without being asked: "Sarah – I love you!"

She saw; she heard. She felt her own body start to behave as if she were not in charge. Her legs lost their strength, and she sat on the scree. Her wings dropped and extended to her sides. They began to tremble. She tilted her head up and opened her bill, as if begging for food.

"Brendan – I love you, too."

VIII

Molly and Zack flew along the South Face of Yamnuska, searching for the best spot in which to build their nest. It was Molly's job to make the choice, and she wouldn't let Zack hurry her. The process could take days, and this was only the first morning. But suddenly she put on the brakes and made a sharp turn toward the cliff.

"Zack! There's a terrific crack over here I didn't see before!" She passed from sunlight to shade, and he lost sight of her for a moment. Then he crossed the same boundary, and he could see her circling at a deep split in the rock. It was big enough to fly into, with a wide, flat ledge on one wall.

"Hey! You're right! I haven't been in here, either." Zack was hoping against hope that this spot would be the one. Maybe the search would be mercifully short, for a change.

"No," Molly said sadly. Zack's heart fell. "It's just too low," she said. "Look – the crack reaches all the way to the bottom. A marten could climb up here all too easily. Let's keep looking." She spread her wings and jumped off the ledge. In a moment her glossy black body passed back into the sunlight. As Zack watched, his disappointment changed to admiration. What a beautiful bird she was! He followed her.

A bowl-shaped part of the cliff was gathering the sun between its curving walls, warm now and promising to be shadowed and cool in the afternoon. Zack and Molly soared back and forth across it. There at the left edge – "Molly! Look at those cracks and corners! Lots of great nesting!"

"Zack, you know as well as I do that humans are up there every day of the summer."

"Oh, right. Climbers. Must have been day-dreaming. Bloody humans! They get everywhere. By the Trees, I just wish –"

"Now *there's* something, Zack." Molly vanished into another shadow. However, she came swooping out again right away.

"Nope. The ledge was good, but no overhang above. Wet nest."

"Speaking of ledges, what about that one over there?" Zack swung back into the cliff. There it was, punched out of a pale-buff wall: an indentation as deep as a raven's wingspan, and twice as wide. He landed in it. "Molly, come look at this."

She flapped down beside him. Together they examined the niche.

"Gee – I haven't been here before," Molly said.

"Me neither. But what a spot! Nice and flat, good overhang above and below, nice size" – he strode from end to end, noting its ample dimensions – "and nothing but blank rock on either side." He picked at the surface of the ledge. "Not even a wood-rat dropping." He walked along the back. "Hey – sticks! There's nesting twigs, here, Molly! Raven nest!"

Sure enough, the ledge had been used as a nesting site. A few weathered gray sticks lay on the dusty rock.

"I wonder whose this was," Molly said, turning a stick over with one foot. "Awfully old twigs," she said thoughtfully. "You know, Zack, this spot looks like it's been forgotten for *years*."

"What do you think, Moll? Is this it?"

She gave him a dark look. "If you don't mind, I'll just take the time to check it out completely, okay?" She sat down carefully on the ledge, twisting her tail as if settling on a nest. "It really *is* the right sort of ledge." She looked carefully up at the ceiling. "I'd say this place has definite possibilities. But I don't know . . ." Zack prepared himself for the letdown. But Molly surprised him. "You're right," she said, ruffling out her neck-feathers. "We're going to take it."

"Whoopee!" croaked Zack. This was the easiest nesting-site trip they'd ever had. He, too, fanned out his neck-feathers. "Uh – how about some lunch? Want to go get some lunch?"

"I hadn't even thought of that. No wonder you were in such a hurry to pick this ledge."

"Now, Molly, you know that had nothing to do with it."

"Oh, sure. Well, we've been lucky, anyway. But I'm not going for lunch. *You're* going to find *me* some lunch, nestmate. I'm waiting here until you get back, just in case another couple arrives – like maybe a pair of crows – and tries to claim *our* spot."

IX

Colin and the Main Raven were soaring along the South Face, feeling the warm updraft under their wings. They were staying low, just above the trees, searching for food along the foot of the cliff.

"I say, Colin," the Main Raven declared, "you've certainly come a long way since you joined the flock."

"Thank you, sir," Colin replied. "It does seem like a lot has happened since I came here." He peered down. "Hey – there's the juniper bush I crashed into on the very first day. The first day I can remember, anyway."

"That's the amazing part, Colin. You seemed so, well, so *lost* at first, if you don't mind my saying so. Honestly, I thought – we all thought – that you weren't going to survive for long."

"Oh, with friends like Zack and Molly – and you of course, sir – there was always someone to help. There were some awfully close calls, though," he said, thinking of the time he fell over the South Face, wounded by the hunter's gun.

"But you've weathered them all so splendidly, Colin! You've not only lived, you've prospered. And several times, C.C., you've been a great help to the flock."

"You're being too kind, sir."

"Not at all. Your constant scouting for food has not gone unnoticed, Colin. And your wonderful ability to sense danger, as you did so well with the avalanche at Carrot Creek. These things have made you a most worthy Raven's Ender."

The Main Raven's words gave Colin a comfortable feeling, a warmth that spread through his body. This emotion was the opposite of fear, he thought. Fear made you feel cold and uncomfortable. Fear made you want to fly away fast and wild-eyed. But this – this made you want to relax. To be coasting along with your friends. That was it, he thought; this feeling had something to do with his companions in the Raven's End Flock. It was . . . it was . . .

"Colin, are you listening?" The Main Raven had been speaking.

"Oh. Sorry. I guess I wasn't. I was thinking about this nice feeling I was having, about how happy I am here at Yamnuska. I really like it in the Raven's End Flock, sir."

"Strange you would say that, Colin. That's more or less what I wanted to talk about. Oh – just a minute."

The Main Raven dipped a wing and swung round to check out a quick movement near the base of the cliff. A small animal had emerged from a crevice. It started to tread nervously out into the sunlight, its nose to the scree. It found something, started to pick it up, then saw the Main Raven coming. In one quick motion it was back in the crack. Its tail, wide-spread and bushy with fright, whipped in after the little striped body. The Main Raven dipped his other wing and wheeled away from the cliff.

"Just a chipmunk. Anyway, Colin, there was a special reason I wanted to fly with you this morning." The Main Raven spread his neck-feathers, the way he did before making an announcement at the Flap. "I have been speaking with Greta about you."

"You have?"

"Yes. She thinks the world of you, Colin. You must know that."

"Oh, I think the world of her, too!"

"Of course. You two seem to understand each other in a way that none of the rest of us does." He turned his head sideways, as if slightly regretting what he had just said. But he continued. "Now, then. Getting to the point, Colin C.C. She was wondering whether or not you'd like to do some apprenticing with her."

" 'Apprenticing'? What's 'apprenticing'?"

"Well, I'm not sure myself. Greta said it had something to do with learning the things she knows."

A chance to learn from Greta! Without thinking, Colin did a barrel roll.

The Main Raven twitched away in surprise, then continued. "Anyway, she wonders if you'd like to spend most of your time with her for a while. You know – follow her around during the day. Roost with her at night. That sort of thing."

Colin was about to say yes immediately, then he thought of something. "Is this a sort of *nesting* thing she has in mind?"

The Main Raven laughed. "Oh, no, Colin. Craw-ha! Not a bit. Greta hasn't nested in all the years I've known her." He laughed again. "She's a very smart bird, but she doesn't seem to know anything about attracting a mate – or even to care about it. Craw-ha! Greta nesting! The very idea! Craw-ha-ha-ha!" The Main Raven laughed so hard, he was nearly out of control. He had to extend his wings and tail fully to recover.

Colin was still thinking. "If she's offering to teach me things," he said, "then I'd certainly like to learn. Should I go and find her?"

"I think that would be most appropriate – ahem – as long as I came along to set everything up, of course. Now where did I see her last? Oh. She was headed down the ridge this morning. I thought she said something about –" The Main Raven suddenly looked distracted. "Actually, Colin, I think I'll just spend the rest of the morning here. You run along and find Greta."

This sudden dismissal of Colin had occurred for a good reason. The Main Raven had just seen the very thing Colin had been looking for that day: a dead wood rat. It was lying at the base of the cliff, melting out of what remained of last winter's snow. Bacteria had immediately attacked the thawing tissues, and the odor alone would have attracted the ravens if the sight had not.

"You'll be off then, eh?" the Main Raven said, hoping Colin hadn't seen the treat.

"Yes, sir. I'm off." He caught the updraft and let it loft him along the cliff face. "Enjoy that rat, sir!"

The Main Raven's bill opened and shut. "He doesn't miss a thing. Not a thing," he said to himself. "So much like Greta."

From his position just above the trees, the Main Raven looked around carefully. Nothing threatening seemed near. He flared out his wings and tail and lit on the snowbank. He danced toward the wood rat, backed away, danced closer, backed away again, then finally hopped right up and took a preliminary nibble at the gray body in the snow.

"Mmmm. Not bad!"

X

"Greta! Hey, Greta!" Colin had caught up with her.

"Hello, Colin," she said. "What's the news?"

"The Main Raven, he – *whew!*" Colin had flown so fast that he was out of breath.

Greta finished the sentence for him. "He told you I was looking for an apprentice."

"Yes! Yes! Here I am, Greta!"

"Don't be so enthusiastic. It isn't going to be all fun, you know."

"Oh, of course not. It's a heavy responsibility, I know, and –"

"Quit talking like the Main Raven."

"Am I? That's what comes from spending the morning with him, I guess."

"Well, from now on you'll be spending your mornings with me."

"And the afternoons, too?"

"Yes, and also the evenings. Is that going to be too much?"

"No, not at all! Can we start right now?"

"Sure."

"What do I have to do?"

"Mainly you'll have to pay attention. Try to remember what I tell you. Be patient with me."

"Oh, that won't be hard at all, Greta. You're the best raven that ever there was."

"We'll see if you still think so after a few days."

Colin felt a cool tickle of fear. He loved and respected Greta more than he did any other bird in the flock, but didn't really understand her. And that was kind of scary. Still, he knew he could trust her. Indeed, there was no one in the flock he trusted more.

He followed Greta as she circled down and alighted in an aspen overlooking the Bow Valley. She spoke again. "So – what shall I teach you, Colin?"

It was a typical Greta question. And he had an answer. "Everything, Greta. Teach me everything you know. All about the world, and the birds, and all the places you've been, and –"

"Hang on, young Colin C.C.," she said, chuckling. "One thing at a time." Her eyes fell on the aspen in which they were perched. It had fuzzy catkins on the twigs. She reached over to one of the catkins and ate it. "What'sh thish?" she said, her bill full.

"It's, uh, part of a tree," Colin replied. He ate some, too.

She swallowed. "Right. But it's also a lot of other things. To a bird, it's food. To the tree, it's the main reason for its existence."

"What do you mean?"

She took a catkin gently in her bill. "Inside each of these is a special part of the tree, a part that is able to produce more trees."

Colin nipped off a catkin himself, held it under his foot and looked at it. "I don't see any little trees in there. It's just kind of soft," he said, feeling it with his long black toes.

"Well spoken, Colin. You're reporting what you see, not what you're told. Very good." She was still holding the catkin in her bill. "Now watch carefully."

She gave the catkin a shake. Colin jumped back. Yellow dust was coming out of it!

"What's that stuff?" he asked suspiciously.

"It's called 'pollen.' Tiny, tiny bits. And each bit, if it finds its way to the catkins on a female tree, can make a seed. And the seed can make another aspen."

Colin's eyes opened wide. "Greta, that's amazing. Do all trees do that?"

"Yup."

So that was how trees mated, Colin thought. He knew how animals produced other animals – by mating – but he had never seen trees mating. Trees couldn't even move. How could they mate? And now he knew: they didn't have to. They sent this "pollen" stuff between them, and the pollen did the mating for them.

"Greta, how do you know all this?"

"Oh, I got started the same as you, by asking too many questions. I *wanted* to know."

"But who taught you?"

"Other birds. Other animals. The bugs on the ground. The clouds in the sky. All you have to do is pay attention."

"Okay," Colin said, paying very close attention indeed.

Greta continued the lesson. "What you learned about the trees is a principle."

"What's a 'principle'?"

"Something that's true for a lot of things. Knowing little truths – like how trees mate – is all well and good, but knowing *principles* is even better." She paused to form her next sentence with care. "The principle you have just learned is this: that everything alive, from the tiniest to the biggest, has come from another living thing just like it."

She let Colin ponder that idea for a moment, which he did, opening and closing his intelligent eyes, raising and lowering his head. At length he stopped and looked up, smiling a raven smile of understanding. Understanding something like this made him feel very good. He was about to tell Greta so, but she spoke first.

"And Colin, this particular principle gets better. If everything alive has come from something else alive, then that means that living things don't really die."

Colin's head jerked up. He shook it. What did she mean, things don't really die? "Greta, that doesn't make sense. Everything dies!"

"Yes, everything dies, Colin. But it doesn't die *completely*."

In a flash of insight, Colin grasped the meaning of Greta's words. Of course! What a wonderful, happy idea! He began to dance. He jumped up and down. He flapped his wings and turned in circles. The aspen branch bobbed about, almost shaking Greta out of the tree.

"Right, Greta! Right!" he croaked. "Nothing ever really dies, because . . . because," he stammered, so overwhelming was the notion, "because . . . it's like *pikas!*" he shouted.

Greta looked at him quizzically as she tried to regain her balance. "Like pikas? What does this have to do with pikas?"

Colin went gushing on. "I met a pika last fall, at Raven's End, and it said something I didn't understand then, but I do now, and it was all about what you just told me, sort of."

"Sort of like what?"

"This pika said that dying was okay. It didn't mind dying at all, not a bit, because there were always lots of pikas left, even if it, personally, was dead."

"What a strange philosophy."

"I thought so, too. But it makes sense to pikas, and now I can see why, because of what you just told me. Pikas must know that part of themselves keeps living, in their babies, and so they don't really die. Not completely. They call it *pikaness*."

Greta smiled broadly. "Pikaness." Her smile became wider than Colin had ever seen it. "I love it." She turned to Colin. "Excellent. Absolutely excellent, Colin. First rate." She looked away, out over the Bow Valley. "Pikaness. Yes, indeed. Pikaness."

"But Greta," Colin began, "Ravens aren't like that –"

Greta's old head swung back toward him. "We are and we aren't. Certainly we value our lives more than pikas do. But a pair of ravens will protect their nestlings even when their own lives are threatened. We'll feed our nestlings even when we ourselves are starving. Same with every other critter I can think of. When you get right down to it, the species must go on, or there would be no individuals, right?"

Colin looked at his teacher rapturously. "Greta, these principles of yours – they are *terrific!*"

"Yes, they are terrific."

"Do you think about them a lot?"

"Practically all the time."

"Do you think of them yourself?"

"Mostly, yes. Some principles I get by asking around."

"I'm going to do that. I'm going to find out lots of principles."

"By all means. You've got the brains for it. After all, you discovered 'pikaness' on your own." She smiled again at the idea. "Of course, I can save you some work by telling you the ones I know."

"Yes! Yes! I want to know them all!"

She smiled. "Oh, by the time summer's here you might have learned a few. Only a few."

"I don't care how long it takes, Greta. I want to know them *all*." Colin looked around earnestly. "I want to know if there's a principle about clouds, and a principle about, about" – he looked down at the ground – "about dirt, and a principle about puddles, and snow, and wood rats, and, and –"

"And ravens?" Greta's brown eyes looked especially bright.

"Yes! Especially about ravens!"

"Then we'll learn something about ravens."

"Greta, you're the best raven in the whole wide world. I've learned that already."

XI

Molly sat on the edge of the ledge, waiting for Zack. "No bird is going to get this nesting spot," she said to anyone and anything within earshot. "This is ours! Do you hear that?! Ours!" Her croak was practically a roar.

Zack arrived with lunch: a hunk of sheep meat so large he could hardly carry it. "Here you are, love." He brought it close to her bill. "The wolves killed a sheep in the valley behind Yamnuska yesterday. Colin found it. Everybody is down there gobbling away."

Molly took a bite. "It's a fine sheep, Zack. I knew you'd bring me something good."

"Only the best for our nest."

"I do love you, Zack."

"I love you too, Molly."

"So start bringing me sticks, dear."

He flew off. He was back shortly, carrying a small branch sideways in his bill. It was old and weathered. The bark had fallen off, or it had been peeled off by woodpeckers, and a tiny wisp of gray-green hair lichen grew near the end.

"How's this for the First Stick?" he asked, setting the branch down carefully on the ledge.

Molly looked at the stick. She touched it with her bill. Then she bit it hard. The stick snapped in two. Without even looking up at Zack, Molly kicked both pieces off the cliff.

"Sorry, Moll. I didn't realize it was punky in the middle."

"The First Stick has to be just right, Zack."

"I'll try again." Spreading his wings, he turned and hopped off into space. Molly went back to her nest-guardian's pose, looking warily about, from time to time announcing to all and sundry that they had better not try anything.

"Here's a better stick, Molly." Zack had another branchlet in his bill. This one was even grayer than the last, and it had more tufts of hair lichen growing on it. Molly tested the branch. She bit it very hard, but her sharp bill could only dent the wood, not break it.

"This will do," she said.

Zack croaked happily as he spread his wings for another nesting-material run. "The First Stick! Then it's the First Stick!" He'd got it right on only the second try.

Molly dragged the First Stick here and there on the ledge, tugging it about until it lay perfectly positioned, as if the bends in it had been moulded to the rock. By the time she was finished, Zack was back with another stick. Molly considered each piece of building material that Zack brought. She refused many of his offerings, which went rattling down the face, even though each stick had taken a good deal of effort to collect. Zack had to fly to the base of the cliff, hunt among the trees for a dead twig, break it off – he wouldn't use any that had already fallen to the ground – then carry it all the way back up to the ledge. For this reason the nest came together very slowly. There was more rejected wood at the foot of the cliff than there was accepted wood on the ledge.

Molly built a solid nest-base, each stick wiggled and teased into position so that it interlocked with the others. Then she built up the sides, especially the side facing outward, by using smaller sticks. She pushed with her feet and pulled with her bill. She turned round and round, making sure the nest was big enough. She settled on it, noting that here was a gap to fill, there was a snag that stuck up too high. She shook herself, making the sticks vibrate into place. If Zack didn't bring her the sort of stick she needed right then and there, she threw it away. Zack sometimes brought the same stick back, hoping that now would be the time to use it. And sometimes it was. Molly would examine the stick as if she had never seen it before, then add it to the nest.

Meanwhile, Sarah and Brendan were engaged in the same process. Without looking very long, they had picked a small ledge at Raven's End. They were having trouble getting started on the nest, though. It was, after all, their first. Brendan was getting impatient. "Aw, Sarah, what's wrong with this stick? It looks okay to me."

"No, Brendan, it's not. It's got bark all over it. A nesting stick can't have any *bark* on it."

"Huh? This hasn't got any bark on it." He turned the stick around in his bill. One side was bare, but the other was covered with flaky, shredding bark. "Oh. You mean *this* bark." He hadn't noticed it. "This bark here."

"Yes, Brendan, *that* bark. Now go get me a different stick." She looked away. "I love you, Brendan," she said softly.

That was all it took. Brendan was off on another search. And another and another, all through the morning and the afternoon.

"We're doing so well," Sarah said to herself. She looked from the growing pile of wood toward the ground. There weren't many rejected sticks there. "Oh, we're doing really, really well."

Late in the day Marg came along to check on the two young ravens. There they were, busily at work on the ledge. "Hi, kids," she said cheerily. "How's it coming?"

"Oh, great, Mum! Just super-great! Look!" Sarah sat proudly atop the pile.

Marg hopped up on it. She looked bewildered. "Uh – where's the nest?"

"What do you mean, 'Where's the nest'? You're perching on it, Mum."

"No, I mean the *nest* part. You've got a big pile of sticks here, but there's no *nest* in it."

Sarah twitched. She closed her eyes and let her head droop. "Oh, jeez. It's supposed to be hollow, isn't it? Like a hollow in the middle, where you sit on the eggs?" Sarah started to wail. "Oh, Mum, we've done it all wrong!"

"Done it wrong?" Brendan couldn't believe what he was hearing. "Wrong?"

Marg was going to explain to the youngsters, but before she could, the nest lurched.

"Something's happening!" Brendan croaked.

The nest moved again. It began to slide toward the edge. Marg jumped off.

"Help! Stop!" Sarah yelled, grabbing at sticks with her claws and her bill. Already bits were starting to fall to the scree below.

Marg looked on in horror. "Oh, no! There it goes!"

The whole mass, with Sarah clinging to it, plunged off the ledge. Sarah flew free as the nest came apart in the air. With a sound like hail, hundreds of nesting sticks bounced down the cliff, some of them catching on other ledges or behind bushes growing in cracks. Brendan dived, snapping at the sticks as they fell, catching one, then dropping it to snatch another in mid-air. Most of the sticks reached the cliff base, where they disappeared into the junipers or bounced down the scree. The last stick landed with a clonk.

"You poor, poor birds," Marg said from a tree nearby. "All that work."

"Mum," Sarah said, her voice quavering, "Mum, I think – I think we, Brendan and me, maybe we're, you know, a little too young to be nesting." She flew over to Marg and huddled beside her.

"No way!" Brendan croaked. He managed to fluff out his neck-feathers. "It was a great nest! A really big nest! We just, uh, kind of built it on a ledge that sort of sloped too much. Sort of." His voice trailed off. The part of nesting that he had been looking forward to most – the *mating* part – was becoming less and less likely. No nest meant no mating, plain and simple. And now there was no nest. With rising anger, he saw it all. Saw it clearly. They had failed. *He* had failed.

"Oh, by the Trees!" He pecked savagely at one of the nesting sticks. "Oh, that makes me so *mad!*" He flipped the stick into the air and jumped on it when it landed, pecking it over and over, his bill missing the stick half the time and clacking on stones. "Awk! Oh, I hate this! I hate this nest! I hate this place! Awk!"

"There, there, Brendan," Marg said. Sarah had tucked her head back under her wing, trying to forget the whole thing. "We all have to learn how to build a nest properly. It took me two years before Sarah's father and I got it right."

But Brendan went on pecking and yelling. A cloud of dust rose around him as he jumped and spun. Peck! Slash! "Awk! Weasel poop! Coyote bums! AWK!!"

"You've got lots of good years ahead," Marg continued. "I can see how much you and Sarah love each other."

At this, Sarah pulled her head out from under her wing. She looked at Marg and blinked. She looked down at Brendan. He had stopped thrashing about and was looking up at her. "Oh, Brendan, we'll try again." Sarah was actually smiling. Brendan began to smile, too.

"Next year?"

"Yes. Next year."

"And next year I'll bring just the right sticks."

"And next year I'll turn them into a nest instead of a . . . a dumb old *pile*." She started to laugh.

So did Brendan. "Did you see that mess go down the cliff? You were right in the middle of it! Craw-ha!"

"Oh, Brendan," laughed Marg, "you looked so funny trying to catch the sticks. Craw-ha-ha!" Soon all three birds were laughing uncontrollably. Sarah convulsed off her perch.

A short distance away along the base of the cliff, a small gray animal heard the laughter and came out from between two boulders. It scurried quickly to the top of one of them and sat there, its large, round eyes watching the ravens.

"Just ravens," thought Okotona, one of many pikas with that name. "Just ravens doing weird things again. Therefore it must be spring." It scurried back down into the rocks to tell the others.

XII

And spring it was. Full-on spring, speeding toward summer. Sugary new sap began to flow in the woody arteries of the shrubs and the trees. The aspen buds popped open and the leaves unfurled. The needles of the conifers, dormant and dark through the dim cold of winter, greened up and got busy.

On the grassy slopes below Yamnuska's South Face, flowers began to appear. First up were the crocus-like pasque flowers. They broke through the ground only a few days after the snow melted. Furry-stemmed as if trying to keep warm, their big purple flowers collected the sun's warmth, encouraging the bugs – the first flies of spring, and the first beetles – to come out from their winter hiding places under the ground and inside hollow trees and back among the rocks. The insects knew it was time. They broke free from their weather-tight pupal cases, discovered their wings and flew toward the brightness of the new flowers. They sampled the nectar and tramped about in the pollen with their six feet, getting bedaubed with yellow dust in one flower before flying on to the next, thereby fertilizing each and all.

Flocks of migrating birds arrived. First came the robins, gobbling insect larvae. As the days went by the robins paired off, building nests and singing cheerily through the spring showers. Then the other thrushes arrived – the hermit thrushes and the varied thrushes and the Swainson's thrushes. More secretive than the robins, they skulked through the brush and built their nests low in the shaggiest of conifers, or right on the ground among the densest tangles. But they would fly up into the trees to sing grandly, especially at dusk; Swainson's with its flutelike melody that spiralled up and up; the varied thrush with its loud, reedy note, sounded low, then high, then in between.

The warblers came next, thousands of little brightly colored birds, singing and singing. They sang in the morning, in the afternoon, in the evening. They loved willowy places, and they flew by the hundred to the Willow Marsh behind Yamnuska. Here they hopped from branch to branch, catching the insects they craved, stopping to sing their complicated, musical songs whenever they felt like it.

And on it went, this invasion from the south, a million warm-weather birds returning to their summer homes to carry out the most important part of their lives: producing nests full of naked, bulgy-eyed babies that cried piteously to be fed and fed and fed some more. Of course, every predator in the woods was preying on baby birds. For the weasels and coyotes and owls and hawks, spring was an enormous banquet. All these creatures had their own babies to feed, and they fed them on the babies of other species. And life went on.

Life went on full blast, like a fire fed more and more fuel. Hot sunlight poured down through the hole in the sky. It fell onto everything green. Grasses and wildflowers and shrubs and trees seized the light, the heat, the photons that crackled into leaves and needles and stems. The sunlight fired the chemical reactions in the cells, producing plant tissues from carbon dioxide and water, growing new leaves, new needles, new wood. From sunlight came stamens and pistils and petals. Everything grew and grew, as fast as it could, impossibly fast.

All of this made Colin tired just to think about it. As he roosted next to Greta, exhausted from another day of his apprenticeship, Colin remembered the slow afternoons of autumn and the long, quiet nights of winter. Yes, the spring was wonderful – remarkable, fascinating – and under Greta's tutelage he was learning how it worked. But it was all so much, so soon, so fast. Maybe it was going to be *too* much. Maybe he just couldn't take it. Maybe – maybe he would just fall asleep, right now, right there on his perch, long before sundown. And he did.

Day after frantic day went by as the solar cycle hurried on toward the summer solstice. Each dawn came earlier, and the sun climbed up out of the night farther to the north. Each day the sun arced higher as it swung round the southern half of the sky, and each evening it took longer to reach the western horizon. It glided down toward the edge of the world at a gentle angle, skimming the wave-like ridges of the Canadian Rockies and crashing into the sea of mountains in a fireball sunset that seemed to go on forever.

When the longest day of the year finally arrived, so did the shortest night, giving little time for rest. It didn't even get truly dark. A band of brightness moved along the northern horizon, illuminating the back of Yamnuska so clearly that even a human would have had no trouble following the trail there at midnight. Soon the sun popped back up, eager for yet another go at trying to stay aloft around the clock. The ravens, like other denizens of the mountains whose lives ran to the beat of dawn and dusk, struggled back to consciousness, prepared – sort of – for another giddy day.

XIII

"Zack! Zack! The eggs are hatching!" Up on the South Face, in a beautifully crafted nest made of sticks on the outside and soft sheep wool on the inside, the only nesting pair of Raven's Enders were about to see what they had bred. Five eggs lay in the nest. They were greenish blue, scrawled with lines of black and brown and red. Molly had sat on those eggs for twenty days. Now whatever was inside was trying to get out.

Pick, pick. The egg tooth of a would-be nestling poked through the shell. Wiggle, wiggle. The baby bird inside lined up for another attack on its container. More picking. More wiggling. The baby had to get out on its own; no help would come from the adult birds.

This was the first of many tests. Could the tiny thing inside free itself? If not, its raven parents would let it die in the shell. Weakness in escaping the shell might be genetic, and every raven knew instinctively that an early death would prevent those weak genes from being passed on.

Molly and Zack watched as first one, then another, then yet another head popped through. Two, three – would there be a fourth? Yes! Four nestlings hatched! This was a very good result, but one egg lay unopened. Molly waited two days, to give it a chance, then she pushed it out of the nest and off the ledge. All the space in that warm pocket among the sticks was needed for the nestlings.

And such nestlings. Their heads were almost as large as their floppy, uncoordinated bodies. Their enormous eyes were tightly shut, a slit through the middle showing where they would open in a couple of weeks. Their bodies lacked feathers. Their skin showed pink and purple, except on their heads and backs, where a skiff of brownish down covered them lightly. Their little naked wings looked like flippers.

"Aren't they cute, Zack?"

"Just dear, Molly, just dear." He perched at the edge of the nest. "You produce beautiful babies, my love."

"They're yours too, you handsome C.C."

"I know," he said, ruffling out his glossy neck-feathers. They flashed proudly in the sun.

The nestlings held their heads up as high as they could when Zack or Molly brought them food. They opened their bills absurdly wide to expose the bright yellow and pink colors within. Down each throat, Zack and Molly dumped enormous quantities of edibles – mostly crushed-up insects – as bird baby-food. All day long, load after load, Molly and Zack stoked those throats. When the nestlings found their voices, the incessant hungry squawking hurried the two adults on their forays. Out, find something, back. Out, find something else, back.

"More? You want more?" Molly touched the leathery bill of a baby.

It opened its mouth wider. "Crawk! Crawk!! CRAWK!!"

"Oh my, sweetums. Such a hungry raven! Here we are." She shoved her bill into the pink-and-yellow gape.

"*Garg! Galarrggh!!*" The nestling fluttered its flippers rapturously as a wad of pulpy beetle parts went sliding down.

"Back in a minute, darlings."

"CRAWK!! CRAWK!!"

Only when both parents were away finding food would the nestlings stop clamoring. Their wobbly heads would sink back below the rim of the nest, and their vocal chords, the strongest part of a baby raven, would relax. The little birds would become completely silent, so that nothing on the hunt for nestlings could find them.

And nothing did. Any crow that ventured within sight of the nest wished it hadn't. Even the prairie falcon, fiercest bird in the valley, kept well clear of Zack and Molly's ledge.

The two ravens were excellent parents. All four of their children thrived, growing larger by the day. On sunny afternoons, when the South Face became baking hot and the nestlings made unhappy sounds, Molly would fly down to one of the ponds at the base of Yamnuska. There she would dip her breast feathers in the water and fly back quickly, to settle cool and dripping over her young. At night she kept them warm under her body and wings.

One morning their eyes opened – all of the nestlings, all together – and in so doing they discovered one another. A few had started to speak in raven nestling-talk, and now they certainly had plenty to talk about.

"Ooo. Ugly. You really ugly."

"So you."

"Me, too?"

Zack and Molly were relieved. The noise would now die down as the young birds began speaking more and yelling less. The brood had figured out the routine – squawk, eat, sleep – and life seemed easy. Black feathers were appearing on their bodies, and Molly showed the nestlings how to preen themselves. Clumsily they practiced, pawing away with their bills, trying to get their big heads over their backs without losing their balance.

"Craw-ha! You fall down!"

"Not funny."

"Me, too."

Molly and Zack were pleased to see that this batch of nestlings, like their others, didn't need any toilet training. Each baby bird knew what to do. It would back up to the edge of the nest and excrete directly into the bill of one of the parent birds. The stuff would come out in the form of a pill-like pellet, not a squirt. Then Zack or Molly would fly a little distance away with the pellet and drop it. Surprisingly clean and tidy, this procedure kept the nest from becoming fouled and smelly, which would have attracted predators.

One day Colin came to visit. Molly didn't like other birds coming to the nest, and Zack enforced her wishes, but when Colin arrived she made an exception. He was almost one of the family.

"Colin! How good to see you!" Molly had missed him. Neither she nor Zack had been with the flock for many days. They had even stayed away from the Flaps and the Flights.

"Gro, Molly. Gro, Zack." Colin stood at the end of the ledge, not wishing to intrude. But he was very interested in this whole bird-raising operation. He had been asking Greta about it. "Go find Zack and Molly's nest and see for yourself," she had said. "Just remember to be extremely polite. They may not want you coming around." So Colin stood humbly, waiting to be invited nearer.

"Come on over, C.C. Have a look at what we've got." Zack was eager to show off his brood.

Colin peered over the rim and into the nest. There were the babies, staring back at him with wide blue eyes. They were all fully feathered now, looking passably like ravens instead of some animal's interior organs. They all began to speak at once.

"Mummy! Mummy! That's not you!"

"Who is it?"

"It's another daddy bird, I think."

"We already have a daddy bird."

"Tell it to go away."

"Go away!"

Colin burst out laughing. These little things were so funny! Their heads were very big, and their bills would open very wide when they spoke, then snap shut. "Craw-ha! These are wonderful!" he said.

"Oh, thank you," Molly replied, showing her pride with a turn of the head. Her eyes shone. This was what she lived for.

"Nice of you to compliment us on them," Zack added. "I guess you wouldn't remember what nestlings looked like. From your own days as a beggar."

That's what raven parents called their young: "beggars." Used with affection, the word described them perfectly. All day long they begged. Molly's nestlings had become quite good at it, each one developing its own endearing version of the head-up, mouth-open, wing-fluttering posture that said, "I'm cute. Feed me." One of them went through its routine now for Colin. Without thinking, Colin coughed up a couple of flies and tucked them into the baby bird's gape.

"Oh, Colin! How sweet of you!" Molly couldn't believe it. Colin had fed the nestling as if he had been doing it for years.

"How did you learn to do that?" Zack asked.

Colin blinked. "I – I don't know," he said. "It just seemed to be the right thing to do."

"It *was* the right thing, C.C.," Zack said, "and it shows that you're going to be – or maybe you have already been – a fine father."

"A father? Me, a father?" He looked at the nestlings again. Another was begging to him. "They really are very cute." He brought up more gullet-goo and fed the little raven. Now the others were starting to squawk. He found that he had just enough to give them each something.

"They ought to be calling you 'Uncle Colin,'" Zack said, with a chuckle.

"Unga Colling!" one of the babies cried. The others joined in.

"Ungle Crawl!"

"Col, Col!"

"Unka! Unka!"

Colin looked at them and smiled. "You kids have a way of winning a bird over," he said.

"Ober, ober!"

"Unka Ober!"

"Colling Ungle! Feed me again!"

"Me, too!"

"More! More again! Do it *agaaaaiiiiin!*"

Colin was out of food. "I'll go get some more," he said.

"Oh, don't bother," Molly said. "That's our job, not yours. Besides, we were just about to leave the little beggars and go for a short flight while they nap."

"Nap?" one of the nestlings said. "Nap now?"

"Nap! Nap!"

"Me, too!"

Instantly the baby birds flopped down in the nest. Their heads rested on one another's bodies. Looking at the pile of birds, Colin had trouble figuring out how many they were. "Do you want me to stay and watch them?" he asked.

"Uh – no. We'd just as soon leave them entirely alone while we're gone." Zack's voice had a slight edge to it. Colin might be a good friend, but, well, he was still a raven, and ravens, you know, had this thing about baby birds. Other species of baby birds, but still . . .

"That's right, Colin," Molly added firmly. "We don't want anybody going near the nest while we're away. Not even you." She smiled. "I hope you don't mind."

"Not at all," Colin said. "I understand." He stepped back from the nest. Nothing could be seen except the fortress of sticks. "They're really lucky to have you two looking after them."

"And they'll be even luckier to have you around when they grow bigger," Zack said. "You're welcome to come around as often as you like – when we're home, of course – and play with our little C.C.s. It'll be good for them. Get them thinking about the flock." He looked over to Molly. "What do you say, Moll?"

She looked doubtful. "Oh, Zack. I don't know."

Colin's happy expression changed to one of disappointment. Molly saw this. It showed the honesty of his intentions. "Yes," she said. "Definitely yes. Colin, from here on you're 'Uncle Colin' to our nestlings."

One of the nestlings looked up. "Uncle Colin," it said, quite clearly.

"Thanks, Molly." Then he remembered that Zack and Molly wanted to escape their charges for a while. "Hey," he said, "I've found a dead marmot. It's just a little way off, around the corner on the back side. Join me for a quick bite?"

"A marmot, Colin? Really?" Molly hadn't eaten marmot meat since last summer.

"Right this way," Colin called, jumping off the ledge and spreading his wings.

XIV

High on the huge face of Wakonda Buttress, which glowered over the valley behind Yamnuska, sat Zygadena, the raven who lived by herself. Today she perched on her roost atop a thumb-shaped piece of rock stuck onto the overhanging cliff. Dolus and Garth flapped to a landing beside her.

"Hi, Zygadena," Garth said.

"H'lo," Dolus said.

"Boys, boys! How nice to *see* you!"

Zygadena was a beautiful raven, her feathers the blackest of black. Her plumage caught the sunlight and glowed iridescent purple and green. She was a large raven, just as large as Dolus. And Dolus found her irresistible. Her eyes were so dark that he couldn't tell what lay behind them. Nor did he dare look directly into those eyes, they were so penetrating, so powerful.

His own eyes flicked about, showing his nervous anticipation. "Zygadena, we have come for more –"

Zygadena interrupted with a laugh. "Ha ha! More *fun*, boys? Would you like to have some more *fun*?"

"Yes!" both the young ravens replied at once.

"Well then, we *shall.*"

Zygadena leapt from her roost and flew up the cliff to a ledge just under the summit. Garth and Dolus followed her. All three had been here before, not once but several times. The ledge was littered with bones, the small, light bones of birds. Above the ledge a crack cleaved deeply into the mountain, and back in its darkness lay the secrets of Zygadena's trade.

"Are we going to have some Magic Meat?" Dolus asked.

"Oh yes, boys. We will, we *will.* We *always* have a little *Magic Meat.*" Zygadena's eyes glittered in the sun. "But first," she said, "tell me more about your *winter.*" She looked at Dolus. "Last time you told me that you went to *Carrot Creek.* What happened on *Carrot Creek?*"

Dolus looked down. He was thinking about his answer. Zygadena always looked for something in her questions. He had learned that, and he wanted to please her with his reply. "Not much. It got cold. An avalanche came down. It killed Cathy."

Zygadena looked interested. "It killed a *Raven's Ender?*"

"Yeah. Cathy. I kind of liked her –"

"– and, and," Garth interrupted, "and she had this cool thing that made a ticking sound!" He looked down. "But she's dead."

"I'm so *sorry* to hear about that. Tell me how it *happened.*"

"Oh, we were all in this big spruce. Snow came down. The rest of us got away in time –"

"Hey, yeah," Garth interrupted. "That was great. Colin, he –"

"I don't want to hear about Colin," Dolus snapped.

Garth babbled on anyway. "So Colin knew it was going to happen, okay, and he warned us about it, and –"

Now Zygadena broke in. "This . . . this *Colin* C.C. You say he *knew* the slide was going to happen?"

Garth looked at Dolus. Dolus answered for Garth. "Well, he said he knew it. I think he actually started it, just to get the credit."

Zygadena looked thoughtful. "I'd like to meet this Colin," she said. Then she shook her head and exclaimed brightly, "So – let's get on with the *fun!*"

A gust of wind swept across the ledge, ruffling the ravens' feathers. Dolus and Garth felt a flutter of excitement as little bones rolled and clinked about their toes. Zygadena spread her wings and flew up into the secret crack. Dolus and Garth waited for her on the ledge, as she had instructed them on previous occasions. They could hear her rustling in the darkness. Then she was back. In her bill she had two wispy strips of dried, blackened meat. She set them down carefully, side by side. "Here you are, boys. Magic Meat." Dolus and Garth positioned themselves beside the strips. Dolus was lowering his bill toward one of them when Zygadena cautioned him. "Now remember, Dolus. Wait for the *Words*." Dolus pulled his bill back.

Zygadena spread her beautiful black wings. As she did, another gust came by. It lifted her slightly, in a stately way, and set her down again. It was as if she had commanded the wind to do that, Dolus thought.

"O now I hear the call of the *Magic Meat*," she said. The words were strong and clear, becoming louder as she spoke.

"And it calls out to my *heart*, and it calls *into* my heart, and it pulls forth from my heart the *power of my body*, the *Magic Meat*."

Louder and louder she spoke, her voice rising in pitch. It was changing, becoming strangely musical.

"And the call of the Magic Meat becomes the *song* of the Magic Meat, and the Magic Meat's song is *strong*, full of *power!*"

Zygadena was shrieking, now, in a voice unlike that of any normal raven. It seemed to echo of its own accord. Then it went even beyond that. Zygadena actually began to sing.

"*O Magic Meat, O Magic Meat, O Magic Meat lies at my feet! O Magic Meat, O Magic Meat, O Magic Meat I now shall EAT!!*"

She plunged her bill down toward the pair of black strips on the ledge. Garth winced. Surely Zygadena would break her bill on the hard stone!

But she checked the downward flash and carefully picked up the wisp nearest her. Tenderly, she swallowed it. Then she picked up another strip and offered it to Dolus. He snatched it from her and gulped it down.

Dolus gave a little shiver and closed his eyes. When he opened them, their color had changed from brown to white. "Yes. Oh, *yes . . .*" he said, throwing his head back.

Zygadena now offered a strip to Garth. He hesitated. He had been through this before, but he still found it frightening. Zygadena stared at him, hard. Garth ate his wisp.

XV

Three golden ravens flew through a sky of gray. The land below was white, white as snow, but it moved in waves like the sea.

"I shall have a place to perch," said the first raven, who was Zygadena. "I shall have it *now*."

And there it was: a tree. A spruce tree. The birds circled down to it. As they landed, Garth recognized it as the big spruce along Carrot Creek. But it was gray, not green.

"I have been here before," Dolus said.

"Yes," said Zygadena.

"Where is the snow?" asked Garth.

"It is here, *now*," said Zygadena. Instantly the tree was heavily cloaked.

"Thank you," said Garth.

Zygadena looked out toward the white land, rolling off toward the gray sky. She spoke over the waves. "I wish to see the young raven *Cathy*," she said.

Cathy flew down to the tree. She perched beside Dolus.

"Hello, Dolus."

"Cathy?" Dolus opened his white eyes wider. "Is it really you?"

"Of course, boys," she said.

Dolus smiled. "Cathy –" he started to say, but Cathy interrupted. "Dolus. Oh, my sweet Dolus," she said, "I have *missed* you."

Dolus trembled. A feeling started in the back of his head. Intensely pleasant, it trickled down his spine. "Cathy, I, I –"

"I know," said Cathy. "I love you, too."

Dolus felt overpowering passion. He took a step toward Cathy.

She took a step away. "Dolus, you may not be with me now."

"Yes! Now! I must!" He moved forward again. Then he saw the terrible power in Cathy's white eyes. He had never noticed that power while she was alive. He stopped.

"Dolus!" she commanded. "If you want me, you must do something for me."

"What?! What must I do?!" He quivered, bending his legs as the feeling came again, the pleasure so strong that it made him weak in the knees.

"You must *bring me* something," Cathy said.

"Yes! Yes! Anything!" Dolus bent his knees again. Oh, the pleasure! It was almost painful.

"You must bring me a *raven*," she said.

"Yes! Yes! A raven! Anyone!"

"You must bring me *Colin C.C.*," she said.

Dolus moaned. "Yes, yes! I will do that! I will kill him! I will kill him and bring him to you!"

"You must bring him to me *alive*," Cathy said.

XVI

When the spell of the Magic Meat had worn off, the three ravens stood again on the bone-covered ledge high on Wakonda Buttress. Garth found that he was having trouble remembering what had happened. There was something about some ravens, and a tree, and – and . . . what?

"Well, boys," Zygadena said. "Was it *fun?*"

"It was good," said Dolus.

"Uh, I liked it a lot," said Garth. He shook his head, trying to get the fuzziness out of it.

"You know," said Zygadena, "some ravens think the Magic Meat is just a lot of *silliness*." She looked at the other two birds. "They think it's nothing but *pretend*."

"Not me," said Dolus. "The Magic Meat works. I can say that for sure."

Zygadena looked at Garth. "Do *you* believe in the Magic Meat?"

"Uh, sure. I mean, why not? It works for us." He shook his head again.

Zygadena brought a glossy eye close to Garth's. "I don't think you really *believe*, Garth, dear."

"I do! I do!"

"What would it take for you to believe, shall we say, somewhat *more strongly?*"

"Oh, I can convince him," Dolus offered.

"No, Dolus," Zygadena scolded. "Garth is your *friend*. We don't hurt our *friends*."

"Tell me that after you've put up with the jerk for a while," Dolus said.

Zygadena turned back to Garth. "I think we can both teach Dolus something about friendship," she said.

"Like what?" Garth asked. "He's pretty tough on his friends."

Zygadena didn't answer his question. Instead, she asked another. "A good friend can do things that *help*, can't he, Garth?"

"Sure."

"I want you to do a favor for Dolus."

"Uh, okay."

"I want you to turn around."

Garth pulled his head in. This was some kind of trick. Dolus was always doing things like this to him. If he turned his back on Dolus, Dolus was sure to give him a peck. A hard one. Garth didn't turn around.

"*Really*, Garth," Zygadena said sweetly. "I won't let Dolus hurt you. This is *different*. This is going to show Dolus how much you really *care* for him, and it is going to show you about the *power* of the Magic Meat. It's going to show you both. Now do as I ask and turn around."

Garth looked quickly over his shoulder. "I've turned around."

"That's not good enough," Zygadena said, closing her eyes and lifting her bill. "You have to turn *all the way around*." Zygadena's voice was soft, but Garth noticed that her eyebrow feathers were raised. Uh-oh.

Garth deliberated. He really didn't have a choice. He turned around, expecting to feel a peck in the back, if not from Dolus, then from Zygadena. But it didn't come. Instead, he saw something that he hadn't noticed before. It was lying among the bones, partly covered by them. He stepped over. His eyes opened wide as he picked the object up by its short chain. As he started to turn around, it swung from his bill and flashed in the sun.

It was Cathy's ticking thing.

XVII

"Hey, Colin!" Colin looked across the circle of birds. The Flap was just breaking up. Who was calling to him?

"Hey, Colin! It's me, Dolus. Over here. I want to talk to you."

Colin had avoided Dolus – and Garth, too – ever since the nasty sheep-watching episode along Carrot Creek. Well, he thought, Dolus probably wouldn't try anything right here, right now. Colin hopped over and Dolus met him halfway.

Colin's tufts were ever so slightly raised. "You want to see me about something?"

"Hey, yeah." Dolus was smiling. "I've got an idea."

"What sort of idea?"

"Oh, a kind of trip idea," Dolus said. "Some exploring."

Colin was immediately suspicious. He didn't care to go "exploring" anywhere with this bird. "Dolus, I'm too busy to go exploring. Greta and I were just about to head down to the ponds below the South Face to learn something about fish."

"Aw, there's always gonna be fish in those ponds. But what I have in mind can't wait."

"Not even until after lunch?"

"Nope."

Colin's curiosity was aroused. He considered. Although he was smaller than Dolus, he was now a better flyer by far – and very quick on the ground, too. Could Dolus hurt him again? Not likely. Colin could probably get away.

"Let me ask Greta if she minds whether I go or not." He looked over to where Greta had been standing. To his surprise, she was gone.

"Uh, yeah," said Garth, walking up to join them. "I just talked to her. She said she had some stuff to do first. She said she'd, uh, meet you later on."

That wasn't at all like Greta, Colin thought. She would have told him herself.

"Look," Dolus said, looking irritated. "Are you coming or not?"

Again, Colin pondered. He had been wondering what Garth and Dolus did all day. Here was a chance to find out. Greta flew so slowly.

He could spend some time on this other thing and still catch up before she reached the lake.

"Um . . . okay. I'll go. But I have to be back pretty soon. Will this take long?"

Dolus was already unfurling his wings. "Naw. Not long at all. C'mon, Garth."

Letting Garth lead the way, Dolus spoke in friendly tones. "I'm real sorry about that fight we had last winter."

"Me too," Colin replied. What was this? Dolus apologizing?

"Yeah, I just kind of lost my cool there. I don't usually do that."

Colin didn't say it, but what he thought was, "You do it all the time."

"Almost there!" Garth called back over his shoulder.

"Almost where?" Colin asked.

"Almost to the buttress," Dolus replied. Wakonda Buttress loomed ahead, its dark walls overhanging the rubbly slopes below, where huge boulders had smashed to pieces after falling free from the heights. Like all the other ravens in the flock except Dolus and Garth, Colin avoided Wakonda Buttress. He had heard stories about Zygadena, and he had no wish to run into her – especially in the company of these two untrustworthy birds.

But now, suddenly, here she was. Zygadena had appeared as if from nowhere.

"*Gro*, Colin C.C.! How *nice* to *see* you! Gro!"

Colin swooped off to the side and started straight back toward Raven's End.

"Oh, Colin – don't go," Zygadena called, sounding hurt. "I wanted to *speak* with you, Colin!" Now her voice changed to one of concern. "It's really *important*, Colin. It's about where you came from before you got to Yamnuska."

Colin turned around so quickly he skidded in the air. "You – you know about that?"

"Yes, *yes*," Zygadena said. "I thought you'd like to *talk* about it." She sounded confiding. "I'm sorry I had to get you over here on a pretext, but the other birds won't let me come over to Raven's End, so I had to invent a little *excuse* for Garth and Dolus to use. I – I hope you're not *offended* –"

Now Colin was really confused. Should he stay? Zygadena sounded so sincere. But with Dolus here, and Garth – this just couldn't be safe.

"I, uh – I think I'll visit some other time," Colin said, his voice shaky. "Nice to meet you. Goodbye." Again, he started flying away. Slowly.

"Well, I'm sorry you didn't want to stay," Zygadena called back. "It's just that your real flock are such *nice* birds, and one of them came by the other day asking about you."

That did it. Colin turned around again. "My flock? My flock?"

"Yes, yes, of course. The Maligne Flock. From north of here."

"The Maligne Flock?"

"Oh, *poor* Colin," Zygadena said soothingly. "You had such a *terrible* experience, didn't you? Something about a *crash*, wasn't it? I guess you still don't remember a *thing*, do you?" She looked at him pityingly. "Let's land over there and I'll tell you *all* about it."

The landing place over there was the bone-covered ledge.

Zygadena lighted on it, followed by Dolus and Garth. Colin had another flash of fear.

"I'm not landing until those two birds have left," he said, looking at Dolus and Garth.

"Of course, Colin," Zygadena replied. "Of course. Some things are *private*." She turned to the others. "You two boys go and amuse yourselves for a while. Colin and I want some privacy here."

Dolus protested. "But, but, you said –"

"What I said was that we need some *privacy*," Zygadena repeated, raising her tufts.

"Uh – sure, sure," Garth said. "Hey, Dolus, let's go check out Bilbo. I thought I saw something dead over there."

"Okay, I guess." Dolus left the ledge.

Garth shuddered. He had known this would be coming. Zygadena wanted Colin all to herself. What was she going to do with him? He followed Dolus off toward Bilbo Buttress.

"*Now*, then," Zygadena said pleasantly as the other birds flew away. "Is that better, Colin?"

"Somewhat, yes," Colin answered. "I just don't trust those two."

"Oh, *I* do," Zygadena stated. "They're really good boys. Just kind of *impulsive*, if you know what I mean." She smiled. "They're always nice to *me*. I've just managed to bring out the *best* in them, I guess."

As she spoke, Colin looked Zygadena over carefully. Her plumage was exquisite, glittering with the iridescence of a raven in her prime. Not one feather was out of place. Her legs were strong, with perfect scales. Her claws were long and very sharp. Her unblemished bill was large and straight. There were no dents anywhere along the opening, the edges of which met perfectly. And her eyes! Her eyes were so dark – so *deep*. Here was the most beautiful raven he had ever seen.

"So I just thought we should get together," she was saying. Colin hadn't been listening.

"Pardon?"

"Oh, Colin, you're so *polite*. Never mind. I'm just glad that you're *here*," she said. Her voice, thought Colin, was alluring – very smooth, with a kind of sweetness. And it showed such intelligence.

"Now," she said in a businesslike way. "About your flock."

"Yes! Tell me about my flock." Colin ruffled his wing-feathers expectantly.

"Well, the *first* thing you should know is that they're absolutely *famous* all over the Rockies," she began. "Really powerful flyers – just like *you* – and they travel a lot." She stopped suddenly and looked around. "Oh, you know what? It's almost time for my mid-morning *snack*. Would you like to *share* it with me?" She looked up toward the crack above the ledge.

"Actually, I *was* getting a little hungry," Colin replied. He hadn't been eating enough lately. Greta's lessons kept him so busy that he was always hungry.

"I'll just fetch a little something from in here," Zygadena said. In a moment she came fluttering back with a couple of dark meat strips in her bill. "I know this doesn't *look* like much, Colin, but it's well-aged bighorn and I think you'll find it *quite* nourishing." Her voice had a motherly tone. "If I have a bit this time of day, it always seems to keep me going until lunch. Sometimes even 'til *supper!*" She presented one of the wisps to Colin. It smelled delicious. He ate it.

And the world fell apart.

XVIII

Greta flew at her usual trolling pace toward the ponds at the base of the South Face. Perhaps, she thought, she might get halfway there before Colin caught up with her. At least this way, by starting early, while he still chatted with the other birds, she wouldn't have to struggle to keep up for the whole distance. She would have to struggle to keep up for only *half* the distance. She chuckled.

Another raven pulled up beside her, but it wasn't Colin.

"Oh, Sarah. You took me by surprise. I was expecting someone else."

"I know, Greta. But I wonder if, like, I could sort of, well, kind of listen in today."

"I can teach only one apprentice at a time, Sarah."

"Really? I was hoping that, you know, I could maybe come along every now and again . . ."

Greta looked at the young bird and smiled. Like Colin, Sarah was very smart. Interested in everything. When Greta was done with Colin, she would have to teach Sarah. After all, a flock lucky enough to have two up-and-comers like Sarah and Colin deserved to have both of them taught well, even if it meant a lot of work for this tired old –

Suddenly Greta felt very cold. She stumbled in her flight.

"Greta, what's wrong?" Sarah moved in closer. "Are you okay?"

"Just – just a minute." Greta's eyes were closed. Her head turned this way and that. She looked to be in pain, and her wingbeats faltered. She lost airspeed. She drifted lower.

Now greatly worried, Sarah started to call out again, but Greta spoke first. Her eyes flicked open. "Sarah! Where is Colin?"

"Oh, he flew off with Dolus and Garth."

"Dolus?! Garth?! Tumbling toad-ticks. Did he tell you anything?"

"He – he just said he'd be back in a little while. Isn't he going to meet us at the lake? Greta, what's wrong?"

"Everything." She wheezed and shook her head. "I'm going to have to land. This is all too much." She wheezed again. "Listen carefully. Colin is in trouble – *huff, puff* – over by Wakonda Buttress – *cough*. Bad trouble. I want you to fly over there as fast as you can, Sarah, and save him."

"Save him?! But what can I do?"

"Whatever you need to do. Everything depends on you. Now go, C.C., *go!*"

XIX

Gray. Everything was gray. The sky was gray. The earth was gray. Even the sun was gray.

Colin felt himself leaving his body. He looked at himself from above. His body was not gray. It was golden, and he was not in it.

"I'm not me!" he cried, more frightened than he had ever been. "Some bird is in my body!"

A quiet, soothing voice responded. "It's all right, Colin. It's only *me*."

The raven that used to be Colin looked up toward the Colin that used to be a raven, but now was nothing but grayness. "See? It's only me. It's only Zygadena."

Colin's eyes zoomed in on the raven. Even though she was far away, he could see her as if she were flying next to him. Her eyes were white, so white against the gold feathers. White and gold against the grayness. Fear stabbed through him again. "What – what is happening to me?!"

"We are travelling together, Colin. We have left this world and gone to another. Do you *like* it?"

"No! No! I want the old world back!"

The voice became harder. "You can't have it back, Colin. Not ever. Everything is *different*, now." Zygadena's golden wings flapped once. Light flashed from the tips. Again the fear struck. Colin thought his heart – whose heart? – was going to explode, he was so afraid.

"But I will give you back your *body*, Colin."

Suddenly Colin was flying beside Zygadena. They were moving swiftly and in unison, wingbeats synchronized perfectly. He was grateful to have his body back. Tears ran from his white eyes. "Oh, thank you, Zygadena. I thought my body was gone."

"Yes, dear Colin, that's what they *all* think when they come to this different world. *My* world. They have to leave their old bodies *behind* to come into my world. Then I give them *new* bodies. Beautiful *golden bodies*, bodies that will never feel *old*, or *sick*, or *unhappy*."

Yes, thought Colin, as the fear died away, replaced by a feeling of assurance. Yes, he was completely certain. Now he understood. He understood everything. This new body was beautiful. It was beautiful because it had no feeling. He reached back and touched himself with his bill. He could not feel the touch. This body was too powerful to feel a touch. It could not feel pain. It was indestructible, immortal. Nothing could harm it. Nothing. Colin wept with the beauty of his new understanding, with the power it gave him. "Zygadena, it's all so *beautiful*," he cried.

"Look at me," Zygadena said.

Colin turned his head. There, at his wingtip, was the golden form of Zygadena. Lightning flickered from her wings with every stroke. Here was strength, Colin thought. Here was grace. Here was wisdom. Here was what he had always wanted. Yes, always!

"Colin, I wish to have you for my *mate*."

Oh, yes! Yes! To be with the golden form of Zygadena, to feel the lightning surrounding them in the darkness! Yes! Yes! Yes! A new feeling of pleasure swept through him. It made his back arch and his wings pull in. Oh, what an incredible feeling! He closed his eyes.

"We must *be together now*, Colin." Zygadena turned upside-down, extending her feet upward toward his. "Take hold of me. Take hold of me now and *draw me in*, Colin, my love."

Colin's mind focussed on Zygadena's beautiful body. My love! The golden raven, she called him "my love"! Yes, he would draw her in. He would pull the golden body of Zygadena toward him, and the golden lightning would flash around them, there in the grayness, up so high, where the only feeling was the feeling of love, so strong, so true!

Colin could feel his feet touch those of Zygadena. Their claws clutched. A surge of golden power travelled up his legs and entered his body. He trembled. He felt everything slowing down. His wings beat slower, slower, then stopped altogether as the pleasure began to build again. This time it ran down his neck, down his spine, causing it to arch again. It gathered under his tail, building there, waiting to explode in a shower of golden sparks. "Oh, Zygadena, my love, are you ready?"

"Yes, I'm ready, Colin. I'm *so* ready, Colin."

Something about Zygadena's voice sent a trickle of fear into the flow of Colin's pleasure. Something was wrong. The words should have carried feelings of love, but they carried something else. Something . . . something like *hatred*.

Colin felt Zygadena's claws wrap around his legs. Tighter and tighter they clamped, working up his legs until he could feel her claws scraping across his belly, replacing the pleasure with pain. What? But his body could feel no pain! His body was golden, immortal! How could he feel pain?

"*Ha ha ha ha!*" Zygadena began to laugh. Her laughter was not the sort that ravens share in fun or happiness. It was a weird, screeching titter that spoke to Colin of the pleasure Zygadena felt in hurting him. He opened his eyes wide. Color was creeping in around the edges of the grayness. He saw a deep blue that he recognized as the sky. He was upside-down. He twisted his head around and saw the forest below, green on gray, coming toward him. He was falling! And Zygadena was falling with him!

Zygadena laughed again as her claws crept farther up Colin's legs. He could feel the sharp tips reaching his breast, stabbing into him now, like the talons of a hawk plunging into its prey.

"*Awk!* It hurts! It's not golden! It's, it's –"

"It's going to be over soon, Colin. *Ha ha ha!* Soon it will be *over*, Colin!" Again came that hideous, shrieking laughter. "*Soon*, Colin! *Soon!*"

Colin tried to extend his wings, but Zygadena's claws had pinned them to his sides. He looked up at her. Her bill was open, coming toward him, closing over his throat.

"*Urk* – Zyg – Zygadena. Why – *choke* – why?"

"Why?" she replied, loosening her grasp just enough to hiss out the words. "*Why?* Because you are *beautiful*, Colin. So fine and beautiful. I must *have* you, Colin. And now I *do*. Because, dear Colin, the most beautiful ravens make the best *Magic Meat!*"

She flexed her claws again, driving them deeper. A drop of Colin's blood blew away in the wind. The air roared by as they fell, faster and faster. Below them now was the top of Wakonda Buttress, a flat summit with a few limestone boulders scattered on it. Eons of rainfall and snowmelt had corroded the tops of the boulders into spine-like ridges of stone, their edges so sharp they could cut.

The surface of one of those boulders, the one perched right at the edge of the cliff, was especially jagged. It was covered with dark stains. Black feathers stuck to it. They fluttered in the breeze.

It was toward this boulder that Zygadena steered their plunge.

XX

Sarah flew as fast as she could. But ahead of her, blocking the way to Wakonda Buttress, lay Yamnuska. Expecting a strong updraft on the South Face, and reasoning that an equally strong downdraft on the back side would fling her toward Wakonda Buttress faster than going around the end of the mountain, she elected to fly straight over the top. Sarah was moving so quickly as she approached the face that she almost smacked into it. But the updraft was, in fact, very strong. She kept climbing within it, beating steadily in tight circles, gaining elevation even faster than the rushing air could.

Soon she crested the top, flying right over the summit. A marmot sitting there ducked its head as she whistled by. She dropped into the downdraft and picked up speed, just as she had planned.

"This is, like, really awesome," she said out loud as she flew on, her wingtips humming. "I'm not even tired! I'm going so far! So fast! And I'm not even tired!"

Then a twitch of dread caused her to miss a wingbeat. What was going on at Wakonda Buttress? What could she do about it? Well, she was going to find out shortly. There, coming into sight, was the buttress. And, yes, there was a raven over it – no, two ravens, clutching together somehow, and – oh, no! – they were *falling!*

XXI

Colin and Zygadena dropped from the sky like a single black stone, gaining speed toward the spine-covered boulder on which many a raven had met its end. Zygadena fell with pleasure, completely in control, preparing herself for the special maneuver she knew so well. It was her own maneuver, perfected years ago and practiced often.

Each time she would wrap her victim in her claws. They would fall together, faster and faster, until, just before impact, Zygadena would spread her wings. The other raven would swing under her and hit first, far harder than she. Her claws would finish their penetration from one side as the stone spears ripped in from the other. Yes, the crash would be jarring for Zygadena, but the crumpling body of her prey would cushion the blow. She would step off the dead raven afterward, a little shaken, as always, but otherwise unhurt. Then she would begin to rip and shred, like a hawk, picking the bloody, broken raven apart, swallowing some of its tender organs on the spot but saving most of the carcass for later – much later – when the flesh had been carefully prepared in the special way she knew so well, infused with the power of exotic substances until it was capable of conjuring up, for whoever ate it, the strange world of golden ravens. Thus did she create her Magic Meat.

Only moments before this scenario was to play, Colin began to struggle.

His mind was clearing, now, his muscles beginning to obey him. Zygadena could feel Colin's strength returning. She shut her bill as tightly as she could on his windpipe. She closed her claws as hard as she could on his breast. More blood droplets spat away in the wind. Grayness crept over Colin's vision again, and this time it had nothing to do with Magic Meat. He was being strangled.

Then, from out of nowhere, came a bird. It was a white bird, not a black one, and it was flying faster than any raven could hope to fly. It shot downward toward Colin and Zygadena at half the speed of sound.

This was a prairie falcon on the attack, with its sharply hooked beak splitting the wind and its lethal talons tucked against its belly, ready to strike. The falcon had seen its target from far off. Now it homed in. The wings canted back, increasing its velocity. As it closed, the falcon made last-minute corrections in its trajectory. The talons swung forward and clenched – two clubs about to deal a killing blow –

WHAM!

The falling mass of raven feathers became two falling masses. One regained control and pulled out of the plunge in time to make a rough landing beside the killing-boulder. The other continued to plummet. It fell past the summit of Wakonda Buttress, just missing the killing-boulder. One wing twisted uselessly while the other worked frantically. The result was a wild circling, like an airplane in a spin. One wing struck the cliff. It caught momentarily in a crack, which slowed the fall. The bird tumbled from the crack onto a ledge just below – the ledge of the Magic Meat.

It was Zygadena.

She was in pain, terrible pain that made her body curl and shudder. Croaking in agony, she rolled among the bones of the ravens she had killed. Something else, though, hurt Zygadena even more. What hurt her more than her broken wing, which hurt a great deal, was the realization that, for the first time ever, one of her intended victims had escaped.

At this moment the prairie falcon came zooming by. It didn't stop, but Zygadena could still make out clearly the crisp communication it delivered to her.

"Raven, this is CZE. Raven, this is CZE. Sorry about that. Do you copy? Over."

Zygadena passed out.

XXII

"Colin! Colin! It's me, Sarah! Can you hear me?" Sarah was shouting at a raven lying among the boulders atop Wakonda Buttress. "Oh, Colin, I hope you're not, like, really hurt –"

"Wha . . .?"

"Oh, Colin, it's me, Sarah! Oh, you can talk! You can talk!" She danced a little jig of joy as Colin struggled to his feet.

"Sarah, I feel terrible."

"But you're alive, Colin! You're alive!"

"I'm also the stupidest raven that ever flew."

"What happened, Colin? Who was that other raven?"

"Zygadena." Colin shook his head, trying to get rid of a lingering poisonous feeling. He checked himself over, finding several deep wounds in his breast. He needed Greta right now more than he needed Sarah. Then he realized why Sarah was there.

"Sarah! You came to rescue me!"

"Well, I guess, sort of . . . yes, I did."

"Sarah, you brave, brave bird. I'll never forget this."

"Oh, but you're getting it all wrong, Colin. *I* didn't save you, that really awesome falcon did."

"Falcon? I didn't see any falcon."

"It was so *fast*, Colin. Just super, super fast. I hardly saw it either. But it hit Zygadena and she let you go."

At this point the prairie falcon arrived. In a rare act of intimacy, it landed near Sarah and Colin. Its fierce eyes regarded the two ravens.

"Thank you," said Colin, simply.

"Raven, this is CZE. Gratitude is appreciated, but cannot be accepted. Purpose of landing was to apologize, over."

"Apologize for what? You just saved my life!"

"CZE to raven. Not intentional. Repeat, not intentional. Collateral damage occurred as unexpected consequence of practice attack. Talons were deployed incorrectly and made contact with civilians. Air regulations require delivery of official apology in such instances. Consider it served. CZE, over and out."

The falcon dived into space. In moments it was a tiny speck in the distance. Sarah and Colin stared after it.

"See?" she said. "It was that falcon, Seize Eddy, or whatever it calls itself. Not me. I was *going* to try to do something, but, well, against Zygadena like that, you know . . . she was going to get you, that's for sure."

"Maybe so, Sarah. Maybe so. But she didn't." Colin touched Sarah's bill with his. "I'm always going to remember this," he said. "How brave you were."

"You were brave for me, once, too. Remember?"

"That time you were in the snowbank? Oh, that wasn't brave. That was –" He wanted to say "second-sight," but he stopped himself.

"Yes, it was, Colin. There you were, all hurt – maybe more than you are now – and you still found me. You came and found me. I'd say that was really, really brave."

"So I guess we're even, then."

"Hey, yeah! I guess we are!"

"Shall we fly back to Raven's End, Sarah? Greta will be worried to death."

"Okay. But what about Zygadena?"

"Zygadena? Oh, by the Trees – what's become of Zygadena?!"

"I saw her fall down there," Sarah said, pointing with her bill to the edge of the cliff. Colin hobbled over to look. There she was, Zygadena, lying motionless on the Magic Meat ledge far below, her left wing bent out unnaturally.

"She won't be giving us any trouble," Colin said. Then he looked up in fright, remembering that Dolus and Garth were somewhere in the valley. If they attacked him now! But he saw no sign of either of them. Instead he saw another raven, flying toward them in a familiar, ungainly style.

"Greta!"

Greta landed beside them, completely out of breath. She had to sit there a while, head down and panting, before she could talk. "Oh – *whew* – thank the Trees you're both all right. I was so worried – *wheeze* – what happened?"

Sarah started in at once, babbling on about Zygadena's attack. Greta listened attentively through the whole story, nodding as if she had heard it before. Colin noted this and asked her.

"Yes. I *have* heard of this before. But up to now, Zygadena has always killed wandering ravens, usually hurt ones. And crows. But never a Raven's Ender. I didn't think she'd be so bold as to take on one of us."

"Now we know better," said Colin. "We'll have to be even more careful – if she's still alive."

"Oh, she's still alive," Greta said. "She looked up at me when I flew by. But I don't know if she'll live for long. Looks like she's got a broken wing. That should finish her off."

"Oh, I hope so!" said Sarah, clacking her bill.

"But I'm not going to get close enough to find out." Greta would tend any hurt raven, even ones she disliked, but Zygadena was just too dangerous to approach, even when dying. Or maybe especially when dying.

"Can you fly, Colin?" Greta had noticed the blood on his breast. "Here. Let me look at that." Gently, she used her bill to push the feathers aside. "Two pretty deep punctures, I'm afraid. Work your wings up and down." He did, gritting his bill to avoid crying out. "Well, at least you've stopped bleeding. That's good. Those claws don't seem to have reached your lungs or you'd be coughing blood. I guess you can fly home. But we'll have to go slowly."

Colin was not looking forward to flying anywhere. But neither did he wish to remain there any longer, because Dolus and Garth were bound to come back. Painfully, he spread his wings and limped into the air. ·

As the three ravens crossed the valley between Wakonda Buttress and Yamnuska, Colin discovered why Sarah had come to find him. He thanked Greta for that, recognizing her power of second-sight without making a point of it in front of Sarah. But Sarah had been thinking about that very thing, and she asked Greta directly.

"Greta, like, how did you know Colin was in trouble?"

Greta answered her honestly. "I knew. I don't really know *how* I knew, but I knew. Sometimes I get feelings about things, just as Colin did about the avalanche. Strong feelings. This one was especially strong, so I was especially sure it was real."

"That's really cool, Greta," Sarah said admiringly. "I wish I could do that."

"Well, maybe you can," Greta said.

"Really?" Sarah sounded excited. "Should I try?"

"Well, *trying* doesn't work," Greta said, "at least not for me. Does it work for you, Colin?"

Colin was following this closely. "No, not really. It just happens."

Greta turned to Sarah and smiled. "So keep your mind open, kiddo," she said. "Maybe you'll get one of those special feelings. And I hope it's not about something like an avalanche!" She thought for a moment. "On the other hand, I hope that if there *is* another avalanche, then you *do* get one of those feelings about it. If you see what I mean."

Sarah understood. She smiled. Then she thought of another question that she wanted to ask Greta, and she stopped smiling. It was a difficult question, one that Greta might not like, but it was important and so she chose to ask it anyway.

"Greta, if you knew that Zygadena was doing this really gross stuff to ravens, how come you . . . how come you didn't tell us about it?"

"Do you mean when you were little, Sarah, to warn you?"

"Yeah. Why didn't you tell all of us fledglings about Zygadena? I mean, sure, you said she was bad and stuff like that, but I didn't think she was *this* bad."

"Sarah, there were two reasons I didn't give you the whole truth about Zygadena." She paused, phrasing her next statement very carefully. "The first is that I didn't think she would actually try to kill a Raven's Ender. I was wrong. The second is that, up until a certain age, I don't think a young raven can deal with the notion of a creature like Zygadena."

"What do you mean, Greta?"

"When you were young you were afraid of many things, were you not, Sarah?"

"Oh, yes. Sure. Lots of things. Everything, really."

"And what did Marg tell you, whenever you were feeling especially afraid?"

"She said, 'Don't worry, Sarah, my dear, I will protect you.'" Sarah giggled.

Greta remained serious. "And did you think that she really could?"

"Protect me? Sure. Of course. As long as *I* didn't do anything really stupid, like sit around where coyotes could get me or something."

"But seeing what has happened to Colin, who is anything but stupid, do you think that Marg could have protected you from a bird like Zygadena?"

Sarah looked worried. "Umm . . . no. I guess not."

"And do you think that you would have wanted to know this about Zygadena back then, when you were little, and so frightened, and needed so much to believe that your mother could always keep you safe from harm?"

There was a long lapse as Sarah thought about this. All three birds flew silently, except for Greta's raspy breathing and Colin's quiet "awk" that he muttered on almost every wingbeat. Sarah looked over to Greta. Greta looked back, and she noticed that Sarah's expression had taken on a different character. She looked older, somehow. Less innocent.

"I see what you mean," Sarah said slowly. "Knowing that stuff would have made me so scared all the time I probably couldn't have *lived*."

"So there's your answer, Sarah. You provided it yourself."

"Greta, then – then there really *is* evil in the world, isn't there?"

"Yes, kiddo, there really is."

"Greta, I think I'm all grown up now."

"Yes, Sarah, you are. I'm sorry to say so, but you are."

With that, the two of them opened their bills and cried. Colin sniffled and said "awk."

XXIII

Dolus and Garth poked around in the nooks and crannies of Bilbo Buttress, the next rock tower east of Wakonda Buttress. They stayed on the side away from Wakonda, where Zygadena couldn't see them and they couldn't see her.

"She wants privacy," said Dolus, "okay, we give her privacy. But not too long. I'm gonna go back there and check up on her pretty soon."

"She'll be angry if you spy on her," Garth said.

"Hey – who said I'd be spying? I'll just fly back and say, 'Is it okay for little Dolus and little Garth to come see cute li'l Zygadena, now, hmmm?'"

"You shouldn't talk about her that way, Dolus."

"Well, she put me off. She made a promise and I'm not so sure she's gonna keep it."

"You mean the promise about Cathy? About you nesting with Cathy?"

Dolus swung his big bill around and pecked Garth. "Shut up about me and Cathy!"

"Okay, okay. Sorry. You don't have to be so touchy. Awk!" Dolus pecked him again.

Working their way around Bilbo Buttress, the two young renegades found a dead porcupine. They ate.

"We should tell the flock about this," said Garth, wiping his bill on the branch of an Engelmann spruce.

"No way," said Dolus. "This meat is ours. We found it. We'll keep it to ourselves."

"Whatever you say," Garth sighed. He had put up with Dolus's selfishness and bullying for so long . . .

Dolus narrowed his eyes and looked around. "Well, it's time to go check on Zygadena. C'mon."

The two birds flew back up the valley. In the distance they could see Colin and Zygadena flying side by side over Wakonda Buttress.

"Hey, they're gettin' along real well," Dolus said happily. "See – Zygadena's not so bad. Even Colin likes her."

"How can you tell that?"

"Oh, if he didn't, he'd be gone like that." Dolus snapped his claws. Then he had an idea. "Hey – let's go get some Magic Meat."

"Dolus, you shouldn't. That's Zygadena's – and she has to use the Words, and all that."

"Aw, those words are stupid. It's the Magic Meat that does it. It makes me feel great, and I want some. Now." He picked up the pace. Garth shook his head, but he followed.

Soon they were standing on the bone-littered ledge.

"Okay. She keeps it in that crack," said Dolus, trying to see what lay back in the cool darkness. "I'm gonna take a peek."

"Be careful," Garth said. He looked up, where Colin and Zygadena were doing something strange. Grabbing feet? Why would they play that game?

"Let me know if she's coming." Dolus disappeared into the fissure.

Garth marked time on the ledge, kicking bones off and watching them fall into space. Then Dolus was back. Several wisps of Magic Meat hung from his bill. "C'mon. We'll eat it over on Bilbo, where she can't see us."

Garth followed. As he flew, two terrible fears grew within him. The first was the fear of what the Magic Meat would do to him. The second was what Zygadena would do to them both when she found out they had stolen from her.

Dolus swung into a dark corner of Bilbo Buttress. Alighting on a dead spruce, he quickly swallowed one wisp. Then he ate another.

"Dolus! You're supposed to eat only one!"

"I'll have as many as I want." Dolus picked up yet another wisp. "Your turn, wimp. Let's see how many you . . ." Abruptly he stopped talking and stood still. The third wisp dropped from his bill. His eyes were turning white. Garth realized that there was no point in talking to him. Dolus was in Zygadena's land of golden ravens.

Something made Garth glance over toward Wakonda Buttress. His eyes widened as he saw two ravens, holding tightly to each other, plunging toward the boulders on the summit. He saw the struggle, the prairie falcon's attack, the outcome. He saw another raven arriving on the scene, then yet another.

He blinked hard, focussing his eyes to their greatest long-distance sharpness. The three ravens on the summit were Colin, Sarah, and Greta. They appeared to speak briefly, then they left. Colin was having difficulty flying.

The raven who had tumbled over the edge – that must have been Zygadena! Garth could see her lying partway down, not moving, on the ledge of the Magic Meat.

"Dolus! Dolus! Snap out of it! Zygadena's been hurt!"

"Huh? What? Zyga – Zygadena, *hurt?*"

"Yes! Hurry!" Garth flapped off toward Wakonda Buttress.

Dolus saw him leave, a golden raven flying away into the void. And that was beautiful. But something was wrong. Something was wrong with Zygadena. Oh, yes. Zygadena was hurt. Instantly, anger swept over Dolus. Zygadena! She was going to die, and she was going to die before she had fulfilled her promise to bring Cathy for him! Seeing the image of Zygadena through a tunnel of rage, he started after Garth.

Garth got to the ledge first. Sure enough, there was Zygadena, lying among the bones. She was a mess. Her left wing hung crazily from her shoulder, which was red with blood. One of her toes was missing its claw, and many of her feathers were bent and tattered. Her bill had a prominent scratch across it, and the tip was split.

Dolus arrived. "Zygadena!" he screeched. "You promised!"

"Dolus," she said, weakly, "oh, Dolus, I'm hurt –"

"I don't care! I want Cathy! I want her now!" He took a step toward her and angrily picked up a bird-bone in his bill. The bone snapped in two. One piece flipped over the edge, and he threw the other after it.

Zygadena raised her head to look at him. What she saw frightened her. This bird, she realized, this big, powerful raven whose eyes were white from eating Magic Meat, this bird could finish her off. She would have to handle him very carefully. She would have to be clever. She would have to ignore her injuries – oh, her wing hurt her so! – and focus only on Dolus.

And there it was: a plan.

She made her voice as strong as possible. "Dolus, listen. I *understand*. I understand *perfectly*. Of *course* you want Cathy. You're worried that I can't bring her to you, since I'm hurt." She winced. "But I still can, you know. *I still can.*"

Dolus looked confused. The power of the Magic Meat was overcoming his anger.

"You will have to *help* me," Zygadena said.

"What do I have to do?" Dolus felt his confusion returning to wrath. "I won't wait, Zygadena! I won't wait!"

"Oh, you won't have to wait, my dear boy. You won't have to wait *at all*. You can have her *right now*."

"Yes! NOW!"

"Just do this. Reach over there by the corner of the ledge and bring me what you *find*." She pointed with her battered bill.

Dolus hopped over and looked. There, tucked into a pocket in the rock, was Cathy's ticking thing. He grabbed it. "Here! Here! I've got it!" The ticking thing dangled from his bill by its chain.

"Now, Dolus. Do exactly as I say. You must *swallow the ticking thing*."

"Swallow it?" The ticking thing seemed much too large to swallow.

"Yes. Swallow it."

"But –"

"*Trust me*, Dolus. The ticking thing is *magic*. You will be *able* to swallow it."

Dolus looked over to Garth, who was looking back at him. Garth's expression was blank.

Zygadena spoke again, more strongly, now. "Dolus, the ticking thing has *power*. You must take the power of the ticking thing into your own body to bring Cathy's body *back to life!*"

Her words brought on another wave of Magic Meat feeling in Dolus. "Yes! Back to life!"

"Then you will both live *forever!*"

"Yes! Forever! We will live forever!"

The Magic Meat feeling was intense, now, creeping down his spine, making his back arch, making his legs weak. He shut his eyes as the wave of pleasure moved through his body. "Yes! Yes! I will swallow it, I will!"

Dolus opened his bill as wide as he could. He tilted his head back and let the ticking thing slide in. He gulped and swallowed, forcing it farther and farther down. Garth watched in horror, seeing the shape bulging in Dolus's neck. The chain was hanging from his bill. Then the chain, too, went in.

"*Ack – kack!*" Suddenly Dolus was choking.

Garth hopped over to him. "Dolus! Cough it up! It's too big!"

"*Ulk – gulk!*" Dolus's eyes bulged and his head went up and down, trying to dislodge the ticking thing. He ran over to the rock face and threw his body against it, once, twice, a third time. He fell down. He picked himself up and did it again.

"*Uh – uh – uh –*" The sounds coming from Dolus grew weaker. He looked around wildly, fixing Garth and Zygadena with white, terrified eyes. Then he collapsed on the ledge.

Garth moved close to him. "Dolus! Dolus!"

There was nothing Garth could do except watch, aghast. The lungs of Dolus still heaved beneath his feathers, but no air would go in. The round shape of the ticking thing formed a perfect plug. Dolus began to twitch. His back arched. His body twisted and writhed, knocking Garth down. His legs flailed. Zygadena dragged herself away from the edge of the cliff to avoid being kicked over it. The chain came up from Dolus's throat and waved about. Yellow slime sputtered from his bill.

"Dolus! This is horrible!" Garth hopped about in dismay. "Try to cough it up! Try! Try!"

At length the spasms ceased. Dolus lay still on his side. Only his eyes showed signs of life, opening and closing, over and over. The intervals became longer, then his eyes stayed open. They looked glassy. As Garth stared into them, the color changed from white back to brown.

"He's dead," said Zygadena. She showed no emotion in making the announcement.

Words came to Garth. "You killed him," he said quietly.

"No, Garth," she replied, "Dolus killed himself. I just helped him along."

Garth understood. "I always thought he might die in some terrible way," he said, looking down at his friend. "He was so strange. So violent. So mean." Garth's eyes found those of Zygadena. "Just like you."

Zygadena didn't reply. She turned her head to stare at the dead raven before her.

A hideous picture appeared in Garth's mind. Was she thinking of Dolus as – as *food?!* This gruesome thought prompted another one. He could just walk over to Zygadena, put his bill around her neck and kill her. Or push her over the edge. Just like that. And the world would be better off.

He took a step toward her. Her head snapped around. Her eyes fixed on his. No words were required; Garth felt the viciousness. The cunning. No, he thought. He wasn't going near that bird. Not ever again.

Garth looked across the valley. There, circling in the warm sun of early afternoon, were the ravens of Yamnuska. Garth didn't hesitate. He jumped off the ledge and flew away – away from Zygadena and the body of Dolus, away from Wakonda Buttress, away from Magic Meat, away from a life that he now saw, with awful clarity, to be wrong. A life that was – what word was he looking for? – *evil!*

"Evil!" He said it to himself over and over, with every wingbeat. "Evil! Evil! Evil!" He looked back at the ledge. It was small, now. He looked ahead, and there was Raven's End, where ravens were decent and things made sense. As fast as his wings could carry him, he headed home.

XXIV

The Evening Flight became the evening news. Several birds had seen Greta, Sarah, and Colin returning from the valley behind Yamnuska that afternoon. Colin was obviously hurt – too badly injured to join the Flight – and the reason came out quickly. Then, when Garth arrived without Dolus, the rest of the story hit the flock. Dolus dead! Zygadena with a broken wing, probably dying at this moment! Well, well, well! Raven's Enders flew back and forth excitedly, trading details and offering insights. For once, food was not the main item of discussion at the Flight.

Busy with their nestlings, Molly and Zack had not attended a Flight in many days. But word reached them, and Zack quickly found the flock. He and the Main Raven soared together, speaking seriously. "Maybe we should just go back over there and make *sure* she's dead, M.R.," Zack was saying.

"Are you implying what I think you're implying, Zack?"

"Bloody right. If she's still alive, let's do her in."

"Absolutely not, Zack. You know the rule. No raven kills another."

"Tell that to Zygadena!" Zack replied, clacking his bill. "She nearly killed a very important member of our flock. And a good friend of mine!"

"In any case, she is almost certain to die on her own," the Main Raven observed.

"I suppose you're right," said Zack, relaxing. No bird could survive for long with a broken wing. But then, Zygadena was no ordinary bird.

Suddenly Garth arrived and flew toward them. Immediately Zack's eyebrow tufts went up, as did those of the Main Raven. Under the circumstances, it was foolhardy for Garth to be there at all, let alone approach such prominent members of the flock.

"Uh, sir," Garth said, easing toward the Main Raven – none too closely – in a submissive way.

The Main Raven looked at him coldly. "Yes, Garth C.C.?"

"Uh, it's about this whole thing with, uh, Zygadena, and everything. I, uh, well . . ." Garth stammered.

"Come on, out with it," the Main Raven snapped. "I don't have much time for ravens who betray their fellow flock members."

"Well, um, I . . ." Garth took a deep breath. What he was about to say required it. "I want to tell you how sorry I am about all of this."

"Go on, Garth C.C."

"I realize now that being with Zygadena was a terrible mistake. She is – was – truly an evil bird."

"Indeed," said the Main Raven.

"And I want to apologize for my part in what happened to Colin, too." Garth looked at Zack, who involuntarily slashed the air with his bill. Garth knew that Zack and Colin were especially close.

The Main Raven turned in flight and looked straight at Garth. He held the connection for a long time. Then, as he broke it off, he made a strange statement. "Garth, I see something in your eye."

"Sir?" said Garth, blinking as if it were a speck of dirt.

"No – not that, Garth." The Main Raven paused. His magnificent voice, capable of conveying so many subtle meanings through its tone and depth, now carried a quality that neither Garth nor Zack was expecting to hear. It carried pity.

"Garth, what I see in your eye is genuine contrition. Real remorse. I think that this whole sorry experience has made quite an impression on you."

"Yes, sir, it has." Garth looked down. "It really, really has."

"And what do you think you will do now, C.C.?" the Main Raven said quietly.

"Well, I thought maybe I could, sort of, be a different raven now," Garth replied.

"Different how?"

Garth's reply was clear and strong. "I want to be part of the flock, sir. Somebody the flock can rely on. Somebody they can trust. Hanging around with Dolus was like being lost. I just didn't know who my real friends were. My real friends were here all along. I thought you were all boring and stupid. But now I know better."

The Main Raven actually smiled at Garth. Loudly, so loudly that everyone in the Flight could hear, he called, "Attention, Raven's Enders. Gro! Gro! I have an announcement." The other birds turned their heads toward him and began to fly nearer. They could sense the importance of what he was about to say.

When everyone was close enough, he said it. "Garth and I have been speaking about what happened today." The Main Raven let his eyes fall on each Raven's Ender, to let the birds know that the discussion had been serious. "Garth is ashamed of his conduct in this affair, and indeed he is ashamed of his life in general since falling in with Dolus C.C., now deceased, and with one Zygadena, whom I am loath to refer to as 'C.C.' at all, and who I hope – nay, we all hope – will soon reach the end of her evil career. If she has not reached it already."

The birds nodded their heads in agreement. The Main Raven paused for effect. This was turning out to be one of his better speeches.

"Now, concerning Garth C.C. He is obviously a deeply chastened individual." He looked toward Garth, as did the other birds. Garth met the hostile gaze of the flock directly and honestly, without flinching. His expression told everyone that what the Main Raven had been saying was true.

"Given all this," the Main Raven continued, "I am willing to accept Garth's humility as genuine. After all, he is a young bird, quite capable of changing his ways. And he says that he wants to remain part of the flock. Do I interpret you correctly, Garth C.C.?" The Main Raven peered sternly at Garth again.

Garth replied immediately. "Yes, sir. If you'll have me." Then, feeling a new burst of shame, he swung his eyes toward the ground, now far below. The birds had let Yamnuska's updraft carry them high over the Bow Valley, up under a swelling cumulus cloud that shone brilliantly in the late-afternoon sun. The birds coasted near the cloud-base, which showed a hint of pinkness as sunset approached. Garth saw none of this. He kept his head down, overcome with the sad implication of his last statement. "If you don't want me, I understand," he said, closing his eyes. "I'll leave right now."

The Main Raven drifted close to Garth under the glowing cloud canopy. He looked to Garth, then back to the flock. He smiled. "I think this bird is worthy of another chance. What do you say?"

Zack said it first, without even thinking. "Rawk-a-taw!"

Within moments, every other bird had joined in. When Garth raised his head and opened his eyes, he found himself surrounded not by enemies, but by the friends he now held dearest in the world: his flockmates.

XXV

Left alone at Raven's End, hurting all over, Colin felt sorry for himself. How stupid, he thought, to have gone off with Dolus like that. To have believed Garth when he said that Greta would meet him at the ponds. To have been led so gullibly to Zygadena, to have eaten that – that *stuff*, whatever it was. He shook his head, noting a few lingering cobwebs. Poison, that's what it was. She'd poisoned him, and then, and then . . . he didn't want to think about the rest.

"Dumb!" he said out loud. "Dumb! Dumb!" He was really angry with himself. "Colin C.C.," he shouted, "you are the dumbest raven in the mountains, you know that?! The very *dumbest!*" He pecked at the scree. "Awk!"

He stopped. He might be the dumbest, but he wasn't going to add to his injuries by breaking his bill. Colin sighed. He hobbled up into the same dead spruce he had roosted in long ago – well, it seemed like long ago – when the mist had spoken to him.

He closed his eyes, remembering. That had been his first experience with second-sight. Then there had been the others. Sarah in the snowbank, the avalanche at Carrot Creek, and the voice that kept breaking in on his life. The voice that turned out to be the voice of the Great Raven. It had been a long time since he had heard that voice.

"Indeed, Colin."

Colin's eyes flew open. He knew instantly who was speaking to him. There was no bird, of course. He didn't expect to see a bird. He simply replied to the air. "You're back!"

"Yes. Sorry I haven't contacted you for so long. Been busy. But I heard about your misfortune today and thought I'd see how you were."

Colin said the first thing that came into his mind, and it wasn't very polite. "Hey, where were you when I needed you? Zygadena almost killed me." He realized as soon as he said it that it was unfair. What was the Great Raven supposed to have done? That whole sorry scenario was Colin's affair, not hers.

The Great Raven's voice sounded sad. "Please forgive me, Colin. I've been so negligent, not checking up on you."

"Oh, Great Raven, no, no. It was my own fault, really. I'm sorry to sound so accusing."

"Well, it's true that I wouldn't have intervened."

"What?"

"That's right. I would not have tried to stop what Zygadena was doing to you."

"But –" The Great Raven didn't care for him? Yet she had just said she was sorry for not paying more attention to him . . .

"I know that sounds strange, Colin, but I have my reasons. One day you'll understand them. The important thing for now is that you survived, as I expected you would."

"But it was just dumb luck that the falcon saw us there, and –"

"Not entirely dumb luck, Colin."

"You told it!"

"No, I didn't."

"But –"

"Look. It's like this. Here are a couple of birds in trouble – fighting, whatever – and they're way up there, plain for everyone to see. That falcon was bound to notice."

Colin found this hard to believe. Considering the source, though, maybe it was true.

"And any falcon would have made a run at you," the Great Raven continued. "That's the way they are. They can't help it. They do it just for practice. But I'm surprised that it actually hit. And even if it hadn't, a near miss would have startled Zygadena and you would have escaped on your own."

"You think so?"

"Sure. You escaped the humans with guns, didn't you?"

"Yes, but –"

"You're impetuous, Colin, and you're a little foolhardy. You've got yourself into serious trouble, no question about it." Colin hung his head. "But," the Great Raven continued, "that inquisitiveness of yours is good for the flock most of the time – look at all the food you've found for them – and you've got the right instincts for getting out of a jam. *And* you're turning out to be very tough, too."

"I – I never thought about it that way." Colin felt a flush of pride.

"Well, don't think about it too much, then. What I mean is, don't get too proud, okay?"

"No. I'm definitely not feeling very proud today."

"Good. Don't. There was a lot of luck involved. Take the episode and learn from it."

"That's for sure." Colin looked around. He had a feeling the Great Raven was very close to him. He half expected to actually see the bird. Instead, he saw Greta coming over.

"Got to go," said the voice.

"But Greta's okay. She knows about you," Colin protested.

"Right, but we had an argument the other day and she's mad at me," said the voice.

"Greta, getting mad at – at the Great Raven?!"

"Oh, sure. Lots of birds do. I'm not so easy to get along with, some-times. Really I'm not." The voice seemed hurried. "But neither is Greta, on occasion. So long!"

Greta flopped awkwardly onto Colin's perch. Darkness was falling, and the flock was returning from the Evening Flight. Greta had flown back early, a little ahead of the others.

"*Whew*," she wheezed. "These Flights are getting to be a lot of work. Maybe I'll stop going." She looked at Colin. "Were you just talking to You-Know-Who?"

"Yes," he replied, "and she said that she'd had an argument with you." He hastened to add, "But she didn't say what it was about."

Greta looked troubled. "That's right," she said quietly. "We had quite a go-round, really."

"What about?"

"About –" Greta caught herself. "Oh, a bunch of things." She looked at Colin with obvious irritation. "It's none of your business," she snapped.

Colin hopped sideways, surprised. This was the first really nasty thing that Greta had ever said to him! She recognized it, too, and apologized immediately. "Oh, Colin. I'm sorry. That wasn't nice." She looked unhappy. "Not nice at all."

Colin tried to fix things. "That's okay, Greta. It was impolite of me to ask."

"Well, eventually you'll find out anyway," she said.

"Me? Why?"

Greta looked testy again. "Let's leave it for now." She turned away. "Colin," she said, "this old world can be *very* unsatisfactory." And she fell asleep. A few minutes later, as Colin mulled this over and other birds settled onto their roosts nearby, he dozed off, too.

PART FIVE

Summer

I

"Uncle Colin! Uncle Colin!"

"Hey! It's Uncle Colin!"

"Quit shoving!"

"Colin, Colin!"

Packed into Molly and Zack's nest, four young ravens shouldered one another aside to see their favorite bird in the flock.

"Hi there, you bunch of big-mouthed beggars," Colin said as he landed. "Big-mouthed" was a hint, happily received, that he had brought them something to eat.

"Colin, what did you bring us?!"

"Colin, show me some more about flying!"

"Colin, guess what I did today!"

"Colin, Colin!"

"Me too! Me too!"

Molly was sitting on a corner of the ledge, looking tired. She was glad to see Colin, because he would entertain her nestlings for a while and get them out of her feathers. "Oh, Colin," she called above the noisy voices, "how nice of you to drop by."

"Well, I missed them yesterday," he said, preparing to poke some food into each wide-open mouth. "Okay, who's first?"

"Me, me!"

"Me, me!"

"Me too!"

He stuck his bill into the closest receptacle. "*Garg! Galargle!* Yum, yum!" Colin had brought the nestlings a cropful of elk guts. He fed the next, and the next, until all four had stopped clamoring. They laid their heads on the edge of the nest and gazed rapturously at Colin. He smiled back. They really looked like ravens, now. Their bodies were fully covered in sleek black plumage. Their wing-feathers had grown in, and so had their long tail-feathers, which kept swiping across one bill or another as the birds turned around in the nest. This would often start a squabble.

"Hey! You whacked me again!"

"Did not."

"Did so!"

"Kids, kids!"

Their eyes were now gray, rather than nestling blue. Soon they would be known as "grays," the raven word for fledglings. One day their eyes would be as brown as those of their parents. But to earn the title of "gray," Molly and Zack's children would have to do the most daring thing they would attempt in their entire lives. Over the next few days each of these nestlings would fling itself off the South Face of Yamnuska and try to fly.

This is what Colin was here for. In preparation for the leap, he was providing the training. Zack usually taught this vital topic, but the kids loved Colin so much, and he was such a fine flyer, that Molly didn't mind if he stood in as instructor. After all, she noted wearily, the nestlings paid more attention to him than they did to their own parents.

"Okay," Colin was saying, "who can tell me the last thing you do before you jump?"

"Get your wings out! Get your wings out!"

"No, that's not it. Your wings are already out. It's something else."

"I know! I know!" One bird was flapping excitedly, trying to get Colin's attention.

"Yes, Zolly?"

Zolly was the brightest in the brood. Zack and Molly hadn't been able to decide at first if she was male or female – the sex of young birds

is so hard to tell apart that even their parents sometimes have trouble
– and thus they had delayed naming her. Colin had noted the problem
and suggested "Zolly," a combination of "Zack" and "Molly."

Zolly spoke in a strong, clear voice. "You always look both ways
before you jump."

"That's right, Zolly. Look before you leap."

Zolly smiled and looked smugly at her siblings.

"You're such a goody-goody, Zolly," said one of the other nestlings.
Another one defended her. "Just 'cause *you* couldn't think of it and she
could, poop-feathers!"

"Ooo! I'll get you for that!"

"Kids! Kids!" Molly was looking forward to the day her whole brood
was safely on the wing.

Colin got their attention again. "Now," he said, "let's practice the
jump together. Everyone up on the edge of the nest."

The young ravens stepped to the rim. They gripped the twigs tightly,
looking uneasily into the void below.

"Okay, wings out."

They all spread their wings, bumping into each other.

"Now, flutter!"

They flapped in short strokes, hitting each other on the head but
concentrating too much to notice.

"That's it! Good flutter!"

They fluttered harder, stirring up the dust on the ledge. A panicked
beetle scuttled away around the corner.

"Now, pick a point to aim at. Pick something in the scenery ahead
of you and slightly below."

They did, their eyes wide.

"Now look both ways. Always look both ways."

They looked. The fluttering was very fast, now.

"And *away you go!*"

On other days, that would have been the end of it. No one would
have leapt. The young birds would have furled their wings and gabbled
excitedly that soon they were going to follow through and leap. Soon,
really soon, but – uh – not right now.

Today, though, one of them did.

"Zolly!" Molly exclaimed. There was Zolly, fluttering out into space.

Colin had known this might happen. He was expecting it, in fact, and no sooner had Zolly left the ledge than he was in the air himself, right beside her.

"Good, Zolly! Good launch!" She had lost some height, but now she was gaining it back, wings beating furiously, as she drew away from the ledge.

"This – *puff, puff* – is really – *whew!* – great," she said in a frightened voice.

"Okay, Zolly, you're doing fine," Colin reassured her. "We have to keep this first flight short, so you don't get too tired." He watched her carefully. "Remember how I told you to turn. Twist your tail left and warp your right wing." She did, skidding a bit as she swung around to face the cliff.

"Like that? – *huff, puff* – Like that, Uncle Colin?"

"Yes! Yes! Just like that! Very good!" Zolly seemed assured of completing her first flight successfully. But Colin knew that the next part was the hardest. What if she couldn't get back on the nest? What if she struck the wall? What if . . .?

Then Zolly reached the ledge. She reached it too well, actually, and flew right into the nest, crashing into her brothers and sisters. They squawked and laughed.

"Zolly! Zolly! You flew! You *flew!*"

"What was it like, Zolly? What was it like?"

Zolly lay in the centre of the nest, surrounded by the others. "It was – *huff, huff* – it was, it was, like, *super!*" She panted some more. "It was harder than I thought, okay – and I had to flap really hard, but . . . oh, I want to do it *again!*"

And she did, this time executing a better landing. She would have tried yet another flight, but Colin warned her not to. She seemed to be tiring.

Molly enforced the warning. "Zolly, dear, if you can't make it back to the ledge you'll have to flutter way down the face and roost all by yourself, and that wouldn't be very much fun, would it?"

"No, Mum." Zolly shivered. The very thought!

"So why don't you lie down and rest for a while? Maybe someone else would like to try." Molly looked at the other nestlings.

"Not me."

"Not me, either."

"Well – maybe I would."

"Hey, yeah, Harry! We'll watch!"

"Go! Go!"

And Harry repeated Zolly's performance, with the difference that Harry figured one flight was enough. In fact, that was enough flying for the whole brood. Worn out by the thrill of fledging, whether or not they actually flew, they were all soon asleep.

Zack arrived with a cropful of ants to find that the intended recipients were dreaming away. "What's this?" he asked. "Everyone napping at this time of day?"

"They've had too much excitement, dear," said Molly. "Two of them fledged just before you arrived."

"Hey, hey!" Zack looked proud. "Which ones?"

"Zolly and Harry," Colin said.

"I knew it!" Zack said. "Zolly for sure. She's so quick at everything. And Harry, too. Right behind her, no doubt." He looked at his offspring. As always, they slept in a pile. Occasionally one would wiggle, and the pile would readjust without waking up.

"These are great little beggars," Colin said. "I mean grays, in Zolly and Harry's case."

"Yes, indeed," Zack beamed. "Grays already. They grow up so quickly."

"Colin was here when they fledged," Molly said. "He helped them."

Zack smiled at Colin. "That's good. No better flight instructor than Colin." He looked squarely at his friend. "It's hard to believe that less than a year ago you crash-landed into our lives, Colin C.C."

Colin reflected. Yes, it had been almost a year. And what a year! So many adventures. So much that was scary, so much that was interesting, so much that was happy and sad, and such a great number of changes. It was almost as if he had lived his whole life in less than a year. Then the chronic question came into his mind. The disturbing question that was always there, waiting just under the surface. *What about before that?* Always his thoughts would be interrupted by this gap in his memory, this hole in his existence. It was getting more and more distressing. He would have to ask Greta about it.

"Colin!" Molly was fairly shouting at him.

"Huh? Oh. Sorry, Molly. I was thinking about something else."

"Colin, you didn't respond at all. I thought you might be having one of your dreams, or something."

"No," he sighed, "but I wish I would."

"Wish you would have a dream?" said Zack.

"Wish I could decide what to do," Colin replied. He hopped to the edge of the ledge and unfurled his wings. "See you tomorrow," he smiled, "and in the morning I'll tell everyone at the Flap about Harry and Zolly."

"Thanks!" said Zack.

"'Bye for now," said Molly, turning to her young ravens. They were waking up. "Say goodbye to Uncle Colin, kids."

"'Bye, Uncle Colin!" they all said together.

"'Bye-bye, you beggars. And you two *grays*," he added, smiling at Zolly and Harry. They looked well pleased with themselves. Then the nest erupted.

"Mummy, Mummy! I'm really, really hungry!"

"Can we eat now, Daddy?"

"Feed me! Feed me!"

"Me too! Me too!"

Colin stepped off the ledge and into the dependable South Face updraft that had helped many a fledgling survive its first flight. He stretched out his big adult wings and soared, feeling his body rise with the vertical wind. He flexed his wingtips ever so slightly, noting with pleasure how the slightest adjustment had exactly the right effect, turning him a little this way, a little that way. Yes, he thought, flying was the greatest thing in the world. He looked down. Below him, he knew, were hundreds of creatures without wings. Coyotes, bighorn sheep, elk, chipmunks, and ground squirrels; the pikas in the rocks and the beavers in the brooks. What a privilege it was to fly. How lucky to have been brought into the world as a bird.

Then the same thought that troubled him at Molly and Zack's nest struck again. He had to know, that was all. He had to find out, and soon. "A raven needs to know where he came from," he said out loud. And he went to find Greta.

II

"Greta, I need to ask you something." Since that is what Colin spent most of his day doing, this was nothing new. But the urgency in his voice told Greta that the upcoming question was special.

"Ask away," she said.

"Sorry to bother you so late, Greta."

"Oh, no bother, Colin. Go ahead." Her reply rang a little false. It was dusk, and she hoped that Colin wouldn't pester her for long. She became very tired on the long summer days and needed her roosting time more than the other birds.

"One thing Zygadena said," he began, invoking a name seldom uttered on Yamnuska, "was that she knew about my flock – my original flock, Greta, from before I came here."

"And you thought she was telling the truth?"

"Well, no. I guess not." Colin let his head drop. "She must have been lying, just trying to get me to stay long enough to slip me that poison."

"But tell me, Colin – what *did* she say about your flock?"

Colin brightened. "She said it was the 'Maligne Flock,' wherever this Maligne place is, and that they were really strong birds, and great flyers, and –"

"You'd like to believe that, wouldn't you?" Greta's voice was kind, but Colin could tell she was patronizing him.

"Oh, Greta, I'd just like to *know*." He looked out into the dimness. To the southeast, evening's violet was creeping in behind the sunset. Colin could see the other Raven's Enders circling, letting the southerly wind carry them back to the South Face after the Evening Flight. Greta hadn't attended the Flight for some days now, and tonight Colin hadn't attended either.

"Greta," he said, clenching his bill, "I have to know where I came from. I do."

"Well, as far as this 'Maligne Flock' is concerned, quit worrying about it. There isn't one."

"None at all?" Colin looked hurt. Greta could be so blunt.

"Nope."

"But where is 'Maligne'?"

"Oh, Maligne is a real place. It's a big lake in the Rockies way north of us. Around Jasper."

"Jasper?"

"A town, kind of like Banff. It's in the Park, too. Ask Scratch and Wheedle about it. They've been there."

"Are there ravens there?"

"Yes, there are. They have their own flock. Far-roaming bunch, too." Greta looked thoughtful. "In a way, Colin, Zygadena was right. The Jasper ravens really are great flyers. And they do roost sometimes at Maligne Lake."

"But there's no separate flock called 'Maligne'?"

"No."

"Greta, this whole thing is really bothering me."

"I can see that."

"What should I do?"

Greta looked closely at Colin. His eyes showed his desperation. She spoke softly, and on a topic that Colin was not expecting. "Colin, did I ever tell you how I came to join the Raven's End Flock?"

"Uh, no." What was this about?

"Well, I arrived in much the same way you did."

"By falling out of the sky?"

She chuckled. "No, not by falling out of the sky. But I, too, had my troubles. I came from Waterton – that's way south of here – just kind of exploring northward, and I got caught in a bad downdraft while I was trying to cross the Bow Valley." She looked in that direction, pointing with her bill. "Got slammed into Lookout Mountain pretty hard. Practically *crawled* across Morley Flats to Yamnuska."

"Were you badly hurt?"

"Yes. Couldn't talk sense for days. Actually broke the last joint on my left wing."

"Awk," Colin sympathized.

"But the Raven's Enders were good to me. A couple named Max and Margaret took me in. Wonderful birds. They're gone now, both of them. And they kept me fed 'til I could fly again. Very generous, those two, like the rest of the Raven's End Flock. Wouldn't have made it without 'em."

"Same for me with Molly and Zack. But –" Colin still couldn't catch the drift of the conversation. Greta never brought up anything without a reason, but what was the reason this time? "Uh, Greta, I don't see what this has to do with –"

"It has everything 'to do with,'" she snapped. "Now listen carefully, Colin C.C. The flock places a certain value on me –"

"Oh, Greta, the flock couldn't do without you. They really couldn't."

"– and they learned that it pays to be kind to strangers. Not that it paid with Dolus and Garth, but still . . ." Her voice faded as she drifted into thought.

"And?" Colin prompted.

"And I have dreams too, you know."

Colin's eyes widened. So that was it! She, too, must have been looking for her past! He had to ask her. "Greta – did you once forget where you came from? Like me?"

"No, no. I've always known where I came from."

Colin's head drooped. "Oh," he said.

"But my dreams have sent me searching for things. That's what I was doing when the downdraft got me."

Colin looked up again, his excitement renewed. "Greta, I'd never known that you came here following a dream!"

"Yes. I did."

"But – but did you ever go on to find the thing in the dream?"

"Yes."

"You actually found it?"

"Yes, I actually found it. And you will, too. And when you do, it will be very, very good."

"The truth about myself?"

"Yes. Among other things."

"I wish I could be sure of that, Greta." Colin looked troubled again. "How do you know I'll find out?"

"The same way *you* know things. From inside. From a place that other birds don't have."

"The second-sight place?"

"Yes, the second-sight place."

"Then . . . what should I do, Greta? My second-sight place hasn't told me any of this. It just makes me feel upset all the time. And the Great Raven is no help. She gets me all excited, then she just *leaves* me here, worrying and fretting. And that dream! That dream about the mountain with feathers?!" Another squawk came from somewhere else along the cliff, reminding Colin that other birds were trying to roost. Colin pecked the rock under his feet. Pain travelled up his bill. It felt strangely good.

Greta touched his wing. "You really *are* in a bad way, kiddo," she said softly. "And it was just as hard for me. The things I used to do to my family and flockmates – oh, I was nasty at times. But try to calm down. This whole thing is going to resolve itself just fine."

Colin spread his toes against the rock of Yamnuska. The ancient limestone felt cool. He gathered himself for one last question. This would be his final question on the subject of his origin. He knew he couldn't stand to ask Greta about it again. He would phrase the question carefully, logically, so that Greta could not weasel out of a direct answer. It would be a simple yes-or-no sort of question. He stood quietly for a long time, thinking.

In the end, though, he gave up. No question would provide a simple answer. He just blurted out the one thing that he needed to know most at that moment. "Greta, what am I going to *do?*"

She chuckled. Colin could have pecked her instead of the rock, but he didn't. Instead, he heard the words he knew so well. "Do what I always tell you to do, Colin. Pay attention –"

"Pay attention to your dreams," he finished, sighing. Well, that was that. He was never going to get a straight-on, forthright answer on this topic. Not from Greta.

But this time Greta's cryptic guidance was exactly right. That night Colin had the most important dream of his life.

III

In the dream, Colin was going somewhere. The lay of the land was unfamiliar – peculiar, even, the way it is in dreams – and his destination was unclear, but he knew he was trying to find something. There were other ravens in the dream, Raven's End ravens. He kept seeing them. He would overtake them. Here was Wheedle, flying in the same direction he was. Colin asked, "Where are you going?" and Wheedle replied, "Out the inside tree, of course," which was nonsense – but it seemed reasonable in the dream. Sarah told him she was "going home by way of the night flowers."

It was scary, in a way. All the other ravens knew where *they* were going, but Colin did not. And he was definitely lost. He kept travelling anyway, watching the strange scenery roll by: forests of moss as tall as trees, streams that ran along the tops of ridges. A growing feeling told him that this dream-flight would take him to some extraordinary place.

And it did. There, right in front of him, was the Mountain with Feathers.

It was a dream-mountain, and thus none too clear, but Colin could see the feathers well enough. They were actually layers of rock that overlapped like the feathers in a raven's wing, pointing upward to a wedge-shaped summit that looked like the tip of the tail.

Colin was ecstatic. "Oh," he cried out, "it's real! I'm there! I've reached it!"

"What? You're where?"

Colin opened his eyes. He was back on Raven's End, perched with Greta in the chilly colorless light that hints of morning. He was embarrassed. "I'm sorry, Greta. I've had a dream. Must have talked and woken you up." Already the dream was starting to fade.

"Well, at least you saw it," she said.

The Mountain with Feathers! The image snapped back into his mind. She had seen it too! Dear old Greta, amazing old Greta, who could share his dreams. And how right she had been to keep reminding him to pay attention to them!

Colin knew that he had to remember the vision of the Mountain with Feathers. He had to keep that picture in a safe place in his mind, because he was certain, now, that he was going to go looking for the real thing. He knew he would find his flock on the Mountain with Feathers.

Morning was about to arrive. This very day, Colin decided, he would start his quest.

"Greta," he said gently.

"Hmm?" She blinked at the world and slowly stretched her wings. Then she looked at him. "Good morning, Colin. Ready for another day of lessons?"

"Greta, I – I'm leaving, Greta."

Her response was short. "Sure," she said pleasantly.

What a bird, Colin thought. She understood perfectly. "You don't mind if I go?"

"Not at all, Colin. When I was young, I, too, paid attention to my dreams. Still do."

"But our apprenticeship thing –"

"Our apprenticeship can break for a holiday. I could go on teaching you forever, Colin. I love it and you love it." She turned to him and smiled. "But you've got the basics, now. Most of them. There are a couple – one in particular – that I can't help you with."

"Do you mean this Mountain-with-Feathers business? I have to find out on my own?"

"Yes." She stretched her wings farther. "Has to be." She touched his bill with hers. "I'm going to miss you, Colin."

"I'm coming back," he said, returning the affection.

"I hope you realize that you might *not* be coming back," she replied wistfully. She looked at him again. "Be careful, Colin." Her voice trembled.

Colin thought about Greta's travels. She knew what dangers awaited a raven far from home. She had survived them.

"You've always made it back, Greta."

"Yes. And I – I think you will, too, dear Colin."

Colin realized that Greta was going to start crying. "I'm off to the Flap, to announce this," he said, trying to sound firm. But his bill quivered.

"I'll be along shortly," Greta sniffled. "Goodbye, Colin."

"Goodbye, Greta." He left the roost before he lost control entirely.

IV

It was a glorious morning for the Flap. Summer sunlight flooded the rocks of Raven's End, and the subalpine firs clustered at its base smelled especially tangy. The night had been cool and without wind, giving the birds a better rest than they'd had in many days. They stretched their wings in the warmth and chatted contentedly.

The Main Raven called the meeting to order. He asked Maya for the news. Her report was brief.

"First, the headlines – a small rockslide in the Runes yesterday destroyed three trees – two Engelmanns and a pine – and left a family of nuthatches homeless – beyond the killed trees, there were no other injuries." She stopped for a breath. "The shrews report that insect larvae of all kinds are especially plentiful this summer –"

"I'll go along with that," Brendan interrupted, running his tongue over his bill. The Main Raven shot him a disagreeable look.

Maya burbled on. "Molly and Zack C.C., of the Raven's End Flock, report that two of their nestlings fledged yesterday afternoon."

The ravens cheered. Colin remembered that he was going to announce this for Molly and Zack, but Maya had found out first, of course. Well, she had saved him from having to make two statements to the flock this morning. Now he had to deliver just one.

"Thank you, Maya," the Main Raven was saying, nodding his bill as he walked about in the centre of the circle. "And now, are there any complaints?"

There were none. All the birds had been getting along very well lately. Garth had lived up to his promise. The change was remarkable. He was now well-mannered toward everyone, and he behaved very responsibly. Brendan and Sarah had become his best friends, and the three of them were together all day long.

The Main Raven was just about to call for the Motion and adjourn, when Colin spoke up. "Gro, C.C.s. I have an announcement."

He sounded so formal that it surprised the other birds. They turned toward him expectantly.

"I will be leaving the flock for a while."

This caused a commotion.

"No, Colin – don't go!"

"No, no!"

"Stay, Colin! Stay!"

"Order, order." The Main Raven had to flap his wings to quiet the circle. "We're sorry to hear that, Colin. Please tell us the reason for your proposed absence."

Colin stepped forward and looked at the other birds. His friends, every one of them. He spoke slowly. "I have had a dream," he said.

The circle tightened. Colin was famous for his dreams. What was this one about? It must have been important, if he was leaving because of it.

"And the dream has shown me an image of a mountain I must find."

Not a feather rustled in the flock.

"So I'm going to look for it. I hope to be gone only a little while. Maybe just a day or two. But if it takes longer, please don't worry about me."

He stepped back into his place in the circle.

Marg spoke next. "Not worry about you? Colin, we'll worry the whole time!" All the other birds joined in, again begging Colin to stay.

"Wait, everyone." It was Greta, joining the Flap late. "Let's be fair, here. You're just making it harder for Colin to do what he has to do," she said. "Part of him really doesn't want to go, because he loves you all so much" – here she looked around at the flock – "but I know how he feels. Been on a few trips myself, you know." She smiled. "And I've always come back, haven't I?"

The other birds nodded. Yes, she had always come back.

"So I think we should wish him well and not make him feel guilty about leaving."

"Greta's right," said Marg, firmly. "A bird has to do what she has to do. Go where she has to go. That's one of the Three Freedoms –"

"Hey, yeah!" Brendan interrupted. "A raven can fly, like, anywhere he wants, right?"

"Yes, Brendan," Marg continued, "and Colin is now making a choice that is hard for everyone concerned. But it's one we will have to live with."

The Main Raven agreed. "Well said, Marg. I think we should close the subject now, and adjourn the meeting with a special Motion to wish Colin a safe journey and a short one, so that he returns to us as soon as possible."

"Hear, hear!"

"The Motion, then?"

The ravens made their wheel. Wing to wing, they each took a big breath of clean morning air and used it to bring forth their familiar call – a special one this day, in recognition of Colin's daring intent. They sent him off with their strength, their goodwill and their confidence that they would see him again. "Rawk-a-taw!"

Colin didn't wait to explain further. He leapt into the air and was gone.

V

But where was he to go? Colin didn't have the slightest idea of where to look for the Mountain with Feathers. It couldn't be to the east, he knew, because there were no mountains to the east. To the east lay the foothills, which were low and gentle. He would have to search to the west, he decided, toward Carrot Creek and Banff. He would get to

Banff, climb very high, and from up there he'd get a good view of everything. Maybe he would see it.

"And if you don't?" came a voice from nowhere.

The Great Raven!

"Then I'll just keep going," Colin replied.

"Good plan." The voice of the Great Raven sounded pleased.

"Hey! Maybe you can help me!" Colin realized that the Great Raven probably knew exactly where the Mountain with Feathers was. "Do you know about the Mountain with Feathers?"

"Yes, of course."

"Hey! Terrific! Where is it?"

The voice chuckled. "That is, as they say, for me to know and for you to find out."

"Oh." Colin's wingbeats slowed.

"But I'll tell you this, C.C. –"

"Yes?"

"You're on the right track."

Colin's wingbeats picked up again. He was going to get some help after all. "Thanks!"

"My pleasure," said the Great Raven. Then she added quickly, "But keep in mind, Colin, that this is *your* adventure. I'll check on you occasionally, but I can't be with you often. I've got a lot of other things to do, too."

"I'll bet you do."

"So good luck. Keep those strokes steady!"

"I will! I will!"

"Goodbye for now." And the voice was gone.

Colin raced toward Banff. He flew high, looking to right and left, hoping to recognize the image in his dream. What he saw were the front ranges of the Canadian Rockies, ridge upon ridge. Off to the southwest were several big peaks: Mount Joffre, Mount Sir Douglas, and the Royal Group, each shining with glaciers. The lesser summits had lost their winter snow, but not these. They were very high. Still, despite their impressiveness, none of these mountains looked like the Mountain with Feathers.

Then, directly ahead, Colin saw Mount Assiniboine. Highest in the region, Assiniboine stuck up like a fang on the horizon. Here was a truly grand mountain, Colin thought; it stood head and shoulders above everything around it. He increased his speed, hurrying to get a closer look. But a little while later, when he was near enough to see some detail on the peak, he had to admit that Mount Assiniboine could not be the Mountain with Feathers. The rock layers did not overlap the right way. Weary, now, and somewhat disheartened, he flew on more slowly.

It was mid-afternoon when Colin rounded the corner of Mount Rundle and landed in the parking lot at the Banff hot springs. There, strutting around, were the Banff ravens.

"Gro," Colin called, alighting a little distance off. Two of the birds turned toward him and began to hop over. One was large, the other small. Colin didn't hesitate. He addressed the big one. "Gro, my friend," he said respectfully. "Perhaps you remember me from last winter. My name is Colin C.C., from the Raven's End Flock."

Surprisingly, it was the smaller bird – a female – who replied. "Gro, Colin C.C.," she said, striding right up to him. She flashed her neck-feathers. "I would like to take this opportunity to welcome you to the Banff area," she said. "I would also like to take this opportunity to introduce myself. My name is Claudia C.C., and I presently hold the position of Main Raven here in Banff." She tossed her head up and down as she spoke. She said each word precisely, the way adult ravens speak to nestlings and fledglings. "I'd like you to meet my assistant, Skerf C.C."

Skerf was the raven, Colin realized, who had beaten Dolus in the fight at the parking lot.

Claudia continued before either bird could speak. "Skerf does my coordinating," she said. "He reports directly to me." She turned to Skerf. "I wish to know whether Colin C.C. was the Yamnuska raven involved in that unpleasantness we had here at the hot springs last winter."

Skerf looked Colin over carefully and replied, "No. It was a different one."

Colin explained, "That was Dolus C.C. He's dead."

"I'm so sorry to hear that. What a shame," Claudia said with mock sympathy. "Did he die in a violent manner?"

"Yes."

"How unfortunate. Well." She fluffed her neck-feathers out again. "May we assume that you are on your way to some other area? Vacationing, perhaps?"

Colin didn't know what "vacationing" was, but he assumed that it had something to do with travelling. To be agreeable, he replied, "That's right. Won't be here long. Just stopping for a bite to eat." Colin hadn't checked the parking lot for goodies yet, but as he looked around he saw that the garbage barrels were overflowing.

"How nice," Claudia said, her bill opening wide with each word. "Well, as you can see," she continued, "we have plenty to share here in the Banff area, with our tourist visitors. As long as they don't stay too *long*, of course."

"Of course." Colin fluttered his feathers like a nestling about to receive food, which was the proper response. He wondered what a "tourist" was.

Claudia told him before he could ask. "Oh, we welcome tourists like you here in Banff. Tourism is a critical factor for us, in terms of our flock. We just love visitors. And we make sure that all our friends from other, less attractive parts of the world, get right into the spirit of Banff!" Her voice had been rising in pitch and becoming more excited as she said this. She finished with a sugary squeak. "And you're invited!"

The big raven now spoke. He seemed more down-to-earth. "What she's saying is that we're about to have our Flap. Would you like to join in?"

"Well, I –"

"We don't eat until *after* the Flap," Skerf added.

"Oh. I see. Uh, sure. I'd love to attend your Flap." This was interesting. It seemed that the Banff ravens had their Flaps in the afternoon rather than in the morning.

"I'm *so* pleased that you'll join us." Claudia raised her head high and called the other birds together. "C.C.s! Round and Round Club! Gather here, birds, by me!"

The others came hopping and fluttering over. One of them seemed particularly keen. He got there first and spoke to Claudia.

"Then eats, right?"

This bird wasn't very large in the usual sense; not very long or tall. But he was big nonetheless. Looking at him again, Colin realized that what he was seeing was a *fat* raven.

"Yes, Dave. First the meeting, then refreshments."

"Okay!"

Claudia waited until all the birds were assembled. They didn't stand as close together as the Raven's Enders did at their Flaps.

"Good afternoon, C.C.s, and welcome to today's Round and Round Club!" she said in her bubbly voice. She paused, obviously enjoying the attention the other birds gave her. Then she poked her bill in Colin's direction.

"I'd like to take this opportunity to introduce you to Colin C.C., of the Raven's End flock. He has stopped in on his way – where did you say you were going, Colin?"

"Uh, west."

"On his way west. I have invited him to join our Flap – I mean the Round and Round Club – on this occasion." She glanced about, smiling sweetly. "So, let's get on with our meeting!"

The format was rather like the Yamnuska Flaps, Colin noted, except that this Main Raven seemed to do all the talking. She gave the news (not as well as Maya, he thought), and she "presented" (her word) to the other birds on a number of "topic areas" (boring stuff about what she had been doing the day before, mostly). She said "in terms of" a lot. Then she called for the Motion.

"Our next priority," she said brightly, "is to utilize all our voices to their *fullest* and have a really great Motion – a super Banff Motion in honor of our guest, Colin C.C. Let's do a Motion any flock of ravens would just *envy!*" She opened her bill so far on this last word that Colin thought it might stick that way.

Colin assumed that the other birds would form a circle around Claudia. He expected that they would spread their wings, so he stepped back to give them room. But he was completely surprised by what happened next.

Each bird shut its eyes and turned around several times. As it did, it made a string of sounds that Colin had never heard before.

"Coo-coo-coo, coo-coo-coo."

What in the world?! Colin felt himself starting to laugh. "Craw — ahem," he said, stifling the impulse.

"Did you like our Motion?" Claudia asked, hopping over to him.

"Oh, uh, *yes*. It's really, um, *different*, isn't it?"

"Of course," she said, beaming. "Everything we do here at Banff is very creative."

"Where did you get this, uh, fascinating Motion?"

"Oh, I have to thank myself for that. And my Tourism Action Committee adopted it immediately, of course. No other flock has anything *like* it. In terms of flock Motions." She smiled. "Why, we're the talk of the mountains. Ravens come from all over just to see it."

No doubt they would, Colin thought gleefully. They wouldn't believe it otherwise.

"And now it's *your* turn."

"What?"

"Your turn to make the Motion."

"Oh, I'm not sure that I really should . . ." Colin wasn't part of the Banff Flock. Why was Claudia asking him to make their Motion?

"It's customary," she said. "We expect it of all our visitors." She said this without smiling, and Skerf moved a step nearer to Colin. His tufts were ever so slightly raised. All the other birds were watching.

"Oh. Okay." Colin turned around a couple of times. "Coo-coo-coo . . ."

Claudia smiled broadly. "Very good, Colin! Very good! Don't you just feel the spirit of Banff?"

What Colin felt was ridiculous. But if he had to do this to get something to eat, and with that big raven making sure he did it — well, it was over now.

Claudia turned to address the rest of the flock, which was waiting silently for her to adjourn the meeting. "Okay, then, flock members. Let us move to the dining facilities."

The other birds hopped over to the garbage barrels, with the one called Dave in the lead. He didn't hop, Colin observed; he waddled.

Very quickly. Colin joined him at one of the barrels, saying, "I'll stand watch up top if you want to go in."

"Hey, great. Really great." Dave flapped heavily up to the edge and flopped in. Right away, Colin could hear the sound of Dave's bill crunching up something. Dave talked as he ate. "Sweet life we got here in Banff," he said, gulping down french fries, "thanks to the humans. I love humans. They make life so easy." Peck, peck. "Too easy, really. No need to look far for goodies around here." Gobble, gobble. "I don't recall having to leave town for food in I don't know how long." *Scrunch, gulp.* "But it can mess you up. Heck, I'm so fat I probably couldn't fly to the top of Mount Rundle if I wanted to!" Peck, peck, *gulp.* "Claudia's trying to get us to cut back. She won't let us start until the afternoon."

Colin waited what he thought to be an appropriate length of time, then he said, "Uh, Dave – when do I get some?"

"Huh? Oh. Sure. Sorry. I'll trade with you."

Colin jumped down to the bottom of the barrel. It was empty. A ruptured packet of ketchup stuck to one of his feet.

"Dave, there's none left!"

"Oh. Are you sure?"

"Yes!" Colin hopped back up to the rim and looked Dave in the eye.

Dave didn't say anything. He just flew off to another barrel. Colin watched him go, wondering how a raven could be so selfish. Well, at least there were other barrels. As he perched there, deciding which barrel to check out next, another bird landed beside him. Colin recognized him immediately.

"Boogs!"

"And a richt guid mornin' tae ye, laddie." It was the raven Colin had met here last winter, the one with the interesting accent and the charming way of speaking.

"It's good to see you again, C.C.!"

"Aye, Colin. How's it gaun wi' ye?"

"Fine. Only I'm still hungry, because Dave, there, cleaned out the fries on the bottom of the barrel for me."

"Aye, he'd dae that, a' richt. He'd dae that." Boogs looked around at the other birds. "Atween ye and me, Colin, maist o' them'd dae the same. The whole fat lot o' them."

"They *are* fat, aren't they?"

"Far too muckle aroond the middle, aye."

Colin laughed. "Muckle," was it? Craw-ha! "But how come they have a reputation for being tough, these Banff ravens?"

"Ach weel, they're *hard*, laddie. Hard."

"How so?"

"Fighters, that's whit they are. An' dirty fighters, too. Och, they *seem* friendly enough, but dinnae tangle wi' them. They're quick on the peck, they are. An' they ken just where tae get ye."

Colin was watching Dave again. He had landed on a barrel occupied by another raven. As Colin watched, Dave and the other raven began to quarrel. Suddenly, Dave's bill shot out and pecked the other bird squarely on the knee joint. It flew off, its hurt leg pumping in the air.

"See whit I mean, laddie?" Boogs shook his head. "Ye'd think the hunger would mak' a bird mean-spirited, but when there's too much tae eat – well, I ken it's worse. Och aye, it's far worse."

"But isn't this your flock, Boogs?"

"Mine? Och, it is, in a kinda way. But, by the Trees, Colin, in another way it isnae. I mostly live by mysel' at Mount Assiniboine. Still, I come tae the toon often, ye ken." He gave Colin a secretive look. "This Banff lot, an' that daft Roond and Roond Club – they're *entertainin'*, don't ye think?"

Colin laughed. This time he didn't have to hold it in. "Craw-ha! What is this 'coo-coo' stuff, anyway?"

Boogs looked amused. "Och, that's nae the half o' it, laddie. Dinnae let Claudia ken I've telt ye this, but I ken for a fact that she didnae think o' it by hersel'."

"No?"

"Not a bit o' it. Have ye ever seen *pigeons*, laddie?"

"Uh, no. But I've heard of them. Pretty stupid, I'm told. Hey, wait!" He was beginning to understand. "Greta told me that pigeons turn round and round! Craw-ha!"

"An' " – by now Boogs could hardly speak, he was laughing so hard – "an' they say – craw-ha! – they say 'coo-coo-coo'! *Craw-ha-ha-ha-ha!*"

Convulsed in merriment, the two birds couldn't hang onto the rim of the barrel any longer. They dropped down to the ground, where they simultaneously spotted a discarded hamburger. This was more important than the joke. Boogs deferred to Colin. "Go on, laddie. Ye're nae doot hungrier than I."

"Thanks," Colin said, tearing off a goodly hunk. "I really *am* ravenous." Having swallowed the chunk whole, he stepped back from the rest of the hamburger. "Help yourself. At Yamnuska we share."

"Why, that's decent o' ye," Boogs replied, taking a bite. The combination of food-in-bill and accent made his next statement incomprehensible to Colin, but he thought he caught a question in it. "Beg pardon?"

Boogs swallowed. "I was askin' ye where ye're gaun frae here – travellin' an' that."

Colin wasn't sure what to say, but he figured that it wouldn't hurt to tell Boogs the truth. "I'm looking for the Mountain with Feathers."

Boogs dropped his next helping of hamburger meat. "Whit did ye say, laddie?"

"The Mountain with Feathers. I'm looking for it." Noting Boogs's expression of surprise, he added quickly, "You haven't heard of it, by any chance?"

Boogs looked thoughtful. "Weel, I – maybe I have, then."

Colin's eyes lit up. He waited expectantly as Boogs tried to remember.

"I dinnae ken if they called it that exactly. But I'd swear there's a mountain o' that description tae the north o' here." He stopped, apparently thinking again. "But I couldnae tell ye precisely where."

Colin was thrilled, despite the vagueness of the other bird's reply. Now he had a direction! "Boogs, thank you very much! You've helped me a lot!"

"I have, have I?"

"Yes! Yes!" Colin quickly ate more of the hamburger. Leaving plenty for Boogs, he spread his wings.

"Ye're fer off already, are ye?"

"I'm not wasting any time."

"If ye're gaun tae fly north, up the Bow River, I'll tell ye where there's a bonnie wee roost." And Boogs described the spot. He smiled. "Awa wi' ye, noo. It'll be gettin' dark soon."

"Goodbye, Boogs. Thanks again. Maybe I'll come by Mount Assiniboine sometime and see you."

"Aye, I'll be lookin' forward tae that, Colin, so I will. Fare thee weel, laddie!"

Colin hopped over to say goodbye to the Main Raven and thank her for her hospitality, which was the polite thing to do.

"Well, goodbye, Claudia C.C. Thank you for sharing your flock's food with me. And your, uh, Round and Round Club."

"Oh, yes, goodbye," she said loudly, "and we hope to see you in our Banff area again very soon. And tell everybody how much we like having visitors. Coo-coo!"

As Colin took to wing and climbed out above the hot-springs parking lot, he looked back at the scene. There were the Banff ravens, walking among the trash barrels and standing outside car windows as food was thrown to them. A couple of birds squabbled over a bag of potato chips. Strange bunch, he thought. He'd take the Raven's Enders any day. Boogs was right. Too much food was just as bad as too little.

Soon the town was behind him, and he was flying into an unfamiliar landscape. The sun lay directly ahead, engaged in its long summertime slide northwestward. Its reflection flashed off the shallow waters of the Vermilion Lakes west of Banff. Beyond, he could see the Bow Valley making a turn to the north.

Boogs had said that he was to follow the river toward a mountain with three big layers in it: two hard layers that formed cliffs and a third one in the middle that was softer, forming a wide ledge. "Castle *Moon*-tain," Boogs had called it, making Colin chuckle. Then he saw Castle Mountain itself far up the valley. He began pulling strongly for it.

VI

Colin slept late the next morning in an alcove high on the cliffs of Castle Mountain. The sun was rising behind him, lighting up the mountains to the west, where range upon range of craggy, glacier-hung peaks stepped off to the horizon. Many of them were much larger than Yamnuska. Things were different here, he realized. He had travelled far enough west to leave the familiar front ranges behind. Now he was in the main ranges, the icy crest of the Canadian Rockies.

Colin left his roost and continued north up the Bow Valley. He followed the river, stopping on the banks a couple of times for snacks – some willow catkins, a couple of trout fry he snapped out of a pool – and for a long drink of cold glacial water. At one of these stops something across the river caught his eye. Here were two ducks, diving and surfacing. They were the most beautiful ducks he had ever seen.

He landed near them. "Gro, ducks!"

"Howdy, raven."

The ducks were small but splendidly marked. Red, black, and white, they were boldly patterned.

"Allow me to compliment you on your plumage," Colin said.

"Thanks."

These were not stuffy types, Colin decided. Polite, but not at all formal.

The ducks busily continued their work, diving below the surface and reappearing a moment later. Colin was impressed by the place in the river in which they worked. It was a rough place, full of boulders. The water roiled through excitedly, shouting and splashing. Colin had never seen ducks in such a rapid.

One of the ducks emerged close by. "Quite a keeper under there," it said.

"A 'keeper'?"

"Yeah. Had to go around twice before I could get free."

The other duck appeared. It shook water from its feathers. "Hoo-whee! Let's eddy out awhile."

"I'm up for that," the first one said. It pointed its bill toward Colin. "This raven, here, seems okay. You wanta talk to it?"

"Sure." The two little ducks stood next to Colin on a rock.

"What's a 'keeper'?" Colin asked directly.

"Ah – you're not a paddler, are you? Well, a keeper is a wave that holds you down on the bottom. Lots of fun, but it *can* be trouble."

"Oh." Colin had bathed in rivers, but he had never swum below the surface.

The duck addressed its companion. "Hey, Willy – did you see any stoneflies under there?"

"No, did you?"

"Maybe. Believe I'll run it again."

"Go for it, Toby."

The duck called Toby flew back out to a big boulder. Then, quick as a splash, it dived.

The other duck watched approvingly. "Strong paddler, that one," it said. "Figures to make the Harlequin championships this year."

Toby popped up again, eating something. "Hey, yeah! Stoneflies for sure!"

The duck named Willy turned briefly to Colin. "Gotta go. Good paddlin' to you!"

"Uh, sure."

"Yo, Willy! Watch this!" The duck that had been eating now put its head underwater and tilted its tail up. It held that position, legs pointed to the sky. This looked to be difficult to do, given the white-water pounding by.

"All-*riiiight!* It's an *endo!*" Willy promptly did the same thing.

On impulse, Colin stuck his head into the water, too. "*Blub* – brrrr!" Cold! Shaking the water off, he looked over to the ducks. They were bobbing on the standing waves, gabbling away, their words lost in the roar of the river.

"You can have it, guys!" he called, lifting off. They tilted their bills upward, acknowledging his departure.

VII

Later that day, Colin cruised high above the Bow Valley. He could now see a long way in any direction, with many peaks to choose from. Was one of these the Mountain with Feathers? He did a slow 360-degree turn, his long-distance raven vision probing the ranges for something that matched the image in his dreams. But there was no Mountain with Feathers. It was going to be farther north, he reasoned. It had to be beyond the distance a raven like Boogs would travel. And Boogs was no stay-at-home. Today, then, was for flying north, far and fast.

And fly he did, wingbeat after wingbeat, all through the day. He followed the valley, watching the Bow River dwindle to a small creek upstream of all the tributaries that made it grow to the size of the river he knew, where it flowed by Yamnuska.

Yamnuska. The thought made Colin homesick. He was very far from home, now. Getting back would take just as long as it had taken to get here. Or maybe not, he realized. This trip was making him stronger. He would be faster on the way back, especially if the prevailing northwesterly wind were blowing. His homesickness turned to pride. On he went, into the next valley to the north, headwaters of an unknown river.

This valley had a dark, malevolent look. The sunless walls were plastered with cold, gray glaciers. As he watched, a huge chunk of ice – bigger, Colin thought, than Raven's End – broke loose and fell. He veered away from the flying ice fragments, the sound shaking his body.

Still, could one of these summits be the Mountain with Feathers? He circled over each peak as he passed it, but none corresponded to the picture in his mind. It's just as well, he thought. The whole place looked downright unfriendly. And there were no other ravens.

Colin soared very high, so high that he could see all the way back to Mount Assiniboine, just barely discernible among the welter of ranges off to the south. He looked north, toward the unknown. In the blue distance he saw a great sweep of snow. It was bordered by huge peaks. Was the Mountain with Feathers one of those? Colin put his shoulders to the wind, his wings repeating the familiar motion: forward, spread, down, back; forward, spread, down, back; hour after hour.

Twenty thousand strokes brought him to the expanse of snow he had seen from so far away. Colin could hardly believe it: here was more snow than he could have imagined, snow blanketing the mountains as it did in the winter. But this was summer. Greta had talked about glaciers with Colin, and she had showed him a small one in the mountains near Yamnuska. But this! This was the Main Raven of glaciers. Then he remembered that Scratch had described such a place: the Columbia Icefield, which he and Wheedle had flown by before they arrived at Yamnuska.

Colin cruised low over its surface, admiring the rolling whiteness. Something caught his eye. Something black in the snow. Then more black things, and more and more. Bugs! Uncountable numbers of bugs, lying all over the icefield. Colin landed. Just before touching down, he noticed how cold it was near the snowy surface. It had been warm only a wingbeat higher – hot, even, as the sun's rays reflected off the snow and heated the underside of his body – but now, as he stepped onto the snow itself, the air felt as cold as winter.

He walked over to a moth and looked at it. The moth's wings began to flutter weakly. It could not fly. Colin ate it. He saw a beetle nearby. Again, the beetle was not dead. Its legs moved slowly, as if they would stop soon. Colin ate the beetle, too.

He realized that all these insects were numb with cold. Numb with cold and trapped here, unable to fly. What an opportunity for a raven! He started gobbling. Flies, mosquitoes, a butterfly, another beetle – it was a banquet, one that turned out to be a supper banquet. The more he ate, the more Colin relaxed, and the more he relaxed, the more he thought he had flown far enough that day. He began looking for a roost. The cold glacial surface offered none, so he flew toward the edge of the icefield. There, a deep valley dropped away. He roosted atop a pillar of rock on a cliff that reminded him of Yamnuska. It was gray limestone, with many cracks and corners. Small trees grew here and there on the ledges around him, just as they did at Raven's End.

Colin longed to be home. Maybe he would turn around and start back tomorrow, he thought. Perhaps he had missed the Mountain with Feathers somehow. Maybe he would see it as he flew back. The idea comforted him somewhat, and he slept.

VIII

BOOM!

Colin snapped awake. The echoes of a thunderbolt were pealing down the valley.

"*Awk!*" The next lightning flash came dazzlingly close, with a simultaneous splitting sound that shook the rock he was perched on. Something had stung his feet.

As he jumped into flight, another lightning bolt lit the scene. Colin's roosting pillar was now tumbling down the mountain, adding its disintegrating crash to the roar of the storm. The sulphurous odor of shattered limestone came up to him on the wind, along with the scream of an Engelmann spruce torn from its ledge and smashed to pieces by the tumbling chunks of stone.

Hail swept down out of the blackness, and the wind flung it hard in Colin's eyes. A gust caught him under his left wing and threw him sideways into the cliff. "*Awk!*" He regained control just in time to hear a boulder fizz past. Lightning struck again. Colin had been in thunderstorms before, but none like this. Instinctively he tried to distance himself from the cliff. The last flash had pointed the way. He groped out into the maelstrom of the sky, where he would not be hit by rockfall or battered to death against the cliff.

But the hail! The hail was firing right through his wing feathers. He would have to land, and it wasn't going to be easy. As each explosion of electricity lit the scene around him, Colin descended through the night, lower and lower, in a series of dives that kept his flying surfaces small. Suddenly he was among the treetops of the valley-floor forest. He put on the brakes as hard as he could and stuck out his feet just in time to intercept a branch that might have broken a wing.

"Whew." Colin clung to the branch as the wind swung it back and forth. "We sure don't have storms like this on Yamnuska," he said aloud, shuddering. The only reply he got was another blast from the thunderheads above. Working his way down the tree in a series of fluttering hops from branch to branch, he reached the middle and moved in close to the trunk to roost. As always, the wind here was light and the hail could not penetrate. He settled over his trembling feet. Morning couldn't come too soon.

IX

When Colin next opened his eyes, he looked out into rain and fog. The storm had arrived in a rage the night before, but now it had mellowed into the gray boredom of an all-day drizzle. Colin sighed. He didn't feel like flying in such weather, and yet he didn't particularly care for where he was, either. He lifted his tail from the branch, noting that his back was sore from being blown into the cliff. He directed a squirt of yesterday's insects at the soggy forest floor. The action fitted his mood perfectly. Maybe he would just start heading back to Yamnuska in the rain.

But where was Yamnuska? And in which direction must he fly? With growing panic, he realized that he had become disoriented in the storm, and he wasn't going to be able to get his bearings in the mist. Then he remembered that the mist had once offered him his first hint about the Mountain with Feathers. He could certainly use another vision of his goal right now. Would the mist offer it again?

Colin tried. "Hello, Mist."

No answer.

"Uh, Mist, this is Colin."

Nothing.

He reconsidered. The experience in the mist had been only the beginning. Later on, the Great Raven herself had spoken to him. Of course! He would contact the Great Raven for help and advice.

"Great Raven, this is Colin," he said to the air. "Can you hear me? I need you."

Colin waited several moments for an answer. The Great Raven had told him that she was often busy. He knew he had to be patient. At length he called out again, louder.

"Great Raven! This is Colin! I'm trying to reach you!"

This time he waited a very long time, perched miserably on his branch. He was wet and cold. His stomach was empty. His body hurt all over from the bruises inflicted by the hailstones, and the Great Raven wasn't responding to his pleas.

"Great Raven, this isn't fair!" he shouted petulantly. "You got me into this, now get me out!"

Still there was no response, and with growing certainty Colin realized that there wasn't going to be one. The Great Raven was paying no attention to him.

He clamped his bill. "All right, then. I'll just have to get back on my own." It was said in anger, and the anger carried Colin off his perch and out into the drizzle. "Bloody well just do it on my own," he repeated, trying to sound like Zack. Zack was a bird who let nothing faze him. Well, he would be like Zack.

First he would have to find something to eat. But he hardly knew what to look for in this kind of forest. It was far wetter and greener than the woods around Yamnuska. Small creeks trickled between banks of moss among the trees. He saw nothing he recognized as edible, and there was no carrion odor on the wind. Yet there was a sweetish fragrance in the air. Colin raised his bill to distinguish it better. It wasn't the smell of subalpine fir, which was sweet in itself. No, this was something different, something that reminded him of . . . of . . .

Berries! Colin dropped to the ground and began looking. Yes, there they were – low bushes with big round blueberries on them. "Oh, yum," he exclaimed as he started in.

A bellyful later he was feeling much better. Maybe he wouldn't turn back after all. He'd come so far, too far to just give up and go home, leaving the great question in his life unanswered. And what would Greta think? What would the Great Raven herself think? He would continue his quest. He would fly north.

The clouds had lifted a little. Colin could see that the valley stretched off in both directions like a long trough, the upper walls hidden by the low ceiling. He had the choice of flying either way in that valley. One way might take him northward toward the Mountain with Feathers. The other would take him back in the direction in which he had come.

"Well, it doesn't really matter which way I go," he reasoned aloud. "If I go the wrong way, I'll come to the glacier again, and if that happens I'll just turn around. So –"

He was stopped in mid-thought by a strange feeling. The second-sight feeling. Something appeared there, dark and foreboding. Something shapeless, something unknown. Something frightening. And it was coming his way!

Colin was off the ground in a wingbeat. Now he had a direction: away from whatever it was his mind's eye had seen. Fear drove him fast along the valley, and he covered a lot of distance in a hurry. After a while he realized that the feeling was gone. He relaxed a little. But what had been the cause? This time there had been no avalanche, no flock member lying under the snow. Maybe, he thought, it was just his imagination. Maybe this second-sight thing played tricks on him occasionally. Regardless, he was certainly going the right direction, for otherwise he would have reached the glacier by now. His spirits lifted.

All day Colin flew northward, following a river that was the same glacial gray as the sky. The valley ran straight, and he seemed to be making good progress – although the low cloud cover hid any landmarks he might have seen on either side. By late afternoon he estimated that he had flown about as far as he had been able to see from the Columbia Icefield the day before. It wouldn't do to miss the Mountain with Feathers, so he considered waiting here for the weather to clear. But a hint of second-sight fear crossed his mind at the thought, and Colin kept going.

At dusk he found himself approaching a town. Worried that he might somehow have wound up back at Banff, he flew here and there looking for the big anthill full of humans, or for the hot springs. But he found neither, so he felt sure that this was not Banff.

Could it be Jasper, then, the place Greta had mentioned? The place Scratch and Wheedle had visited on their way to Yamnuska? Tomorrow he would try to find out. Colin sought a cliff on which to roost, but the clouds had descended almost to the treetops, and the valley sides could not be seen. Colin settled into a tall pine on the edge of town. He slept uneasily.

X

"Who's this, then?"

Colin awoke to a dozen ravens landing on the branches around him. "Uh, gro," he said cautiously.

"Gro, C.C.," came the pleasant-sounding reply. Colin fluffed out his neck-feathers a little, to look assured but not arrogant, and introduced himself to what he assumed to be the local birds.

"Gro, my friends. I am Colin C.C., of the Raven's End Flock."

"Gro, Colin," said the bird who had first spoken to him. "My name is Angie C.C., Main Raven of the Jasper Flock."

So this was indeed Jasper! He had made it all the way to Jasper!

"Gro, Angie."

"So. Where's 'Raven's End'?" Angie asked. Her voice was kindly.

"On Yamnuska," Colin replied.

"And where's 'Yamnuska'?"

Colin blinked. He was now so far from home that the ravens hadn't heard of Yamnuska! "Yamnuska is along the mountain front south of here. South of here by three days of flying."

At this several birds gasped. Three days of flying! This Colin C.C. was a long-distance traveller.

Angie spoke for them all. "You've come a long way, Colin. What brings you to Jasper?"

Colin thought he might as well state it directly. "I'm looking for the Mountain with Feathers," he said seriously.

"Aren't we all!" said one of the ravens. "Aren't we all!"

"Beg pardon?!"

The same bird replied. "I guess anyone who takes journeys like you do is looking for the Mountain with Feathers, eh?" The raven gave him a knowing look. "But I doubt that you're quite ready to find it, right?" At this, several of the birds laughed.

What was going on here? Colin decided to try to straighten things out. "I wonder if we're talking about the same mountain. The one I'm talking about is a sort of dream mountain. I see it in my dreams. That's why I'm looking for it."

The other birds fell silent. They looked to their Main Raven.

"It might be the same one, Colin." Angie smiled. "Some of us believe that's where ravens go when they die."

Colin twitched. Ravens go to the Mountain with Feathers when they die? He had never heard this before. "Oh," was all he could say.

He decided not to inquire further about the Mountain with Feathers right now. The Jasper ravens seemed strange – friendly enough, but strange – and he didn't want to offend them. So he asked the next question that was on his mind. "Where does a raven get his breakfast around here?"

"At the human cache, mostly," Angie said. "We're just on our way there now. Care to join us?"

"I'd love to." He joined the flock as they took to wing. He was surprised to discover that he was not stiff this morning, despite his long flights of the previous days. The farther he flew, the better his body seemed to like it.

This day was just as cloudy as the one before. Colin had hoped to check out his surroundings from the air, but all he could see was the forest stretching off in every direction. Was he just in a wide valley, or was he even in the mountains at all? The cloud cover was so thick he couldn't tell.

The other birds noticed right away what a strong flyer he was. For every two flaps of their wings he needed only one to cover the same distance – except for Angie, who seemed to be as strong as Colin.

"You're a fine flyer," Angie complimented.

"Thank you. So are you. Seems to make a difference, if you go day after day."

"Indeed it does."

The birds were now over the town. Jasper was smaller than Banff, and it didn't have the hemmed-in feeling about it that Banff did. That observation brought to mind the question Colin had when he arrived the evening before. "Where do you roost, Angie – if you don't mind my asking?"

"Oh, here and there. We've got several roosts. We use one, then another. Gets boring otherwise, you know?"

Colin told Angie that at Yamnuska the ravens had their favorite perches and used them all the time. She seemed surprised.

"I'd like to visit Yamnuska sometime," she said. "See how ravens live in your part of the Rockies. Though it's hard to take much of a break with this crew on your tail every day."

The other ravens laughed. Colin could see that they genuinely *liked* their Main Raven.

By this time the flock had reached the place they called the "human cache." It was surrounded by a fence. Outside the fence lay a normal-looking forest of lodgepole pines, with clearings full of wildflowers. But inside the fence all was chaos. There were no trees, no shrubs, not even any grass. The earth had been gouged into raw-looking humps and hollows. Black bags full of something delicious – Colin could smell well-ripened food – lay in a pit, and a machine with a human on it was pushing dirt over the bags. The machine made a roaring sound, very loud, and dust followed it around. Also following it were dozens of seagulls. Long-winged and white, they wheeled gracefully about. They seemed quite out of place in the cratered landscape inside the fence.

"Breakfast is served," Angie said as she glided over to the pit with the black bags in it. Quickly she plunged her bill into a bag and ripped it open. Before the huge, clanking machine could push dirt over both Angie and the bag, she made off with a rib to which nearly all the meat still adhered. Angie landed on the ground, well away from the machine, and began stripping the rib.

As Colin watched, the other ravens made their own attacks on the bags, scattering gulls as they landed. Each tore and tugged, retrieved something to eat and flopped away with it.

"I guess I'd better get in there," Colin said to himself. His first attempt failed. The machine bore down on him and he had to fly away empty-billed. But on his next try he came away with a bunch of grapes.

"Mmm, sweet," Colin croaked happily as he popped each one and let the juice run down his throat. Wow! These Jasper ravens had it made!

Angie hopped over to him. "You've got the hang of it, I see."

"Anything to watch out for? Besides that horrible whatever-it-is the human's on?"

Angie looked over her shoulder at the machine. "Yeah, be very careful of that thing. We lost a flock member to it earlier this summer. It's slow, so you take it for granted. Then *crunch*."

Colin shuddered, imagining what it would feel like to be flattened under the treads. "I'll be careful, all right. Oh, and Angie –"

"Yes?"

"Why do you call this the 'human cache'?"

Angie threw his question back. "Haven't they got one at Yamnuska?"

"Well, uh –" Colin couldn't recall seeing anything like this around Yamnuska. "No, not really. What do the humans do with it?"

Angie gave Colin a look that told him he had just asked a very stupid question. But she answered it anyway. "Humans cache stuff here. You know, store it for later."

"Bury it in the ground? The way wolves do?" Colin was catching on. He knew that wolves sometimes buried their meat. And he, like other ravens, often hid small items of food that couldn't be eaten at the time.

"Well, yeah. Like wolves. Only they bury lots more than just meat, and they bury it really deep, and they –" Angie hesitated. She looked puzzled. She glanced back at Colin. "And you know," she continued, "I just realized that I've never seen any of them dig it up again." Angie closed her eyes, thinking deeply. "How strange. I'll have to ask . . . uh, I'll have to ask somebody about it." Then she flew off to open another bag.

Colin went back to eating. He had learned what this place was, and that was enough for now. How long the humans left their food cached was of no concern to him. They could leave it buried for a year, for all he cared. He laughed. No raven could wait that long to recover something he had cached – he'd have forgotten where it was! Craw-ha!

After breakfast, Colin expected the Flap. When it didn't occur, he asked Angie about it.

"Oh, the Flap. We've decided to combine the Flap and the Flight today. Sometimes we do that."

"Why today?"

"Well, because of you."

"Me?"

"Yeah. On the way to the Flap somebody spotted you and everyone had to come right over. So much for the Flap!"

Colin nodded in agreement. It was easy to interrupt a Flap at Raven's End, too. What surprised him was that Angie was taking it so well. The Main Raven at Yamnuska hated having his Flaps disrupted.

"Doesn't it bother you when something goes wrong with the Flap?"

"Aw, I don't care," Angie replied. "That's one less Flap to have to referee. We'll get caught up this evening, anyway."

"So you have your Flights at sundown, just like we do."

"Yup. Doesn't everybody?"

Another raven came up. "Hey, Angie!" he called.

"Hey yourself, Kootenay." The two birds touched bills.

Angie looked toward Colin. "Colin C.C., meet Kootenay C.C., my nestmate."

"Gro," said Colin.

"Gro," replied Kootenay. Then he turned toward Angie. "Should we take him to see Uriah?"

"Good idea. If there's anyone here who can help Colin, Uriah can."

"Who's Uriah?" Colin asked.

"The strangest bird you'll ever meet," Angie replied.

No stranger than Zygadena, Colin thought. And not as dangerous, he hoped.

XI

Colin, Kootenay, and Angie flew southeast across the Athabasca River, gray with rock flour from the glaciers upstream. A fish leaped from the milky water, alerting a nearby osprey to its presence. A moment later the big bird had the fish in its talons. As Colin watched the osprey fly off to its enormous nest of sticks, he felt the first drizzle of the day.

The three ravens were headed toward a side valley, where Colin could see a gorge. Angie got there first. She landed in a dead pine over-looking the deep gash in the bedrock. This place reminded Colin of Carrot Creek Canyon, but this gorge was even narrower. And deeper, too. He couldn't see the bottom. He could hear a river pounding through, pouring over waterfalls and raising mist. The mist sprinkled the sides of the gorge, keeping them wet and glistening.

Colin felt himself both attracted to the gorge and repelled by it. He lifted his eyes from the spectacle in front of him and turned to the other birds. "This is a strange and beautiful place," he stated.

"You bet," Angie said. "That's exactly what it is. Strange and beautiful. Precisely."

"It's called 'Maligne Canyon,'" Kootenay offered.

Maligne! The name Zygadena had used! Colin shivered. He stuttered out the obvious question. "Do – do you know anything about . . . about a flock of ravens called the 'Maligne Flock'?"

Angie surprised him with a laugh. "Sure. It's a flock of one. His name is Uriah." She looked up. "And here he is, the whole flock of him!" She laughed again, and so did Kootenay, as a raven landed clumsily on the branch. He was a small raven, and an old one. His plumage was dull, and his feathers were tattered. His bill had several notches in it, and, as Colin noticed when the bird turned his head toward him, one eye was missing.

"Greetings, all," said this odd-looking raven in a raspy voice. Then he turned to Colin. "Gro, my young friend. My name is Uriah C.C. Do I know you?" He tilted his head this way and that, fixing Colin with his good eye.

"Uh, no. My name is Colin C.C. I'm pleased to meet you." Colin wasn't sure how pleased he actually was.

"Colin is from Yamnuska," Angie said.

"Ah, yes. Yamnuska. Marvelous place," Uriah said, looking thoughtful. "Terrific place."

"You've been there?"

"Yes, indeed. And everywhere else in these mountains."

Colin let his guard down a little. Uriah seemed to have a lot in common with Greta.

Kootenay spoke next. "Uriah, Colin is looking for something. We brought him along to you because we thought you might be able to help him find it."

"Help him?" Uriah turned his blind side to Colin. "Of course I can help him." He turned back to Colin and looked as if he were about to say something to him, but he spoke to Angie instead. "Would you like to just leave him here with me for the afternoon?"

Colin started to object. "Oh, I don't know that I –"

But Angie only laughed. "No worries, Colin. He's harmless. Aren't you, Uriah?"

"Yes, I suppose you're right. By the Trees, Angie, I hate being harmless. But I am. I'm so old I have trouble pecking at bugs these days, never mind pecking at another raven."

"You'll find him quite interesting," Angie added.

Colin wondered what he should do. The trap that Dolus had set for him with Zygadena had nearly taken his life. Could he trust Angie and Kootenay, whom he barely knew? And what about this Uriah, whom he knew not at all? He looked at the circle of birds. He looked at their eyes. He saw honesty in the eyes of Angie and Kootenay, and something else in the one eye of Uriah. He wasn't sure what it was, but at least it wasn't evil. Colin knew the look of evil.

He decided to take a chance. "Okay. I'm just kind of leery after a run-in with a very nasty raven earlier this summer."

Uriah chuckled. "I should be just as leery of you, stranger." He gave Colin the same sort of penetrating look that Colin had given him. "But I'm not," he said, smiling. "Heck, these days I don't care much about myself at all."

"We'll see you at the Flight, Colin," Angie said. "Look for us right here, over the canyon, at sundown. It's one of our favorite places." She spread her wings.

"'Bye for now," Kootenay called as he left the branch. Colin let out a gasp – Kootenay was free-falling into the canyon! From the depths of the gorge a moment later, Colin heard him croak "whee!" as he pulled up just above the water.

"That Kootenay," said Angie. "He's such a daredevil. It's frightening to watch him."

"Just imagine what it must feel like to *be* him," said Uriah thoughtfully.

XII

Colin and Uriah sat together on the branch of a dead pine overlooking Maligne Canyon. Clouds had moved in, obscuring everything in fog. Light rain fell steadily. Neither bird said anything for a while, then Uriah broke the silence.

"Now then, Colin. Tell me the worst thing that ever happened to you."

"What?" Colin had never been asked anything like this.

"It's just to help me get to know you better."

"Oh." This was a strange way to make an introduction. But Colin was willing to cooperate. "Uh, let's see. Worst thing. Well, that was probably when I got shot by humans."

"Shot? Tell me about it."

"Oh, a couple of hunters on Yamnuska. I didn't know what they were. Got too close to them, and *bang!*"

"Were they hunting ravens?"

Colin hadn't considered the possibility. "They could have been, I guess." Clearly, Uriah was a very perceptive bird.

Rain pattered down. "I've been hunted a lot," Uriah said offhandedly.

Colin looked puzzled. "Really? Here in the Park?" Greta had told him that Jasper was in the Park, just as Banff was. "That can't be right, Uriah."

Uriah turned his good eye toward Colin. "Well, my young friend, perhaps it *wasn't* in the Park. But you obviously know far more about these things than I do." He turned away again.

Colin didn't know what to say next, he was so embarrassed. He could imagine Greta lecturing him along the lines of "a travelling raven has to be tactful at all times."

Uriah may have been insulted, but he resumed the conversation. "So. Tell me what it is you want to know."

"Well, I'm trying to find a particular mountain."

"I know. I have been there."

"You have?" Colin's feet gripped the branch hard.

"Of course. I have been everywhere."

"But how did you know which mountain I'm looking for?"

"Oh, I have my ways. You don't even have to tell me the name."

"It's the Mountain with Feathers."

"Ah. Indeed. The Mountain with Feathers. Yes, yes."

Colin's heart leapt. Uriah had been to the Mountain with Feathers! Now if he could only provide directions to it . . .

Uriah raised his head and ruffled out his neck-feathers. He took a deep breath. "The Mountain with Feathers is a grand and glorious mountain. It is higher and more beautiful than any other. Its base is surrounded by dense forest of the deepest green. Its sides are covered with glaciers that shine in the sun. Its top is lost in the clouds."

He glanced at Colin. Colin was listening eagerly.

"If you seek this great mountain, you must be pure of heart and strong of body. You must have *spirit!* Many ravens have tried, but few have succeeded." He peered again at Colin, who was enthralled. "It requires a lifetime to reach the Mountain with Feathers." He waved a wing in the air for emphasis. "A lifetime. And even so, for most of us the trip is a failure. We begin at hatching, when we know not where we are going or why. We continue through the innocence of youth. Ah, wonderful youth!" Here he looked knowingly at Colin. "But as we mature we lose that innocence and start on the hard part of the journey, the journey through adult life. Through wind and storm, through beauty and ugliness, through happiness and grief. And then, when we reach the end of life, we see, still distant and unattainable in our final weakness, the great mountain that has been our goal."

A feeling as gray as the weather began creeping over Colin. The message had gone from inspiring to sad. In fact, Uriah himself seemed overcome with the sadness of it. He stopped speaking. His head drooped and his eye closed.

Colin's darkening mood brought forth dark words. "Uriah, do you think that the only way to reach the Mountain with Feathers is to *die?*"

The eye stayed closed. "Indeed, my friend."

"And most ravens don't reach it, even so?"

"That is true."

"But you said you have been there."

"That is also true."

"But —"

"I know. How can I still be alive if I have been to the Mountain with Feathers?"

"Yes, Uriah. How can you?"

The eye opened. "My life has been harder than most, Colin. I have been ill, and injured, and starved and frozen." He ruffled out his neck-feathers again. "I have known the hunger of the Hard Winter, and the bitterness of the Year Without a Summer. I have fallen from my perch in fever and been seized between the jaws of a coyote. Death has stalked me closely, Colin, and caught me on several occasions."

"And you survived?"

"Yes. Just barely. At the very last moment, strength flowed into my body and saved me."

"Where did this strength come from?"

"From the Trees themselves."

Colin had never heard anything like this. His anxiety deepened. "Uriah, if I keep seeing visions of the Mountain with Feathers, does it mean that I am going to die?"

Uriah looked thoughtful. "It may," he said.

"Soon?"

"Possibly."

"How soon?"

"There is no way of telling."

"But — but what should I do about all of this, Uriah?" Colin was despairing. "I mean, I've come all this way just to *die?*"

"What will be, will be. The Trees may spare you. After all, they spared me. Everything is the will of the Trees. If I'm lucky, when I die, the Trees will send the Great Raven to take me to the Mountain with Feathers. If I'm lucky."

The Great Raven would take him to the Mountain with Feathers? Everything was the will of the Trees? Colin grappled with these ideas. But much of what this old, half-blind bird was saying didn't make sense to him. Greta had told him that life went on after death in a different way, through seeds and such. And what Uriah was telling him didn't agree with any of his dreams. Yet the Great Raven herself had told him to pay attention to his dreams.

Colin had never been so confused. He stared desolately into Maligne Canyon, hearing the water thundering below but unable to see into the swirling mist. This was like his life, he thought. Voices urging him on toward something invisible. If Uriah was correct, it was also unreachable. Maybe the voices – that of the fog long ago, or the wind during the Cold Blow, or the Great Raven's weird pronouncements – maybe they were all for naught. Maybe the world just didn't make sense in some very basic way, and no matter what you did there was no point to it.

Second-sight, for example. What was it good for? Seeing ahead toward death, that's what it was good for. Sure, he had been able to save some lives with it. But what had it meant for *him?* He was no closer to answering the big question, the tormenting question, the question that was driving him to desperation: *Where had he come from?!*

Colin shivered in the rain. Water ran off the end of his bill and dripped away into the roaring depths of the canyon. He watched the droplets disappearing into the darkness of the gorge below.

Clearly, he had failed. Failed to find out where he had come from. Failed to find the Mountain with Feathers. Failed in everything. His whole life – what he could remember of it – was a failure. It was all so hopeless. Perhaps he would just stop all this futile searching. Perhaps he would just let go . . .

Colin closed his eyes. His feet loosened their grip on the branch. He began to tilt forward.

XIII

"Chirrup!"

Who was that? Colin opened his eyes. He was slipping off his perch in the dead pine above Maligne Canyon. He grabbed on hard with his feet and straightened himself up.

"Chirrup! Chirrup! Bzeet!" The sound was coming from inside the canyon. It grew louder. Colin looked down to see what was making it. There, barely visible on a ledge far below him near the bottom of the gorge, just above the churning water, was a bird.

It was small and gray. Standing on the ledge, head held high, the bird began singing in earnest – "Bzeet! Bzeet! Chirrup, chirrup, chirrup! Bzeet, bzeet!" – bringing forth a long, happy song. Colin couldn't understand all the words over the noise of the water, but he caught the gist: "I am a dipper, and this is my home, the home that I love."

Colin blinked. A bird living in a place like this? What –

"Bzeet! Chirrup!" The dipper dived from its ledge into the roiling currents. Colin flinched. Surely it would drown! But a moment later the bird was back on the ledge, flexing its legs in a bobbing motion that sent the water streaming off its feathers. In its bill it held a water insect. Rather than eating the insect, the dipper flew with it down the canyon toward another sound Colin was now starting to hear: similar, but higher pitched. There was more than one voice. "By the Trees," Colin said aloud, "that bird must have nestlings in the canyon!"

The realization brought him a feeling of wonder. Birds raising their young in a place like this! Little gray birds *living* in a place like this, singing happily amid the torrents! Truly, Colin affirmed to himself with growing delight, birds could live anywhere, could do anything. Birds could live in the bottom of Maligne Canyon and sing about it. Birds were just, well, the *best!*

And he, Colin, was a bird. A bird who had been slipping into a deadly reverie moments ago, but now a bird who felt as if he had just awakened. He looked over to Uriah, who was sleeping. He looked up into the fog. And suddenly he knew what he was going to do.

"Up!" he yelled to the dripping canyon walls.

"*Up, up, up . . .*" they echoed.

Colin spread his wings and shot upward from his perch like a black rock flung from a volcano. Up! Up! Up! He pulled hard against the fog, gaining elevation faster than he ever had before. His lungs set the pace – inhale! exhale! inhale! exhale! – and his heart kept up, although it felt like it was coming loose in his chest. Up! Up! Up!

Then he burst through the cloud-tops and into the sun.

"Free!" he cried. "I'm free!"

Yes, he was free. He was free of the fog. He was free of the canyon. He was free of Uriah. He was also free, he realized, of all the worries he had been carrying on this long journey. The frightful agony of *not knowing* had left him. In its place was the certain knowledge of his great avian heritage, the strength and joy of his wings, the comfort of just being a raven, alive, up in the sky.

Now he could stop his frantic flapping. He levelled off and soared in the sunlight. He recalled something Greta had said last winter, during the Flight before the coldest night, when she had told Zack that the reason to live was – how had she put it, exactly? – oh, yes; the reason was "to be part of all this." How true! Colin could now see clearly that the "this" she was referring to was the world of ravens. Her world and his world. And what a world it was! So rich in beauty. So rich in experience, there for the taking. So rich in knowledge, there for the learning.

So rich in ugliness, too, and evil, and pain and suffering – yes, he had certainly suffered – but he had endured suffering; he had survived evil. He would undoubtedly encounter these things again, and gladly, for they were part of the world, the *real* world in which he lived. The world of ravens.

Colin felt satisfaction. He pictured himself falling numbly into Maligne Canyon, his senses shut off, his mind paralyzed with self-pity. How silly! He found himself laughing.

At that moment something caught Colin's attention.

Something out of the corner of his eye.

There, off to the right, not so very far away –

"It's the Mountain with Feathers!"

Colin heard the sound of his voice croaking happily. "The Mountain with Feathers! There it is! It's real!"

And so it was. Higher than its neighbors, reaching well above the clouds, the Mountain with Feathers was instantly recognizable. The sun glinted on its angled slabs, which overlapped one another just like the feathers on a raven's wings, exactly as in Colin's dreams. "Oh, yes! It's real! It's perfect! And . . . and I'm *almost there!*"

Then he heard another voice in addition to his own. "Well done, Colin. Well done," said the Great Raven.

XIV

The cloud deck was breaking up as Colin flew toward the Mountain with Feathers. Except for some filmy stratus still clinging to the peak, it was now visible from base to top. He could see that it was carved from a single, enormous block of limestone. The west face was the slabby side, a vast inclined surface of bare rock, recently wetted with rain and dark as a shadow. On the other side, Colin could see a glacier shining white in the sunlight. Rock on one side and ice on the other; Colin could not imagine more perfect symmetry.

How should he approach the Mountain with Feathers? Colin chose the west side. Here he would probably find an updraft, and as he drew near the slabs he felt himself lifted skyward as never before. He soared ecstatically, circling in the rising wind, feeling the power that abided in this peak.

Far above the summit, black dots drifted among wispy bits of cloud. Ravens! In a few moments, Colin was among them.

"Greetings, Colin. You're just in time for the Mythical Flight." It was Angie. And here was Kootenay.

"Kootenay? Mythical Flight? But —"

"And so we finally meet, Colin C.C." The voice of the Great Raven — and a bird to go with it!

Colin was surprised to see how ordinary she seemed. Ordinary, that is, until she looked at Colin. Her beautiful brown eyes were so clear, so deep — deeper, even, than Greta's — that it seemed to Colin that the knowledge of the ages must be stored there. Yes, this truly was the Great Raven. He wanted to speak, but he didn't know what to say. The Great Raven spoke instead.

"It's all right to be tongue-tied, Colin. I imagine you'll be doing more listening than talking in the next little while anyway. Just let me say how pleased I am that you're here."

A ripple in the airstream bounced the birds about. They made the most of it, croaking playfully.

"Wing-over! Yay!"

"Immelmann! Immelmann!"

"Let's go a little farther east and grab the downdraft. It's going to pack a wallop today!"

"Yes, let's do that," said the Great Raven, "but first, don't you think we ought to welcome Colin C.C.?"

"Aye, an' that we should, G.R." By the burr on the *R*, Colin could tell who was speaking. Sure enough, it was Boogs, the raven he knew from the Banff Flock. What was Boogs doing here? And Angie and Kootenay?

"Let's land at the Loft and do this properly," the Great Raven suggested. All the birds immediately pulled in their wings and hurried downward. Colin could hardly keep up, they flew so well.

The Loft was a platform near the summit of the Mountain with Feathers, the only flat place on what was otherwise a knife-edge of rock. On one side lay the slabs that Colin had circled beside. On the other an equally steep slope of glacial ice fell away. Despite the westerly wind that rushed over the mountain, the air at the Loft was calm. Colin fluttered as he dropped out of the updraft along with the other birds. Two-dozen strong, they formed a loose circle around the Great Raven.

"Who wants to explain?" she asked.

"Oh, you do it," said Angie. "You've had the most practise – craw-ha!" The others echoed her laugh.

"All right, I will." The Great Raven turned to Colin, who was looking both eager and fearful. "The first thing, Colin, is that there's no need to be frightened. We're not going to hurt you." She smiled. "Come close and look into my eyes."

Colin looked, but from a safe distance. What he saw – kindness beyond words, limitless generosity, boundless love – brought him over in a single hop.

"That's it. Now keep looking into my eyes. Stare hard."

He did. A peaceful feeling came over him. "I – I feel sleepy," he said.

"You're supposed to," the Great Raven reassured him. "Just let the sleepy feeling grow. Pretend that night is coming. It's a warm summer evening at Raven's End, after a day without a single cloud, and the wind feels soft. You're on your favorite roost. Everything is comfortable and warm. Your head is back under your wing, and you can feel the warmth spreading through your feathers, making you so sleepy . . ."

Her voice trailed off as Colin, head tucked away, seemed to fall asleep.

The other birds had been watching intently. One of them whispered to the Great Raven. "May we do it, too?"

"Certainly." She turned her eyes toward the rest of the flock. Every bird stared into them, and in a few moments the Loft was silent. The Great Raven, in her own special way, began to tell Colin's story. There were no words. Instead, there was a dream shared by all.

XV

High up on Yamnuska, two humans – two climbers – stood on a ledge.

"Last pitch," said one to the other. "Twenty metres to the top, give or take. Want to lead it?"

"I – I don't know, Colin. This looks weird. It's totally overhanging. There's not supposed to be anything this steep on the route, is there?"

"Who's to say? We've lost the guidebook."

"Sorry about that."

"Aw, no worries. Remember when I dropped the guidebook off Castle Mountain? We got up okay."

"But maybe we're not on the route, Col."

"I'd say we have to be." Colin was looking up. "That crack is so obvious."

The other climber was also inspecting the crack. He craned his neck back. "Well, maybe that *is* the route. Really steep, though."

"So you want to lead or not?"

"Well, no. Really, I don't. And I don't like this belay. I mean, here we are, way up here, and I'm anchored on only one piton."

Colin glanced at a metal spike sticking out of the rock at waist level. He touched it. Flakes of rust fell away as he wiggled the ring in the end. Not good. But they had nothing to put in its place.

"It'll have to do, that's all." Colin's voice was firm. "Look – the sun's setting, okay? We'll be trying to get down in the dark." He stepped away from the rope piled about his feet. He checked the knot that tied him to one end of the rope. His partner was tied to the other. "You got me, Ted?"

"Yeah." Ted glanced at the rope in his hands. His knuckles were scraped and scabby. He looked Colin in the eye. "Be really careful, okay?"

"Not to worry, Ted. It's in the bag."

Colin began to climb, up there in the late-afternoon shadows. He found a handhold, swung up onto a tiny ledge, and balanced against the vertical wall, his nose to the rock. He could smell the rock. It was earthy, the odor of moss and lichen and cold stone.

Colin's fingertips brushed across the rough surface, finding a hold here, a hold there. The toes of his rock-climbing shoes touched lightly, cautiously, seeking a nubbin, a hollow, a bit of cliff that sloped less steeply than the rest. One careful move at a time, Colin was gaining ground. His rope dangled down to Ted, who watched intently from the ledge, feeding the rope out as Colin tiptoed higher, higher.

And here was the crack in the rock. It ran straight up to the sky. Colin could see the blue at the top of the crack, the top of the South Face, the top of the mountain. It was so close. They were going to make it – if he could climb that crack. As wide as his thigh, the crack split a wall that leaned toward him, beyond the vertical.

Colin stuck his arm into the crack. A bit of winter's chill lingered there, hiding from the August sun. Feeling around, Colin's hand bumped into a stone. The stone was wedged tightly in the crack and just the right size to grab. The perfect handhold. He sighed in relief. This would make all the difference.

"How's it look?" Ted called up.

"Off-width. But there's a chockstone. Just have to get up high enough to stand on the thing."

Just, just. Colin leaned out on his arms, trying to rest his muscles before making the difficult move up and over the chockstone. He was tired. Tired all over. He and Ted had been climbing since daybreak.

Colin took a deep breath. He reached up and grabbed the chock-stone with his right hand. He pulled hard on it, feeling his body rise. Plenty of strength left in that arm. He pressed his lips together in a tight smile, getting ready for one of his great pleasures: doing something demanding, and doing it well. Such was climbing, he thought. There was something like this on every mountain, every cliff, every frozen waterfall, every –

The chockstone pulled out.

He saw the wall rush back. His hand shot out, grabbing for the edge of the crack, but it was gone. He shouted – "*TED!!*" – and saw the sky in a place it shouldn't be.

Ted had the other end of the rope. Now it was up to Ted to save Colin's life. Having climbed upward a dozen difficult moves, Colin was falling downward that same dozen, then a dozen more before Ted could do anything about it. Ted braced himself.

The weight came on the rope, a lot of weight, generated by the force of the fall. All that weight hit the little aluminum belay plate on Ted's climbing harness. It went "click" and stopped the rope from sliding through. The plate was attached to Ted, so the force now tugged at Ted's body. It jerked him forward. In the next instant he would be hurled off the ledge and into space. Unless . . .

There was one hope left for these two climbers. Driven into the cliff beside Ted was the piton, an old, rusty blade of steel. Ted had tied himself to it. Would it hold?

Perhaps it would. The great Brian Redman had driven that piton many years ago, when he had peered up at the overhanging rock and had told himself, "That crack looks too difficult. I'm going to work my way over to the right and check around the corner. But first I'm going to get a good, solid peg in."

So Brian Redman had hammered in the piton – *ping, ping, ping* – until only the ring had stuck out. He had clipped his rope through it, then he had traversed rightward. He had found a good hold over there, hidden around the corner, and he had climbed easily to the top. So he never had to climb the overhanging crack. Nor did he fall as he finished the climb, so he didn't have to put his piton to the test.

But Colin was testing it now. All in an instant the ring distorted under the strain, becoming an oval. The piton bent. It shifted forward in the crack . . . it held. This bit of metal, worth a few dollars in a mountaineering equipment shop, had done its job. Colin and Ted stopped falling.

But all was not well. Colin was dangling on the cliff face twenty metres below the ledge. And he was not moving.

"Colin! Are you okay?"

No answer.

"Colin!"

No answer.

Ted squinted down the cliff. He could see that Colin's yellow helmet had a big dent in the top. "He must have hit something," Ted said to himself. And then he saw the blood running from under Colin's helmet, dripping away in the wind, blowing back across the rock in red spatters. He tried to calm himself, to think about how he could get Colin back up to the ledge. Colin was so heavy, hanging there in that harness. The harness went around Colin's chest, and the nylon webbing squeezed his ribs. Under Colin's ribs were Colin's lungs, trying to breathe.

"Colin always climbed like the Europeans, in a chest harness," Ted caught himself saying. He was speaking of Colin in the past tense, and well he should, for as he watched he saw the harness working its way upward on Colin's body, creeping under his arms. He saw Colin's arms start to rise, helplessly.

"No! No! Colin, wake up! Keep your arms down!"

But the harness crept up and up, until suddenly Colin's arms shot straight overhead. His body dropped through the web of nylon and fell free.

XVI

Colin the raven awoke with a twitch, as he always did from a dream in which he was falling. The other birds, affected the same way, opened their eyes, too.

Angie walked over and touched his bill, saying, "Great story, Colin, great story. Much more exciting than mine." She looked over to the Great Raven. "Fabulous, G.R. These dreams you do get better every time."

"Thank you," the Great Raven replied.

He knew. Finally, after all this time, Colin knew where he had come from. The dream had been very clear. Yet it was incredible. To have been a human climber who fell from Yamnuska? A flood of questions swept through his mind, but before he could sort the torrent into words, the Great Raven spoke.

"Colin, you are one of us. You have been one of us since the moment of your appearance as a raven, and you shall remain one of us as long as you live." She paused to let that sink in. "And, like the rest of the Mythical Flock, you can live as long as you like."

Colin's eyes had started to widen with her first statement, and they practically popped out at her second. "As long as – I can live as long as –"

"As long as you like," the Great Raven repeated. "Colin, with membership in the Mythical Flock comes the privilege of immortality."

Colin opened his bill, but nothing came out. The Great Raven gave him a moment to absorb this vast idea, and none of the other birds interrupted. Then she continued.

"It's like this, Colin. No aspiring mythical raven knows where she or he came from. And you haven't either, until now. And it hurts. It hurts a lot. You suffered more than most, and I'm sorry. But it had to be. You are all the stronger for it." Some of the other birds nodded, saying "yes, yes" and "quite so."

"Like all other mythical ravens, Colin, you started as something else. Lately they've been starting as humans."

Humans becoming ravens? This was impossible! When you were dead, you were dead. Something ate you!

"Of course it sounds impossible," said the Great Raven, thereby reminding Colin that she could know his thoughts. "But that's the way it is. The Trees are the ones behind it, and you know what sort of power they have. Impossible power. The power to make crazy-sounding things into real things."

The swish of wind over the slabs a few metres away became a roar, taking her words away. Yet the breeze on the Loft barely ruffled her feathers. Presently the gust passed.

"Colin, you were very, very lucky. You were the one among many millions of humans given a chance to become mythical. I guess you just happened to fall off Yamnuska at the right time, when the Trees were watching."

"The other human climber – the human who was my climbing partner – what happened to it?"

"Your partner was rescued by other humans." The Great Raven looked admiringly at Colin. "And it's a sign of your character, Colin C.C., that you would want to know that."

He lowered his head, embarrassed by the compliment but honored all the same.

"So how do you feel now?"

Colin took a moment to think. What came to him was a question. "I feel very relieved," he said, "but I wonder if I could ask you something, Great Raven –"

"Of course."

"What was it like for you, before you knew where you came from?"

The other birds tittered. What a personal question! Colin looked mortified, but the Great Raven just chuckled. "Now, now. I'll bet everyone here would like to know that. Am I right?" She looked around. The tittering had turned into expectation. "I can remember when the Trees first explained my origin to me. And they took their sweet time getting around to it. A thousand years or so."

Colin gasped. How could she have stood it?

"Barely," she replied to his unspoken question. "But eventually the Trees did tell me. They didn't make me from a human, you know. There weren't any humans back then. They made me from a dinosaur." She smiled. "I'll bet *that's* not something you hear in those Great Raven tales they tell in the mortal flocks."

No, indeed, thought Colin. And what was a "dinosaur"?

"Big lizard. Anyway, I've always felt that the Trees made a mistake when they granted me immortality. It complicated things, both for them and for me. But they're a vain lot, the Trees, and they wanted to keep their handiwork around. 'This was our first,' they'd say, showing me off. 'Don't you think it's terrific?' And they'd congratulate each other. For a long time I thought my only purpose was to feed their sense of superiority. My only purpose besides scratching their itchy limbs, of course." Here she gave a little snort of a laugh. "But in time they left me alone. Just plain forgot about me, I guess. *I* had to go to *them* with my problem."

Another gust whistled over the birds, forcing the Great Raven to pause.

"My problem was that my flockmates kept dying." She looked wistful. "Worse, my nestmates. I'd have a mate for a few years – had one for twenty years once – and then he would die. It just crushed me every time. I went back to the Trees and demanded the right to die, too."

No one laughed at this.

"But the Trees, in their typical way, refused. 'No,' they said. 'We like you alive.' So that was it. I couldn't even kill myself. I tried. They'd haul me back. It was horrible."

Another roar of wind over the slabs.

"But you know, the Trees are terribly clever, even if they are the most self-centred things in the world, and they came up with a pretty good solution."

"What was that?" Colin asked.

"You. All of you. All the immortal members of the Mythical Flock. From among you I have chosen my nestmate. Which reminds me," she said, turning to a distinguished-looking raven standing beside her, "Would you like to introduce yourself now, Archie?"

"Certainly. Greetings, Colin C.C. I am Archibald C.C., mate of G.R. here." He touched her bill.

She touched his, then turned again to Colin. "A raven needs a flock, too, and mine is the Mythical Flock. Unless you are careless, Colin, and I hope you're not, you can be part of the flock as long as you wish. That is to say, forever."

Forever. Colin smiled broadly. "Thank you," he said.

"Don't thank me. Thank the Trees."

"Thank the Trees? How can I, uh . . ."

"Just keep on scratching 'em. That's part of the deal. We mythicals get an awful lot of practise, so we do it best."

As the wind rose again, a gust of elation swept over Colin. To live forever! To live forever, and in the company of ravens such as this! Think of what he could *learn!*

"Oh, there's something I forgot to mention," the Great Raven said, "something that you may find interesting. That bit of cleverness – the creation of the Mythical Flock – is what you hear hinted about in the Great Raven tales as the 'Request.' In fact, a fair bit of my story has escaped over the generations into the mortal flocks, in spite of my trying to prevent it. The Trees warned me about that. They've seen what loose knowledge of immortality can do in other species. So the Trees have made sure that the true nature of the Request doesn't become known."

Those were Greta's words almost exactly, Colin recalled. He wondered how much Greta knew of all this. Then it dawned on him that Greta might be a mythical raven. Of course! She had to be!

"But be aware, Colin, that even mythical ravens can be killed. And the Trees won't bring you back if that happens. Mythical ravens are immune to aging and disease, and they have great healing ability, but a really severe injury can be fatal. That is why the Trees create new mythicals occasionally. You've had some close calls, right?"

Colin nodded, but he said nothing. He noticed, though, that several of the other birds looked sympathetic.

"In fact, most aspiring mythicals don't make it," the Great Raven continued. "They have accidents along the way. We lose a hundred potential flock members for every one we gain. But if a candidate mythical raven survives the first year, then there's a good chance the bird will be with the flock for a very long time. So we go ahead with the induction."

She smiled at Colin. He looked back at those splendid eyes, grateful to have lived long enough to see them. Now he would have a chance to get to know this bird well. It was an exciting thought.

"So, I guess it's time for the welcoming," she concluded. "Shall we induct Colin?"

The other ravens croaked their approval, and the circle closed around Colin and the Great Raven. She made the pronouncement.

"Colin Corvus Corax, we welcome you as the newest member of the Mythical Flock." She touched his bill, then turned to the others. "Shall we have a Motion?"

The other birds were quick to assent.

"Yes! Yes!"

"Hear, hear!"

"Oh, I love this. A new member!"

As at Yamnuska, the flock moved in, covering Colin protectively with their black wings. The wheel of wings fluttered eagerly. Then, led by the Great Raven, the wings rose up in unison. The birds raised their heads high, and out came the flock call.

"Rawk-a-taw!"

Colin's bill opened in disbelief. It was the same call used by the Raven's Enders.

XVII

Colin, now a full-fledged member of the Mythical Flock, was mobbed by the other birds. They all wanted to hear more of his story, and he wanted to hear theirs. He learned that Angie and Kootenay were both mythical, but that they had not been humans in their previous lives. They were too old. Like the Great Raven, they had lived before the Trees had invented humans.

"What were you and Angie before you became mythical?" he asked Kootenay.

"Oh, I was a sort of armadillo. Angie, now, she was a really weird sea creature. I can hardly even pronounce the name. 'Ammoloid sethfal-loop' or something like that."

"Ammonoid cephalopod, Kootenay. I've told you a thousand times —"

"Literally," said Kootenay. "And I'll never remember it. Anyway, the whole lot are extinct now. Except for Angie, of course. Who's kind of extinct, too —"

Angie pecked him.

Boogs, the Banff raven, welcomed him warmly. "It's a real treat, so it is, seein' ye here, laddie. I was surely hopin' ye'd mak' it, so I was."

"But Boogs – why didn't you just tell me where the Mountain with Feathers was?"

"Ach, it's no' allowed, laddie. Ye have tae get there by yersel'. Mind, I *was* kind enough tae gie ye a wee hint, was I no'?"

"Well, yes. And it saved me from wasting my time going west from Castle Mountain, which I surely would have done otherwise."

"Aye, weel I'm glad I helped ye, then."

"And where did you –?"

"Where did I meet ma end as a human? It was daft! I fell through a snow cornice, climbin' wi' nae rope."

"So you were a climber, too."

"Aye, an' wi' a wife and wee babe at hame." He looked sad.

"But can you visit them?" Colin asked.

"Och, indeed I can," Boogs replied, brightening. "I'm for makin' the flight tae their hoose in a day or two."

"But they can't know it's you."

"Weel, no, they cannae, that's true. An' it wouldnae be proper for them to. But it doesnae stop me from keepin' an *eye* on them, eh?"

One of the other birds hopped up to Colin. "Gro, Colin C.C. I'm Laurel C.C., from the Squamish Flock." She touched his bill with hers.

Colin responded in the proper way. "Gro, Laurel C.C." He returned the touch. "Uh, where is Squamish? I've never heard of it."

"Oh, it's out about ten days southwest of here. If you fly."

"Ten days? If you fly? What –?"

"Hey, far out to meetcha, Colin. I'm Jon-Jon C.C., from the Calgary Flock."

"Calgary Flock? But I thought this was the Mythical Flock –"

"Howdy, Colin C.C.," said a bird with a peculiar, drawly accent. "I'm Rick C.C., from the Pikes Peak Flock." The initials "C.C." sounded like "Say Say."

And so it went. He tried to remember all the names, but there were so many that he quickly lost track. Oh no, he thought, they would think he was a boor if he couldn't remember! His head was spinning.

The Great Raven saw his worried expression, looked briefly into his mind and understood immediately. "Oh, just look at him, C.C.s. Don't you know how he feels? How you felt the first time?"

"For sure, for sure," said Jon-Jon, the raven from Calgary. "He's coming to grips with a whole new plane of existence here. Immortality is kind of a heavy trip to lay on someone all at once. It *can* throw a bird off." Several of the other ravens giggled. Colin cringed.

The Great Raven addressed the whole flock. "I'll tell you what, C.C.s. Why don't all of you be off for a while so Colin and I can talk one-to-one, okay? Just for a while, to get him all sorted out."

They didn't want to go, but they went. And they didn't go far – just out of earshot at the other end of the Loft.

Colin, the insatiable asker of questions who was now overwhelmed with answers, said, "Thank you, Great Raven. It was really getting to be a bit much."

"You can just call me G.R., Colin. Everyone else does."

"Okay, uh, G.R."

"Now. You're wanting to ask me why the Trees chose humans to become mythical ravens, right?"

"Well, yes." Colin was already formulating his next question: where did she get her power to know what other ravens were thinking?

"Well, Colin," the Great Raven began, "I'll get to your second question in a moment. But about the humans. The Trees don't even *like* humans much. After all, humans cut down trees. Inventing humans was the worst mistake the Trees ever made. But they know that only a very intelligent creature can be turned into a raven, and when humans came along it was only natural to use them. After all, humans are the third-smartest things in the world, next to ravens and the Trees themselves. Humans are also a lot like ravens, in some ways. Humans can eat almost anything, same as us, and they aren't happy unless they're amused, same as us. They have great memories, perhaps even better than ours. And so on."

"But why not just pick ravens in the first place? It would be easy for the Trees to make a raven immortal, wouldn't it?"

"Yes, of course. But not very kind."

"Not very kind?"

"Most aspiring mythicals don't survive their learning period."

"And – and –" Colin's mind was racing ahead. "And the Trees thought it would be cruel to put a raven through that? All that worry and uncertainty? And then another death?"

"Yes. The Trees are pretty obtuse sometimes, but they do care about ravens. It just seemed improper to make them suffer. Besides," she said, "they tried a few ravens early on and botched it. Made me terribly unhappy. And I sure let them know it. So they started using humans. Humans don't matter much to the Trees."

"Why did they pick climbers, like Boogs and me?"

"Well, climbers are the most suitable kind of humans to be made into ravens. Think about it. You know a fair bit about climbers, don't you?"

"Yes, I do." Colin recalled his memories of John and Linda, and the many other climbers he had watched on Yamnuska. They seemed to love the mountains as much as he did. And they certainly liked ravens.

"Exactly," the Great Raven continued. "The Trees thought that climbers would really enjoy being able to fly among the peaks."

Colin remembered his second question. "G.R., how are you able to –"

"How can I do the things I do? Speak to you from wherever I am? Know what you're thinking? All that?"

"Yes. All that. Did the Trees give you those powers?"

"No, the Trees don't give anything away they don't have to. I had to learn to do those things myself."

"You did?!"

"Well, let me put it this way. If you had lived as long as I have, you'd have learned a few tricks, too."

"So any raven can do what you do?"

"I imagine. They just have to stumble on the techniques. I say 'stumble' because these things aren't at all obvious. I mean, look how long it took the humans to learn how to fly."

Humans could fly? Colin wanted to pursue this subject, but the other birds were getting restless. Some were edging over to listen in. Quickly he asked the Great Raven the one other question he had to know the answer to right now. "G.R., it's about Greta. Is she –"

At that moment another raven arrived at the Loft. Colin shrank away in horror. It was Zygadena C.C.

XVIII

The Great Raven's eyebrow tufts went up in a flash. "Zygadena, you know you're not supposed to come here."

"Oh, is that *so?*" Zygadena replied sweetly, turning her head to the side. "And who *says?*"

"It was decided long ago, C.C."

"Well, I'm asking for an *exception.*"

"No exceptions."

Some of the other birds had moved backward to the edges of the Loft. They seemed just as afraid of Zygadena as Colin was. Others in the flock were moving closer, tufts raised.

Colin now realized what his second-sight had told him the day before. That strong feeling of impending evil – it must have been Zygadena following him! But he wondered how Zygadena could still be alive. Somehow she had overcome her injuries from the falcon attack. Her left wing showed no sign of being broken. Her bill was now healed. Her plumage, her legs – she looked to be her usual, beautiful, deadly self. How could she have done that?

The Great Raven spoke quietly to Colin, but she kept her eyes on Zygadena. "Just stay cool, Colin. This particular bird was kicked out of the Mythical Flock for bad behavior. But she comes back from time to time. We know how to deal with her."

So that was it. Zygadena was mythical. No wonder she had such incredible power. No wonder she healed so quickly.

"I have my *reasons,*" Zygadena was saying.

"This had better be good," Archibald responded. His voice was threatening.

"Oh, it *is*. It *is*." She preened a feather that was slightly out of alignment. "It's about this Colin C.C. you seem to care for so much."

Colin cowered. What was going to come next?

"He's *not* what you think he is," she said slyly.

The Great Raven sighed. She was well acquainted with Zygadena's lies. "Out with it."

"He's an *imposter.*"

"Oh, Zygadena," the Great Raven began, trying not to laugh, "that's the most ridiculous thing I've ever hea –"

Zygadena's bill flashed out and caught the Great Raven by the throat.

"*Awk!*"

Archibald started for Zygadena, but she tightened her grip and quickly dragged the Great Raven away from him. "Keep your distance or I'll kill this bird right now," she hissed, forcing the Great Raven's neck into a nasty twist.

Archibald scoffed. "Zygadena, you know you can't kill the Great Raven. The Trees will just bring her back."

"Oh, and are you *sure?*"

"Uh . . ." Archibald stepped back. No one moved, for fear that Zygadena would actually break the Great Raven's neck.

No one moved – except for Colin.

"Kill me instead," he said, stepping forward. "You always wanted to kill me, Zygadena."

"Oh, not as much as I've wanted to kill *her,*" she replied, clamping down harder on the Great Raven's windpipe, "the way she's treated *me!*"

Oh, come come, Colin's eyes said to Zygadena.

She blinked.

Look at me.

Zygadena's eyes met Colin's.

Surely you'd like to keep looking at me, his eyes continued, locked with those of Zygadena. **Surely you'd like to keep looking at me, wouldn't you?**

Zygadena kept staring at him.

And now don't you think you'd like to come over here, where I am?

"Yes. Yes. I would like to come over there where you are." Zygadena's voice had gone strangely flat. She was loosening her grip on the Great Raven.

Well, then. Please come closer. Much, much closer. I am waiting.

"Yes. I am coming." Zygadena's bill opened as she spoke, and the Great Raven pulled away.

Instantly, several ravens seized Zygadena. Angie had her by the throat. Boogs grabbed one of her legs. The bird named Rick grabbed the other. Zygadena extended her wings as if to fly, but other members of the Mythical Flock jumped on her, dug in their claws and held her down.

The Great Raven was getting back on her feet. "Oh, my – *cough* – how could I have been so stupid – *cough, cough* – oh, Zygadena." She stretched her neck and shook her feathers back into place. She looked toward her worried nestmate. "I'm okay, Archie – *cough*."

"Now we're *even*," Zygadena gasped out. "We're *even*. Let me go, G.R."

"Let you *go?!*"

"I'll stay away from now on."

"You bet you will," the Great Raven said gruffly. She spread her wings and closed her eyes, then she lowered the left one only, curving it in an unusual way.

Zygadena disappeared.

Angie's bill snapped shut on the empty space that had been Zygadena's neck a moment before. The bills of Rick and Boogs likewise closed on thin air. The three birds who had been standing on Zygadena's back dropped onto the ones that had been holding her. There was a flurry of feathers and claws as the ravens untangled themselves, then they looked at each other and started to laugh.

"Craw-ha! That was quick! Here one minute, gone the next!"

"Way to go, G.R.!"

"By golly, Rick, you sure looked funny hangin' onto a bird's leg that wasn't there!"

"So did you, up on her back. Planning to *mate*, maybe?"

"Craw-ha!"

Then one of the birds turned to Colin and looked quite serious.

"Colin, how did you do that? That thing with your eyes?"

The laughter ceased.

"Uh . . . I learned it from a lynx."

"A *lynx?*"

"Yes." Colin was aware of every bird in the flock staring at him incredulously. "It – it just sort of happened," he said. "I didn't really think about it." He was fumbling for further explanation when the Great Raven broke in.

"Friends," she said. "Never mind how he did it. I for one am just glad that he did."

"Yes, and we are all just as grateful as G.R. is." The voice was Archibald's. He hopped up to Colin. "Many thanks to our newest flock member. Shall we tell him what we think of him?"

"Rawk-a-taw!" came the universal reply.

XIX

"Yes, I'm fine. I'm just fine." The Great Raven was trying to reassure the Mythical Flock. She decided to change the subject. "Some birds will do absolutely anything to get revenge. Zygadena is one such."

Archie spoke next. "You know, a bird like Zygadena – thank the Trees there aren't many – a bird like that operates under a different set of rules than we do. She cares only for herself. Worse than that, she has to have power over everybody else. And she knows the way to get it."

"What way is that?" Laurel, the Squamish raven, asked.

Archie answered. "Ah, Laurel. Lucky you, never having had to deal with Zygadena. Well, she kills ravens and crows and turns their flesh into a poison. She calls it 'Magic Meat.' Her victims take more and more of it, and after a while they'll do anything to get it. Anything at all – even killing their flockmates."

Several birds shook their heads in disgust.

"Of course, this 'Magic Meat' eventually makes Zygadena's slaves so sick they can't serve her. Then she kills them. And she uses them for more Magic Meat. She's vicious, utterly vicious. As she proved once again today."

Laurel looked astonished. She turned to the Great Raven. "And you let this bird live? You just – you just *sent her away?*"

"Yes. We could easily have killed her just now, but I would never allow it. For one raven to kill another is evil. It's evil in the same way that Zygadena herself is evil. And to kill the killer just spreads the evil further. It spreads and spreads. I have seen it and I know."

Laurel still wasn't convinced. "But you said that you already banished her . . ."

"Yes, I did. We all did. Threw her out of the flock by unanimous agreement."

"But she came back!"

"She has come back several times, claiming to be reformed. Not that she couldn't be, you know" – Colin thought of Garth – "but she has lied, just as she did now."

"So where did you send her this time?"

The Great Raven chuckled. "Oh, someplace that will keep her out of our feathers for a very long time. Away from every other raven in the world, actually. Although it's kind of unfair to the penguins."

"Penguins? What . . .?"

"Oh, I sent her off to Antarctica."

XX

The long light of late afternoon lay warm on the Mountain with Feathers. Colin was talking with Angie and Kootenay.

"You two didn't give a thing away when I came to Jasper, did you?"

"'Course not," Kootenay said. "We've been through this before. We've seen other aspirants heading for the Mountain with Feathers."

"But why don't the locals know about it?"

"Oh, they do," Angie said. "They fly here all the time. I even take them. The soaring is really terrific, don't you think? But they know the mountain by a different name" – she stated it for Colin – "and the Great Raven makes sure they never see her or the Mythical Flock. It works out fine. Uriah has them all convinced that the Mountain with Feathers is the place where ravens go after they die, and we play along with that."

"Then why did you send me to see Uriah?"

"Uriah is an interesting character. I'll tell you his whole story sometime. Or you can ask him yourself. Anyway, we thought Uriah would test the strength of your convictions. And he did."

"Did he ever! I almost wound up in the bottom of Maligne Canyon, Angie!"

Angie stayed unruffled. "Yeah, I heard. We weren't expecting that, and we're sorry it happened." She touched his bill with hers.

"Well, I got here anyway," Colin said, accepting the apology.

Angie looked at Kootenay. "You know, Koot, we've got to go. It's time for the Flight back at Jasper."

"Should I come along?" Colin asked.

"Sure, if you like," Kootenay answered, "but why not stick around here? Archie and G.R. might let you roost with them." The pair flew off.

"Anyone up for a Flight?" asked the Great Raven. By way of an answer, all the remaining birds immediately took to wing. The Mythical Flock, Colin among them, soared along the west face of the Mountain with Feathers. A cloud-rich sunset glowed over the Canadian Rockies, coloring everything red-orange. Colin flew beside the Great Raven and her mate. "Where do we roost?" he asked.

"Oh, most of the mythicals go home," Archie replied.

"Home?"

"Yeah. Didn't you notice that they were all from different mortal flocks?"

"Yes, but I don't know why."

"G.R. likes it that way. Tell him why, G.R."

"Well, if you're immortal you learn a lot as the years go by. And that's good for ravens generally – if the knowledge gets passed along. So I make sure it does. A lot of mythicals are Main Ravens. Uh, but not the one at Yamnuska." She had known what Colin was going to ask next.

"Hey, Colin. G.R. and I roost here on the mountain – sometimes we use the Loft – and we'd be pleased to have you join us. Especially after what you did for us today. Eh, G.R.?"

The Great Raven agreed. "Of course. But I'm a little sore in the throat" – she coughed – "so we'll have to limit the questions, okay? Besides, even mythical ravens need to sleep. Especially new ones."

Colin was, in fact, feeling very tired. "Would you please answer a question for me right now?"

"My pleasure."

"All these mythical ravens I met seem to come from very far away. Way too far to get back before dark –"

"Well, most of them don't fly here. They ask and I bring them."

"You 'bring' them? How do you do that?"

"Same way I sent Zygadena off to cool her claws south of Tierra del Fuego. I kind of bend the world a little."

Colin was trying to bend his mind around this idea. The Great Raven tried to explain. "It's something I learned to do quite recently. Just a couple of thousand years ago. You do it with space, and time, and –" She looked at Colin, who was twitching with confusion. "Let's talk about it another day, my dear."

Colin shook his head, trying to clear it. "Will you be able to send me back to Yamnuska?"

"Certainly. And when you want to visit, just ask. Sometimes I'll have to say no – too big a crowd here already – but usually it's no problem. You know how to get in touch with me, right?"

"Uh, sort of. I just think about you? Without trying to think about you?"

"Yes. You'll learn how to do it. And it helps to non-think of the Mountain with Feathers, too. That way the signal comes in stronger."

Most of the other ravens had left the Mythical Flight by now. Colin hadn't realized they were leaving, but he just happened to be watching when Boogs departed. Boogs didn't fly away. He simply called, "Aye, an' fare thee weel, G.R.!" then winked out of existence. The Great Raven had curved her left wing.

"I can't believe all the amazing things you can do, G.R."

"Oh, it's not so much. Whales, for example. You know about whales? Biggest fish in the sea, although they aren't really fish, but never mind. Whales can talk to each other all the way across the ocean. And they're mortal." She smiled, thinking about the long-distance squeaks and whistles of the whales. She liked to listen in on the whales.

Colin had no idea what a whale was, and only a vague notion of the sea. He interrupted the Great Raven's thoughts with yet another question. "I'm sorry, G.R., but there's something else."

"Okay. Let's make this the last question for now, Colin."

"It's awfully nice of you," Colin said as politely as he could. "I was surprised to hear the flock call."

"Ah. 'Rawk-a-taw.' The Motion of the Mythical Flock. You know it, don't you?"

"Yes, I do. It's the same one we use at Raven's End."

"Does that surprise you?"

"Well, yes, because I thought all the flock calls are different."

"And that's true, Colin – which should tell you something about the Raven's End Flock."

"The Raven's Enders are mythical?" This was intriguing, but it didn't make sense.

"No, no. The Raven's Enders are mortal. The reason we mythicals use the Raven's End call is more obvious than that. Think about it."

He thought, and moments later he had the answer. The Great Raven knew it as soon as he did, of course. "Colin! You delight me!" She touched his bill with hers. "Yes, that's right. Yamnuska is where I came from. I was the original raven of Raven's End. Pretty soon we had a flock there, and we invented the idea of the Motion way back then. I just kept it for the Mythical Flock."

"Oh! That brings up a really important question!" Colin had almost forgotten. He held his breath, hoping the Great Raven would answer it.

"Very last one, Colin, okay? Someone's trying to contact me."

Colin let his breath out. "I really appreciate this. What I need to know is why Greta isn't here."

"Oh. Greta." The Great Raven looked pained. "Greta is not mythical, Colin."

"Not mythical? But –"

"I know. She seems mythical. She knows a lot about us, too. She really wants to be mythical, and I don't blame her. She'd make a great mythical raven. Remember that argument I was telling you about? The argument between Greta and me? Well, I've tried to get the Trees to grant her honorary mythical status several times, but they won't do it. She blames me for not trying hard enough, I guess. But she doesn't know the Trees like I do. I don't want to get their back branches up over this. We've been through it before. Greta's not the first bird to discover the Mythical Flock."

The Great Raven looked wistful, then she smiled at Colin. "Greta had you pegged immediately, kiddo."

Kiddo. A term Greta used, Colin recalled. "But how could she find all this out? About you, and – and about mythical ravens, and all that?"

"Greta is the smartest bird I have ever known, Colin. Smarter than me, that's for sure. I've had eons to figure all this stuff out. Greta has done it in a single lifetime."

Colin felt admiration for Greta spreading warmly through his wings. Oh, how he loved that bird! When he got back he would tell her so. "So that explains why she looks so old and the real mythicals don't?"

"Yes. Greta must be – let's see now, I'll have to add this up – um, about fifty years old. She's probably the oldest raven around right now, among the mortal flocks."

The Great Raven seemed distracted for a moment, then she turned to Colin with a troubled expression. "That bird I was talking about? The one who was trying to contact me? It was Greta herself. She said she's been having trouble reaching me, and she was glad we thought about her just then or she might not have been able to get through at all." The Great Raven hesitated. She looked greatly distressed. "Colin, I'm going to send you home. Greta says she's dying."

XXI

The Great Raven had curved her wing. Everything in Colin's world had gone brown for a moment – the same sort of brown he saw in the Great Raven's eyes – and then he was soaring over the summit of Yamnuska.

Bands of pink and purple clouds, the glowing filaments of day's

end, decorated the mountain front from horizon to horizon. But no ravens played in the sunset here. Colin tucked his wings and dived for Raven's End.

There he found them. Zack, Molly, Scratch, Wheedle, Marg, Sarah, Brendan, Garth, and the Main Raven all stood in a circle. At the centre was Greta. She lay on her side, with one wing partly extended. Her eyes – her wonderful eyes, Colin thought, so much like those of the Great Raven – were shut. No one was speaking. No one was moving a feather. Colin landed quietly a few hops away and walked grimly over.

"Colin!" Molly saw him first. "Oh, Colin!"

"Is she dead?" Colin stepped through the circle of birds. They blinked as they recognized him.

Marg touched his bill. "We don't know," she said, looking down at Greta. "She hasn't moved since sundown. But I could hear her breathing until just a moment ago."

Too late, Colin thought. Too late!

"Col . . . Colin?" Greta opened her eyes. They were clouded.

"Greta. Oh, Greta."

"Colin." She took a breath with each half of his name. "I'm . . . so glad . . . you're back. Did you . . . did you see the . . .?"

He knew what she was unable to say in front of the flock. "Yes, Greta, I saw her. I saw them all. They took me in."

"Oh, that's . . . that's so . . . so grand, Colin." Greta closed her eyes. "So grand."

Colin turned to Scratch. "What happened to her?"

"Aw, it's a cryin' shame, Colin, it really is. She took sick not long after ya left. Told us it was her lungs, like. Said they was jest too old, eh? Said they was gonna quit workin', like. An' sure enough that's what happened."

Greta took several wheezy breaths before she could speak again. Her words were labored.

"I guess . . . I guess this is . . . it. Old Greta's . . . *cough* . . . old Greta's . . . off to the ants."

Marg couldn't help herself. "Crawwwwwww . . ."

"It's . . . okay, Marg," Greta said. "The ants . . . the ants have had to wait . . . *wheeze* . . . way too long already." She coughed again. "And . . . and the way I feel right now – oh, that hurts – I'm happy to go."

Marg closed her bill. It hung down. So did that of every other bird in the flock.

"Before I . . . die . . . here's what I . . . what I want you to know." She gasped, and her wing twitched. "So listen up . . . C.C.s."

They listened as never before.

"The Main Raven . . . the Main Raven's real name . . . his real name is . . ."

"Greta!" The Main Raven's eyes were wide in astonishment. "How could you?!"

She smiled. "Oh, M.R. You know I . . . I really wouldn't . . . *cough* . . . do that to you. Just . . . just a last joke, okay? . . . I did love . . . making jokes . . ."

The Main Raven turned his head away.

Greta opened her eyes and spoke again. Her voice was stronger than before, and what she said came out all at once. It took any strength she had remaining. The feathers on her breast shook with every word.

"C.C.s! You live in the most beautiful . . . of all worlds. Enjoy it . . . while you may . . . for we are here . . . only for a little while. Be kind to each other. And Colin . . . this is meant for Colin . . . where is he? I can't see him any longer . . ."

"I'm right here, Greta. Right beside you."

"Colin . . . do you remember . . . 'pikaness'?"

"Yes, Greta. Of course I do. And all the other things we talked about."

"So you won't forget . . . all those . . . other things . . .?"

"All those things you taught me, Greta. I'll never forget."

"Raven . . . ness. There's . . . ravenness, Colin . . . at Raven's End. Lots of raven . . . ness . . ."

"Indeed there is, Greta. We will make sure it goes on. On and on."

Greta closed her eyes. "Take care . . . take care of these birds, Colin . . . I've loved them . . . so well."

"And we have loved you, Greta." Colin's bill was quivering. He touched it to hers.

"Goodbye, all . . . oh . . . weasel widgets . . . this is it . . . goodbye, G.R.!" Her bill opened a little wider. "Rawk . . . rawk-a . . . rawk . . . a . . . taw." Greta's wings spread themselves slightly and she lay still.

The other birds knew the time had come. "Craaawwwwww . . . craaawwwwwwww . . . craaaaaaawwwwwwwwwwww . . ."

Through it all, and over the sound of his own sobs, Colin distinctly heard the voice of the Great Raven. It trembled.

"Goodbye, Greta. Goodbye, my dear. Oh, I'm going to miss you so much." The voice broke, and it blended with the others in the flock.

XXII

Many years have passed. Some of Zack and Molly's nestlings are still raising their own broods on Yamnuska, but most have lived out their lives, as have Molly and Zack and the rest of their generation. All but one.

It is late in the day, and the sun lies low over the front ranges of the Canadian Rockies. Near the top of Yamnuska's South Face we hear a familiar sound.

"On belay, John."

"Keep an eye on me, Linda. This looks kinda tricky." John steps up from a ledge onto vertical rock.

"Yeah, that's what everyone says about it, This is where that guy fell off and died, remember? About twenty years ago? Fell out of his harness."

"Thanks for reminding me." John steps back down to the ledge.

"Sorry." Linda looks worried. "You want me to check the guide-book?"

"Mmm – not a bad idea. Is it handy?"

"Got it right here."

Linda reaches into her small rock-climbing pack and extracts a slim volume. If it weren't for the tape all over it, the book would be falling apart. She turns the dog-eared pages and reads.

"It says, 'Step right, around a corner, and feel for a sharp but good handhold.' Whatever that means. 'Alternatively, climb the difficult overhanging wall above the belay.'"

"I'll pass," says John. "That's how that guy got killed." He peers upward. "Sure. Off right has to be the way to go. Straight up looks about two grades harder than anything I'd care to lead this afternoon."

"Whatever you think. Anyway, I've got you."

John steps back up from the security of the ledge to the small holds on the wall. His nose is close to the stone, and he must hang on with both hands to avoid falling over backward. On impulse, he sticks out his tongue and licks the rock. It tastes earthy.

He moves to the right and notices a piton there. The piton protrudes from an outside corner, as if driven into the edge of a building. John can't see around the corner, but he reaches out with his right hand, feeling for holds. His fingers find only blank rock.

"Gee, it seems unlikely over that way," he reports. His voice falters.

"Take your time, John."

"Yes, my dear – hey, I found it!"

"Found what?"

"That hold they talked about in the guidebook."

"Yeah?"

"Yeah. 'Sharp but good,' is exactly right. I can't see it, but it feels like the edge of an axe. I'm almost afraid to pull on it. Might lose my fingers."

Hanging onto the mystery hold with his right hand, John picks at his climbing gear with his left. He mutters to himself. "Big move coming up. Believe I'll just get something in beside this old peg."

Jingle, jingle. He tries various items in the crack. "Hmm. Small cam might go in. Nope. Too big. Maybe a size three . . . Aha – perfect placement." Then he calls down to Linda. "A little slack, please."

"Here you go."

The sound of rope sliding against rock. A click.

"Okay, I'm going to step around the corner and see what I'm hanging onto."

"Fine by me."

John moves carefully up and right. He swings a leg around the corner. His foot brushes the rock, searching. It finds a hold at knee-level. He transfers his weight to the hold, ducking his head under the overhang. He looks down.

"Hoo-*wee!* Check this out when you're up here, Linda. You can see all the way to the deck. Clear drop."

"Let's not do any dropping, okay?"

Finally John can peer past the edge of rock. He likes what he sees, pulls on the sharp hold and brings his other foot around the corner. Now out of Linda's sight, he calls back.

"Absolutely gorgeous move! Looks hard but really isn't. You're gonna love it."

"How's the continuation?"

"Piece of cake."

"Good going, John!"

The rope pays out faster, now. A few minutes later Linda hears John's voice from the top. "Off belay."

"Belay off." Soon the rope tugs gently at Linda's waist, and she follows her climbing partner's path up and rightward toward the over-hanging corner. She removes the gear John has placed in the crack. She feels for the secret hold, but her reach is shorter than John's and she can't locate it.

She inches up under the stone ceiling, where her arms must bear more of her weight. Her muscles are tired from climbing all day. She cannot cling this way for long.

"Keep me tight!" she shouts to John. He takes up the slack in the rope. She feels around the corner again, and this time she can just barely touch a hold that might be the right one. She can't see it, though, and she can't get her whole hand on it.

Linda's strength is fading. She must decide what to do, and soon. She takes a deep breath and lets go with her left hand, throwing her off balance momentarily, then she stretches her right hand toward the hold. Her fingers close and lock on the blade of rock.

"Whew!"

She swings around the corner as John did. She takes a look straight down to the base of the cliff far below. "What an incredible place to be," she says softly to herself. Then she follows the rope to the summit of Yamnuska.

John is waiting for her there in the last of the day's sunlight. His helmet is off and his hair is gray.

"Oh, John – what a fine climb," Linda says, sitting down beside him. He kisses her. She kisses him back. She takes off the pack and finds their water bottle.

"Two swallows left. One for you and one for me." She tilts the bottle and drinks. Her knuckles are scuffed, but she has lost no skin. Her hands are tough from a summer of climbing the rock of the Rockies.

John points out a large black bird soaring beside the South Face. "There's that raven again."

"Do you suppose it's the same one we keep seeing on these Yam climbs?"

"Well, you're the one who says you can tell the ravens apart."

"Just one, John. I can tell just one. But I know it really well. I can tell by its eyes."

"Here it comes. Have a look."

The raven has decided to coast by the climbers. It has spent the afternoon drifting contentedly in the updrafts. Now it has decided to land on the summit and enjoy the happy feelings it senses in the humans sitting there. It lifts its wings high, flares the feathers at the tips and drops onto a boulder near the climbers. It regards them, first with one eye, then with the other.

"That's it! That's the one!"

"Oh, come on."

"No, really. Look at his eyes. Look at his eyes!"

John looks. "Gee. You know, Linda, there *is* something about those eyes –"

"See? That's the one, John! That's him!"

She digs into her pack and finds some raisins loose on the bottom. It is the only food that she and John have left. She holds it out.

The raven stands there. A feather on its back flips up and down in the breeze. It won't come closer. It recognizes these humans, and it would be easy to hop over and accept the gift, but there are some rules a raven never breaks. Besides, the raven knows that the food will be thrown to it shortly.

Linda tosses the raisins to the raven. The raven picks up as much of the offering as it thinks polite. It isn't hungry. It will leave the rest for some other creature.

With a mild thank-you croak, Colin Corvus Corax spreads his wings and rises off the boulder into the warm wind. He will make his way back to Raven's End. The others will be waiting for him to announce the Evening Flight.

ACKNOWLEDGMENTS

To Cia, my wife, for her helpful ideas and her eagle eye. And for her patience.

To John Blum, Toby Gadd, Amber Hayward, Crawford Kilian, Rose and David Scollard, Jill and Basil Seaton, Janet and Chris Smart, Paulette Trottier and Volker Schelhas (and Nicolette and Danyelle), all of whom read drafts of the manuscript and made many useful comments.

To Shura and Mike Galbraith, who gave the character "Boogs" his Scottish accent.

To Bernd Heinrich, for writing *Mind of the Raven*, which is the best book on these wonderful birds.

To J.R.R. Tolkien, who may have been delighted to learn that several names from his *Lord of the Rings* would wind up on the real-world map of Yamnuska and its surroundings.